A note on the author

Denzil Meyrick was born in Glasgow and brought up in Campbeltown. After studying politics, he pursued a varied career including time spent as a police officer, freelance journalist, and director of several companies in the leisure, engineering and marketing sectors. Previous novels in the bestselling DCI Daley thriller series are *Whisky from Small Glasses* (Waterstone's Scottish Book of the Year, 2015), *The Last Witness*, *Dark Suits and Sad Songs*, *The Rat Stone Serenade*, *Well of the Winds*, short-story collection *One Last Dram Before Midnight*, *The Relentless Tide* and *A Breath on Dying Embers*. Denzil lives on Loch Lomond side with his wife Fiona.

Also available in the D.C.I. Daley thriller series

eBook only

JEREMIAH'S BELL

A D.C.I. DALEY THRILLER

Denzil Meyrick

First published in Great Britain in 2020 by Polygon, an imprint of Birlinn Ltd.

Birlinn Ltd
West Newington House
10 Newington Road
Edinburgh
EH9 1QS

www.polygonbooks.co.uk

1

ISBN 978 1 84697 520 2
eBook ISBN 978 1 78885 279 1

British Library Cataloguing-in-Publication Data
A catalogue record for this book is available on request from the British Library.

Typeset by 3btype.com

Dedicated to the memory of
Tommy Morran and John Mactaggart.

'Not all those who wander are lost'

—J.R.R. Tolkien

PROLOGUE

The old woman stood on the jagged promontory, the strong wind catching her plaid shawl, sending it flapping round her shoulders. She drew it over her bony frame as she shivered in the late November chill. The sea was pale green, almost luminous in the gloom of the day. A storm had hit hard the previous night, and high above its tail was curling like a celestial whip ready to crack its full wrath against them once more before the next dawn.

In the distance, a fishing boat struggled through the turbulent swell, a determined prow cloaked in the white crash of waves, the safety of port still to be gained. The silhouette of a lone gull rode the gale almost motionless under the pale glimmering disc of a shrouded sun. Framed by it, the bird hung like a dark crucifix in the lowering sky: the absence of benediction. The thrash of the tide crashed over the Barrel Rocks, calling to the ghosts of the many mariners who had perished on them through the ages; a desperate lament for the departed, ripped from the world like leaves from an autumnal bough, lost souls never to settle or rest, but to rot unremembered in the turbulent depths.

She hefted the bell in her right hand, and with no little difficulty swung it to and fro. This was far from a call to prayer;

more like the summoning toll to children at play in the schoolyards of long ago. Its peal caught on the wind and the modulated chime cried plaintively against the tumult all around. Nonetheless, three figures stirred against the dark rocks and the washed lime sea, their ears long since attuned to the urgency of its call. Slowly, begrudgingly, they turned in the direction of the bell's insistent demand, swaddled arms laden with driftwood bleached white like old bones by the unforgiving wuthering wind and waves.

Satisfied, the old woman let the bell swing loose in her bony hand, then turned for the weather-beaten cottage across the rocks and beyond the dark rampart of seaweed which had been forced into the cove by the sheer ferocity of the storm. Here it would stand sentinel before the low dwelling until the spring tides and warmth of the sun ate away at its wasted, rotting edifice.

She trod on, her worn boots sinking into the black soft cleft of the weed until the rough shingle afforded surer footing. A brief turn of her head was enough to register the lurching shapes close together in her wake, quite indistinguishable now, slouching forward, almost as one foul beast, headed for an ancient little town.

1

They were all there; at least those who had taken the trouble to say goodbye to the man now encased in the wooden casket. Old friends and new – faces from the past and the present.

Hamish was huddled in a voluminous black woollen seafarer's pea jacket. Suddenly he looked frail and old in a garment that seemed to draw what little light there was from the grey sky and hid an off-white shirt and a badly knotted black tie. Beside him, Annie took a handkerchief from her handbag and wiped tears from her eyes. Though she was dressed brightly – she refused to wear black – her heart was stifling sore.

Brian Scott's dark suit did nothing to hide the neatly laundered collar from which his wife now banished a dark mote blown there by the gusting wind. His hand darted to loosen the top button of his shirt, but a look from Ella was enough to make him withdraw it hurriedly. He stared into his wife's blue eyes behind the short black veil of her hat and gave her a weak smile. She whispered something into his ear and clutched his hand hard enough to help him choke back the tears that were making his throat ache unbearably.

Carrie Symington stood at the head of a rank of police officers, all dressed in their best uniforms, white-gloved,

3

heads bowed. The gold braid on her cap caught a shimmering shaft of sunlight that faded as quickly as it had arrived. Her chin jutted determinedly forward, face expressionless; but anyone close enough would have been able to see the tears brimming her dark eyes.

The large coffin was poised above the gaping hole in the ground on two stout planks of wood, red winding cords sprouting from the gleaming brass handles round its sides. The white hair of Kinloch's undertaker was tugged at by the wind as he solemnly handed out little white cards bordered by black edges to some of those gathered by the graveside.

The saddest sight of all was that of the beautiful woman holding the little boy by the hand. She was bare-headed; a break with tradition that had seen some shaking of heads in the town's chapel during the funeral service. But everyone had averted his or her eyes when her sad, hypnotic gaze caught theirs. The child pushed back a lick of dark hair from his forehead and looked up at his mother, bewildered by the unfamiliar ritual of it all. He opened his mouth to speak, but was interrupted when the man in the flowing robes of a Roman Catholic priest called those present to order.

The small throng fell silent. All that could be heard now was the distant cry of gulls, as beyond the serried ranks of gravestones a wailing wind whipped whispering waves on to the shore at Kinloch.

Despite the silence, though, the name on the polished brass plate of the coffin shouted loud as thunder.

James Francis Daley.

He sat bolt upright in bed, the sweat that covered his body making him shiver in the darkness. Beside him, a figure stirred, slowly propping herself up on one elbow. Her face was suddenly illuminated by a slash of white moonlight through a chink in the curtain.

'Jim, it's okay. A dream – another nightmare.' She embraced him, feeling the clammy dampness of his skin against hers. 'Have you taken your pills?'

He didn't reply, choosing to sit forward, his head bowed, breathing heavily. It had all seemed so real, as though he was actually looking at the mourners at his own funeral. It was a spectre that had been haunting him for weeks. The panic attacks when he was awake, the nightmares when he slept. The first was when he'd fallen on to the pontoon beside the boat called *Wisdom*. He'd had a few since, but though these wakeful attacks seemed to be decreasing in number, the dreams of his own interment were with him every night still.

'I'll get some hot milk. That helps you get back over,' said Liz. She slipped from the silken sheets of the bed and padded out of the room, her shape seeming to flicker like an old black and white movie as she walked through the shaft of moonlight.

Daley lay back. His head had made the pillow damp, and the sensation of lying on it was an unpleasant one. He was trying to slow his breathing; somehow the sound of his wife busy in the kitchen helped, and soon he began to feel slightly better.

Better – would he ever be able to say that and mean it? If this was the path his life was to take, Jim Daley wasn't sure that the constant anxiety and dread of his own mortality was something with which he could cope. Though he'd always felt melancholy about the end of life, he could no longer free himself from the fear of its cloying bonds. It was with him night and day – every night and day. He'd always thought of himself as brave; well, brave enough to face what life as a police officer threw at him. But this was something he couldn't face with anything other than horror. He'd seen the dreadful finality of death all too often, and it always made him recoil.

Soon Liz was back with the hot milk. She sat beside him on the bed and helped him sit up and hold the mug in his shaking hands. 'This can't go on, Jim. You're going back to work soon; you have to be honest with Carrie – with everybody!'

He took another sip and looked at her through the darkness. The months since the brutal attack perpetrated on her by the man she would no longer talk about had banished her cuts and bruises. Her face was flawless again, apart from the sliver of a scar across her left cheekbone where her attacker's signet ring had ripped through the flesh.

Sometimes, Daley was ashamed that he'd lost control, beaten his wife's tormentor mercilessly. But more often than not, the thought helped restore some equilibrium to his soul. He'd been quite prepared to face the consequences, face justice for what he'd done, but his victim refused to make a complaint, no doubt worried about his own culpability, and given the circumstances the Procurator Fiscal had decided that there was no case to answer, despite the PIRC report.

'Jim, you're not listening. You can't go on like this. How on earth are you going to function back at work when you hardly get any sleep?'

'Being back at work will help.'

'You think?'

'Yes, *I think*.' He finished the hot drink and his wife took the empty mug back through to the kitchen. In all honesty, he didn't know how he would cope, but he had to try. His job was all that kept him tethered, and the months without it had seen him plumb the depths of despair.

Surely he could find himself again.

As Liz Daley slid back between the covers, the howling wind sent a flurry of heavy rain against the bedroom window from clouds that suddenly obscured the moon. Another storm was brewing, and DCI Jim Daley was going to have to face it.

2

Alice Wenger was fifty years old, but could easily have passed for someone fifteen years younger as she sat in the Executive Lounge at Heathrow Airport. Her skin, though tanned, bore none of the signs of premature ageing that ravaged regular sun worshippers. Yes, she'd had some work done, but her plastic surgeon was good, his work subtle.

Her soft grey leather jacket was tasteful, yet fashionable – the best Beverly Hills could offer – and it complemented the well-cut pale jeans and Roman sandals she'd worn to make the flight from Los Angeles. As she checked her phone, she ran her hand absently through her honey-blonde hair, her finger, as always, then exploring the tiny lump above her right eye. It was her touchstone, the link from her privileged present back to the past from which she had escaped. But life was a circle, and everything came round again – if you were lucky enough to survive the first spin, that was. It was her turn to ride the wheel, and she was determined that on this occasion those who had made her suffer the first time round would face her once more.

'Speak!' she said into the phone after it buzzed in her hand, then listened intently for a few moments. 'How much do I pay you, Janneck? No, that's not a question you need to answer, honey, it's rhetorical. I'm sure I don't have to explain what that means to a man with an Ivy League education. Just do what you're paid to do – direct, manage, work the fucking problems, and do what I tell you when I tell you, you got that?' She listened again, briefly, then clicked off the call without ceremony.

Though Alice had spent almost twenty years in California, the sibilant tones of Kentucky still sounded strong when she opened her mouth. She knew she could change her voice – after all, she'd done it before – but she liked the way her adopted accent played across her lips, and the impact it had in the rarefied circles in which she now moved. Very few people wanted to cross the acid-tongued Southern girl who'd made her way up in the hotel and leisure industry with such speed and efficacy. That pleased her, and it had made her rich – very rich.

'*British Airways flight 194 to Glasgow Airport is now boarding . . .*'

Alice ignored the rest of the message, heaved the large handbag over her shoulder and made her way towards the aircraft that would take her back to a country she'd not seen for a very long time. The wheel of life was about to turn again, but this time it was firmly in her grasp.

'Gie me a break, Ella,' said Acting DI Brian Scott as he knotted his tie. 'The big man's coming back, and I don't know if I'll be an inspector, a janitor or a chief bottle-washer. Anyway, I've hated every minute o' it.'

'Why, what's there to hate?' replied his wife, pouring milk on her cornflakes.

'The paperwork, for a start! Have you any idea what's

involved in a' that? Bugger me, it's bad enough in the polis these days for everyone, but see when you're a gaffer, it never ends: forms, rotas, reports, assessments. I've even had tae count money!'

'Aye, well you've never been any good at that, mind you.'

'Naw, and I've no' improved, neither.' He took a bite of white toast and washed it down with some black coffee. 'I joined up tae be a polis, no' some pen-pusher.'

'You joined up for a bet, Brian.'

'True, it started off as that, but I got in, didn't I?'

'I never thought you'd pass the exam.'

'Listen tae it! You encouraged me, if I remember.'

'Huh, I didnae think you would end up as target practice for all and sundry. You're safe in an office. You might no' like it, but that's a fact.'

'I'm an acting inspector – acting, Ella. That means when I stop acting I'm back tae plain DS, and no' a moment too soon.'

The couple consumed the rest of their breakfast in silence, Ella staring at him resentfully over her mug of sweet tea.

'Right, that's me away,' said Scott.

'Aye, see ya, *inspector*.'

'You know, you amaze me, Ella. Never stop miscalling Lizzie Daley, yet you're gettin' just as bad. What's got intae you?'

She looked out of the kitchen window. 'Maybe I liked having a husband who was an inspector – the extra money's certainly been welcome.'

'Aye, well, a' good things come tae an end, dear.'

'And what's so special aboot Jimmy Daley? When we were up for oor dinner last week he looked like the ghost o' Christmas past.'

'He's been through a lot, Ella. His heart, then that caper o'er at Inverkip. They fainting fits he's been having.'

'You got shot – twice – and you just had tae get on wae it!'

'You know me, Ella. Where there's nae sense, there's nae feeling.'

'You do yourself doon a' the time.'

'Maybe, but I know what I'm good at and what I'm no'. And let me tell you, I'm no' good at being a manager.' He marched out into the hall.

'You'll need your raincoat; it's throwing it doon oot there.'

'Aye. I'll see you later!'

Ella Scott heard the front door open and close, then sighed. It had been nice to boast to her friends that her Brian was an inspector. She had a picture of him in his new uniform on the mantelpiece. It made her proud.

But he was right: Brian Scott, the man she'd loved, argued with, huffed at, been exasperated by – been to hell and back with – wasn't cut out to be a senior officer, and she knew it. But hope sprang eternal; it was just that this hope's spring had sprung long ago.

She sighed again and began the weary task of clearing away the breakfast dishes.

3

Sergeant Shaw drew his finger across his forehead mimicking the braid on Symington's cap, alerting Scott to the fact that his superior was in residence. Scott returned the favour with a wink.

The Acting DI hated waiting, so he knocked on the door of the office Symington used when she visited the subdivision. Better to get things over with, he thought. In any case, with Daley's return imminent he'd been half expecting her arrival.

'Good morning, ma'am,' he said, poking his head round the door at her call.

'Brian, the very man!' she returned. 'Come in and take a seat, please.'

Scott sat in front of her, ready to be not only relieved of his temporary rank but also admonished for some mistake with the overtime sheets, holiday roster, or any of the other obscure and frustrating tasks that had fallen to him in Daley's absence. But if Brian Scott was used to anything in the job he'd worked at for so long it was being hauled over the coals. The result of years of such experience had instilled a certain sangfroid on facing the music.

'Now, as we know, Brian, DCI Daley should be back with

us in a few days.' Symington smiled broadly as she passed on this information.

'Aye, he said he'd be back soon, right enough.'

Symington sat forward in her seat. 'This conversation is strictly between you and me, Brian. Off the record, so to speak.'

Scott's stomach began to churn. When a senior officer told you something 'off the record' it was rarely anything good. 'Aye, fire away, ma'am. You know me, tight as a drum, an' that.'

'That's why I know I can trust you with this, Brian.' She looked at her desk, almost apologetically. 'I haven't forgotten our little experience on Gairsay, or what you did for me – despite what you may think.'

'In the past, ma'am, as far as I'm concerned.'

'Yes, quite.' She cleared her throat. 'This matter is just as – delicate.'

Fuck me, thought Scott. What other skeletons does she have in the closet? But he made sure his expression remained neutral and nodded his head sagely, ready to meet the great revelation with as much gravitas as he could muster.

'I've had to fight tooth and nail to get Jim back, you know. It's been bloody hard. There were plenty who wanted him put out to pasture, let me tell you. Especially after that incident on the boat.'

Scott shrugged. 'I cannae say much aboot that, ma'am; I wisnae there. But if it's good enough for they c— I mean, them in Discipline, it's good enough for me.'

'Oh come on, Brian, we both know DCI Daley beat that man within an inch of his life. He had to have dental reconstruction!'

'Surely he could just have done that himsel' lookin in

13

the mirror, like? Him a dentist an' all. Let me tell you, Lizzie's face wisnae too pretty when he'd finished wae her.' Scott felt the bile rise in his throat.

'That's not the point, Brian. Jim was lucky – very lucky. He could be behind bars now, never mind coming back to work.'

'Och, we've a' got something we'd rather folk didnae know – eh, ma'am?'

'Yes, indeed.' It was time for Carrie Symington to clear her throat again. 'But as I say, it took a great deal of persuasion and personal guarantees from me in order to make this happen.'

'Good of you, ma'am. I'm sure the big fella will appreciate that.'

'Yes, well, we'll see. However, one of the guarantees I had to give was that DCI Daley would be under close scrutiny during his first few months back at work.'

'Oh, aye.'

'Now, clearly I can't be in Kinloch all the time, so the task of keeping an eye – and writing regular reports – on DCI Daley will fall to someone else.'

'So, another new face, eh?'

'No, Brian, an old face.' She stared unblinkingly at the man across the desk.

'Wait, you're saying you want me tae spy on oor Jimmy – write reports on him?'

'Yes, that's exactly what I mean.' She silenced Scott's protests with a wave of her hand. 'Nobody knows him better, and there's no one he trusts more.'

'Exactly! See where I come fae, that's called being a sneaky rat bastard, if you pardon the language, ma'am.'

'From where I'm sitting – and trust me on this, Brian – it's the only way back for your friend. If you won't do this – well, I don't think I can make HQ wear it. Simple as that!'

'This is blackmail. How can I spy on a man who's been my best friend for so many years? If he ever found oot it would break his heart, and I couldnae blame him.'

'But if he doesn't get to come back to work, or gets kicked into the long grass to some shit desk job, how will he feel then, Brian?'

'He'll cash in his chips and resign – who wouldnae?'

'This job's all he has, and you know it. The only way I can make this happen is if you agree to monitor him. That's the bottom line.'

Scott shook his head. 'You've left me wae nae choice, haven't you? You knew I'd have tae agree under these circumstances. But let me tell you now, ma'am, I'm sick tae my stomach at the thought o' this. And I mean sick!' Scott banged his fist on the desk.

'You're doing the right thing for your friend – and for me, Brian. He'll probably fit right back into the swing of things, and this will be forgotten. We'll be back to normal.'

Scott recalled the last time he'd seen Jim Daley. He had looked pale, agitated and nothing like his normal self. Scott wasn't at all sure that coming back to work was the right thing for his friend to do, but he had to give the man who had done so much for him a chance. 'Aye, I'll dae it. But I want tae register my reluctance – aye, an' disappointment, tae.'

'There's a silver lining, Brian – well, two, when you think about it.'

'Which are?'

'Well, firstly, you'll be helping in the rehabilitation of an old friend.'

'And?'

'Once this period of observation is over, I'm instructed to inform you that your move to inspector will be made permanent.' Symington smiled broadly.

'You can tell them at HQ where tae stick their promotion. I feel bad enough having tae dae this in the first place. I'm certainly no' taking thirty pieces of silver for the privilege. I'm mair than happy as a DS. Now, if you'll excuse me, ma'am, I've a sub-division tae run. For the time being, at least.'

Before Symington could reply, Scott thrust back his chair, made for the door, and slammed it in his wake.

'Well, that could have been worse,' said Symington quietly to herself.

Even Alice Wenger had been anxious as the small aircraft approached the runway at Machrie side-on. Frequent flyer though she was, the belting rain and high winds made her doubt the decision to allow the flight to go ahead. She was further alarmed when the pilot casually informed the dozen or so souls aboard that he'd have a go at landing, but if that proved impossible it was back to Glasgow.

Alice clutched the arm of her seat firmly as the plane hit the tarmac four times before landing was complete. She recoiled as a young man in front of her spewed copiously on the floor, and an elderly couple across the aisle screamed in unison. But as the plane came to a halt on the wind- and rain-lashed runway, her anxiety soon dissipated and she began to feel more like herself.

It was ironic in a way. The last time she'd seen this place

she'd had to flee with her heart in her mouth. Now, after all this time, she was back, experiencing much the same sensation, albeit for very different reasons.

The small party was ushered down the few steps from the aircraft and huddled across the short distance towards the terminal building. Through security, Alice collected her luggage and addressed an elderly man in overalls marked with the airline's logo.

'I need a cab. You got any numbers?'

'No need tae worry on that score,' he replied. 'McLintock's always have some taxis waiting – especially on days like this. Just go oot the main door there and you can't miss them.'

She nodded by way of a thank you and made for the exit. The elderly man watched her leave, stroking his chin thoughtfully, before returning to his luggage duties.

A red taxi sat behind a low fence. Alice Wenger leaned into the wind and made her way through an open gate to jump into the back seat with her luggage, thankful to be free of the dreadful weather. 'You take me to Machrie House Hotel, yeah?'

The young man behind the wheel smiled at her in the rear-view mirror. 'Aye, nae bother, missus. Hooroa day, eh?'

Alice smiled at the expression she hadn't heard for so many years. 'Yeah, it sure is, kid.' She studied her driver: squat, red hair and blue eyes. 'Tell me, are you Duncan's boy?'

The driver looked puzzled for a few moments until the penny dropped. 'Dae you mean my grandfaither?'

'Your grandfather – wow!'

'Aye, dae you know him? It's still his taxi company, but he doesna dae much driving now on account of his knees, you know.'

'We went to school together.' She was pleased to note the look of disbelief in the young man's eyes. It clearly seemed impossible to him that the woman now sitting in the back of his taxi could possibly be the same age as his grandfather. 'How is he?'

'Jeest an' auld bugger – if you pardon my language, missus. My name's Duncan tae. I'm called after him.'

'I can certainly see the resemblance.'

Her driver laughed. 'You obviously havena seen him for a few years. Bald as a coot noo.'

As they drove through the rain, Alice rubbed some of the condensation from the window with the back of her hand. She could make out the hills she'd known so well, looming ghosts in the gloom. They were shadows, mere glimpses, but in her time she'd come to know every path, burn and glen. Walking in the hills had been an escape, the need to free herself of other people in an attempt to find peace. Though she couldn't see them clearly, she could picture them vividly in the full glory of a bright summer's day. The way they cosseted the town had in turn made her feel warm, protected – somehow in their care. She even remembered the names of some of the farms they passed on the road to Machrie. Nothing seemed to have changed, but everything had changed. She was no longer the frightened girl dressed in rags with holes in her shoes, the butt of her classmates' jokes and barbs. That was another life.

They pulled up at the hotel, the taxi's diesel engine shuddering to a halt.

'I'll get they bags in for you,' said Duncan, opening her door.

'Thank you, young man.' With Alice taking the lead, they made their way up a short flight of steps to a large glass door, which was opened by a liveried doorman.

'Welcome to the Machrie House Hotel,' he said with a smile. 'I'll take those bags for you, madam.'

Alice watched Duncan hand over her luggage as she delved into her handbag. 'What do I owe you, Duncan?'

'We'll call it seven quid, missus, if you don't mind.'

'Here, take this for your trouble,' she said, giving him a fifty-pound note.

'Are you sure?' Duncan stared at the note as though he'd never seen money before.

'Sure. I picked up some UK cash at Heathrow. It's yours, kid.'

Duncan turned to go, but stopped. 'Can you tell me your name – jeest so I can tell my grandfaither, like?'

Alice thought for a moment. 'Oh, he won't remember me, but nice meeting you, yeah?' She showed him the card she had picked up in the taxi. 'I've got your number, so if I ever need a cab . . .' She smiled and turned towards the large reception desk.

Duncan shrugged and made his way back to his taxi, making sure that the large denomination banknote was tucked safely in the bottom of his trouser pocket.

'Mrs Wenger, welcome to the Machrie House Hotel,' said the receptionist, perfectly turned out in a kilt and matching dark blue jacket.'

'It's Ms Wenger.'

'Oh, I beg your pardon.' The young woman began to blush.

'Hey, don't sweat it. Take my advice, marry some rich bastard then get rid of them as quick as you can, honey.'

'Right, I'll remember that. I'm Daisy. We have your suite ready for you, Ms Wenger. Tommy will take you upstairs. If I could just ask you to sign the register and have your credit card details, please?'

'Sure thing.' Alice handed over her Amex Black card and signed the register. Her journey had been a long one: not just the flight from California, the journey of her life. But now here she was back where it all began. Automatically she ran her hand through her hair and let her forefinger linger again over the lump above her eye. 'Oh, I'll need to hire a set of wheels while I'm here. Can you do that for me?'

'Yeah, certainly,' said Daisy. 'If you can let me have your driving licence and passport for ID – I have your card details. I'll sort it out now. Mason's in Kinloch hire cars; I'll get them to deliver.'

'None of that stick-shift crap, either. I want an automatic, okay?'

'Certainly, Ms Wenger.'

'Good stuff. You look after me, Daisy, and I'll do the same for you.' She handed the receptionist twenty pounds. 'First of many, yeah?'

'Thank you, Ms Wenger.' Daisy smiled. Maybe her new guest wasn't such a bitch after all.

4

The thin old woman sat in the rocking chair, her fingers working nimbly with a pair of thick knitting needles. The chair creaked rhythmically as she rocked to and fro, eyes staring not at her work but at the three large men who sat round a rough wooden table. They were dressed in matching jumpers, oily black, with food stains spread liberally over the front of all three. Each man had dirty brown hair in various stages of retreat. The slightest of them had only three strands that stood on end from a balding pate. At his temples slivers of grey speckled nature's tonsure. It was hard to put an age on any of them, but this man was clearly the eldest, possibly in his mid to late fifties, though he looked older.

Without warning, the largest of the three – with the most hair and likely the youngest – burst into fits of laughter as he threw the dice, jumped up and clapped his hands manically.

'Enough!' the old woman shouted, and looked on with pleasure as the men at the table cowered and the laughter stopped abruptly. 'You boys would be better served getting ready tae get they sheep in before the weather gets worse, instead of sitting rolling dice like children.'

'Aye, Mother, jeest going,' mumbled Three Strands, his voice slurred like a drunk's.

'See that you do. It'll be dark soon and I want they sheep in the fank noo! I hope you sorted that fence, tae, or you'll be chasing them up the hill.' She hesitated, watching them with a steady, malevolent gaze. 'Well, whoot are you waiting for?'

She watched them troop out one by one, pausing only to collect three filthy black capes from hooks on the wall. They shrugged them on and left, the gale already sounding a braying lament as the old door opened and closed.

'You're too abrupt with them.' A thin man appeared at her side, his loose-fitting trousers held up by braces over a grey vest. He had a lick of shaving soap on his scraggy neck and a cut-throat razor in his hand. 'It'll be worse tonight than last,' he commented, looking through the small panes of the filthy window. On its ledge sat a handbell, the brass tarnished but the name *Jeremiah* still plainly etched in black on its mottled surface.

'Why don't you take mair responsibility for them, then?'

'I'm working, you know that.' The man looked at her with an expression that was hard to gauge. Though his face was grey and old, his bright green eyes still shone below a deeply furrowed brow. There was something about the way he spoke that didn't quite match his surroundings. His refined, modulated tones clashed with the hovel. An old brick fireplace stood at the gable end of the room. Under the window the roughly hewn table sat behind an ancient couch from which the stuffing fought for freedom out of age-worn holes in the faded brown fabric. The floor was of bare boards, not the polished, prettified affairs so in vogue, but rough, uneven planks, punctuated only by two sheepskin rugs that had clearly once belonged to beasts long since deceased. It was as though the modern world had been cast aside, and the cottage was held fast in time, as sure as the hills under which it nestled.

As the pale light of day bade a premature farewell from the lowering sky, the peat fire and an old storm lantern began to hold sway in the musty space as another lash of rain broke against the thin glass of the windows.

'You could take a whip tae them and it would make no odds, husband. We both know fine that's the truth.'

The man walked over to a wooden clothes horse by the fire, from which he picked a worn jumper similar to those that adorned the three younger men of the house, though newly laundered. He slipped it over his oval head and was immediately enveloped in the homespun garment, the hem almost reaching his knees. 'They're still strong, Ginny. But if we're to survive they must be taught how to look after us. The years are rolling on, and I have no intention of spending my last days in the geriatric home in Kinloch. They'll have to learn to think for themselves.'

'Maybe so, Nathaniel. But hark at this: they are what they were intended tae be. We're damn sure o' that. And all considered, we'd maybe be better spending oor last days in the retirement home, eh?'

He shrugged and left the room. Soon, the sound of a typewriter tapped in counterpoint to the gathering storm outside, like the rattle of bullets in a desperate battle.

Ginny continued to rock back and forth in her chair, her eyes now staring blankly into space, lost in her own thoughts.

Annie and Hamish eyed the two men in suits with growing suspicion. One of them was standing on a stepladder, examining the ceiling of the cosy bar at the County Hotel with a small bright torch. He muttered something to his youthful companion, who wrote quickly on a clipboard, then descended the steps and looked around.

'Now, Mrs . . .'

'Annie, Mr Foreshaw, that'll dae just fine.'

'Yes, Annie; of course, you did say earlier. I realise that you will have residents, but I'd like to see the empty rooms now and the others when the guests leave tomorrow morning, please. We're staying overnight, as you know, so that shouldn't be a problem, yes?'

'No, no' a problem, Mr Foreshaw.' Annie swallowed hard and with her best effort managed a weak smile.

Foreshaw muttered something else to his younger companion then addressed the hotel manager again. 'Can you direct me to your facilities – Annie?'

'Eh? You've seen the cellar, have you no'?'

'No, I was meaning the bathroom – the Gents?' Foreshaw raised a brow at the misunderstanding.

'Doon the corridor and to your right,' said Hamish sharply. 'One door's got a woman on it and the other a man – though his legs are missing since wee Arthur cut them off and replaced them wae a spectacle I'll no' discuss in polite company.'

'Aye, the bastard,' said Annie, a look of fury now on her face. 'I'd tae ban him for a week. We managed tae get it off wae some Vim and vinegar, but we never got roon tae drawing the legs back on. But the lassie's still got her skirt on, so you'll be fine. I got tae him before he could deface her, thankfully.'

'I dread tae think whoot would have been the result if you hadna,' observed Hamish, sucking at his unlit pipe, face grim.

'I'm sure I'll manage to work things out,' said Foreshaw, before disappearing from the bar in search of the elusive toilet.

Hamish eyed the remaining man with suspicion. 'You'll be here for the health and safety, eh? Man, that's becoming fair dictatorial these days, right enough. The boys on the boats tell me they canna make their breakfast withoot having tae fill in numerous forms. All aboot the quality of the eggs and the like, I shouldna wonder. Auld Adolf would be rubbing his hands with glee, so he would.'

'What gave you that idea?' The young man sat on a barstool. 'We're surveyors. We do a lot of old hotels and the like.'

'I jeest got a call tae book yous in for the night and let you look at whootever you wanted,' said Annie, polishing a beer font.

'So, for whoot reason would you be surveying the hotel?' asked Hamish, his head cocked to one side.

'Well, usually it's for a sale, or remortgage, or that. Let me see.' He consulted notes on his clipboard. 'Ah, here we are. It's a feasibility study – preliminary, of course.'

'A feasibility study intae whoot?' asked Hamish.

The young man again consulted his notes. '*For the purpose and intent of conversion for habitation, dwelling and utilisation of same.*' He smiled.

Annie scowled back. 'Gie us it in English, young fulla.'

'Flats, probably – or maybe one big house, but that would be unusual.' Again he smiled brightly, looking between Annie and Hamish.

There was a choking sound before Hamish began a barking cough, tears coming to his eyes as he wheezed for breath.

'Here,' said Annie, quickly pouring some dark beer into a wine glass. 'Gie him this o'er, would you, son?'

The junior surveyor handed the drink across to Hamish, whose face had turned a shade between red and purple. He grabbed the glass, drained it in one gulp and made to speak, though nothing emerged from his mouth other than a coarse whisper.

'Whoot's he saying?' asked Annie. 'Is he after an ambulance?'

The youth jumped from his stool and leaned into Hamish's face, trying to make out what the old man was attempting to convey. 'I think he wants a pram – a big one.' He shrugged his shoulders, a confused look on his face.

Annie narrowed her eyes, took a small glass from a shelf and held it under a large bottle of whisky on the optics gantry. 'Here, gie him his *pram*,' she said, handing over the large measure.

Hamish took another deep draught, and seemed to regain his equilibrium, though his face was still an unhealthy hue. 'An auld man like myself shouldna be facing such dilemmas.' He took another gulp at the whisky. 'Enough tae take life fair away, a shock like thon.'

Foreshaw walked into the bar and immediately focused on the old fisherman. 'What on earth's happened?'

Annie flung her bar towel aggressively over one shoulder and glared at her newly returned guest. 'I think you're the one tae be answering that, Mr Foreshaw, don't you?'

The surveyor thought for a moment, then addressed his young charge. 'Anthony, a word, please.'

5

Alice Wenger had considered the rain lashing against the windows of her hotel's dining room with impatience. She had things to do, self-set tasks to accomplish, and rain like this would most certainly impede her. Still, as the motto of much of her life had been 'nothing is impossible', she decided to adapt her plan.

On finishing her first meal of the day – light fare of coffee, cereal and fruit, as opposed to the fat-fest that was the 'Traditional Kintyre Breakfast' – she walked across the tartan carpet to reception, where Daisy was already in place, her permanent smile seemingly painted on.

'Ms Wenger, good morning. How can I help you today?'

'I need some wet weather gear. You know, gumboots, rain jacket. I forgot how shit the weather could be around here.'

Daisy thought for a moment. 'Not something we have in the hotel, I'm afraid. But there's a place in Kinloch – McGryffe's – they supply all that type of stuff. Your 4x4 should be arriving shortly.'

'Well done, just what I need. I remember McGryffe's – the bottom of Main Street, right?'

Daisy looked slightly taken aback. 'Yes, next door to the newsagents.'

'You look as though you've seen a ghost, honey. Yeah, I've been here before.'

'I hadn't realised.' Daisy retained her composure.

'No, I'm quite sure that will apply to quite a lot of folks. It's been a long time. Give me a ring when that car arrives.'

Alice took the lift back to her room and flung herself on the bed, mind working overtime. She had always been an early riser, and here in Machrie she'd made no exception. She'd been the first at breakfast at six-thirty, having already been up for two hours sending emails and making notes to ensure things went smoothly back in California. Even though she enjoyed frequent vacations, she never really let go of the reins of power. In any case, it was so easy now with Skype calls, email, smartphones. There were few places in the world in which she felt cut off from her business, and that's the way she liked it.

As she contemplated an hour in the hotel's gym, the unfamiliar tone of the phone at her bedside sounded. She greeted the call in her habitual style. 'Wenger, speak.'

'That's your car arrived, Ms Wenger. Would it be okay if you came down to sign the paperwork?'

'Yeah, sure thing.' Alice heaved herself back to her feet, pocketed the entry card to her room and took a deep breath. There'd be no time for a workout. Things had to be done, things that had preyed on her mind for far too long. As she opened the door to her room, though, she felt her hand tremble. Shit, still after all this time, she thought. Without warning, five faces filled her thoughts.

Alice Wenger closed her eyes, banished the unwanted image and left the room. Soon, the hatred that had plagued her, driven her through most of her adult life, could be addressed.

And there was no time like the present. Automatically, she reached for the lump above her right eye, and, as always, its presence reinvigorated her.

Scott was leafing through some papers in the glass box, nine constables along with Sergeant Shaw standing before him.

'I cannae see how it's happened. It took me half the night tae work oot this week's shift roster, what wae annual leave, re-roster rest days, sick days, court appearances and a' that. Mind you, Ella was in my ear. She was watching some crap on the telly – thon cooking programme, quite good – so I was finding it hard tae concentrate, know what I mean?'

'Well, basically we're three up today and five down tomorrow,' said Sergeant Shaw.

'I'd to cancel a weekend away with my boyfriend,' said Constable Janice James. 'We were going to the Lakes – a lovely wee cottage, too. Lost a fortune on the deposit, so we did.'

'Oh, it's great down there, Janice,' said Constable Mike Fearns. 'Me and the wife have been down about five times. Great for the kids; but you don't have that problem yet.' He smiled.

'We're trying for a baby, but what wae Alex's shifts on the ambulances and mine, well, it's hard going, you know.'

Fearns nodded in sympathy. 'My other half's a midwife; she can be off at a minute's notice.'

'Aye, but reassuring, is it not? Especially when she was having her own, eh?' commented Constable Bob Fletcher. 'I mean, she knows fine what she's at, and all that.'

'She didn't haul the wean out by herself, if that's what you mean,' replied Fearns. 'We're not talking DIY plumbing here.'

Janice James was about to speak when Scott banged the desk with his fist. 'Would yous shut up! I'm trying tae think.' He shuffled some more papers, reading glasses perched at the end of his nose.

'Mind I'm going to the Christmas markets in Germany in three weeks. I handed you a leave request,' said Fletcher.

'Is this *Holiday '86* – do I look like Barry fucking Norman?' said Scott impatiently.

'He was the film guy, Brian. You're thinking of Cliff Michelmore,' remarked Shaw.

'Oh for fuck's sake,' shouted Scott. 'Whoever it was, it's no' helping the fact we've got far too many bodies the day, and bugger all tomorrow! Fletcher, James, can yous jeest go home the noo and come back in tomorrow morning instead?'

'No can do, sir,' replied James. 'I've got an appointment.'

'Well, you'll just have tae cancel it.'

'Can't do that, sir.'

'How no'?'

'It's personal, sir. A medical matter.'

'Listen, I'll have a look and see what I can do,' said Shaw with a sigh. 'I'm sure we can come up with something.'

'Well, you better take this pile o' crap then.' Scott handed the desk sergeant a bulky, untidy pile of papers all bearing his familiar spidery handwriting.

'You'll need tae bring in one of they experts from the university to decipher that,' said Fearns, making his colleagues giggle.

'Smart arse, eh?' Scott glared at him. 'Just you wait until you've got some responsibility, see how you'll like it. Any bastard can cloak aboot gathering up drunks or helping auld dears across the road. This is the sharp end here, son!'

'Sorry, sir – just a joke, you know.'

'Right, is that it sorted, Sergeant Shaw?'

'Yes, I'll work something out,' replied Shaw doubtfully.

The door swung open to reveal Chief Superintendent Symington in all her finery. 'Problem, DI Scott?' she said, looking round the crowded room.

'Naw, just planning the Christmas party – och, you know what it's like.' Scott smiled guilelessly.

'I hope I'm getting an invitation?'

'Oh aye, goes without saying, ma'am.' Scott turned to the assembled company. 'Right, so we all know what we're at, just get oot an' arrest some bas— I mean get stuff done in an orderly fashion, an' that.'

Symington did her best to suppress a smile as her officers trooped out, most acknowledging her with 'Ma'am', or an incline of the head. 'Everything fine, then, Brian?'

'Oh aye, hunky-dory, ma'am. Well oiled machine here, as you can see.'

'Big shift out today. Is there something on?'

'Noo that's a good question, ma'am. Reports o' a motorcycle gang at Lochgilphead. Might be heading doon here. You cannae be too careful.'

'No, absolutely, DI Scott, absolutely. Anyway, I'll let you get on – almost lunchtime, I see.'

'Aye, I'm fair ravenous, ma'am.'

'Okay, we'll see you once you're fed and watered.'

'Yes, will do.' Scott smiled happily.

Symington turned to leave, then checked herself in the doorway. 'Jonathan Ross.'

'Who?'

'He's the first guy I remember doing the film programme.'

She turned on her heel, closing the door gently in her wake.

'Every bugger's a comedian, here,' muttered Scott to himself as he shrugged on his jacket. Ella was having lunch with some new friends she'd made at a library book group, so Scott decided to treat himself to lunch at the County Hotel. He left the office, passing Shaw with his head down over work rotas.

'Good man. Just you make sure you get something tae eat, noo,' said Scott as he pressed the buzzer and left Kinloch police office.

'Sure thing, Brian. In a hundred years, once I've managed to work this out,' the sergeant said to himself with a shake of the head.

6

Alice Wenger was toiling up a muddy path, her newly purchased walking boots making light work of her trudge, despite the conditions underfoot. She was dressed in a matching storm jacket and rain trousers – one of the best brands. The young man in McGryffe's had smiled broadly as she paid for the goods. Probably the best single transaction they'd had in a while, she reckoned.

On the way to Kinloch, under clearer skies, she realised that things had changed. During the five-mile journey into the town she spotted a number of new houses and a couple of dilapidated farmsteads that had once been thriving little businesses, homes to some kids with whom she'd been to school. When she drove through the town change was even more marked. Old familiar shops had gone to be replaced by places she didn't recognise. There was even a tattoo parlour, something she couldn't have envisaged in her youth. By the same token, she silently mourned the loss of the greengrocers on Long Road, the old bookshop on Main Street, and the little Italian café on the seafront. She'd known all these places so well; she could still smell the musty bookshop and the old woman who seemed to have been behind its counter for ever.

Books were the only things that had made her life bearable back then. Those and the little transistor radio her best friend had given her – a prized possession that Alice hid away carefully and listened to through a single earpiece late at night when she knew nobody else could hear.

One dreadful day her mother had discovered her pride and joy, and when Alice returned home from school the woman had taken a mallet to the little radio, smashing it to pieces on the big old table, a broad smirk spreading across her face at her daughter's evident distress.

'You've no need for this tool o' the devil. You've no' got long left at school, mind: then you'll see the error of your ways.'

As she reached a thicket of trees she couldn't remember having been there before, Alice shuddered at the memory. She could see that face in her mind's eye as though it were yesterday. The small dark eyes, black almost – well, to her anyway. The hair pulled into a tight bun, the mole sprouting hair on her left cheek, and the tight, cruel mouth, more often than not downturned in a perpetual scowl.

Despite herself, Alice Wenger had to stop for breath. The very thought of this woman had forced the air from her lungs.

Thankfully, the heavy rain had eased to a light drizzle, though the storm hadn't yet blown itself out. A stiff breeze rustled the dark branches of the trees all around her, the very last leaves of autumn tossed in its wake and dashed to the muddy ground. These bare trees reminded her of her mother's thin gnarled fingers as they gripped her arms, the malicious cuts left in her young flesh by the woman's razor-sharp fingernails.

Alice plodded on. She had been able to take the large 4x4 further than she'd expected. But in a way she was grateful to make the last part of her journey on foot, feeling the elements, breathing the air, stoking her hatred with every step.

Soon the little glade of trees thinned out, and Alice found herself on a bare hillside, a storm-tossed sea far below. She walked up a rise, picturing in her mind the sharp drop at its far side. In a few minutes she had reached the summit, and the wind caught the collar of her jacket so that it flapped in her face. She pushed it away with her gloved hand and edged as close to the almost vertical drop as she dared.

Her gaze was still elevated, staring across the waves to the horizon, where she could make out the bread-shaped mound of Ailsa Craig through the smir. Slowly, she lowered her head, just as a gust of wind caught her, making her take an involuntary step forward to resist its push. There, far below, sat the little cottage, a deep strand of seaweed banked up on the shingle at its front, a sharp finger of black rocks poking into the surf like a defiantly drawn, malevolent sword. Alice fancied she could already smell the taint of seaweed on the wind.

She took the small but powerful binoculars from her pocket and held them to her eyes. She was angry with herself when the image before her began to jump and jar because of the trembling of her hands. She would have liked to blame the chill wind for that, but knew it was the visceral emotion of fear, the like of which she hadn't experienced since she was last in this place.

She willed her hands to stop trembling and soon she was able to pick out the dwelling more clearly. Beside a broken plough sat the remains of an old Transit van. It was kilted to one side, a back wheel arch propped up on bricks. Though the ruined vehicle sported one wing that looked light blue, almost white, the rest of the bodywork bore the red-brown of rust, though she could still make out a shadow of the bottle green it had once been.

Where would I be now without that van, she wondered. She hadn't expected to see it, but there it was, decaying like the rest of the property, but present still. Parts of her life that, no matter how hard she tried, she could never banish from her darkest thoughts and worst nightmares.

She scanned the shingle beach, swallowing hard when she noted three hulking dark figures hauling a little boat along the pebbles nearer to the bank of seaweed. They were a blur now, her tears obscuring the view despite the quality of the binoculars. She let them hang by the strap around her neck as she sobbed.

This was unexpected – unwanted. But it had happened.

Alice spoke to herself, her voice suddenly changed; gone now the Kentucky drawl. 'Gie yersel' a shake, lassie – come on!'

Just as she forced herself to stop crying, something else grabbed her heart with icy cold fingers. Distantly, on the wind, a bell tolled. Jeremiah's bell – it could be no other.

Alice Wenger sank to her knees and curled up in a ball on the soaking ground.

Jim Daley looked himself up and down in the mirror. He was glad to have lost some weight, but unhappy about the reason for doing so. But this bittersweet feeling encompassed most of his life now, he reckoned, so he tried to make the best of things. No struggle this time to button his trousers – in fact he had to draw his belt in a couple of notches.

He tied his tie in the habitual Windsor knot then sat on the end of the bed to put on his shoes, polished to perfection the night before. This wasn't going to be his first day back at work, but he was to see Chief Superintendent Symington, and that was enough to set his pulse racing. It was as though she had the power of life and death over him, to give, or to take away. The notion disturbed him greatly.

He looked at the picture of his wife and son on the dressing table. Despite himself he couldn't remember when it had been taken. Liz had gone, come back, then gone again. Now, it seemed, she was determined to come back for good. But remembering the song, he wasn't sure if that was what he wanted. Still, she'd kept him safe, nursed him through one of the most difficult times of his life, and he felt he owed her a deep debt of gratitude.

But was that enough upon which to base a marriage?

'Right, that's me, Liz,' he called as he found his car keys on the table in the hall.

She emerged from the lounge in sweatpants and a long jumper, newly acquired glasses on the end of her nose as she appraised him. She smiled and walked the short distance to kiss him on the cheek and wish him well.

'I hate this,' said Daley.

'Of course you do – why wouldn't you?'

'It's like going to see the headmaster.'

'In that case you should ask Brian for tips. I'm sure he stood before a fair number of headmasters in his time.'

'Of that there can be no doubt.' He smiled and kissed her on the forehead.

'We're okay, aren't we, Jim?' She looked up at him hopefully, large eyes magnified by the spectacles.

'Of course we are,' he replied with as much conviction as possible. But he could see a shadow of doubt pass across her face, more than likely reflecting a similar expression that had just passed across his own. 'One day at a time, eh?'

'Yeah, you're right, Jim. One day at a time.'

She wished him good luck as he walked down the steps to the SUV parked under the raised decking beside his house on the hill. Before him, across the lime green waters of the loch, the familiar march of gravestones was picked out in flashes of sunlight from behind scudding clouds. The smell of the storm was strong in the air; everything renewed, a fresh start. That's what he was hoping for – wasn't it?

He sat behind the wheel, drew a smaller length of seatbelt across his stomach than he was accustomed to, and started the car. He made his way slowly down the rough track that took him out on to the main road. As he drove through the town he was surprised by the bustle. He reasoned that the last two stormy days had kept folk indoors and now they were taking advantage of the favourable elements while they could. The forecast was for more bad weather.

In minutes he was driving through the gates of Kinloch police office. He smiled, noting that Brian's car was occupying his parking space. He didn't mind; in fact the thought of his old friend being acting sub-divisional commander made him chuckle. But he knew that was unfair. Instant choice for the next chief constable he might not be, but Brian Scott – despite his many failings – was one of the best cops he'd ever worked with, as well as being his oldest and dearest friend.

As Daley punched in the security code to access the office via the rear door, a whole new set of thoughts entered his head. Had things gone another way he could have been standing at a similar door while someone else entered the security code. Regardless of the noble revenge for a hideous crime, he knew he was lucky not to be behind bars himself. As he walked into the dim light of the corridor, the familiar bleep and crackle of radio traffic made him feel like a fraud. Had he any right to be here, any right to be discussing his return to work?

Any bastard would have done the same, Jimmy. Brian Scott's words echoed in his mind. *If he'd done that tae my Ella, he'd have been wearing his bollocks for earrings, I'm no' joking!*

Heartened, Daley strode down the corridor towards the charge bar, where Sergeant Shaw was looking puzzled as he worked on a set of papers, his hair standing on end where he'd been scratching his head for inspiration.

'You at the *Times* crossword?'

'Jim – sir, no, not at all. I'm trying to make sense of our acting inspector's roster sheets.' He grimaced.

'Ho! Good luck with that.' For the first time in a long while Daley felt a smile spread across his face. 'Is she in – the real boss, I mean?'

'I think so – unless she's in your box arguing with Brian again.'

'Arguing? What about?'

Shaw shrugged his shoulders. 'No idea, but they were going at it hammer and tongs a while ago. Brian was giving as good as he got – I could hear them from here.'

Daley raised his brows. 'Oh well, I'll leave you to it. No time like the present.' Shaw gave him a wink of encouragement and Daley walked along the corridor until he reached what had been John Donald's office. In a way he would have been happier at the prospect of facing his dead boss and bitter enemy. There would have been no sense of guilt or unworthiness when confronting a man who cared nothing for morals and even less for the law. But as he composed himself and knocked on her door, he knew Carrie Symington was a different proposition altogether.

7

Brian Scott entered the bar at the County Hotel, his stomach rumbling. He hadn't enjoyed his breakfast because of bickering with his wife, so he'd decided to treat himself to something substantial rather than his usual filled roll and crisps.

Two or three people were dotted around the room. A young couple sat at one of the back tables, and the wafting aroma of their fish and chips made the detective's mouth water. At the table nearest the bar, Hamish and another man sat deep in conversation, their expressions less than sanguine. Likewise Annie, usually animated and welcoming, merely nodded and said a subdued 'Hello'.

'Has somebody died, or what?' Scott asked.

'It's yourself, Brian,' said Hamish. 'Come on over and take a seat.'

Scott accepted the invitation and sat down beside Hamish and his companion. 'Can I get a menu, Annie? I'm fair starving, so I am.'

She reached below the bar and stretched over to hand him a laminated single sheet that served as the lunch menu. 'No special on the day, Brian.'

'Oh, why not?'

'Och, big Peter couldna be bothered – whoot wae a' the goings-on, an' that.'

'What's been going on?'

'A fair tragedy, Brian,' said Hamish. 'No other way tae describe it.'

Scott's heart lurched in his chest for a moment. If any kind of disaster had befallen the community he should have known about it. 'What are you on aboot?'

'Och, I can hardly let the words form in my ain mooth,' said Hamish. 'You tell him, Annie.'

'Bad news, Brian – the worst, in fact,' she said.

'Will somebody just tell me what's happening!'

'There's men here – *surveyors*, if you please,' said Hamish, clearly now ready to tell the tale. 'They're upstairs going through the bedrooms at this very moment.' He shook his head and downed what was left of his glass of whisky.

'What are they aboot?'

Annie made to speak but Hamish beat her to it. 'They're here to work out how they can turn the hotel into flats, that's what they're aboot!'

'Eh? Surely no'. This place does well, what wae meals an' drink, guests and the like.'

'No' well enough, Brian, that's clear,' said Annie, her head bowed, leaning on the bar. 'I phoned the owners last night. They didnae say much, mind you, but I could tell fine whoot they're at.'

Scott shook his head in disbelief. 'Hard tae think o' Kinloch withoot this hotel.'

'I've been coming here since the end o' the war,' said Hamish. 'I was jeest a nipper, mind you, but my faither brought me in after that German submarine got washed up on the causeway. Fair upset, he was – even though it was the enemy who perished. Mind, there's a fair solidarity between men o' the sea, regardless o' ideology, though he was tight tae admit it at the time. I was greetin' fit tae burst, so we came in here as a treat. My, I remember that like it was yesterday.'

'Aye, an' you've been in jeest aboot every night since,' said Annie.

'I've graced this establishment a fair number o' times o'er the years, it's true. For all its faults, mark you.'

'Faults? Whoot faults?' Annie was suddenly on the defensive.

'Well, for a start, you've always been mair expensive than Jenny's, and the beer's never been as good as in the Douglas Arms. Something tae dae with the drawing distance fae the cellar, I'm sure.'

Annie tried to speak, but her mouth flapped open and closed like a landed fish.

'You've been coming here for a whiles yoursel', Erchie, eh?' Hamish addressed the other man at the table.

'Aye, since I was posted here from Clydebank,' Erchie replied.

'Posted?' asked Scott.

'Yes, posted. I was in the polis. I served as a constable here for a good four years. Long before your time, mind you.'

'Why did you leave?'

'Married a local lassie. Her family weren't so keen on polismen, so that was it. Either the job or the lassie I was in love with. So I chose her.'

'No regrets, I bet.'

'Ha! No regrets, my arse. We lasted about eighteen months before she ran off with the cobbler.'

'Willie Johnson. Would shag a barber's floor, that bugger,' observed Hamish with a sour look.

'They moved to Australia, and that was that – left high and dry.'

'And naebody tae mend so much as the sole of your boots in the whole place. Auld Mr Quinn in the shoe shop rubbed his hands till they was red-raw, so he did.'

'Did you apply tae join up again?' asked Scott.

'No, it wisnae really for me, to be honest. We'd a right bugger o' an inspector back then – everybody hated him. I didnae want tae go back tae that. I was a farm labourer up until a couple o' year ago.'

'And what are you at these days?' Scott had noticed his boiler suit.

'Just part time oot at the airport. I do odd jobs – help with the luggage, clean the loos, that sort o' thing. Gets me oot o' my bed in the morning, and pays for the car; that's about all I can say tae recommend it.'

'Here, tell Brian whoot you telt me earlier, Erchie,' said Hamish. 'We're both needing a wee libation, Brian – jeest tae force the sadness oot, you understand.'

Scott ordered a round of drinks and fish and chips from the menu. 'Right, I'm all ears,' he said, after taking a gulp of ginger beer and lime.

'Just something that troubled me yesterday; like seeing a ghost, so it was,' said Erchie.

'Here we go.' Scott raised his eyes to the heavens.

'Noo, hear him oot, Brian. This might be o' interest tae yourself, mind.'

'If you must, but get it o'er before my fish an' chips arrive.'

Erchie adopted a faraway look. 'We're going back – och,

mair than thirty years. It was my last year in the polis. A lassie went missing; disappeared intae thin air, so she did.'

'One o' the Doigs fae the black croft,' Hamish interrupted.

'The black croft? That's a cheery name tae call your hoose,' remarked Scott.

'That's no' its right name. It's Rowan Tree Cottage – but it's been known as the black croft since long before I was born.' Hamish took a gulp at his whisky.

'How so?'

'Well, the Doigs got a bad name – the worst.'

Scott sighed. 'So it's a family saga, noo. Mind my fish an' chips are near ready.'

'They were wreckers, Brian, the lowest o' the low. Lured fine seamen tae their deaths, an' profited from what was washed ashore. Despicable, that's a' a man can say.'

'That's jeest auld wives' tales, Hamish,' said Annie.

'Not a bit of it! My faither telt me, and his telt him. And let me tell you, we're no' a family prone tae fancy.' There was a brief silence while those gathered absorbed this fact.

'And what aboot this lassie, then?' asked Scott, desperate to shorten what promised to be a long tale of Kinloch lore.

'The day after she left the school, she just disappeared. Took their van fae the cottage, and that's the last that was seen o' her – until yesterday,' said Erchie.

'Yesterday?' Despite himself Scott's interest was piqued.

'I was busy unloading the cases fae the trolley at the terminal. This lassie came up tae me – American like – asking for a taxi. I'm prepared tae swear that it was Alison Doig.'

'How can you be sure?'

'I spent my last year in the polis looking for her. Yous must have records back up the road still. We found the van

45

abandoned at Tarbert, but that's as far as we got. It's as though she just evaporated.'

'Hard tae tell after all these years, I'd say. The woman must be in her fifties by noo.'

'I'm telling you, if that wasn't Alison Doig I'll eat Hamish's bunnet.'

'You bloody well will not, Erchie!' said Hamish, pulling the Breton cap down on his head by way of security.

'And these Doigs, are they still aboot?' asked Scott.

'Yes, very much so. The mother and faither are a fair age, but still oot at the black croft, so they are. Auld Doig was a smart bugger. Went tae Glasgow tae be a doctor, so they say. But his faither didna like the idea, so it was back tae the croft. Never sat his exams, so I believe. He married a MacKechnie lassie fae up Firdale way. She was a right horror – could turn milk sour wae jeest a look. My faither crossed himself every time we passed the black croft when we was oot on the boat – an' him a Protestant, tae. They've got three big hulking lads, but naebody hardly ever sees them. No' jeest quite right, so I've heard. Live off the land and the fishing. Don't even have electricity, so they say.'

'So it's the blacked oot croft,' said Scott with a chuckle.

'I'm telling you, it was her,' said Erchie as Scott's meal arrived.

Two men entered behind the waitress. The older of the pair handed Annie two sets of keys on the familiarly over-large wooden hotel fobs. 'That's us, Annie. We'll not stay for lunch, we're on a tight schedule.'

'Good!' said Annie without looking him in the face.

'Aye, off tae ruin someone else's lives, I shouldna wonder,' said Hamish.

With a shake of his head the surveyor left the bar, his young colleague behind him looking apologetic.

Almost oblivious of this, Brian Scott savoured his lunch and silently resolved to have a look at the case of Alison Doig back at the office.

'And you're sure you feel fine, Jim?'

'Never felt better, ma'am. The tablets have fixed the heart arrhythmia. The doc calls me a model patient.' Daley smiled weakly.

'Well, the force MO agrees. You seem to be in good shape – lost a bit of weight, too, I see.'

'It's been a stressful time, ma'am.'

'I know – I absolutely acknowledge that. Things must have been so hard for you both. How's Liz?' Symington knew she would have to raise the subject sometime, but she was dreading it.

Daley folded his arms. 'You know. She's being Liz.'

'Which consists of?'

'Carrying on as though nothing has happened. She's been doing it all the way through our marriage, so why stop now?'

'I wish she'd taken it further – what happened to her, I mean.'

'Me too – though I doubt I'd be sitting here if she had.'

'Is that why Liz wouldn't proceed, you think?'

'No. If I thought that, I would have persuaded her to make a complaint.' Daley shifted in his seat uncomfortably. 'She doesn't want her family and friends to know. Nor does she want to go through the hell of the trial and all the publicity that would surround it. You know the score: rich businessman and top cop's wife. I can see the headlines myself.'

'And how does that make you feel?'

Daley angled his head towards the ceiling. 'With the greatest of respect, ma'am, this isn't a therapy session. In any case, I don't know how I feel – about anything.'

'Sorry.'

'No need.'

'But you think you're fit to come back?'

'Raring to go! My job – well, I've realised that, like it or loathe it, it's become my life. You're a cop; you must realise that too.'

Symington nodded feebly. 'Yes, it does become rather all-encompassing. But it's up to us not to let that happen, Jim.'

'You might be able to, but it's too late for me. I've felt completely rudderless over the last few months. Yes, the illness made me uneasy, but not having a reason to get up in the morning is the worst feeling in the world.'

'You could try other things.'

'What are you trying to say?' Daley's look was intense.

Symington sighed. 'Sorry. I'm not good at this, Jim. Of course I want you back – we all do. You're one of the best men we have. I just want you to know that you have other options than to come back to this.'

'You know what's funny, ma'am?'

'What?'

'For years I felt out of place in this job – it's not so long ago I resigned, or tried to, at least. But that would have been on my own terms. When the decision is made for you, it's as if you're helpless – nowhere to go. Like a naughty child being punished by having toys taken away. It's only since then I've realised how much this means to me.' He passed his hands through his hair. 'A long time ago someone told me not to let this happen – the job become my life, I mean.'

'But you didn't take the advice?'

'No.' He paused. 'It came from a man who was sitting in a shed at the bottom of his garden. He'd retired, but he was still as involved with being a policeman as he'd ever been – but only a few knew it.'

'DCI Burns, yes?'

'Yes.'

'And that's how you see your life now?'

'Not in a shed, no!'

'Okay, okay, Jim, I understand. I'm here to tell you that it's here for you whenever you want – work, I mean. You have medical clearance and PIRC have no objections.'

'Huh. Not since the PF threw out the case against me.'

'You know how complicated that was. Everyone just had to follow the rules – unlike you, Jim.'

'I know I've been lucky, ma'am.' His tone was now one of contrition.

'One day I'll tell you a story about my life. Trust me, I'm not judging you.'

Daley looked puzzled for a moment, but decided to carry on. 'So, back on Monday? Is that too soon?'

'No – not at all. I'm delighted we've managed to get to this place.' Her expression changed.

'But?'

'But I have to tell you something.'

'Go ahead, ma'am.'

'It's a trial period, Jim. Best I could do.'

'The trial being in what form?'

'Nothing complicated – just to make sure you can cope, that's all.'

'So I'm treading on eggshells.'

Symington leaned forward. 'Listen, with your health scare – and everything else – I had no choice but to agree. We give it six months, then your situation will be reviewed. Nothing sinister.'

'I suppose I knew it wouldn't be as simple as going straight back to normal.'

'It will be normal, Jim . . .'

'Just don't knock the shit out of any dentists or fall over, eh?'

'Something like that.' She smiled. 'Monday it is, then?'

'Yes, Monday it is, ma'am.'

They stood – the big detective towering over his superior – and shook hands.

'It'll be good to have you back, DCI Daley.'

'You're just saying that because I'm good at roster sheets.' He laughed.

'Yes, that has been a bit of a problem. Not Brian's thing, really.'

'Oh yes, I can understand that.'

'Don't get me wrong, though; he's done a good job.'

'Underneath it all he's one of the best cops out there, ma'am.'

'Don't worry, I know. And one of the most decent people, too.'

As though on cue, an urgent knock sounded on the door and Scott's face appeared round it.

'Jimmy boy!' He rushed over and enveloped his old friend in a hug. 'Good to see you, big man. I was going tae take a run up last night, but Ella was in my ear aboot cleaning oot the garage.' He stepped back for a moment, looking between Daley and Symington. 'Everything okay?'

'Monday, Brian,' said Symington.

'Monday what?'

'I'm back on Monday, Bri.' A broad grin transformed Daley's face. He grabbed Scott's hand and shook it vigorously.

'Steady on, big chap – you'll dislocate my shoulder!'

8

Alice Wenger lay on her bed in the Machrie House Hotel. Absently she was studying a small fly trapped in a spider's web in one corner of the high ceiling. As it weakened and became resigned to its fate, its desperate attempts to be free slowed to a stop.

Though she couldn't reach the web, even standing on a chair, Alice resolved to free the tiny creature. She opened a drawer in her dressing table and removed a pair of climbing socks, rolled into a ball, bought from the shop in Kinloch with the rest of her wet-weather gear. She padded across to the corner of the room and took aim at the web.

On the first occasion she missed the silken prison by a few inches, but her second attempt was more successful. The ball of socks scored a direct hit, and she was pleased to note that the web had been destroyed and there was no sign of the wretched insect. She bent forward to collect the socks, but was dismayed to find the fly lying only a few inches away, its legs still entangled in slivers of grey web. Carefully she picked it up and walked to the large sash window, which she forced open to let the fly fall from her hand into the sea-tanged air. It was a tiny gesture of kindness – setting a soul free – but to her it mattered. It was only when she returned to her bed that she considered the possibility that the fly had been killed by the blow of the heavy socks.

She lay back, troubled still. This tiny moment seemed like a metaphor, an encapsulation of her life in one act. Or at least that's what it promised to be. For the first time she asked herself the question: had coming here been a mistake, likely to do more harm than good? It was possible, but she knew she couldn't draw back now. For her, freedom was precious. For years she'd shied away from thinking about the course her life would have followed had it not been for the decision to flee, to be free of the web that entangled her. But as she'd watched the three shambling shapes far below the cliff and heard the tolling of the bell, the truth had confronted her like a kick to the guts. In another life, a middle-aged woman was gathering driftwood on that beach, her mind blank, responding only to the summoning toll of the bell.

On her nightstand, her cell phone pinged and she reached for it with a sigh.

Need your authorisation to transfer tax payments. J.

No, he didn't! Alice had made provision for that; she'd told Janneck.

Her phone pinged again, this time just a spam email. This tiny device was her bell, she realised. Its call was irresistible.

But Alice Wenger – Alison Doig – was no lumbering figure on a windswept beach.

Scott keyed the name Alison Doig into his computer. He was searching Kinloch's cold case archives. Almost instantly, the details appeared on the screen, mostly scans of typed reports and case notes by the officers who had investigated the girl's disappearance at the time.

As he scrolled down, an image appeared. The girl was a teenager. Her cheekbones were high, exaggerating a gaunt, pale face, flecked with acne. Her light brown hair hung in straggles almost covering the shoulders of a faded blue chemise. Her black-and-yellow-striped school tie, frayed and badly knotted, was hanging loose, though her blouse was still buttoned to the neck. She looked like many of the kids he'd been to school with in Glasgow's East End; there was poor, like his family, and then there was piss-poor. Alison Doig certainly fitted the latter category.

Her eyes drew him in, though. Large, green – wary, but bright, reflecting intelligence, he thought.

As Scott scanned the case notes, it was clear that Erchie had been accurate in his brief summation of events more than thirty years before. It appeared that Alison had taken an old Ford transit van without the knowledge or permission of her parents, abandoning it near the pier at Tarbert to the north end of the peninsula. It also appeared in a scanned photograph. Though faded, Scott could tell the vehicle was green, and was pictured on its own beside a muddle of nets, creels and buoys. A couple of interested young fishermen stood nearby smoking cigarettes and sporting haircuts redolent of the time – mullets. Scott found this an appropriate style for men of that occupation and chuckled to himself.

As he reached the end of the case notes he came upon a final statement, written by an Inspector Innes.

It has become clear over the last few days that Alison Doig was unhappy with her domestic circumstances. That she took the decision to abscond is an assumption, but

seemingly a sound one under the circumstances. She will
remain categorised as a missing person.

She is known as a wilful, difficult pupil by her teachers,
and had few companions at school, save for two or three
girls with whom she appears to have struck up an unlikely
friendship. The foremost of these is Sheena Cunningham,
daughter of a prominent businessman in Kinloch, but she
has been notably unhelpful to the officers investigating
this case.

Scott read on, unimpressed by the off-hand manner of the
man writing the report. But as he knew, that was the way
things had been back then. Invariably, cases of missing
teenagers were seen as merely troublesome, meriting little in
the way of investigation at any serious level. The basic attitude
was that they'd chosen to leave the family home, and – being
considered adults at sixteen in Scottish law – would have to
abide by that choice. This attitude was confirmed in the last
line of Inspector Innes's report: *Though we have taken every*
step possible to locate Alison Doig, and will leave the case open,
I can justify spending no further time or expense on tracing the
aforementioned, who by now could be almost anywhere.

Scott leaned back in his chair and shook his head. That he
was a police officer of the old school there was no doubt. But
he was the first to acknowledge that things had changed for
the better during his many years in 'the job'. Not all, by any
means, but most.

It was always worth listening to ex-cops and he'd been
convinced by Erchie's theory. Brian Scott resolved to have a
chat with the woman his lunchtime companion had identified,
if she was still in the area.

Symington knocked lightly on the door of the glass box and entered. 'You busy, Brian?'

'Not really, ma'am. Just looking at some old case notes on a missing person. I've reason to believe she's back for the first time since she disappeared – or at least it's a possibility.'

'Interesting. Keep me informed, if you don't mind.'

'Aye, will do, ma'am.'

Symington took a seat opposite the acting sub-divisional commander. 'So, Jim. What do you think?'

'In what way?' Scott remembered how unhappy he was about being used to judge the current state of his old friend and colleague. 'Is he up to coming back? He's been tested by a' the docs, hasn't he?'

'Yes, of course.'

'Well, if you don't mind, why ask my opinion?'

'You know him, Brian. I mean really *know* him.'

'He looks fine tae me. Wee bit pale aboot the gills, but who wouldnae be, after what he's been through, eh?'

Symington pushed a piece of paper across the desk.

'What's this?'

'It's the email address for the person in HR who's dealing with Jim's case.'

'And what dae you want me tae dae with it?'

'We've discussed this, DI Scott. Every day I want you to send a short report as to DCI Daley's – well, his fitness for duty. I want you to copy me in, too.'

'Something like *Oor Jimmy was quite cheery this morning. He'd a ham roll for his lunch and took a shite aboot half three*? Is that what you're after?'

'Don't play the fool all the time, Brian. It doesn't suit you.'

'And as I've told you, this doesn't suit me, neither – ma'am.'

'It's the way things are, Brian. Make no mistake: if you don't take this seriously it will harm Jim. I hope you realise that?'

'Aye. I've been in this job mair than twice as long as you. I know the score – wae fucking bells on.'

'Well, do your job, DI Scott!' Symington's voice was raised, her face red.

'Fine, point taken.'

'Good! And it's *wae fucking bells on*, ma'am.'

'Toupee!'

'It's touché, Brian.'

'Och, I knew I hadnae got it right. It's one o' Jimmy's favourites.'

Symington leaned across the desk and grabbed his hand. 'Do it for him, Brian – please.'

'Aye, I'll do it.' Brian Scott knew when he was beaten; it was his default position in his marriage and his job.

9

Nathaniel Doig had three failed attempts at starting the old pick-up before the diesel engine rattled haltingly into life. The Peugeot had replaced the rusting Ford Transit that was slowly decaying into oblivion in their yard. Now, though, this vehicle sported almost as much rust as its predecessor, with only flecks of red paint visible here and there to identify its original colour. He doubted it would last much longer.

Slowly, nursing the ruined pick-up over the bumps and potholes that punctuated the unkempt lane from their cottage, he eventually reached the smooth tarmac of a single-track road. He turned right, hoping the Peugeot would still be capable of negotiating its way up hill and down dale until he reached Kinloch.

As the engine spluttered at the top of the longest climb, he looked across the restless sea. No sign of Ailsa Craig, far less the Ayrshire coast, on a day like this. The world felt enclosed, as though the walls of his existence were slowly but surely tightening in around him, ready to smother his life away.

Life? Did his experience of existence even merit the name, he wondered. Ambitions thwarted by a brutal father he never dared disobey, who was succeeded by a wife who'd ruled the roost since Nathaniel had been foolhardy enough to marry her. But Nathaniel knew that he was no hapless innocent when it came to the dynamics of his family – perhaps he'd even made them all what they were. He'd certainly started the process. There is no more demanding master than stifled ambition that eats away at the soul; he'd read that once. Certainly, it makes a man – or woman – do things at odds with a normal life. He'd always recognised that, even when all that had gone on around him became so abhorrent. No blame to him, then – no, that was firmly the responsibility of others.

The familiar syncopated knocking from his offside front wheel sounded as he turned right on a corner and the island at the head of the loch hove into view. He'd often wondered when the telephone box at the causeway would be removed; he knew that with the advent of mobile phones such things were rapidly becoming an anachronism – a bit like himself, he considered. But as he drove along the straight section of road next to the seaweed-slathered shore the red box soon became visible, and he pulled up in the little lay-by beside it, tugging hard on the handbrake in order to make sure it held.

Inside, the box reeked. Someone had pissed in it, and there was a used condom on the floor. Disgusted, he pushed it into a corner with the toe of his boot, before reaching into his pocket for the handful of pound coins he'd placed there before leaving home.

The call took moments to connect. He cleared his throat ready to speak. Sure enough, the confident tones of a young woman sounded on the other end of the line.

'Williams, Strong and Hardacre, how can I help you?'

'I'd like to speak with Mr Hardacre, please,' replied Doig.

'Oh . . . I see.' The confidence seemed stripped from the woman's voice.

'Is there a problem?'

'I'm sad to say there is. We lost Mr Hardacre three months ago.'

'Lost?'

'He passed away, sir – sorry, can I ask who's calling?'

Ignoring the question, feeling rather stunned if truth be told, Doig carried on. 'Well, who has taken over from him – taken on his old clients, I mean?'

'That's young Mr Williams – Blair Williams.'

'In that case I'd like to speak with him, please.'

'As I say, I need your name. Mr Williams is a very busy man ...'

'He'll find time for me. Please tell him that Jeremiah is calling.'

'Mr Jeremiah, or is that your first name?'

'Just Jeremiah.'

Surprised by the abrupt nature of the conversation, Karen Milne sighed. She was used to awkward people; they seemed to be attracted to lawyers like moths to a flame. She recalled a woman arriving recently in the office shouting, swearing and threatening. She'd called one of their clients a psychopath; clearly the idiot hadn't looked in the mirror herself recently. Karen had had to deal with all sorts – including clients who were much ruder than this *Jeremiah*. 'I'll put you through, sir,' she replied for want of a better title.

'Yes, Karen, what do you have for me?' She could hear the playful smile in Blair Williams's voice. He was a very attractive man – married, but then so was she. They'd been having an affair for months. She knew him well enough to reckon that she would be called upon to fend off this call.

'It's some bloody weirdo who calls himself Jeremiah. Won't tell me if that's his surname, or what. One of Hardacre's old clients – do you want me to give him the polite brush-off, Blair?' She spoke his name slowly, as though savouring the syllable.

Williams hesitated. 'Jeremiah?'

'Yes, just that.'

'Put him through, Karen – always put him through. Don't ask him any questions – or me, come to that. Got it?'

'As you wish, *Mr* Williams.' As she pressed the button on the console to put the call through she wondered what on earth had caused the change in her lover's attitude. He usually swaggered – everywhere, whether in court or at a party. Karen could have sworn she had heard fear in his voice, something that had never happened before.

The young lawyer answered the call. 'Hello, Jeremiah. Blair Williams; how can I be of service?' He was trying hard to keep his voice steady.

'You've been briefed – by Mr Hardacre, I mean?'

'Yes – yes, absolutely. Something he made very sure of – he was very emphatic on the subject, in fact.' Despite himself, Williams gulped.

'I'd have thought a client such as myself would merit one of the more senior partners.'

'Oh, I am a partner. My father has retired, and Mr Strong is taking a back seat these days. He's still senior partner, but he picks his own fights, as it were.'

'I should have been informed.'

'I think we did try, but the only number we had just rang out. Perhaps you could give us your address, Mr – sorry, Jeremiah.'

'No. But I'd like you to listen carefully. You have long-standing instructions from me. This and other services have been paid for in advance, as I'm sure you know.'

'Yes, yes, absolutely.'

'It may well be time to put in motion what is described within those instructions, Mr Williams. Do you understand?'

'Yes, I do – of course.'

'Good.'

'One question, if I may, Jeremiah?'

'Go ahead.'

'How . . . when will we put the wheels in motion? Your instructions, I mean.'

'Every week I want you to buy a copy of the *Kinloch Herald*. It's available online, so just subscribe to the bloody thing.'

'Yes, certainly. But what am I to look for?'

'Go to the obituary section. If you see the death notice of a Mr Nathaniel Doig, be sure to put everything in place as has been arranged.'

'Yes, certainly. Shall we just go through that – now that Mr Hardacre is no longer here – just to make sure?' Blair Williams listened. 'Hello – Jeremiah?'

No reply was forthcoming. Jeremiah had ended the call without ceremony.

Blair Williams replaced the receiver and thought for a moment. He lifted the handset again. 'Karen, get me Mike Strong, now!'

Brian Scott was quietly impressed by the efficient roster Sergeant Shaw had produced. Everything fitted in nicely: overtime, leave, court dates, contingency plans for emergencies.

The screen flickering on the desk made him feel inadequate. 'A fine job, eh? I'm buggered how you could make head or tail o' it.'

'Just a case of keeping on top of things, Brian. I used to do this before you lot arrived.'

'Under MacLeod, you mean?'

'Aye. And the boss before that.'

'How did you no' say? I've been struggling with the bloody thing since oor Jimmy took a heider in his lounge!'

'I didn't want to stand on your toes – you with the new pips and all.'

'Bugger that! I'm no' proud, in case you havenae noticed.'

'*The worst thing in the world is inertia*, that's what an old gaffer of mine used to say.'

'Aye, you're no' kidding: Kilbirnie, Cumnock, Dalry an' all these shitholes. Tell me aboot it.'

'No, *inertia*! As in standing still – letting things mount up. Not *in Ayrshire*!'

'Aye, okay. I was only pulling your leg,' said Scott unconvincingly. 'I'm a polis, no' some clerk. That's the problem wae this job, if you ask me. There's oor Jimmy, fair embattled wae forms and rosters – all kinds o' useless paperwork – when he should be oot doing what he's best at.'

'Knocking the shit out of some dentist on a yacht?'

'Aye, well, that wisnae his finest hour. Cannae blame him, mark you.'

'We all feel the same – in the office, I mean.'

'No' the first time he's near buggered up his career, neither. Or the last, likely.' Scott thought for a moment. 'Here, dae you know these Doigs at this Rowan Tree Cottage on the back road tae Blaan?'

63

'Only from hearsay. Their daughter went missing. Long time before I arrived.'

'Aye, well it sounds as though she might be back – according tae Erchie Meikle. He used tae be a cop here back then. Reckons he clocked her at the airport.'

'Good man, Erchie. I have a pint with him now and again. If he thinks that, I'd take it seriously. He's not prone to flights o' fancy. He was a good cop, so they say.'

'What happened tae them?'

'You're still here, Brian.'

'Aye, cheers! For that lovely compliment you now have the honour of producing the weekly roster.'

'But DCI Daley's coming back, no?'

'Aye, but best he takes the next few months easy. As little pressure as possible.'

'Your wish is my command, inspector.'

Scott flicked Shaw a playful V sign as the desk sergeant left the office. The sudden reappearance of people rarely boded well, in his experience. He'd already discovered that the mystery visitor had been taken by taxi to the Machrie House Hotel, and was now going by the name of Alice Wenger. Alice – Alison. Too close to be a coincidence, thought Scott. He decided to pay Ms Wenger a visit.

He poked his head round the door of the glass box. 'Right, Potts, me and you are off tae solve a mystery, son.'

Acting DS Potts rolled his eyes. 'If you say so, sir.'

'I dae say so. And if you're lucky, you can buy me a ginger beer an' lime.'

'My lucky day.'

'Shit rolls doonhill in this job, son. You must have picked that up by noo. I've been swimming in it for thirty-odd years.'

'I'll get my goggles, sir.'

'Ain't you the bright boy? Just goes tae show the benefit o' a university education. Come on then, let's go.'

10

Mike Strong sat in a leather recliner chair in his wood-panelled study. He was wearing a sports jacket, the open-necked shirt beneath revealing crinkled jowls. This sign of age was balanced by a thick head of wavy white hair, brushed back from his square, tanned face. Books – mainly leather-bound legal tomes – sat on shelves on every wall bar one. His desk was old walnut with embossed green leather on which a writing pad sat in front of a row of ornamental fountain pens placed evenly in their inkwells. Behind him the light of a bright Edinburgh day poured through the sash window.

Strong eyed his junior partner critically. The subject Blair Williams had brought before him was a vexing one; something he'd tried not to give much thought to before Charles Hardacre had come to him, his face gaunt with the cancer that would very soon take his life. His old colleague's tale had been amazing – not only for its content, but for the way he'd managed to keep it a secret in their exclusive but tight-knit law firm for all these years. Now, here was this fresh-faced thirty-six-year-old, who bore no resemblance to his father, but had his mother's deep brown eyes.

But that was a story that would eventually be lost in the annals of Williams, Strong and Hardacre.

The younger man spoke. 'I must admit to being rather out of my depth here, Mike. I mean, is what we're about to do strictly legal . . . has it ever been?'

Strong thought for a moment, taking the time to light a large cigar and send clouds of pungent smoke into the study. 'If we could go back in time, I dare say Jeremiah is not someone we would have considered as a likely client, regardless of the financial reward. However, Charles didn't afford me – or anyone else, come to that – the courtesy of being able to say no.'

'It is a lot of money.'

'And it came at a time when our firm was struggling. I know Charles did what he thought best, but . . .'

'And now it's my problem.' Williams's expression was taut. 'I had wondered – and please forgive me for this notion – if Jeremiah is this Doig chap, who will know about the arrangements when he dies, except for us?'

'You and Charles got on well. He was always uptight about some damned thing.' Strong smiled.

'Yes. I liked the old boy.'

'Birds of a feather.'

'Steady on, Mike! I'm just trying to work out what's best for us – the company. This could backfire on you and me.'

'Oh, it very well could. That's why while you deal with Jeremiah, I shall talk to the third party.'

'Who – I mean, what?'

'Unfortunately you're not in full possession of the facts. This isn't just a case of disposing of a large amount of money to various places. Jeremiah has something more specific in mind. Though what that is I cannot tell you.'

'Fuck. It's not legal, I bet.' Blair Williams's face was ashen.

'I don't know – I suspect, but I don't know. And the less you know the more you are insulated from any potential action.'

'But what about the money? We haven't followed any of the protocols, I know that!'

'Now, calling it money isn't quite right – if one decides to be a pedant, that is.'

'Oh, fuck – it's not drugs, is it?'

'No. Try to stick this up your nose and you'll find you require more than Vicks to set things right.'

'Well, what on earth . . . ?'

'Gold, Blair, pure gold – well, as near to pure as it gets.' Strong quite enjoyed the look of horror that passed over the face of his arrogant junior partner. He quietly disliked the confidence of this young man: his sports car, his state-of-the-art home in a trendy part of Edinburgh, and his beautiful wife. He was also envious of his relationship with their secretary, who was just as alluring, if not quite as conceited, as the man now standing before him.

In reality, his envy was born from the fact that Blair Williams was the new model of Mike Strong. Mike had always wanted children, but his wife had proved to be infertile. This was a young man he would be proud to call a son, despite the jealousy he felt. There was no doubt the absence of a family had left a hole in his life. And while age found him richer than he'd ever imagined, he'd happily have given it all away to scroll back the years and live this young man's life on the hoof from one bed to the next, one party to another; thrill upon thrill. Old age had its merits, but they were poor fare when compared to the overflowing banquets of gilded youth.

'I have to scan this damned newspaper every week now. It's like waiting for the bloody hammer to fall.'

'You take care of the newspaper, and when the time comes, tell me.'

'And?'

'And it's best you don't know. I owe it to your father – and your mother, come to that.' He searched Williams's face. 'How are they, by the way?'

'Fine – the last time I saw them.'

'Go more often. They won't always be here, you know. And please, give them my regards.' Strong took another puff on his cigar, sucking hard to re-ignite it.

'I will – most definitely. I know you and my parents have always been close.'

'Oh, yes.'

'And thank you for – well, helping out, Mike. I was pretty worried for a while there – after Charles's revelations, and now what you've told me. Why didn't he just leave this with you? That's what I'd like to know.'

'You know Charles. Belts and braces chap – always was.' Though he said the words, Mike Strong knew the real answer. Charles Hardacre didn't trust him – never had. How ironic life is, he thought. The younger, teetotal, fitness fanatic had lost his life to cancer, while here he was, with his dodgy ticker, an habitual consumer of old malt whisky, Cuban cigars and fine champagne, still alive. There was still time for one last hurrah, he was sure, and Jeremiah may well be its genesis.

As a rule Alice Wenger hated dining alone. But she had so much going on in her head, much of it unexpected activity, that she welcomed the peace and the chance to enjoy decent enough food and an exceptionally good champagne.

The bubbles that filled her mouth helped to clear the froth from her head, and by the time she was halfway through a main course of pheasant in a port jus and further through the bottle, she had relaxed sufficiently to think properly. Alice liked alcohol, but she had always been careful with its use, especially if its consumption revolved around a relief of stress rather than her social life. She knew all too well how easily it could change minds – alter personalities – and she was comfortable with the ones she had, though that had by no means always been the case.

She was dragged from her thoughts and the lull of the soothing background muzak by what sounded like something of a commotion at the door to the hotel restaurant. When she looked up, a range of emotions welled up inside her, a mixture of mercies, unsettling but in a way joyful.

'Alison! It is you, isn't it?' The middle-aged woman was chubby, but reasonably well dressed, and her face was instantly recognisable. 'It's me – Sheena – do you remember?' She rushed forward to embrace the other woman.

Alice's first instincts were to shake her head, deny it all: a case of mistaken identity. But she'd been prepared for something like this – she knew how Kinloch worked, and in a way she'd drawn attention to herself by her conversation with the young taxi driver. At the time she had wondered why she'd given herself away so readily, but the need to be known for who she really was had been strong for so long.

'Sheena Cunningham! I can't believe it!' Wenger got up from her chair and embraced her long-lost friend.

'Sheena McKay now. I married Bertie – you know, the fisherman we all fancied?'

'Fuck, yes I do. He was a catch, eh?' Alice could hear her

voice slipping back easily into the accent of home. 'Streaked blond hair – a mullet!'

'Huh! Grey, what's left of it now – but he's still a lovely guy. We've had a good marriage – ups and downs, you know how it is, but we've been blessed with lovely children, and a grandson now!'

Momentarily, Alice felt a flash of jealousy, but it passed as quickly as it arrived. Talk of children always made her feel the same way. But, as usual, she forced it to the back of her mind. 'Take a seat, Sheena. Can I get you something to eat – a drink?'

'Can I have a gin and tonic – a large one, please. I think I need it. This is so – so unexpected!' She took the seat across the table from Alice in a flurry of too much sweet perfume, an off the peg dress and badly cut hair. Alice had to remember this wasn't Beverly Hills.

'Sure, my pleasure. How did you know I was here, honey?'

'Oh, you know – the local gossip machine. I didn't believe it.' Sheena cast her eyes to the floor. 'I'm ashamed to say it, but most of us thought . . .'

'Thought what?'

Sheena sighed. 'We thought you were dead.'

'I can understand that – my folks, right?'

'We all knew how they were to you and your brothers. When you just disappeared like that – well, you know how folk talk, Alison.'

'It's Alice now.'

'Oh, right – Alice, sorry.'

'Nothing to be sorry about. Alison had bad memories, but I wanted to keep a bit of it, you understand?'

Sheena paused again, looking around the plush room.

'I pleaded with my dad – to tell the police to keep looking for you. He had influence, if you remember?'

'He was the big cheese back then. The petrol station, the bookmaker, that building company; I remember. How is he?'

'We lost him two years ago. He had Parkinson's. It was terrible.'

'Shit, I'm sorry, Sheena. You know, when you come back to a place – especially a place like Kinloch – you expect nothing to have changed, everything to be frozen in time. But I walked down Main Street yesterday and I didn't recognise anyone. It was as if the buildings were still the same, but everything else had gone. Still got Michael Kerr the baker, I suppose.' Alice laughed and took a gulp of champagne.

'I think everything's much the same at Rowan Tree Cottage, Alison – Alice, sorry.'

'Yeah. I went for a walk up the hill yesterday – looked down on the old place. Everything looked, as you say, just the same – a little worse, maybe.'

'They're still alive – your folks, I mean; and your brothers. Nobody sees much of them, but I know that for a fact.'

'Did anybody ever see much of us? If my folks hadn't been forced to send us to school we'd have been totally invisible.'

'Yes, I suppose you're right. They always kept themselves to themselves.' Sheena sighed.

'Hey girl, this isn't a wake! I'm so pleased to see you again. Let's get drunk – talk about back in the day, yeah? I could use a friendly ear right now.'

'You – you've changed so much. You're beautiful, Alice.' Sheena put her hand to her mouth. 'I mean, not that you weren't before.' She blushed.

'I was a ragged-arsed kid with holes in my shoes and no hot water for a bath. I won't even mention the rest. You must remember that.'

'It doesn't matter – it never did in my book. When my gran died, you were the only one who understood what I was going through.'

'We were the same in a way – though from opposite directions. You had everything and everyone was jealous, and I had – well, I had shit.'

'But you've turned things around. Look at you, the clothes, the hair – that jewellery. Plus you look ten years younger than me!'

'I've had work done.'

'Oh – wow! You must be better off than me too, then.'

'What happened to all your old man's money?'

'Dad was ill for a long time. You remember my brother Allan, aye?'

'Sure I do.'

'He took over the business, but he was more keen on drinking whisky in the Island Bar than working. We lost everything – it broke my father's heart.'

'I'm sorry, Sheena. He – you – didn't deserve that.' Alice took another gulp of champagne. 'Listen, order something – we'll eat and then we'll talk. We've got a lot of catching up to do, me and you.'

'I'll have to get back in an hour or so – Bertie's coming to pick me up.'

'To hell with that! You got a cell phone, right? Call him and tell him it's a girls' night out. We'll eat, drink, be merry – talk the pants off each other. Fuck knows we have plenty to talk about. I'll get you a room for the night – c'mon.'

'I couldn't. That would be so unfair.'

Alice Wenger grabbed her old friend's hand across the table. 'You remember that little transistor radio you gave me?'

'Yes, the red one. I remember it well.' Sheena smiled at the thought.

'It was one of the best things anyone has ever done for me. I owe you – and not just for that. It's my turn to treat you, Sheena.'

'What can I say? Okay, you've twisted my arm. Let me give Bertie a call.'

Alice watched the dowdy middle-aged woman who had once been a pretty girl fish into her handbag for her phone. Though her smile remained intact, her heart broke. She hated the passage of time. She felt as though she'd lost so much of it to poverty, cruelty and the shit life had thrown at her. Despite the plastic surgery, the money – everything she had – nothing could bring those years back, not ever.

'I'm looking for an Alice Wenger,' said Scott to the tartan-clad receptionist.

The girl looked flustered at the mention of the name.

'You okay?'

'Yes, it's just that Ms Wenger is at dinner, and she already has one unexpected visitor. Can't this wait, DI Scott?'

'No, it can't. I'm following up an old case, and I've reason to believe that Alice Wenger can help me. So, if you don't mind, where can we find her . . . Daisy?' said Scott, glancing at her nametag.

'Right, if you say so.' Daisy sighed. 'Follow me, please.'

They made their way along a corridor and then up a short

flight of stairs. Daisy pushed open the restaurant doors and turned to the detectives. 'If you don't mind, I'll ask her if she'd rather speak to you in private.'

'Up tae you, dear. As long as I get to speak tae her, I'm no' bothered where it is.'

Potts was moving uneasily from foot to foot. It was a habit Scott had noticed before. 'What's up wae you?'

'I just feel a bit uncomfortable – you know, disturbing her evening like this, sir.'

'You mean you're itching to get hame.'

'No – well, aye. But couldn't we have done this earlier?'

'This is the polis, son, no' the social work department.'

As Scott was about to expand this statement, Daisy reappeared. 'If you don't mind giving her a couple of minutes, Ms Wenger says she'll speak to you. She's in company so has to excuse herself. You can have a word with her in the office down there.' Daisy pointed to a door marked *Private*. 'Just go in and make yourselves comfortable.'

In the small office, Potts looked round. 'There's only two chairs, sir.'

'Well spotted, son. I've always said you was Crime Squad material.'

'Where will this woman sit?'

'She'll sit doon there – opposite me. You'll stand up an' take notes.'

'This isn't how I imagined the life of a DS.'

'Enjoy it while you can. We're a' aboot to take one step back again.'

A resigned look crossed Potts's face just as the door swung open.

'You're the cops, right?' said Alice Wenger.

'That's right, Ms Wenger. I'm DI Scott and this is DS Potts.' Brian stood to shake her hand, but she ignored the gesture. 'Anyway, take a seat, please.'

'No thank you, Inspector Scott. I don't intend to be here for long, so ask your questions and I'll get back to my friend.'

'Okay. I have reason to believe that you're Alison Doig, formerly of Rowan Tree Cottage. You went missing almost thirty-four years ago. I need to ask you some questions about that, please.'

Wenger was dressed in trousers and a jumper, a pair of cowboy boots the only nod to her adopted homeland. Scott tried hard to see the pale face of Alison Doig, but struggled to make the picture fit in his mind.

'Yes, I was Alison Doig. So what?'

'You went missing – nobody's seen you for years.'

'Is that a crime here now? I was over sixteen – just. I could do what I wanted.'

'You stole your parents' van.'

'I borrowed it.'

'You drove it without permission and with no driving licence.'

'Okay, inspector, charge me then. I can assure you of one thing: I will get an attorney who will make your head spin.'

'We just need to know more about what happened, that's all.'

'Then why don't you take a trip to Rowan Tree Cottage and ask my so-called parents why I left the way I did?'

'Now I've established your identity, it's only right I inform them that you've been found, Ms Wenger.'

'Found?' She laughed heartily. 'You asshole! If you want to charge me, get on with it, honey. But I don't want you to *inform* my parents of anything. I'm no kid now, inspector. If you want to right some wrongs, as I say, you take a trip to see them. Apart from that I have nothing to say.' She turned on her heel and opened the office door.

'Here, I've no' finished yet!' shouted Scott.

'I have!' Alice Wenger slammed the door in her wake.

'She's a nippy-sweetie,' said Potts.

'Aye, you can say that again.'

'What are we going to do – I mean, I can't see a traffic charge sticking after all this time, can you?'

Scott was thinking. 'No, we're hardly going tae try that. We'll take a wander doon tae this Rowan Tree Cottage tomorrow.'

'To let her parents know she's turned up?'

Scott shrugged.

'Don't tell me: something's not right.'

'Bang on, son. At last you're getting it.'

As Scott got up off his chair and made for the door, Potts shook his head. 'Not really, to be honest.'

11

1925

The little steam puffer had plied its trade up and down the west coast of Scotland for thirty-four years, but rarely had she sailed in weather like this. In fact, her gnarled old skipper Fergus Donaldson would never had put to sea in such a gale under normal circumstances.

But these were not normal circumstances.

The two large men with the American accents were menacing, even though both were now below emptying the contents of their stomachs into old tin pails. They'd left Donaldson no choice other than to abandon his plan of riding out the storm at anchor in the relative safety of the little cove. His passengers had made that abundantly clear. When his protestations had been met with a revolver pointed straight at his head, the decision to face the gale blowing huge seas from the nor'east had been made for him.

'Time's money, fella,' said Frank, the bigger and uglier of the pair. Somehow his slow New York drawl made him seem even more menacing, and was enough to send first mate Sammy McMichael and the ship's boy running to seek the relative safety of the over-pressed engine room.

Donaldson sucked on his pipe and merely nodded. 'Aye, if that's what you want. But hark at this: it might no' be that far to Kinloch – a few hours in fine weather – but, I tell you this, these seas are the most dangerous they can be right noo!' He had to shout to make himself heard against the howl of the wind and lash of the great waves that were breaking over the bow of the vessel.

Frank waved the pistol at him again, closer this time, almost touching his temple. Though he was a stubborn man, Donaldson was in no doubt that these men were ruthless enough to carry through their threat of killing him and forcing his first mate to sail the rest of the way to the bay near Kinloch from where they were to pick up their illicit cargo and make the deal.

'You ain't no Billy McCoy, captain, but you'll fucking do this thing!'

Donaldson had to grab the ship's wheel to stop himself falling as another huge wave thrashed across the prow. His tormentors weren't so lucky, both careering to the deck. For a split second, Donaldson considered the iron jemmy bar he used to prise open the hold when it got stuck, but these men – distressed as they might be – were tough. They were back on their feet in seconds, Frank's companion, Tony, now with a nasty cut on his brow.

'Look at this! I'm bleeding here,' he shouted, examining the smear of red left on his palm when he had tentatively touched his forehead.

'Go find a nurse then,' replied Frank sarcastically. It was clear that his wrath could be directed at anyone, friend or foe. 'You'll do this, old man. You're getting a good taste – more than this tub is worth. Just keep sailing, you got it?'

Knowing when he was beaten, Donaldson, still gripping the wheel, nodded and squinted out of the wheelhouse window.

'You see anything out there?' Frank demanded.

'Nothing but the blackest hell you can imagine.'

'You're a great guy to be around – all the fun of the fair over here. It's like Coney fucking Island.' He turned on his heel, making sure he was holding on to the chart table in the cramped cabin. 'C'mon, Tony, we're going back below.'

'Let me die!' Tony wailed.

'You know, I wish I'd brought Big Patsy from AC to do this thing. You do nothing but moan, you asshole.'

Together, they forced the door open, confirming the full force of the storm as seawater and spray crashed into the tiny space.

Making sure the door was secure behind them, Donaldson turned his attention back to the turbulent dark of night, desperately searching for the lights that were now their only salvation.

Jim Daley sat at the big window of his house on the hill looking across the loch. It was almost three in the morning, but he couldn't sleep. His mind was awash with problems, both real and imagined. How would his colleagues react to his being back – especially following his attack on the man who had raped Liz? The answer was, he couldn't be sure.

Back in the old days, it would have been different. Nobody would have turned a hair at the thought of a police officer giving someone a good hiding. He'd have been a hero, in fact. But in these days where university graduates were the standard recruitment ground, who could be sure what they would think? The irony was that he'd turned into those he so despised: the cops he'd worked with in the past who took pleasure in breaking the rules – were proud of it, even.

He took a gulp of the whisky that he knew he should have left in the bottle. But for all the medication he was now on, nothing worked to calm his soul like the water of life. He remembered how Brian had struggled with his alcoholism – would probably always struggle. That set the big detective wondering if he too was an alcoholic. They'd asked how much he drank in the hospital; he'd lied – standard procedure. But in his heart, he knew that he looked forward to popping the cork of a good malt every evening – looked forward to it far too much.

And then there were the lingering doubts about his health. They'd told him not to look up his condition on the internet, which of course was the first thing he did. There were so many horror stories of people with months or a couple of years to live, terrible deaths, woeful disability. He had shut the lid of the computer and vowed never to look at this stuff again. But he had. Searching for the good news the worldwide web always seemed so reluctant to provide – unless you liked cat videos, of course.

Then there was Liz. Hard as he tried, the feelings he'd had for her would not return. Yes, he was fond of her – she was the mother of his child. His heart had broken when she'd eventually told the truth behind her battered face, about the man who had brutalised her.

Though he'd been asked a similar question by numerous doctors he'd seen in the last few months and always responded in the negative, he wondered about his state of mind. Yes, he'd always tended towards melancholy, feeling at odds with the world, an alienation made worse by his chosen profession. But now he felt a real sadness, a pain in the pit of his stomach that only whisky seemed to cure, albeit temporarily.

He looked at the phone on the table, walked over and picked it up. As he dialled the number, he realised that he would probably not have done this sober, but he needed to speak to someone, and he could think of no other.

'Jimmy, is that you?' The voice was slurred with sleep.

'Yes, Brian. Listen, I'm sorry to call you at this time . . .'

'No worries, big man – open twenty-four hours a day waiting for a call from you, mate. You know me.'

Daley felt instantly happier. He could hear the smile in his friend's voice, despite the hour.

'Right, I'm just going doonstairs. I don't want tae wake oor Ella.'

Daley heard shuffling, then the padding of feet and the creaking of stairs.

'What's up, Jimmy – you're no' ill again, are you?' There was genuine concern in the voice on the other end of the phone.

'No, I'm just – och, I just don't know what I am, Bri.'

'Listen, Jimmy. You've been through a lot, and that's putting it mildly. No man or woman can carry on as normal under they circumstances, and you're no different. Though I know you think you are.'

'What does that mean?'

'You gie yourself too high standards, big chap. You always have done. Even when we was starting oot you were the same – worried aboot things that never crossed my mind, so you did.'

'And still don't, eh?'

'Where there's nae sense, there's nae feeling. We all know that. I just said the same thing tae Ella recently.'

'You do yourself down.'

'You think? Listen, just try an' take life as it comes. Worrying aboot shit won't make any difference, you know that.'

'Do you think I should come back – to work, I mean? Wouldn't it be easier to cash in my chips?'

'Aye, it would be easier – of course it would. Then what – open a wee bookshop? I mind you sayin' that years ago when we was in some strife or other.'

'It's true – I wouldn't know what to do. I've missed the job more than I ever thought was possible these last few months.'

'See! Just get they big feet o' yours back under the table and you'll be fine.'

'I suppose.'

'And can I gie you a wee bit o' advice – and don't call me thon hippo thing.'

'Hypocrite?'

'Aye, that's the one.' There was a short pause. 'Go easy on the bottle, big man. And before you start shouting aboot me having a cheek, take it from somebody who knows an' doesnae judge. There's nothing better than sitting wae a glass in your hand feeling all your problems disappear. But let me tell you, see in the morning once you've had a skinful the night before, well, they just seem worse than ever.'

Daley sighed, swirling the whisky round in the glass. 'I know – but just the chance to get some relief, Brian . . .'

'When you're back at work, the world will all seem like it was, trust me.'

'Shit! Now I am worried.'

'Get tae your bed, get some kip and I'll come over and see you tomorrow. We can have a proper chat, Jimmy, eh?'

'Yes. Good idea, Brian.'

'Right. Goodnight, buddy.'

Daley clicked off the call. He looked at the whisky in his hand, walked to the kitchen and emptied the glass in the sink. He was smart enough to know when people were speaking sense – even when it was Brian Scott.

As Scott tiptoed back up the stairs his heart was heavy. He knew how it felt – knew exactly. Even now he yearned for the soothing effect of booze to take the edges off a hard day – any day, come to that.

He pondered on the reports he was supposed to write about Daley. Over the years in the police, he'd had to do a lot of things that hadn't sat easily on his shoulders. But this was by far the worst.

Had it not been for the memory of the sheer despair he'd felt when his drinking was out of control, he'd have gone back downstairs and poured himself a bumper. Instead, he slipped back under the duvet and cuddled into the back of his wife.

'No!' she said emphatically.

'No what?'

'If you think you're on a winner at this time o' night, think again, buster.'

'Away – I'm just wanting a cuddle. It's brass monkeys doon that stair.'

'That's because you'll no' have the heating come on until the last minute.'

'You need tae be Rocker-feller tae pay they heating bills.'

'Go to sleep, Brian.'

'Yes, boss,' said Scott, already drifting away.

12

1925

Now that the American mobsters had gone below to suffer seasickness out of the storm, first mate Sammy McMichael felt it safe to return to the wheelhouse. He was now sporting a large bruise where a solid storm lantern had careered off its hook and collided with his face. He looked into the darkness through the tiny windows as his skipper also squinted determinedly into the tumult. The noise of sea and wind was deafening as the little puffer lurched from one massive wave to the next.

'Glad you're here, Sammy!' shouted Donaldson. 'I could fair do with another pair o' eyes.' Just as he said it, a massive wave engulfed the whole vessel, crashing into the wheelhouse and engendering a creaking from the hull that sounded loud despite the wail of the storm.

'Where do you think we are, skipper?' said Sammy.

'Too damn near the Barrel Rocks and Thomson's Point for my liking. I'm hoping they've been able to raise the light.'

To his right Sammy thought he could see a pinprick flash on and off. 'That'll be the Ailsa Craig light,' he roared.

'I bloody well hope it is, because if it's no' we'll likely end up sailing doon Kinloch Main Street before long.'

'We should never have done this!'

'Aye, fair enough for you to say that now, but in two weeks when you've no money to put food on the table and nothing to scrape together for a dram or three, you'd have been crying foul. Aye, and I'd have been the target of your righteous anger.'

Sammy nodded his head solemnly as the little vessel breasted another great wave.

'And anyway, I've been out in worse than this many a time and got us back safely into port.'

'You have that,' replied Sammy, though both men knew it was a lie. He cupped his hand round his eyes the better to see any light that would guide them between the ragged point and the deadly rocks.

'If we see anything it'll have to be soon. I cannae be just sure where we are, but judging by the light on Ailsa Craig I think I'm right.'

Sammy picked up a pair of old binoculars encased in a box under the brass compass. He put them to his eyes, desperate to see anything that could indicate their position. He was a local man – from Dalintober – and knew this coast like the back of his hand, but in this weather every sailor was on a strange tide.

'At least we don't have to worry about the Yanks,' shouted Donaldson.

'They're too ill to be a bother. Though I'll be glad tae see the back o' them, skipper, and that's no' a lie.'

'We just pick up the casks o' whisky, let them do their business and bide a while in the cove tae let this storm blow over. You know what like it is; tomorrow the sun will likely be splitting the sky and the sea a millpond.'

'I've got something!' Sammy pointed ahead.

Donaldson followed his line of sight. 'Well done, Sammy, my boy! That'll be Thomson's Point. We'll give it a wide berth then sail back in near the coast to avoid the Barrel Rocks. Man, I know where I am now. I could do this in my sleep, storm or no bloody storm!'

Outside the wheelhouse, despite the thunder of waves and the roaring gale, Jeremiah's bell tolled of its own accord; but whether in celebration or warning, only the Almighty knew.

Brain Scott left DS Potts in the car and ascended the steps to Jim Daley's front door, on which he knocked loudly by force of habit as all police officers are wont to do.

'Brian! What a nice surprise,' said Liz, opening the door to let him in. 'I'm just taking the wee man to nursery. Jim's in the lounge.'

'Thank you, dear,' said Scott, kneeling down to pat James junior on the head, messing up his hair. 'How are you, young fella, eh?'

'Hello, Muncle Brian.' The child gave him a hug.

'You behave at that nursery – nae high jinks, mind.' Scott smiled, said goodbye to Liz and made his way down the hall. He leaned his head round the corner of the door. 'Are you decent, big man?'

'I heard you. Anyway, do you think I parade about here in the scud when nobody's about?'

'As we both know, some folks have right strange habits, Jimmy.'

'Take a seat, Bri.'

Scott did as he was asked and flopped down on a large

recliner. 'I was wondering, what wae you coming back on Monday and all, would you fancy a wee warm-up?'

'A warm-up?'

'Aye. I've got to go and see these buddies at a place called Rowan Tree Cottage. Thought you might like tae come and take charge, get back in the swing o' things, like.'

'I don't know the first thing about the case.'

'Och, I'll fill you in on the way. It's no' much o' a case at the moment, it has tae be said. But there's something nagging at me – you know what it's like, Jimmy.'

'I do.'

'Right, get yourself oot o' they jogging troosers and intae something more respectable and we'll get going.'

Daley smiled. He knew Scott was right, but the thought of being a policeman again seemed odd, somehow. There was no reason why he shouldn't accompany his old friend on an inquiry – after all, he'd done that more times than he could remember. Symington had returned his warrant card, and there were only a couple of days left before he returned to work officially. He nodded to Scott and went to change.

Scott looked about the room as he waited. Liz had already tidied the place up and it looked more like a home again, rather than the refuge from the world it had appeared in her absence. In a way he was glad she was back, while in another he wished she'd made a decent life with someone else and left Daley alone for good. He wasn't at all sure that his friend felt the same way about his wife as he had for so many years, and Scott feared another fracture in their relationship could prove too much for the big man.

Idly, he checked his phone and played a new game he'd

found where a snake chased around a maze trying to eat up little dots. It reminded him of his youth in the arcades in Glasgow. He'd never been good at these games then and he was worse now, but at least it passed the time.

'Right, that's me good to go,' said Daley, appearing in a suit that looked as though it had been made for another, much larger man. Scott eyed him up and down.

'I think you'll need tae go an' get some new threads, Jimmy.'

'Why?'

'That bloody suit's hanging off you! It's like these adverts in the paper, you know? The fat bloke and the thin bloke after he's lost the weight.'

'You mean "before and after"?'

'Aye, though in this case it's "before and *way* before"!'

'Huh. First time I've felt comfy in a suit for years.'

'I could see it in your face, but what wae you slobbing aboot in these jogging bottoms and sweatshirts, I never realised how thin you'd got.'

'It's the same way I felt when you stopped drinking.'

'In what way?'

'Well, it was like being with a stranger, you know?' Daley's face was unreadable.

'Away!'

'Come on, I'm only kidding.'

With Scott still smarting at the comment he thought bore some truth despite Daley's shrugging it off as a joke, the pair made their way back to the car.

'You get in the back, Potts. Let the DCI in the front wae me.'

'I'm fine in the back, Brian.'

'Since when? You hate being in the back of cars. What's changed?'

'A lot.'

With that they headed off to find Rowan Tree Cottage, Scott explaining what he'd discovered as they went.

13

Annie looked miserable sitting in front of the owners of the County Hotel. They'd arrived unexpectedly, and now she was sitting in the cramped back office as they looked through various accounts and till receipts.

'We've had a great couple o' weeks: two hame darts matches and a wedding last Saturday. The place was going like a fair, so it was.'

Mrs Ramsay looked at her sadly 'Aye, but there's not enough weeks like that, Annie. You must see it yourself: takings have gone down steadily over the last few years.'

'I can see it right enough. But sure, every place is jeest the same – in the licensed trade, I mean.'

Mr Ramsay, who had once sported a fine crop of wavy auburn hair, now only had a thinned grey tonsure. He peered at the accounts through half-moon spectacles, shaking his head and making his jowly face wobble. 'It's not just the drop in income, Annie. And before you get all overheated, it's nothing to do with your management of the place. You know how grateful we are.' Annie waited for him to continue, but suddenly he seemed lost for words.

His wife came to his rescue. 'What Eric is trying to say is that he's sorry you found out the way you did – what our intentions were, I mean. But we're not getting any younger, Annie, and the simple truth is we want to retire – find somewhere warm to enjoy our last few years.'

'Rita has the right of it there,' said Mr Ramsay. 'We're planning a move to Florida. Once we maximise what we can from the hotel and sell our other business interests, well, we should have enough to go and buy a modest place there and live reasonably comfortably.'

'Our David and his family have been out there for eleven years now, as you know. I miss not seeing my grandchildren.' Rita Ramsay looked every bit the granny, a plump face under a nest of neat grey curly hair.

'Right. I see,' said Annie, head downturned.

'Of course, we'll make sure you get the redundancy money you're due. And it goes without saying that we'll give you a glowing reference,' added Mrs Ramsay quickly.

'A manageress of your calibre will find another position in no time – you'll likely make money on the deal, eh?' her husband said unconvincingly.

Annie shook her head. 'Dae yous know how long I've been here?'

'Since my father's time, I'm sure,' said Eric Ramsay.

'That's right, aye, and I used tae work wae your grandfaither, tae. He liked tae keep his hand in behind the bar noo and again. Taught me the ropes, so he did.' She wiped a tear from her eye. 'You see, this place has been my life – aye, and the life o' a good few others, let me tell you. I know fine that fashions change, but you wait: folk will soon get fed up jeest staring at their televisions drinking cheap wine fae the supermarket, and start coming oot for a meal and a few drinks again. All this stay-at-home stuff is jeest a passing phase.'

'Even if it is, we still want to go to Florida, Annie. And at the moment, the way business is now and with the hotel in desperate need of refurbishment, we wouldn't get what we need,' said Mrs Ramsay.

'Turning the place into well-appointed flats and selling them off one by one means we'll make much more. I hope you understand.' Eric Ramsay closed a ledger, and patted its leather cover in an almost ceremonial way that said – to Annie at least – *that's it, it's over*.

There was silence in the room for a few moments, during which the Ramsays looked at each other uncomfortably, while Annie blew her nose loudly into a white hanky.

'So, when is this all going tae happen, then?'

'We've some functions on the books that take us through the Christmas period and into the New Year. Hopefully we'll make a bob or two then. So, to answer your question, we intend to close the hotel in February. Bloody awful time of year, anyway – certainly in this trade.'

'But we've got three weddings booked for the summer,' protested Annie.

'Yes. I've spoken to the parties involved and told them they'll have to find other venues. They were all very understanding, if a little upset, being locals, of course.'

Annie stood, sniffed, and looked between her bosses. 'Well then, there's nothin' tae be said, obviously. I'll need tae get oot an' find myself another job. Though at my age it's no' going tae be as easy as you think it will be, that's for certain sure.'

'We were rather hoping you could stay on and see us through until closure,' said Mr Ramsay.

'Aye, and I was *rather hoping* yous widna close the place and leave me oot o' a job. If you want a captain tae go doon with the ship, yous can look elsewhere – maybe dae a bit o' work yourselves. I canna guarantee whoot kind o' welcome you'll get, mind you. No, fair's fair. Yous have made up your minds to dae whoot's best for yous, and noo I'll dae the same.'

'If you leave, you risk your redundancy payment, Annie. I think it's only fair to warn you.' Eric Ramsay's face reddened as his wife glared at him.

'If you don't mind, I have a hotel tae run – for the time being, at least.' Annie turned on her heel and left the room, blinking back tears as she went.

'Well done, Eric. Another fine example of your diplomacy. If she goes, what will we do over Christmas?'

'She won't leave. I know Annie of old, her bark's always been worse than her bite. Anyway, she'll see sense about the money. At her age, she'll struggle to find a job – certainly one that pays as well.'

'That's if she doesn't take us to court over constructive dismissal.'

The drive to Rowan Tree Cottage – or the black croft, as Hamish had it – took Scott longer than he'd expected. The coast road to Blaan was a hilly single track. The view, though, was magnificent. The sun was shining and the air had turned cold. The storms over the last couple of days seemed like a distant memory as the three policemen looked across to the southern tip of the Isle of Arran, with the mound of Ailsa Craig standing solid in front of the distant blue line that was the Ayrshire coast. The sea, though, looked cold and dark, as if brooding quietly after days of angry turbulence.

Scott followed the directions Sergeant Shaw had written down and DS Potts was calling out as they went. Soon they came to a tumbledown gate to which was nailed a rough wooden sign with 'Rowan Tree Cottage' daubed in white paint across it. Potts opened the gate to allow Scott to drive on to the rutted lane ahead. As he closed it, he was doubtful that the construction would have been able to stop any but the least determined sheep or cow, but nonetheless he made sure it was secure before jumping back into the car.

They bumped along what was more like two tracks worn in a field underpinned by some gravel than a legitimate lane, Scott cursing as the car lurched from side to side over large potholes or the odd small boulder. Soon the ground dropped away before them and the track meandered on towards a distant cottage perched before a rocky promontory, a line of shingle beach to its side, and seaweed backed up in an impromptu wall in front of it.

'Nae wonder Hamish calls it the black croft. I can smell that seaweed fae here,' said Scott as the car bumped through another pothole.

Daley screwed up his face as they came to a halt beside the remains of an ancient Transit van and a pick-up that looked almost as decrepit but at least had four wheels. As Potts made to get out of the car, Brian Scott waved him back inside.

'Me and DCI Daley will deal wae this, son.'

As Potts watched them walk into a muddy yard, he shook his head. 'Fucking great,' he said to himself.

As Daley and Scott made their way to what they supposed was the front of the dwelling the stench of rotting seaweed was almost unbearable. Scott cursed further as his shoe squelched into what he identified as a cowpat, but could have been almost anything that was dark green, cloying and rancid. An old barrow sat by a rickety front door that had recently been painted blue, the only hint of colour in the place.

Scott knocked more loudly on the door than he had on Daley's earlier that morning, while trying to rub whatever it was that had attached itself to his shoe off on a clump of grass growing at the bottom of a rusted roan pipe.

'Here, maybe it'll be like Frank MacDougall's; mind, Jimmy? A wreck ootside and like a palace once you stepped o'er the door.'

'I wouldn't bet on it,' replied Daley. 'Wait, I hear someone coming.'

Sure enough, the sound of keys turning in at least two locks and the ring of bolts being pulled open could be heard from within.

'Why bother wae a' that? A gust o' wind could blow this thing in,' whispered Scott.

The door opened to reveal a small wizen-faced woman who could have been any age between seventy and ninety, it was hard to tell. Her hair was pulled back in a tight bun, and she wore an old-fashioned apron patterned with faded flowers that covered her almost from scrawny neck to scraggy ankle. Her eyes, though, were of a piercing green, with threatening depths. She shifted her gaze between the detectives, her head angled up to face them. 'What can I dae for you?' she said with little warmth.

'I'm DCI Daley, this is DI Scott. Can we come in, please, Mrs Doig?'

'If yous must.' She led them straight into a room that could have looked the same a hundred years ago, replete with storm lanterns, ancient furniture and a fire over which hung a blackened kettle. Dominating the room was a large, roughly made table under the window, around which were set five wooden chairs of various designs, none of them new. 'Take a seat at the table, if yous want. If it's aboot that auld truck, I don't drive it, so there's nae point asking me anything aboot the thing.'

Scott sniffed the air and could still smell the rotting seaweed outside, now overlaid by the smell of cooking fish and a musty overtone that made him want to sneeze. He was about to speak, but Daley beat him to it.

'You're the mother of Alison Doig, I believe?'

'Aye, I was until she ran off.' The answer was flat, without emotion.

'Ran off, you say?' said Scott.

'Aye, jeest so.'

'But she was reported missing at the time – thirty-four years ago.'

'You don't need tae remind me how long ago it was; I was here, remember. The only reason she was reported missing was they buggers at the high school. She ran away, plain and simple. She even stole oor van.' Her piercing eyes remained fixed on Scott, making him shiver involuntarily.

'So, you think she ran away – from what, here?' Daley asked.

'She was a selfish wee bitch, aye, and too keen on getting her hole. Nae respect for God or man. I was glad tae see the back of her, and that's the truth.'

'Well, regardless of how you feel, Mrs Doig, it's my duty to tell you that she's returned to the area. Temporarily, at least. To put your mind at ease after all this time,' replied Daley doubtfully.

Her face remained almost inscrutable, though for a moment her mouth opened slightly, something she hastily corrected. 'Well, tell her not tae bother coming here!' Her croaky voice was raised.

'What aboot your husband – her brothers?' said Scott. He was looking at his notebook. 'I believe you have three other children.'

'Aye. They're oot at the creels. If you care tae take a walk roon the back o' the place you'll see them in the bay.'

'And your husband?'

'He's oot for his walk. He goes this time every day, rain, hail or snow. He'll no' be back for a couple of hours, I would say,' she said, looking at an old grandmother clock against the wall.

'And he does this every day?' said Daley.

'Like I says, in rain, hail or snow.'

'Will he no' be interested to hear that his daughter is safe and well?' Scott asked.

She stared at him balefully. 'You'll have tae ask him that yourself, officer.' She folded her arms. 'Noo, if that's what you came tae say, I thank you for your time, but I've things tae be getting on with – so if yous don't mind.' Mrs Doig looked pointedly at the door.

'And you'll be sure to tell the rest of the family that your daughter has returned?' said Daley.

'Of that you can be sure. But I say again, she's no' welcome back here, and none of my family will feel any different. Feel free tae pass on that message tae her.'

Scott walked over to the window. 'What's the bell for?' He was examining the name *Jeremiah* boldly stamped on its side.

'My voice isn't whoot it was. It's for getting the boys in oot the fields or the boat when I've a meal on the table. I'm no' answering any mair questions. As I say, I've things tae get done, so if you please.' This time she walked to the door and pulled it open.

'And you've no other message for your daughter?' said Daley.

'Jeest tae stay away from us, that's all that needs tae be said.'

Daley handed her a card from the pocket of his jacket. 'If you don't mind, I'd be grateful if your husband could phone me on this number. It doesn't matter when, just as long as he does. I'd like to speak to him, please.'

'How many phones can you see?'

'Sorry?'

'We don't have such a thing – no, nor any modern gadget.'

'Well in that case, I'd like him to report to DS Scott at Kinloch police office at his earliest convenience.'

'For what reason?'

'Just to have a chat about Alison, that's all.'

'If you want him tae come tae your polis station in Kinloch you'll have tae come and arrest him.' One corner of her mouth tilted up, giving her a sly look. 'But I'm guessing that you've no lawful reason tae do so, in which case you know what to do.' She opened the door further.

'That's fine, Mrs Doig,' said Daley. 'I made that request to preserve your privacy. But I'll be back soon – I take it evenings are best? I'd like to speak with the rest of your family then.'

Scott followed Daley out of the door, being careful to avoid whatever it was he'd trodden in before as they made their way across the yard back to the car. 'She gives me the shivers, Jimmy,' he said as they took their seats in the vehicle.

'Not the most welcoming of folk, it has to be said,' Daley agreed.

'Look, she's still staring,' said Potts.

'And what aboot that hoose, eh? I've been in museums that don't have stuff as old as that in them.'

'Brian, how many museums have you been to – outside work, I mean?' Daley asked.

'Huh. Easy seen you're feeling better. Let's leave the Little Hoose on the Prairie and get tae fuck.'

As they drove off, the diminutive yet malevolent figure of Mrs Doig stood resolutely in her doorway, watching them go.

14

Nathaniel Doig stood at the edge of the hill. He'd been coming here every day for most of his life; the place drew him like a magnet. Though he wasn't a man prone to bouts of boundless enthusiasm – far from it – today he felt a particular melancholy.

He looked down at the sheer drop on to the rocks below as he had done hundreds of times before. It was strange, he thought, how people were drawn to the edge of the abyss in so many ways. Was it some ancient self-destruct button located deep in the mysteries of DNA, or merely a human tic akin to a typing error in a sentence? He didn't know the answer, but he could still feel the pull of the void.

Despite his best efforts to stay away from Kinloch as much as possible, he was sometimes forced to make the short trip to purchase the essentials of life. Had this not been the case, the town that hugged the loch might have been as far distant as the Alps or New York for all he cared. But as it was he was forced to endure the glances from cars and shop windows, the odd cat-call, or – as had been the case the last time he'd gone to the ships' chandlers to purchase lamp oil – the malicious gossip.

Above, a flock of gulls rode on the thermals, wings outstretched, soaring or swooping, their cries echoing along the hillside. He'd seen this place in all its moods: the soothing blankets of snow that made the world look soft and forgiving; the bright days like this one when he could easily have been standing on a Mediterranean coast; or the last couple of days, when it looked as though the wrath of God could be visited upon it at any moment. Broiling, dark seas flinging massive waves against the cliffs and hills like clenched fists battering an unprotected face.

As he considered this, he remembered the stories his father had told him, with that glint of madness in his eyes. He recalled the craggy, unyielding stare of the man who was happy to take a belt to his son whenever the fancy took him, before his strength was sapped by the cancer that feasted on his frail body: a punishment he richly deserved.

And what of him – what of Nathaniel Doig? The boy who dreamed of escaping this place, but had been pulled back in the same way he was drawn now to the edge of the cliff. He'd done what he thought was right – thought was right then. But ever since, his conscience had eaten away at his soul. He wrote every day, a long, unending missive of mitigation, a plea to God to forgive him for what he'd done. A meandering story, one he would never have the nerve to speak, but one that would see his soul burn in hell once others came upon it. And they would – he'd made sure of that. It was his eternal struggle between damnation and redemption. A struggle he could never win.

But he knew now that time was short. At least he could make some meagre amends for his sins.

He thought of his three sons. He could see them distantly across that dark sea, labouring mindlessly at their tasks. And he could see his home; he pictured his wife within, her withering looks, her sharpness, her ill temper. But there was more.

Perhaps it was the chill of the wind, perhaps some elevated primeval sense, that made him turn round; he didn't know. But turn he did.

Though in reality, with his failing eyesight and the distance involved, he couldn't recognise the figure climbing the slow green slope towards him, he knew exactly who it was.

He turned back to face the sea, the jutting point, the ragged finger of rocks to his left that had so shaped his life, and would now, in its own way, shape what was left of it. When he turned back from the vista of rocks and sea, the figure was growing larger as it approached, each stride bringing Nathaniel, too, closer to the destiny he knew he could never escape.

'Ach, it's jeest a terrible thing,' said Hamish, before taking another sip of his tea from the takeaway cup. He was sitting in the unmarked police car with three detectives, two of whom were demolishing bacon rolls, the third nibbling at a salad from a clear plastic container. 'I suppose it'll be the Douglas Arms for me, though wae a' those young folk aboot there and the racing on the TV non-stop, no' tae mention the racket they fruit machines make, well, it doesna make for a happy prospect at all.' He paused to reflect on the horror of the closure of the County Hotel. 'Thanks for the tea, Brian. At least that was a happy coincidence, me bumping into your young assistant here in Michael Kerr's.'

'Aye, the highest paid message boy in Scotland, that's me,' said Potts under his breath.

'Huh. When I was your age I was on points duty in Glasgow in the pissing rain,' said Scott.

'No you weren't. You were off having a fly pint with me. You were well in the CID by the time you were his age,' Daley pointed out.

'And look where that got me, eh? Green flamingos an' haunted hooses in my heid every night – no' tae mention the wee Mexican at the bottom o' the bed wae the huge guitar. You should count yoursel' lucky that you're sitting in here having a roll and a cup o' coffee, son.'

There followed a short silence while the other three occupants of the car processed this information.

Hamish was the first to break the silence. 'How come it was specifically a Mexican, Brian?'

'What about the green flamingos?' added Potts.

'Och, me and Ella went tae this place in Yorkshire when the weans was just wee. I cannae remember the name noo,' said Scott.

'Flamingo Land, by any chance?' said Daley.

'Aye, that's the one. Here, that's how you've got a' they pips on your shoulders, Jimmy, and the young fella here's just got a chip on one o' his.' Potts tried to retort, but Scott carried on. 'Of course, in a place called Flamingo Land there was a fair scatter o' they birds.'

'No' green yins though, surely?' said Hamish.

'No, there wisnae any green ones. But then again there were no three-feet-tall Mexican guitarists neither. Though they had one o' they Mexican bands. What are they called again? You always remember, Jimmy.'

'Mariachi.'

'Aye, that mob. How come I can never remember that?

Anyhow, there was one o' they bands playing in the wee nightclub when I used tae go doon for a drink. Och, it took Ella ages trying tae get the kids off tae sleep.'

'So that was her job, then?' asked Potts.

'You're no' kidding. What, after them knocking back fizzy drinks, sweets and candyfloss a' day, they was hyper. I'd tae get oot tae preserve my sanity.'

'I'm glad to know that there's still one unreconstructed male on the planet,' said Daley.

'See, there you go wae they things I don't understand again. I'm sure in a' the conversations we've had o'er the years, I've only understood maybe half o' them.'

'Tell me what you know about this black croft, Hamish?' Daley was anxious that Scott's tales of his struggle with the DTs should go no further.

'I telt Brian aboot them, but I maybe forgot something.'

'Like what? Don't tell me, they howl at the moon every Thursday,' said Scott rather unhelpfully.

'They might well do something akin tae that, Brian. I wouldna put anything past them.'

'No, me neither, especially having been doon at the place.'

Daley gave Scott a look and continued. 'So, Hamish, what did you forget to tell Brian?'

'The rumour is that they're as rich as Croesus.'

'You would think they'd spend something on the hoose, then,' said Scott. 'Like buying another one.'

'Carry on, Hamish,' said Daley with a sigh.

'Maybees jeest old wives' tales. But you know how I telt you they was wreckers. Och, jeest the lowest o' the low.'

'And?'

'Well, so the story goes, a long time ago they wrecked one

o' the Spanish Armada ships. Laden wae gold it was. Somewhere the place is full o' Spanish doubloons, or the like. They've been hoarding it a' these years.'

'How on earth did they get a hauld o' the Spanish Armada up here, when it was in the English Channel? Plus they're still living in a place like that. I think we can put that doon tae local pish,' remarked Scott.

'Well, now, you see, it's easy to say that – jeest being fair dismissive. It's well known that some o' the Armada escaped up the east coast, then came roon the top o' Scotland. Och, they were in hellish form by the time they got tae the North Channel. Many perished long before, the great galleons hitting rocks and that. I'm sure maist o' the folk on Mull are descended fae they sailors washed ashore in one way or t'other. A right sallow bunch they are up there – swarthy, you know. Some o' the tales that you hear are true, Brian Scott. And as I always say, there's nae smoke withoot fire.'

Scott remembered something. 'Here, have you ever heard of a boat called the *Jeremiah*?' he asked.

'Now, that rings a bell, right enough.'

'Funny you should say that, Hamish.'

'I canna jeest bring it tae mind – ach, it's a bugger getting old. I go into the scullery for something, and by the time I'm in there I've no clue why I went. But let me think on this *Jeremiah*, Brian. I'll get back tae you.'

'Once you've remembered what you wanted fae the scullery.'

'This salad's crap,' said Daley with a grimace.

15

'Hello, Faither.' The voice was almost lost on the wind. Even Alice Wenger was struck by the way it sounded as the words whirled back at her. It was as though the intervening years had never happened and she was back, standing here as the teenager she'd once been.

Nathaniel Doig looked at her, his face showing no emotion. 'Alison, it's good to see you.'

'The name's Alice now.'

'Yes, so I hear.'

She was momentarily taken aback. 'How do you know that?'

'I see you've forgotten the place from which you sprang. In Kinloch there are few secrets.'

'Apart from ours.'

He didn't reply, but turned back to face the sea, the breeze tugging at wisps of his grey hair.

Alice had forgotten what his voice sounded like. Not the casual burr of the locals, of the place where he had been brought up. No, it was the accent he'd acquired at university: refined, well spoken. She was astonished that she hadn't remembered that. The people she'd met since coming home had all sounded as she remembered them, apart from the man standing on the edge of this hillside – her father. 'Well, have you nothing to say?'

He looked over his shoulder at her. 'What do you want to hear?'

'Anything. Shout at me, cry – do something! Shit, we've not seen each other for decades!' Her raised voice sent the wheeling gulls high above into a frenzy of calls.

'Why have you come back?' He was facing her now.

'You know why.'

'If I knew I wouldn't have asked.'

'There are too many things left unsaid – undone. You know that's true, Faither.'

'Please don't call me that.'

'Why?'

'Because I've never liked the way you've said it.'

'Am I too folksy, Daddy?' she replied coquettishly in her adopted southern drawl.

'So you've been in America. That's what I heard – the accent.'

'What the hell do you care where I was?'

'I've always cared.'

'Oh yeah? Well, I wish to fuck you'd told me that when I was here!'

'Please, no profanity. You sound like your mother.'

'That old witch.' She stepped towards him and instinctively he backed away. 'What, you running scared of your little daughter?'

'No.'

'I knew you'd be up here. I'd bet my last cent you've been coming here every day since I left.'

'No. I was ill for a few months, but it passed. Otherwise, yes, you're right.'

'The scene of the crime; don't they say criminals always return to the scene of the crime?'

'I committed no crime here.'

'You asshole!'

'I'm glad to have seen you again, Alison.'

'Alice, you prick! Just ignore everything. It doesn't matter to you, does it? You've absolved yourself of any blame.'

'Sorry, Alice. I do beg your pardon.'

'You should have begged me a long time ago – and not just for pardon.'

'Maybe that's true. But have you ever thought about blame and how it should be apportioned?'

'You're still the same sanctimonious hypocrite you always were!' Alice spat on the ground.

'They tell me you're rich now.'

'Yeah, I'm wealthy. So what?'

'Enjoy it while you can, daughter.'

As Alice opened her mouth to speak, her father backed further away from her. Arms outstretched, he closed his eyes. Slowly, almost like a tall building being demolished, he toppled backwards into oblivion.

Alice rushed to the edge of the precipice. Already the broken body of her father was lying on the rocks far below, his face staring back up at her, pale and bloodied in death.

His daughter's screams echoed round the green hills of what once had been her home.

Liz Daley had begun to feel better – or so she thought. As she struggled to get her son to put on his clothes, though, she felt a tightening of her chest.

'I don't want to go!' The little boy stamped his feet.

110

'It hurts!' he wailed, tears now spilling down his chubby cheeks.

'Well, toothache hurts a lot more. Ask Daddy. He's always hated dentists.' As she spoke she felt herself gasping for air, and had to lean her head against her son's tiny chest as she kneeled before him in order to stop the room from spinning.

'Mummy, what's wrong?' James Daley junior had stopped crying now, his unwillingness to visit the dentist replaced by worry for his mother.

Liz breathed deeply. She'd expected Jim to take their child for the check-up, but he'd disappeared with Brian. She hadn't made a fuss when he'd called to say he would be gone most of the day; that he had effectively gone back to work early. Part of her had wanted to scream at him for his insensitivity, but she knew that he would have been angry with himself for failing to think of the significance of the situation, and anyway he'd had enough to deal with over the last few months.

She sighed and cuddled her son. 'Don't worry, James. Mummy's just a bit tired. Come on, we have to get ready. I promise it won't be sore. There are just some things in life you have to do.'

Finally, he was ready. Once he was securely fastened into his car seat, Liz drove off, making steady progress down the rutted lane until they reached the main road.

'It's bumpy, Mummy,' said the little boy.

'Yes, Mummy will have to speak to Mr Galbraith and see if he can fix it.'

'He's a farmer, Mummy. Will he do it with his tractor?'

'Oh, I expect so, James. Farmers do most things in their tractors in my experience. Just you sit tight; we're on the road now. It'll be much smoother.'

As they drove along she began to feel hot and turned up the air conditioning.

'Mummy, I'm cold.'

'Sorry, darling.' She turned it back down, but the sweat on her brow was a cold one.

They avoided the centre of town, driving along the little dual carriageway and up a rise. After passing two small hotels she pulled in at a convenient space just outside a big sandstone house. On one of the pillars that guarded the entrance was fixed a polished brass plate: *D. A. Skelton, Dentist, FRCDS*.

Liz's hands began to shake; she felt her throat tighten and tears begin to fall down her cheeks. She felt the pain, the helplessness, the paralysing fear, the nausea – everything she had suffered at the hands of another man in this profession. He always smelled the same; whether it was antiseptic or one of the many other tools of the trade she didn't know, but the underlying stench of his job lingered like the base note of an expensive perfume.

'Oh, they're closed today. I must have made a mistake, James,' said Liz with forced jollity. 'It's your lucky day, son.'

'Yay!' roared James Daley junior as they drove away from the dentist's and headed for home. All the time Liz was doing her level best to keep her silent sobs from her young son.

Alice Wenger's hands shook as she tried to dial the emergency number into her phone. This was her second attempt, there being no signal at the place her father had chosen to take his own life.

'Emergency, which service do you require, police, ambulance or fire and rescue?' The voice on the other end of the line was calm, measured.

Alice hesitated. What should her reply be? The ambulance was of no use to her father now. 'I – I'm not sure,' she stammered.

'Please try to tell me what's happened,' said the operator in a soothing tone.

'He's dead!' Alice put one gloved hand to her mouth.

'You're breaking up slightly. Did you say someone was dead?'

'Yes, yes – my father. He fell – jumped – I don't know.'

There was more urgency in the operator's voice now. 'Please tell me where this happened.'

Alice looked around. For a second the hills and fields were anonymous in her mind, the places where she'd run and played as a child suddenly forgotten as she tried to process the trauma of seeing her father plunge to his death. Then it clicked. 'Thomson's Hill. I'm on Thomson's Hill.'

'And you mentioned your father, where is he?'

Her voice was quaking now; despite her expensive outdoor gear she was freezing, cold enough to send her teeth chattering. 'He's – he's on the rocks – below the cliff.'

'I need your name, madam. Are you safe?' Concern now on the other end of the phone.

'Yes, yes, I'm safe. Oh, just please, please help me!'

16

Daley and Scott were following an ambulance as it made its way along the winding single-track road towards Thomson's Hill. Ahead, vehicles coming from the opposite direction reversed into the nearest passing places or pulled up on the grass verge to let them past. Both Scott's car and the ambulance were attending the scene to the wail of sirens and flash of blue lights.

The ambulance slowed at the gate. A woman in a green uniform jumped out and opened the gate to let both vehicles on to the hill.

'Shit, I don't think I'll make it up the rise in this jalopy,' said Scott as the car began to slip and slide alarmingly on the slick grass. 'We should have gone for your SUV, Jimmy.'

Ahead, the ambulance was having similar problems. Both vehicles stopped at the foot of the hill. The paramedic jumped from the ambulance and made her way to Scott's car.

'No way we'll make it up there – you neither, by the looks of things. The field's like a bog after the storms.'

'I was kind o' thinking that myself,' Scott replied.

'But it's not far over that hill until we get to the cliff. My father used to take me up there birdwatching when I was a wean. We'll take the essentials. Nothing we can do for

Mr Doig by the sound of things, but we can see that this Ms Wenger is cared for. The lifeboat's on its way; they'll retrieve the body, I think.'

'Oor forensics team are coming doon on the helicopter. You tell they lifeboat boys not tae touch anything until they arrive,' said Scott.

'What if he's still alive?'

'Does that sound likely tae you? He's no' moved in half an hour, no' tae mention falling two hundred feet on tae rocks. Are you expecting him tae bounce up an' say that he's okay and it's just a wee cut?'

Daley leaned across Scott. 'We'll call the lifeboat and let them know the procedure, Mrs Shanklin. You feel free to do your job with Ms Wenger. We'll follow you on foot up the hill.'

'You've got the knack wae these folk, Jimmy. I don't know how you do it.' Scott scratched his head.

'It just involves not being rude, Brian.'

'Aye, right. You're the master o' diplomacy when the red mist descends, eh?'

Scott's mobile rang and as always he had to squint at it before he could see to answer the call. 'Yes, ma'am.'

Daley looked on as he nodded without speaking. 'She can't see you nodding, Brian – it's a phone!'

Scott nodded a couple more times then handed the phone to Daley. 'Here, it's the boss. She wants tae speak tae you.'

Daley raised his eyes as he took the phone. 'Yes ma'am?'

'Jim? I didn't think you were coming back until next week?'

'I just popped into the office. DI Scott was getting me up to speed on what's been going on.' He winked at Scott.

'Okay. I'm glad you're there. A suicide, I hear?'

Daley hesitated. 'I don't think we can immediately jump to that conclusion. Under the circumstances, I mean.'

'What circumstances?'

'I'll call you when we get back to the office, ma'am. This could be more complicated than it appears. Might not be, but there's a possibility.'

'I'll leave it in your capable hands then, Jim. Let me know what's happening as soon as you can.'

'Certainly will do, ma'am.'

'And Jim?'

'Yes, ma'am?'

'It's good to have you back.'

He thanked her, ended the call and handed the phone back to Scott. 'Right, DI Scott, time to get up that hill.'

Liz was back home, gazing out of the window as James junior played on the floor with his toy cars. She'd been warned by her GP that life wouldn't – couldn't possibly – return to normal after her ordeal, but she hadn't listened. Overall, she'd been happy with how she felt. No bad dreams or panic attacks – she even managed not to think about it, though that had been difficult during the investigation into her husband's attack on her tormentor.

But today had been different – very different. She was still shaking from head to toe, and her mind was a whirl of memories of that evening, flashing before her as if they were taking place now, right in front of her. She could see the pitiless look in his eyes, feel the pain of the blows, then the humiliation.

She looked at the time: almost three o'clock. She went to

make herself a cup of coffee to see if caffeine would magically restore her equilibrium and banish the images from her mind, but when she returned from the kitchen with a steaming mug and a glass of juice for James, she headed across to the drinks cabinet and poured a large measure of whisky into her drink.

As she gulped it down a merciful calm descended upon her, almost akin to an embrace. Liz laid her head back against the sofa and stared at the ceiling, trying to think of nothing for a few minutes. Soon, however, the sights and sounds of the attack on her returned, and this time she decided to forget the coffee and just poured herself a large measure of the good single malt her husband always kept to hand.

Just one more, she thought. Just to take the edge off.

As she took a gulp at the raw spirit she screwed up her face, the whisky burning her throat. Liz Daley was more used to expensive wine than fine whisky, but it was hitting the spot, so she persisted.

She thought of her life. Growing up in a privileged, well-off family; a private school, university; then her marriage to Jim Daley. It hadn't been plain sailing by any means, and in truth most of it had been her fault. She wondered what had driven her to have so many affairs; to have destroyed the man for whom she would always have the deepest affection. But the past was just that, immutable, like a mountain or the stars: no matter how much she wanted to push against it, change what had happened, it wasn't possible and she knew it.

She'd nursed Jim Daley through his health scare and the investigation by PIRC into his conduct and she knew that he was grateful, happy to have had the care, a shoulder to cry on, someone to talk to when he was at his lowest ebb.

But she also knew that something had changed.

Gone was the big man who looked at her with puppy dog eyes; gone the husband who would forgive her outrageous behaviour every time she threatened to leave; gone the man who would shake at her very touch. Gone, all gone.

He had become cold, not to others, like Brian Scott, but to her. The changes were barely perceptible; nobody but her could possibly have noticed them. But Liz knew in her heart that Jim Daley, the man she loved, had cheated on, had treated like shit, no longer loved her. Tears filled her eyes, and for want of something else to do she headed back to the bottle and poured another large measure.

'Mummy, why are you stealing Daddy's special drink?' asked her son, looking up at her with a confused expression.

'It's not just Daddy's, James. It's mine too.' She knew, though, this was a lie. Nothing of Jim Daley belonged to her now; certainly not his heart.

While the forensic team were busy at the rocks below, Daley had made sure that nobody went near the cliff edge from which Nathaniel Doig had plummeted to his death. Indeed, a young cop, wrapped up against the cold, was now standing guard awaiting the arrival of SOCO.

'What are you thinking, Jimmy?' Scott asked.

'I don't know. We'll have to wait until the boys in the paper suits have done their work.'

'Aye, but what's your gut telling you?'

'My gut's been away from this for a while, Brian.'

'But it's possible, right?'

'What?'

'She comes over here tae take revenge on her dear old dad.

It's clear tae me that's a dysfunctional family, if ever I saw one. It's 1842 in that hoose!'

Daley thought for a moment. There was no doubt that the likely circumstances in which Alison Doig, now Alice Wenger, had grown up were unusual ones, but why wait all these years to come back and kill her father? Though he hadn't met the man, Hamish had called him a *gent*, and seemingly he was more refined and much better educated than the rest of his family. Somewhat unkindly, Daley considered Alice Wenger's waspish mother to be a more likely candidate for murder. But within families ran complex, often impenetrable dynamics. Who knew what relationship the woman now shivering in the ambulance down the rise had had with the man who'd just died?

With Scott in tow, Daley walked carefully down the slick mud of the hill. Alice Doig was wrapped in two blue blankets, her teeth still chattering.

'We'll be off to the hospital in a couple of minutes,' the paramedic told them as she asked Wenger to lie down and strapped her into the on-board stretcher.

'Just a couple of questions, then you can be on your way,' said Daley.

The paramedic opened her mouth as though she was about to object, but a stern look from Daley saw her close it again and disappear from sight round the side of the vehicle.

'I know what you guys think. Cops are the same all over the world,' said Alice, defiant though obviously still in shock.

'And what do I think?' Daley asked.

'That I've come all this way after such a long time to kill the father I've always hated.'

'Did you hate him?'

119

'There wasn't a whole lot of love going on in our house. But since you've asked me a direct question, no I didn't hate him.'

'And your mother?'

'I don't want to talk about her.'

'Why?'

'Are you deaf? I said I don't want to talk about her!' Alice Wenger spat the words out.

'Tell me what happened today.'

'I knew he came here every day. He did it all the time I was a kid. I knew him, so I was sure he'd be here, just like always.'

'Why not go to the cottage?'

'I wanted to speak to my father.'

'What about your brothers?'

'Have you met my brothers, detective?'

'No, but I'll be speaking to them soon.'

'Well, good luck with that.'

'Tell me what happened – on the hill, I mean.'

'We spoke – he was very calm.'

'Were you?'

'No, not really.' She drew the blankets tighter round her shoulders. 'It was as though he'd seen me yesterday. He didn't . . .' Her voice tailed off.

'He didn't seem surprised to see you after all this time?'

'Huh, no. Some of the local gossips had gotten to him first. He knew I was here – even knew I'd changed my name.'

'What, then?'

'We exchanged a few words. I shouted, he said very little. Then he just walked backwards, held out his arms, closed his eyes and fell off the edge.'

Scott screwed up his face. 'Backwards, you say?'

'Yup.'

'Was your faither a drinking man, Ms Wenger?'

'Never touched a drop when I knew him. His father was a drinker. I think he'd suffered – you know, the old guy used to get tanked up and beat the shit out of him, that sort of thing. My eldest brother is named after him – Thorbin. I've seen my fair share of men who like to drink, but he certainly didn't appear drunk to me.' She lowered her head.

'Okay, Ms Wenger – Alice. Let's get you to the hospital and we can talk some more once you've been checked out,' said Daley.

'If you think you're going to make a name for yourself by pinning this on me, you can think again, asshole!'

'I'm not in the habit of pinning anything on anyone. We'll speak later. I'm sorry your father's dead.' Daley turned on his heel and walked towards Scott's car. His old friend nodded at Alice Wenger and followed him.

'What now, Jimmy, back tae sleepy hollow?'

'Yes. While she's being checked out we'd better go and inform Mrs Doig that her husband's dead. Didn't think we'd be back there so soon. Looks like I'm having a baptism of fire.'

Scott started the engine and pulled away, making slow progress towards the gate and the road beyond. 'It's no' just Symington that's glad you're back. I am too, big man.'

'Thanks, Brian. Much appreciated.' Daley smiled.

'I don't fancy passing on the bad news tae that old witch, I'm telling you.'

Daley sighed and looked up at the sky, a patchwork of grey clouds and flecks of blue.

'What's up wae you, Jimmy?'

'You spoiled the moment, Brian.'

'Eh? You're as bad as Ella. It's like speaking tae a crossword: you never know where you are.'

'While I remember, I'll need to get to grips with all the roster sheets. I'll take a look when we get back to the office.'

'Och, nae bother. Shaw's your man for that.'

'I thought you did them.'

'Nah, I was, but he was keen as mustard. He's done his best – you know, under the circumstances, like.' Scott gave Daley a side-on look and changed the subject as quickly as he could.

17

1925

As the tide went out what was left of the steam puffer *Jeremiah* was to be found lying on her side, held fast by the black finger of rocks that had brought about her end.

The day was fresh now, a strong wind the only remnant of the storm that had raged all through the previous night. The air, cleaned by gales, wind and rain, was salt-tanged by the sea, and seabirds soared, glad to be able to take their heads from under the wings that were now spread in flight. In the small bay lay the body of a man, face down where sea met sand, tiny waves still pulling and pushing him as they came and went.

The three figures, all male, one of early middle age, the other two little more than boys, looked on dispassionately. The man stroked his beard, already flecked with grey as he squinted against the early morning sunlight at the wrecked puffer.

'You two, go take a look at thon body. Remove anything he has in his pockets – leave nothing. Then make sure you float him back out to sea. You understand?' As the boys turned to do as they were bid, he grabbed the arm of the elder. 'Did you do what I asked up on Thomson's Hill, Thorbin?'

'Aye, Faither, exactly as you said. I covered the burned grass wae some boulders, then branches and that.'

'I hope it's convincing – jeest like I showed you.' He tightened his grip on Thorbin's arm.

'Aye, just like you showed me the last time. You wouldna know there'd been a fire there, I promise.'

'Good. Get down there and help your brother.'

When Thorbin arrived by the body of the dead man, his brother had already turned him over. His skin was sallow though deathly pale – a strange sight. His face was battered and bruised as though he'd been in a fight. One of his legs lay at an impossible angle, clearly broken.

'You go through his pockets,' said Thorbin, attempting the same authority of voice his father displayed.

The younger boy grimaced. 'Dae I have tae?'

'Aye, Ethan, you do. Check everywhere, and make sure there's nothing left on him. Then we'll have tae haul him back oot.'

Swallowing hard to keep the bile from rising in his throat, Ethan went about his task as effectively as he could. The man's sea jumper was sodden, and he had to pull hard to lift it above the corpse's waist, the dead weight of the body making things even more difficult. He pushed two fingers into the right pocket of the dead man's trousers and using them like tweezers pulled out what he had found. Though the cigarette packet was sodden, the writing on it was still discernible. 'Lucky Strikes?'

'It's they Yankee cigarettes. Mind we saw them in that film at the cinema?'

'Aye, when you were trying tae get Elsie MacBride tae gie you a kiss. I mind.'

'Hurry up, you pair!' The distant voice of their father carried on the wind.

Satisfied that there was nothing more in that pocket, Ethan turned his attention to the other. Again he fished out what he found: first a short black comb, then a small leather wallet containing only a business card for an olive oil company, and finally a clump of sodden paper held together by a clip. He looked again at his elder brother. 'What's this?'

'I don't know.' Thorbin looked at the gold clasp that held the paper together. 'It looks like money.'

'But no' oor kind o' money, eh?'

'Faither will know whoot it is. Right, are you sure that's all in the front pockets?'

'Aye. You get doon an' gie it a go if you're so keen.'

'I'll gie you a kick in the teeth if you don't hurry up. And that's nothing tae whoot Faither will dae if we don't get this sorted quick smart.'

Both of them knelt by the body and flipped it over as the waves lapped at their rubber boots. This time Thorbin hauled the sodden jumper up and nodded to his brother, who probed into the back pocket of the trousers with the same two fingers. 'Nah, nothing in there,' he said, looking relieved. 'Right, we'd better wade out an' get rid o' him like Faither said.'

'Hold on,' said Thorbin. He lifted the jumper up further, revealing something black and metallic poking out of the dead man's waistband. He hauled at it and a stubby pistol was soon revealed.

'It's a gun!'

'Aye, it's a gun.' Thorbin held it by the handle, being careful to keep his finger off the trigger. He was old enough to know what guns could do; he'd spent plenty of time hunting rabbits with his father. 'Right, throw this stuff up the beach. We need tae get him back in the sea.

The boys grunted as they pulled at the body, gasping harder the further into the cold water they went. It wasn't until the water was above Thorbin's waist and under his younger brother's arms that they felt their load lighten.

'Right, let go,' said Thorbin. Sure enough, as though now held by an invisible hand, the body of the dark-haired, sallow-skinned man began to drift away on the surf. 'We'll take what we found to Faither, then we'll have tae get intae thon puffer. The tide's on the turn.'

Daley and Scott made their way back along the rutted track towards Rowan Tree Cottage. If anything, the stench of rotting seaweed was stronger than on their last visit. As they made their way to the front door, Scott nudged Daley.

'Here, there's the three stooges doon on the beach.'

Daley looked where his colleague was pointing. Sure enough, three dark-clad figures were on the shingle shore, hauling a lobster boat clear of the surf. 'Good. We can have a chat with them after we've spoken to Mrs Doig.' Daley made a fist to chap the door, but before he could reach it the grim-faced old woman had opened it.

'Yous again. What dae you want this time? This is harassment, so it is. I suppose my rich daughter put money in your pockets tae make my life difficult, eh?'

'We need to speak to you, Mrs Doig,' said Daley. 'It's a serious matter – concerning your husband. Can we come in?'

'Naw, you can't.' She folded her arms resolutely, standing small but immovable in the doorway. 'Whoot you have tae say you can dae here. Get on wae it, for I've nae time tae waste.'

'Very well,' said Daley. 'It's my sad duty to tell you that your husband was involved in an accident a short time ago.'

'Whoot? Are you going tae tell me he fell vaulting o'er a fence? For I tell you this, he's no' got the energy.'

'No, I'm sorry to say that he's dead, Mrs Doig. He fell from the cliff on Thomson's Hill. It's too early for us to give you any more details.'

For a moment Ginny Doig's face changed. Whether it was a flash of surprise or sadness Daley couldn't tell, but very quickly she composed herself.

'Bit o' a coincidence, is it no'?'

'What?'

'My dear daughter arrives after all these years and my husband conveniently falls off a cliff. I hope your next port o' call will be tae have words wae her?'

'We've spoken to Ms Wenger already, Mrs Doig,' Daley told her.

'Huh.' The old woman laughed mirthlessly. 'She's got you in her pocket right enough. Instead o' coming tae see me first tae tell me my husband's dead, you rush tae see her. How much did she gie yous, eh?'

'Your daughter was at the scene.'

This time Ginny Doig's eyes flashed, a look of pure hatred enveloping her face. 'Well, there we are. She came here for one reason and one reason only, tae kill her ain faither. I don't care how much money she's got, I want yous tae arrest her for murder!' She took a step towards Daley, wagging her finger up in his face.

'If you don't mind me sayin', you don't seem too upset that you've just lost your husband,' said Scott.

'And how would you know whoot I feel? Did yous jeest

127

come tae see me collapse in a heap, greeting like a wee lassie so yous could pass it all on tae Alison? Well, yous can think again. I'm no' one for tears; what's done is done. But I want her in chains in your cell, DCI Daley.'

Ignoring her, Daley turned round. 'We saw your sons when we arrived.'

'And?'

'I want a word with them.'

'I'll tell them what's happened to their faither. We don't need you – we don't need anybody.'

'You can come with us and tell them, if that's what you wish. But a man has died, and I'm carrying out an investigation. One way or the other, Mrs Doig, I will speak to your sons. In the light of these tragic events I'd much rather it be this way. But if you try to stop me I'll make sure that I do what is necessary to speak to them, whether you like it or not.'

She eyed the police officers balefully. 'We'll do it your way. But I don't want you to mention their sister.'

'Don't they know she's here? That she's safe – alive?'

'My boys are simple lads. They don't need the upheaval of knowing that their long-lost sister has just killed their faither!' She screamed the last few words.

'Lads?' said Scott. 'They don't look like lads tae me. Grown men, mair like.'

'I dare say there's a newfangled term for it noo, but I just call it as I see it. My boys aren't quite the full shilling. They might look like adults, but they've got the minds o' children. I'm no' ashamed o' it, that's jeest how they are. But I don't want yous speaking tae them.'

'I'm afraid you've no choice in the matter, Mrs Doig. Now, shall we?' Daley started walking towards the beach.

18

1925

The father and his two sons made their way in a lobster boat out to the wrecked vessel that lay on its side at the end of the spur of jagged black rocks. They could hear creaking as the puffer settled in this unnatural state on its side, held fast until the tide would set it free only to send it to the depths. A great gash in the vessel's side would guarantee that.

They anchored by the wreck and made their way gingerly on to the rocks. The man threw a grappling hook up the side of the puffer. He failed at his first attempt, but the hook caught a rail on his second try. He pulled at the rope to make sure it was secure.

'Thorbin, you go first. Your brother and I will come after you.' He watched as his elder son quickly scaled the rope and pulled himself on to the slanting deck. Ethan followed, but with less agility than his older sibling.

The vessel was a mess: the taff rail was broken in two places, no doubt by the impact of hitting the rocks; one of the heavy doors into the hold had sprung open and was torn from one great hinge. A brass storm lantern lay smashed against a bent funnel. Part of the ship's wheel, like a wedge of cake, lay trapped against a strongbox under the few steps up to the wheelhouse. The man bounded up them, followed by his sons.

All the windows in the wheelhouse were smashed. Half in, half out of one lay the body of a man who had almost been cut in two by the broken glass, no doubt flung against it as the vessel was wrecked on the unforgiving thrust of the coast. Ethan looked away, appalled by the sight.

'Don't be a fucking lassie!' His father caught him by the neck of his jumper. 'Go through his pockets just like you did with the man on the beach. Quickly now!' He turned to his elder son. 'Get below while I check the hold.'

Thorbin made his way back on to the deck and forced open the hatch that led to the crew's quarters. Against the bulkhead sat a blackened stove with a guardrail that had failed in its task. Burnt coal and cinders were scattered across a mess of hessian sacks containing potatoes and carrots; pots and pans littered the deck. A box of herring had been upended and tins of all shapes and sizes were gathered against one side of the vessel, having rolled there with the cant of the stranded puffer.

He stepped through a bulkhead door. He had to cover his nose against the stench of sickness and blood. Two men lay on the floor in a pool of seawater, vomit and gore. He prodded them one after the other with the toe of his boot, but both were dead, eyes staring lifelessly, bodies bloodied and battered. Despite the horror of the task, he automatically went about the process of searching through their pockets.

One man was sandy-haired, the left side of his face battered to a pulp leaving one eye hanging from its socket. He was strangely familiar, and Thorbin thought he was probably a local, though he couldn't put a name to him. His pockets were empty, save for a few coins and a briar pipe.

The other man had sallow skin like the body on the beach, though his hair was of a lighter hue. He had an old scar running down one side of his face and a fresh gash in his forehead. The impact must have been a heavy one as his skull was cleft in two and a slick of grey matter infused with red blood oozed from it. Thorbin gagged as he realised this was the dead man's brain. Again, though, putting his revulsion aside, he delved through his pockets, this time finding a leather wallet thick with the same notes he'd seen held within the golden money clip of the corpse on the beach. Probing further, he discovered what looked like the hilt of a knife.

Thorbin examined this odd implement, and jumped when he pressed a button on the side of the handle and a wicked blade shot up with a snap. He looked round to make sure there was no sign of his father before slipping the stiletto into his pocket, blade retracted. It would now be his and his alone.

As he stood up, eyeing the rest of the cabin he was startled when his father appeared through the bulkhead door.

'Nothing in the hold worth a shilling! Fuck all apart fae a few miserable bags o' coal and a deid engineer. No' worth hauling o'er the side. Bastard!' he roared.

Thorbin was about to speak when both his and his father's attention was drawn to one of the top bunks. From it came a weak voice, groaning and pleading for help.

Thorbin's father pulled himself up on the side of the bunk and looked over the edge. A boy, no older than his own son, lay lashed to his bed, blood still pouring from a wound on his cheek. He gazed at the older man with half-shut eyes. 'Help me, please, mister,' he croaked.

Letting himself down from the bunk the man looked around. On the mattress below lay a sodden pillow. He hauled it into his arms and this time made his way up the short ladder to lean over the stricken boy in the top bunk. Without expression, he forced the pillow on to his face. The boy's wails were muffled as he was slowly smothered, struggling against his bonds. Soon, the movement stopped, and when his attacker removed the pillow the dead boy's eyes stared still and empty into the face of the man who had taken his life.

Watching, Thorbin could take no more. Removing items from the pockets of dead men was one thing; this was quite another. It was the murder of a child, plain and simple. He spewed copiously on the deck, over the dead men.

'Pull yourself together, boy!' His father struck him hard in the face with the back of his hand. 'There's no place for pity in whoot we dae. Aye, I've just killed that boy, but the minute you set that fire on Thomson's Hill you killed all the rest of these men. So don't look at me like that!' He hit his son again, this time with a balled fist, sending Thorbin spinning to the floor, where he landed amidst the blood, vomit and gore.

'Get up, you useless bastard. There's nothing for us here apart from what we've already found. We'll get what we can fae the wheelhouse and be on oor way before this tub is refloated on the tide. She'll sink, but that's a good thing.'

'Won't anyone have reported it?' said Thorbin, struggling to his feet, his face already bruising where his father's fist had connected with his cheek.

'Aye, maybees so. But the fishermen in Kinloch will be slow tae the task o' manning the lifeboat this day. They'll have enough on their plates wae their ain boats after that storm last night. They'll find her if she doesna sink quickly, but that's unlikely, and in any case we'll be back at the cottage. Come on.'

As Thorbin pulled himself back on to the deck, the sheer shock of seeing his father kill a boy began to sink in. He swallowed the bile in his throat, shamed by what his father had done but aware that he was right: Thorbin himself had set the fire that lured these men to their deaths. He was as guilty of murder as the man with the greying beard who was now searching the deck for anything of value.

'That old boy had a gold pocket watch!' shouted Ethan, emerging from the wheelhouse. 'And I thought I might as well take this.' In his other hand he held a small ship's bell, hanging by a short length of rope he'd hacked at with his penknife.

'Aye, well, at least there's something. We'll get some money for the watch up in Glasgow.' His father spat on the slanting deck as he looked around. 'Here, that strongbox. Get it open, Thorbin.'

Still nursing his shock and revulsion, Thorbin pulled at the lid of the metal box under the wheelhouse steps. It was sturdy, the size of four fish boxes placed together, though slightly taller. 'It's padlocked, Faither,' he called.

'There's a mallet up here,' said Ethan from the wheelhouse.

'Don't jeest stand there – bring it doon here, you halfwit,' said his father, holding out his hand for the metal tool.

Watched by his two sons, the middle-aged man swung the mallet at the clasp and padlock. After five or six attempts the lock sprang open. He unhooked the ruined padlock from the clasp and forced up the heavy lid, letting it clatter against the base of the wheelhouse. He stood back for a moment, taking off his greasy sailor's cap as though mourning a dead friend, face blank. Gradually, he cracked a smile that quickly broke into a wild laugh.

'Whoot is it?' said Thorbin, rushing to his father's side. As he looked into the dull metal box the butter-yellow ingots glowed in a shaft of light, almost as though they were infused with some inner force all of their own. 'Is that . . . is that what I think it is, Faither?'

'You're damn right it is, son. Gold! Aye, and damn plenty o' it, tae.' He cackled with laughter again. 'We're rich – the Doigs are rich at last!'

Thorbin stepped back from the box and the treasure within, his mind swirling at the sight of the gold and the horror of seeing his father take the life of a child – of all the death he'd seen that day. His father was now holding an ingot in two hands, lifting it up to the light of the sun like a sacred offering.

Thorbin reached into his pocket and felt the slick wooden handle of the blade he'd found in the pocket of the dead man below. If his father could kill one child for money, what else could he do? He remembered the beatings, the long days without food, the punishments, the torments he'd suffered at the hands of this man for as long as he could remember. He heard the screams of his mother as, in drink, the man in front of him now tossed her frail body against one wall then another. He heard the muffled wails of the boy strapped to the bunk as his father suffocated the life from him.

Something in Thorbin Doig's head snapped. In one easy motion he delved into his pocket, removed the knife and clicked the switchblade into the light. It too glinted in the sun before it was slathered with the blood of his father as again and again he plunged it between his shoulder blades.

Ethan screamed and ran at his brother, desperately trying to pull the knife from his hands, as their father staggered and dropped the ingot to the deck with a clatter. Without thought, Thorbin pulled the knife from his father's back and thrust it between his brother's ribs.

Ethan stared at him wild-eyed as he took a step backwards, then looked down at the hilt of the switchblade still sticking from his chest. He tried to speak but only a rasp sounded as bubbles of dark blood appeared at the corners of his mouth.

The act had been instinctive, without any force of will, as though some other hand had turned the knife on his younger brother. With his father in his death throes on the deck, Thorbin leaned over Ethan's motionless figure and pulled the knife from his chest. A slow flow of dark blood trickled from the wound.

Thorbin Doig stepped back. He remembered his mother's words as he had tried to bathe the wounds inflicted on her by his father.

'The Doigs are monsters, son. Don't be like them. Don't be like them.'

He'd promised her that he wouldn't, but in that moment he knew the promise was broken, was nothing but a lie. For Thorbin Doig was the biggest monster of all, and now he knew it.

19

Hamish was sitting beside another elderly fisherman, quietly remembering the halcyon days of the County Hotel. They both swirled the whisky in their glasses as though using the spirit to conjure up images of past and future, a divination. A young couple – holidaymakers – looked on as they picked at their food, the atmosphere of gloom and despondency making them wish they'd chosen another venue for their meal. Behind the bar, Annie was polishing a pint tumbler, but with none of her usual gusto. The task was perfunctory, as she too stared into space looking for an answer that wouldn't come.

'Bugger me, it's like a badly attended wake in here,' said Charlie Murray as he entered the bar. He was wearing an old sports jacket with leather pads on the sleeves over his dungarees, all powdered with sawdust from his work as a joiner, made more obvious by his protruding belly.

'Whoot's there tae be cheery aboot?' asked Annie. 'Enjoy the place while it's here, Charlie, for come February it'll just be so much bricks and mortar, gone for ever. Aye, and me oot o' a job intae the bargain.'

The local councillor, Kinloch's own political tour de force, sat down heavily on a stool, leaning forward, his elbows fixed on the bar. 'Aye, I've heard the rumours, right enough. The owners are going tae turn it intae flats, so the gossips say.'

'Aye, they are that.' Annie put down the glass she was drying. 'What can I get you, Charlie?'

'A pint o' heavy, please. You get a fair drooth wae all that dust in the air.'

'I thought you retired long ago?'

'I did. But they sons o' mine – och, they're good enough tradesmen, gifted, in fact. But when it comes tae business, well, they might as well be toddlers. I go in two days a week and keep them on the right track. Aye, and it's good tae keep my hand in wae the tools noo and again.' He brushed some dust from his dungarees as he spoke, and Annie quickly wiped it from the bar with a wet cloth before she laid the pint of beer in front of him.

'It would seem that fiscal jurisprudence doesna run in every family,' said Hamish from his seat at the table. 'Certainly not the one that owns this place, at any rate, Charlie.'

Murray took a long draw of his pint, wiping foam from his lips with the back of his hand. 'My, but you're a right defeatist. If we'd had that attitude in the war we might as well have surrendered.'

'At least we had a fighting chance in the war. We've got hee-haw, noo. They've made up their minds. Off tae live the high life in the sun on the money they make fae this place once it's carved up intae flats.' Annie looked around the bar. 'This hotel has been my life, Charlie – for better or worse. I'm fair heartbroken, so I am.' She brushed away a tear.

'Turning a place intae flats insna as simple as you might think,' said Murray.

'Why, whoot do you mean?'

'They have tae get permission from the council planning department. I'll have a look at it. Who knows, for some reason this building might no' be suitable for conversion, eh?'

For the first time in days, Annie felt her spirits rise. 'Your pint's on the hoose, Charlie,' she said, smiling.

'I thank you, Annie. But mind, while I'll dae my best, I canna make any promises.'

Hamish piped up. 'Any port in a storm, Charlie Murray – any port in a storm.'

Daley and Scott eyed the three men in front of them. Though they were of varying heights and ages, they were all big and overweight, the youngest nearly as tall as Daley. They stood looking at their diminutive mother, almost as though the policemen weren't there at all. Behind them, a small lobster boat was pulled up on the pebbled shore, a haven for empty creels, curls of rope and a couple of orange buoys. The boat, however, looked as dilapidated as Rowan Tree Cottage.

'Right, yous jeest listen tae me,' said Ginny Doig. 'There's bad news.'

'Whoot, Mother?' slurred the smallest and oldest-looking of her sons, a few strands of hair sticking up almost vertically from his otherwise bald head.

'Your faither's deid.'

Scott raised one eyebrow. 'Don't you break it too gently, noo,' he muttered under his breath, eliciting an elbow in the ribs from Daley.

The men's reaction was hard to gauge. Never taking their eyes off their mother, the only real show of emotion at the news their father had passed away was a gaping mouth or a sigh between them.

'And there's mair, tae. Your sister – the one that ran away all they years ago – she's back. She killed him!' Ginny Doig spat the words out.

'That's enough, Mrs Doig!' said Daley. He looked around the three men. 'Your sister is back, yes. And though we're carrying out investigations, we don't know what happened to your father yet.' Though he spoke to them directly, they still stared at their mother with expressionless, empty faces, seemingly devoid of any emotion or feeling, apparently entranced by the tiny woman in front of them.

'So you say,' said Ginny Doig. 'As I telt you, there's no coincidence that she disappears for mair than thirty years, then the minute she's back her faither plunges tae his death off Thomson's Hill. Aye, and her at that very place, tae.' She addressed her sons. 'Yous go and get on wae your chores.' Then to the policemen, 'You've done what you came tae do. Yous can go.'

Daley watched as Ginny Doig's sons shuffled back towards the small boat. He noted that despite the tragic news about their father not one word appeared to pass amongst them as they went about their 'chores'.

'I'm not happy with what has happened, and we will be investigating the death of your husband, Mrs Doig. But to do that, I want to speak to you all one by one. Out of respect for your loss that can wait until tomorrow. We'll return then – around noon, if that's convenient for you?'

'And whoot if I tell yous tae fuck off?'

'Then you'll be making your statements at Kinloch police office. One way or another, Mrs Doig, you and your family will all answer my questions. And I'll want to know more about the disappearance of your daughter Alison.'

'Jeest ask her!'

'I want to ask you, Mrs Doig – and your sons. You have my sincere condolences. Until tomorrow at noon.' Daley turned on his heel and walked back up the pebble beach, Scott in his wake.

'That was just weird, Jimmy.'

'I've seen more effusive displays of grief, it has to be said.'

'And boys tae men, that's no' right, neither. You've just been telt your father's gone and they never cut a light!' He shook his head. 'Aye, and did you notice their eyes?'

'No, not really.'

'Each one o' them had a droopy right eye. You've been away too long, Jimmy. I spotted that a mile off.'

'Some family trait or other, I expect – probably genetic. I was keener to gauge Mrs Doig's behaviour. Anyway, all your nephews have red hair.'

Scott nodded. 'Mind you, so has their mother.'

Daley stopped and turned back towards the sea. Standing with her arms folded, Ginny Doig stared darkly back.

Daley and Scott went straight to Kinloch hospital where Alice Wenger was being assessed following her ordeal. They were ushered into a side room, where they found Wenger sitting up in bed having an animated conversation on a mobile phone. Whoever she was speaking to could have been in no doubt that she wasn't happy with the way things were going – whatever those things were.

As she waved the detectives in she ended the call abruptly, not bothering to say goodbye.

'Ms Wenger,' said Daley. 'I hope you're okay?'

'You know hospitals, detective. They just love sticking needles into you and making you wait for results. Apparently my blood pressure is too high, so they want to keep me in overnight. But that's not going to happen. As soon as the doc arrives, I'm outta here!'

'Are you sure? Better safe than sorry,' Daley remarked from experience.

'I have a thorough medical every six months in a state-of-the-art hospital in LA. I think if there was anything wrong with me they would be more likely to pick it up than this quack's paradise. Who wouldn't have raised blood pressure when they've just watched their father die by his own volition? Just normal, wouldn't you say?' She reached for a bottle of water on her bedside table and took a gulp.

'Well, if you're sure. We can put this off and speak to you at the office once you're discharged, if you'd prefer?'

'Heck no, let's just get on with it.'

Daley and Scott sat down on either side of the bed. Scott consulted his notebook. 'So, you're back here to make some kind o' contact with your family, right?'

'To tell you the truth, Mr Scott, I don't know why I came back. I guess outta curiosity, a bit of nostalgia maybe.'

'You had no firm plans to make contact with your family?' Daley asked.

'Not really.' She closed her eyes. 'I missed my father – Faither, as I used to call him.'

'What aboot your mother?' said Scott.

'What about her?'

'You didn't want to see her again? I mean you made a special effort to go and see your father up on Thomson's Hill, rather than at home. You weren't sure if he'd even be there.'

'Home? Shack, more like. But no, I didn't want to see my mother, not now, not ever.'

'Was she the reason you ran away?'

'One of the reasons, yes.'

'What about your brothers?'

'I take it you've been to see them, yeah?'

Daley nodded.

'So, you make up your own mind as to whether I wanted to see them or not.' The reply was flat, without emotion.

'They're no' much like you, Alice,' said Scott.

'You bet they're not. Leastways, not now.'

'Meaning?'

She didn't answer the question, merely shrugging her shoulders.

'What did you and your father talk about?' asked Daley.

'As I told you, he knew I was here, wasn't surprised. I forgot what this place was like, no secrets. We talked a whiles, then . . .'

'You said you argued.' Daley stared at her, looking for a response – looking for anything.

Wenger folded her arms. 'I said, I was pissed that he didn't seem bothered he hadn't seen me in all this time. You kinda hope you'll get some reaction, some kinda emotion from a father who's not seen you in half a lifetime.'

'Not much emotion to be found in your family, it would appear,' said Daley.

'So yous did argue?' Scott asked.

Alice Wenger laughed. 'You cops. Like I always say, you are the same all over the world. I also know, with the kinda tech you have now, you'll be able to see that I never stepped nearer than ten feet to the man, if that.'

'You've had experience of the police?' said Daley.

'Some – enough to last me all my life.' She ignored a ping from her mobile and sighed. 'I was a kid when I first landed in America, Mr Daley. Raw, stupid – I had no idea about the world. I got in tow with the wrong guy. He had a motorbike, he was handsome – in the biker kinda way. He was kind for a while; until he beat the shit outta me, that was.'

'You went to the police?' asked Daley.

'They came to us. He let me go, but he wouldn't surrender to them.' Alice Wenger stared into space, everything passing before her mind's eye. 'They shot him dead.'

Slightly taken aback, Daley swallowed hard. 'I'm sorry.'

'No need, he was an asshole.'

'So that was Mr Wenger?' asked Scott.

'Hell no!' Her laughter filled the room. 'I was young then but I soon learned. I got me a job as a nanny in a big house in Louisiana. Two kids to look after, but compared to my brothers they were no problem. Jack and his wife – well, they fought a lot.'

'Jack?'

'Jack Wenger.' She smiled at the expression on their faces. 'Yeah, he became my husband. One day his pretty wife and his two kids just upped and offed. She came from old money, so they disappeared. Jack, well, he was different. He'd made it from nothing – from a bellhop to the owner of ten hotels – good ones, too. Anyhow, there was just me and him rattling about in this big ol' house. One thing led to another; I'd learned what men liked in a woman by that time, and I suppose I made it easy for him. I don't regret it. Trust me, I'd paid my dues.'

'Why did he keep you on – when his children left, I mean?'

'He hoped they'd come back, he really did. But he never saw them again from the day they left until the day he died.'

'By which time you were Mrs Wenger, aye?' said Scott.

'I sure was. He was more than thirty years older than me, but he treated me well. Yeah, I saw guys my own age – had a tumble in the hay more than once. But on the whole we were happy.'

'He died?' Daley asked.

'Took a liking to the bottle when she took his kids away. He could hold his liquor, I'll give him that. It wasn't until the end that I realised just how much he was stowing away. But by then it was too late.' Her eyes filled with tears. 'He died in my arms. He was no more than the weight of a child. You see, his liver and his kidneys had gone and shrivelled right away, and he just kinda disappeared. Sometimes I think he was glad to die. He missed those kids so much.'

'And you inherited the hotel chain?' said Daley.

'I did. He taught me all he knew, and I learned real quick. I realised that while we made a good living where we were, LA was the place to be.'

'What aboot Las Vegas? Some cracking hotels oot there. Me and the wife went on holiday a few years ago. Must be a goldmine,' said Scott.

'Sure it is, but once you've paid off the mob, you'd be surprised how little there is left.'

'I thought that was a thing of the past,' said Daley.

'You think? Oh, they don't go around toting guns and burying folks in concrete any more. It's all smart suits and smarter accountants. Still an' all, if you cross them they soon show their true colours. Try as they might to hide behind big corporations, the Mafia still runs Nevada, trust me. Atlantic City too, come to that.'

'You just had an aptitude – for business, I mean?'

'Sure helps when you have some money to play with; and

Jack was a good teacher. But my family has always been good at business.'

'They hide it right well,' said Scott.

'Oh, they do. But if you dig a little deeper than that shithole shack, those three dummies and my witch of a mother – well, you'll see.'

'What do you mean?' Daley asked.

'Nothing I can be sure of, Mr Daley. But I'd bet everything I have on the fact there's money hidden away. And before you suggest I'm here trying to bag some of it, you know I own Wenger Leisure Inc. One thing I don't need is money.'

'Where did your family's money come from, and mair importantly where is it noo?' asked Scott, looking bemused.

'You'll have to ask my mother that – or on second thoughts, probably easier to ask folks around here. I'm sure you'll hear some grand tales about the Doigs, that's for certain sure.'

Daley looked at Scott. 'Okay, Ms Wenger, we'll let you rest. And again, I'm sorry about your father.'

As the two detectives prepared to leave the room Alice Wenger looked troubled. 'One more thing, officers.'

'What?'

'My father. All my life he used to go into the back room and tap away on this old typewriter. I don't know what he was writing, but, like walking up Thomson Hill, he did it every day. If you can set your hands on that, well, who knows what you'll find.'

'Thank you. Oh, and I'll need your passport, Alice. Until we find out what happened to your father . . . I'm sorry, just procedure.'

'It's back at the hotel. If one of your constables wants to drive out tonight, I'll hand it over. But I tell you this, Mr Daley.

I'm fixing to get the best lawyers Scotland has, so don't be too confident you'll have it for long.'

As the policemen made their way back to the car, Scott shook his head. 'What do you make o' that, Jimmy?'

'She knows more than she's letting on, that's what I make of it.'

'Huh. Great minds think alike.'

'And, Brian, fools seldom differ.'

20

Mike Strong had loved the wireless since he was a boy. Not only did he like listening, he collected radio sets, to the extent that he now had around two hundred of varying make, model and vintage. Every couple of days he'd head down to the basement of his large home and select a different radio to sit on his desk.

Today, it was a 1970s Hacker Sovereign, clad in black leather, one of his favourites. It sounded as fresh as the day he'd bought it, and he noted with pleasure the satisfying clunk as he switched it on.

Looking at his TAG Heuer watch he noticed that it was almost time for the afternoon news magazine programme on BBC Radio Scotland. Carefully, he pulled up the aerial and tuned into the station just as the news bulletin was about to begin.

He shuffled papers on his desk, listening absently to the usual round of politics, violence on the streets of Scotland's towns and cities, dire warnings regarding the environment, and so on. However, one item interested him so much that he dropped the papers on his desk, where they fanned out unevenly.

Police in Kinloch are investigating the death of a seventy-nine-year-old man. Nathaniel Doig was last seen on Thomson's

Hill near the town, from where he fell to his death earlier today.
If anyone was near the hill at around midday, please contact
DI Brian Scott at Kinloch police office, or . . .

Before the piece ended, Strong rushed to switch off the radio. He walked over to a low cupboard at the far end of his study and opened it to reveal a sturdy safe. Clicking in the code, he sprang the heavy door open and delved in, his back aching as he leaned down at an awkward angle. He knew by the feel of the envelope – rough and dry – that he'd set his hand upon the item he was looking for. He removed it from the safe and closed the door, then the faux wooden fascia.

Back at his desk, he removed some papers from the envelope. They were yellow and faded, having spent a long time in the possession of his late partner Charles Hardacre. He could only imagine the trepidation with which that man would have approached the task they set, but for Mike Strong this was an opportunity, not a dangerous chore.

Nevertheless, as he read the information contained within, reacquainting himself with the peculiar details of the business, an involuntary shiver went down his spine. But thoughts of financial advancement soon replaced any doubts.

His young colleague didn't know the whole story. Charles Hardacre was too canny to let a young buck handle something like this, despite his life-long dislike for his more senior partner. Mike Strong realised what he had to do.

Caldwell, New Jersey

Vito Chiase sat back in his large recliner, sighing as the big chair took his weight. He felt every bit of his sixty-eight years today. His knees throbbed, his back ached and his hands were painful, some fingers held tight by the unseen bonds of arthritis.

He picked up the mug from the table beside him and drank the brew he'd just percolated. It was a rich Italian coffee, the kind he'd been drinking all his life – well, ever since he could remember. But that wasn't always so easy these days; not just the act, the will of remembrance itself was painful. There were too many things he wanted to forget, too many regrets; too many faces from the past that would never return. Some he missed, most he was glad he would never see again.

Now, he had few things to fill his day. He could go hang out with the guys down at the pool haul, or the bar in Newark. But these places were nothing like they had been when he was young. The guys who made up the family of which he was still a member were either high on drugs or coming down. There was none of the camaraderie, none of the laughs, the breaking balls they'd had when he was a kid coming up. But that was a long time ago. In any case, what with wiretaps, listening devices and the many tools now at the disposal of the Feds, everyone had to talk in code if they talked at all.

He yearned for the days when fat Vinnie had been the boss and he a captain. They had lived the high life, never worrying about what the next day would bring – or trying not to. Wives and families at home in the suburbs, goombahs stashed away in apartments in New York, or somewhere off Bloomfield Avenue – far enough away to be sure that the two parts of their lives could never coincide.

But the inevitable had happened. He'd been busted for fraud and an assortment of other crimes, bundled together as a RICO Predicate. Ten years in Sing Sing had been tough, but he was a stand-up guy. Though the FBI had tried to flip him, he was old school; he'd rather have died by his own hand than become a rat.

Trouble was, he was one of the last of the old-school guys. Hell, there wasn't even a boss any more, the family being run by a committee of capos, a committee on which, despite having once been one of the best earners in the organisation, he wasn't invited to sit. In his day, the old men were at the top of the tree. Now they were in the garbage.

They let him have a little money on the streets, but it was at subsistence level, and he had to kick more up to the new 'bosses' every week. If he hadn't owned the house in which he was now withering away, he'd be in some rundown retirement community, stinking of piss and reeking of death. That was another thing he didn't want to think about.

Trying to banish these thoughts, his eyes flicked to the photograph of his dead wife above the big stone fireplace. She'd been in her early thirties when it was taken; in her prime. Gina had been a beauty, of that there was no doubt. Sure, he'd cheated on her, but that was his way of life. In his heart, he loved only her.

The photograph was almost forty years old – where had all that time gone? He'd had one last year with Gina when he'd made parole. Their last few precious months together were spent as she withered away with the cancer. But still he missed her.

As for his kids – huh, who needs family? He'd brought them into the world, made sure they had a better life than his, a college education, a nice home – all they'd ever wanted. Now, his son was a lawyer in New York City so anxious to forget his criminal father that he'd changed his name. His daughter was married to an accountant in Chicago, and though she kept in touch, he rarely saw her or his grandchildren.

This is where being a stand-up guy had got him. Sitting in a big house, badly in need of repair, with too many ghosts. No more dinners with Gina looking like a movie star; no more cookouts in the back yard by the pool that held nothing now but stagnant rainwater. No more breaking balls with the guys, no more fun, no more life.

Vito Chiase was just killing time until he died.

Then his phone rang.

21

As she'd promised Daley and Scott, Alice Wenger was now being dropped off at the Machrie House Hotel, having signed herself out of the Kinloch hospital. As she was paying the driver, a police car arrived behind her taxi. She walked up to her room with a young woman in uniform in tow and as requested handed over her passport.

She'd seen every eye on her as she'd made her way through the hotel. She knew the whole place would be aware that her father had died earlier that day, and, in the words of the locals, 'something wisna right aboot it'.

When the police officer had left with her passport, she kicked off her shoes and lay back on the bed, staring at the ceiling. When she closed her eyes she could see her father falling backwards, arms outstretched. She'd heard stories about such events appearing as though they were happening in slow motion, and now she knew what that meant. It was as though his fall had been unnaturally slow; surreal, almost. She wondered whether if she'd rushed to his side it would have been possible to grab hold of him, to save his life. But she soon reasoned that this would have been an impossible task – wishful thinking. What she was now remembering had in fact played out in real time, obeying every law of physics. It just didn't seem that way.

Alice Wenger's next instinct was to cry, but why? She hadn't seen or spoken to this man, her father, for more than three decades. It was clear her family had made little or no attempt to find her. She'd made sure the task was easy, leaving a trail any decent private investigator could have followed. She'd wanted them to seek her out, just so she could laugh in their faces when they pleaded with her to come back.

But she knew in her heart of hearts that would never have happened.

Instead of crying, Alice picked up her phone and dialled the office in LA.

'Janneck, I want you to drop everything you're doing. Get me the best damn lawyer you can find in Scotland, and be quick about it. Tell them money's no object.' She listened for a minute. 'I know that, and I know what time it is here, just get it done as soon as you can. I don't care if you have to stay up all night to do it!'

It was only then that the old fear gripped her heart. She felt the sharp point as it cut into her flesh. The pain, the horror of it all was real, as though it was happening to her now.

Then she saw the face of her mother. She was younger, stronger. The pain ended as quickly as it had begun when her father appeared. But that had been a long time ago. Instinctively, she ran her middle finger across the lump above her eye, and renewed hatred filled her soul.

It had been Jim Daley's first day back at work, and it had been an eventful one. Though weary, he was pleased not to have suffered any panic attacks, or even felt ill. In fact, he felt the best he had in months. He was tired, though, as he trudged up the front steps to his home on the hill. The house was in darkness, though Liz's car was parked under the decking.

He took the key from his pocket, but as he leaned on the handle ready to unlock the door it opened. For a few seconds, his heart lurched in his chest. He rushed into the bedroom. Their bed was empty, neatly made. Sometimes his wife would sleep with their son if he'd had a bad dream, or was restless. But the child's room too was empty.

Daley could hear his pulse in his ears as he flung the door to the lounge open. Only the bright moon lit the room, but he could see a shape on the long couch. He flicked on the ceiling lamps, flooding the room with a bright light that made him blink.

Something stirred under the blanket and his son's head popped out. The boy rubbed his eyes, squinting in the glare.

'Daddy!' he exclaimed sleepily.

Daley hauled his son from under the blanket and into his arms. Liz was lying on the couch, her mouth open, a trickle of saliva at one side. For a split second the policeman worried that she'd taken another overdose, but when he leaned into her the smell of whisky on her breath was plain.

'Liz!' He shook her by the shoulder and she mumbled something incoherent.

'I'm hungry, Daddy,' said the little boy.

'Okay, James, Daddy will get you something to eat. What do you want, eh?' Before he took his son into the kitchen, Daley noticed an empty bottle of malt whisky on the dining table beside a single glass. He wanted to shake Liz awake to tell her how irresponsible she was being in the care of their son. But he knew he'd get no sense from her now. He knew she'd been drinking, but this being his first day back at work, quickly realised that she'd likely been hiding the full extent of it from him.

With James in the crook of one arm, he tucked the blanket back under her chin. She mashed her mouth, and for a few seconds opened her eyes.

'Jim,' she slurred.

'You sleep it off, Liz. I'll go and feed our son. We need to talk – tomorrow!'

Though she mumbled something else, Daley walked away. He knew how tempting alcohol could be as a salve against the constant onslaught of problems, worries, even fear – he'd used it as such far too often himself. But Liz had never been much of drinker. He knew she needed help following her ordeal at the hands of the man who had brutalised her. She refused to seek any, and the man had walked free – well, apart from the hiding Daley had meted out to him. But she was still suffering; would do so for ever. He felt useless.

As Jim Daley busied himself making his son a meal, he knew he'd have to persuade his wife to speak to somebody – anybody – who could help her.

New Jersey

'Why the fuck can't I just speak to somebody on the telephone?' he swore to himself as he leaned towards the flickering screen of the laptop. It appeared to Vito Chiase that the world had become a more difficult place since the arrival of technology, rather than enjoying the promised ease of communication. He cursed again as he took the wrong option on the menu and had to start again in order to try to book his flight.

Then something occurred to him. He had an old friend who'd been in the travel business. Well, perhaps friend wasn't the best appellation, but he'd picked up his vig every week for decades, and they'd managed to maintain a more or less workable relationship – one of the less troublesome businesses in his corner of Newark.

He reached across the desk for an old roller deck, filled with frayed and yellowing business cards. He had to peer through his glasses to see the cell number, but soon he was dialling it.

'Henry – Henry Rogan, is that you?'

'Sure. Who's this?' said the voice on the other end.

'It's Vito, Vito Chiase. How you doing, my friend?'

There was silence for a few moments, then the reply, the voice much quieter, less effusive. 'Vito, this is a surprise.'

'For me, too. I thought you might be dead by now.'

'What?' There was sudden panic in his voice.

'Hey, at our age, who the fuck knows the minute, eh?'

'Oh, yeah, I get it, Vito. What – what can I help you with?'

'Listen, do you still have that travel business?'

'Just two shops – my son runs them now.' The words were laden with regret.

'Two shops! You used to be all over North Jersey.'

'Yeah, and a couple across the river, too. You know how it is, Vito. We're living in a different world. This internet, it killed me. I thought it wouldn't last, you know, guys having to book their own holidays – all that shit you have to go through. Guess I was wrong.'

'I hear yah,' replied Vito, staring at the computer screen with disdain. 'So you'd welcome a little business, yeah?'

'Hold on, I can't put my son at risk. He's got a young family

– it's not like the old days. He's finding it hard enough to make it.'

'Who said anything about illegal? This is straight up. I need to book a flight and get to a place, that's all. Isn't that what you still do?'

'Sure it is, Vito. But, the way things are, I can't get you the old discount, if you get what I'm saying?'

'Who said nothing about discount? Listen, I'm sitting here in front of a computer, and I ain't got a clue what to do. I'll pay you up front, no strings. You have my word, Henry.'

'Well, okay. Tell me where you wanna go and when. I'll get the details back to you tomorrow.'

'Needs to be faster. I want to leave tomorrow.'

'Okay.' He paused. 'Where you going, LA, Miami, Vegas?'

'No, Glasgow.'

'You mean Glasgow in England?'

'Sure, but ain't it in Scotland? That's what it says on my computer. Where did you think I was going, Glasgow Illinois?'

'I didn't know they had a Glasgow there.'

Vito pulled the phone from his ear and glared at the handset. 'If you don't mind me saying, you don't seem to have your old edge. A little squirrely, maybe. When you was arranging trips to the desert for me and the crew, you was all over this shit, remember?'

'Oh, I remember.' Again, regret.

'So, can you do this thing?'

'Okay, Vito. But you gotta give me a couple of hours. And I'll need the money up front, I'm sorry.'

'Have I ever let you down over money, Henry?'

'Well . . .'

'Hey, listen, you do this thing for me. You send your boy round; he picks up what I owe plus twenty per cent for the favour. Hows about that?'

'What class?'

'What?'

'What class you wanna travel? You know, business, first, economy?'

'Hey, you breaking my balls? Economy, you kidding?' Vito thought for a moment. 'What's the next up?'

'I dunno, economy plus nowadays, I suppose.'

Vito gritted his teeth. Gone were the days when he could travel on private jets and helicopters. He used to take a chopper to Atlantic City at the drop of a hat. Now he was reduced to this. But, he reasoned, it would be worth it. 'Okay, I'll take this economy plus. But don't let me down, Henry, okay? I'll be hearing from you – soon!' Before there could be any argument he put the phone down. It was this guy's job, his line of work. If you want a flight to Chicago, you go see Henry Rogan. You want somebody clipped? Well, that was another matter. You go see Vito Chiase.

22

Daley was unhappy with himself as he drove through Kinloch to work. He'd done exactly what he'd promised himself he wouldn't do and that was have an argument with his wife. Though the sun was shining, it glared off the roofs and spires of the town, all frosted with a garland of ice that showed no sign of melting.

Liz was still fast asleep when he got up. Once he'd given his son his breakfast and got him ready for the day, he woke her.

Liz was sullen. She didn't need help. Yes, she'd had a few drinks, but when had that become a crime? How long had he spent in the County Hotel in the last few years? Yes, she'd replace the whisky, don't worry.

The words ran through his head again as he drove through the big blue gates and into the car park at the rear of Kinloch police office. He noted that Brian Scott was already at work and his spirits rose. If anyone could brighten his mood, it would be Brian.

'Good morning,' he said in passing to a young cop as he made for his glass box. The blinds were down, and when he pushed at the door it was locked. He knocked at it sharply with his big fist. 'What are you doing in there, Brian?'

In seconds the door swung open, but it wasn't just Brian Scott who was behind it.

'Jim, good morning. Bright and early, I see.' Symington smiled at him broadly.

'Ma'am, I beg your pardon. I can go and get a coffee if you and DI Scott are busy.'

'No, we've had our little chat. I'm just down on a flying visit. I've things to do in mid-Argyll, so I thought I'd make sure that everything was as it should be ahead of your return – well, the official one, that is.' Symington looked at the bags under Daley's eyes. 'Everything okay, I hope?'

'Yes, absolutely. The wee man was a bit restless last night.'

'Oh, I see. Well, I won't hold you up, DCI Daley. I know you'll want to get your teeth into this Doig business. All sounds very strange, from what DI Scott has told me.'

'Yes, ma'am. I think there's much more to this than meets the eye.'

'And your reasons for this?'

'Give me a day or so to gather my thoughts. As Brian probably told you, we have Alice Wenger's passport. For the time being, at least.'

'There could be a problem with that. I'll leave DI Scott to fill you in. Welcome back, Jim.' She held out her hand and shook his. 'Remember, any problems at all, just call – at any time.'

'Thanks, ma'am, I'm sure I'll be fine.'

She marched off, leaving a miserable-looking Scott in her wake.

'What's up with you, Mr Happy?'

'Ach, I've been in the polis near before she was born. I'm fed up her wanting tae hold my hand every two seconds.'

'Well, you've got me to hold it for you now.'

'Aye, thanks a million.' He leaned forward, propping his head in his hands on the desk.

'So, do you want me to sit here now?' Daley pointed to the empty chair.

'No, here big man. Sorry: force of habit, if you know what I mean.' He stood and let Daley sit behind his desk. 'Aye, it's good tae see you back at the coal face.'

Daley was momentarily disorientated. Everything seemed wrong. The computer screen was too close, as was the keyboard. He moved a jar containing pens, pencils and other office implements further away, and pushed the phone unit nearer the edge, but still something wasn't right. He reached down and lowered his chair. 'Okay, that's better,' he said, smiling at Scott, who had taken the seat across the desk.

'We're no' all giants, you know. Took me ages tae get that right. I was moving that chair up and doon for aboot three weeks until I nailed it.'

'What was Symington on about – something to do with Alice Wenger's passport?'

'Oh aye.' Scott brightened slightly. 'She's got Grant Dunwoody representing her.'

'*The* Grant Dunwoody?'

'The very man. He's on his way here, if you please. He's no' happy we took her passport off her at all.'

Daley thought for a moment. There was little doubt that Grant Dunwoody was one of Scotland's most high-profile and effective lawyers. But he came at a price, a price Alice Wenger was obviously prepared and more than able to pay. 'Right. So what about SOCO? Did they get anything from the Doig case yesterday?'

'Aye. Her footprints are at the edge of the cliff, but right at the edge. That would fit with her story that she looked o'er tae see what had happened tae her faither – obvious reaction according tae SOCO. She was examined at the hospital. No signs o' a struggle, bruising, or the like. Harder tae tell wae his remains, I dare say. We'll get the results o' the PM later today.'

'Any witnesses yet?'

'There was one phone call last night, but the guy was foreign. He's coming in at two tae tell us what he saw, but we'll have tae find someone who speaks Greek because his English is shite.'

'What language does he really speak?'

'Greek!'

'Oh, I thought you just meant *it's all Greek to me* sort of thing.'

'Nobody seems tae get what I'm saying today!'

'Symington on your back, Bri?'

'Something and nothing, Jimmy. She picks through everything, you know, every dot and comma. I don't know how you manage tae dae this shit. I'd have had three heart attacks by now.'

'I agree, it can be tough.' Daley studied his friend's face. 'But what aren't you telling me, Brian?'

'Nothing – just the usual shit you get fae gaffers. You must know what it's like; you had John Donald looming o'er you for long enough.'

'Very true. Symington's a pussy cat compared with him.'

'But she's got rare fangs,' murmured Scott.

Daley decided it was time to change the subject. 'Well, if this witness is Greek we'd better get a translator sorted. Can you give HQ a shout? We can do it online.'

'I've done that.'

'Good man, Brian. Sorry, I'm forgetting you've had to deal with all this. I need you to keep going, if you can. It'll take me a wee while to find my feet, you know what I mean?'

'I do, Jimmy. Mind, I've been shot and had tae come back fae that – twice!'

Daley nodded. He knew now exactly how Scott had felt. Despite having been a police officer for so many years, he felt out of kilter. Nothing seemed normal. What had been mundane for so long now appeared strange, like the first day at a new school. He hoped the feeling would pass.

The phone on his desk rang. 'Don't tell me, it's Grant Dunwoody, Sergeant Shaw?'

'No, sir – not even close. I have a Mrs Doig at the front desk. Says one of her sons is missing.'

'Bring her through, please, sergeant.'

'What now?' said Scott.

'It's Ginny Doig.' Daley sounded as surprised as he looked.

'Bugger me. Bring oot your deid!'

It was early – very early – for Vito Chiase. As he boarded the aircraft he was ushered to his right, the cheap end. He was dismayed to have been allocated an aisle seat. At the window sat a fat man in a T-shirt that was at least four sizes too small. He seemed to have no neck at all, his head apparently erupting from his shoulders amidst rings of chins. The boy next to Chiase – the other man's kid, he reckoned – was nearly as obese as his father. He was eating a candy bar, much of which was spread across his round bloated face. Chiase looked on in disgust as the boy wiped his hand on the armrest they shared.

'Hey, kid! Clean that shit off there,' he said irritably.

Before the boy could reply, his father leaned across him. 'Did you swear at my son?'

Vito Chiase eyed the man up and down. 'I did. He's spread his filthy paws all over my armrest. And if he doesn't clean it up, I'll stuff him up your fat ass, you got it, dough ball?'

The man opened his mouth to reply, but something in the old man's gaze made him think again. 'Here,' he said to his son. 'Use this to clean that up. How many times have I told you not to spread food all over the joint?' He handed him a wet wipe.

'Better yet, starve yourself for a couple or three months and you might live to be an adult,' said Chiase, looking straight ahead but speaking loudly enough to be heard.

One thing the modern world had come up with that was worth having was the portability of music. He took the phone from his pocket, made sure it was in flight mode, then selected the music his daughter had downloaded for him on one of her rare visits. He popped in the ear buds and watched other passengers board to the swirling accompaniment of Tony Bennett. It wasn't so bad. He had enough legroom – just about – and with his fellow passengers suitably subdued, the flight promised to be a long but reasonably comfortable one. 'Excuse me, miss,' he said to a female member of the cabin crew as she passed by. 'Could you tell me where the peeshado . . . the restroom is?'

'It's just ahead, to your right, sir. Do you need to go now, or can you wait until we take off? It shouldn't be long.'

'No, I was just making sure I knew where it was. At my age, when you need the peeshadoo, you need the peeshadoo, right?'

She smiled and walked back down the aisle. Nice ass, thought Vito Chiase as he settled back, ready to endure the flight to Glasgow.

Ginny Doig was wrapped against the cold in an old coat and a knitted shawl. On her hands were red woollen mittens with holes, and she wore an old pair of green wellington boots. Though Daley was speaking, she stared malevolently at Scott, her green eyes narrowed.

'So he went missing last night, you say, Mrs Doig?' said Daley.

'Aye, that's whoot I telt you.'

'It was pretty cold out there. Why didn't you report this sooner?'

'The pickup wouldna start, and as you know, we've nae phone. We managed tae get it going this morning and I came as soon as I could.' She tore her gaze from Scott. 'No' that you'll have tae look very far tae find oot who's responsible, right enough.'

'What do you mean?'

'I would have thought that was pretty obvious, is it no'?'

'If it was obvious I wouldn't have asked the question.'

'Huh. Amazing whoot a bit o' money can do. She killed my husband yesterday and noo she's likely done the same tae her brother.'

'You're talking about your daughter, Alice Wenger?'

'Alison Doig tae me! And aye, that's who I'm talking aboot.'

'These are very serious accusations, Mrs Doig.'

'But you've got her passport, aye?'

'That's a precaution. Procedure. And anyway, how do you know that?'

'I might live in the back o' beyond, but I'm no' stupid. And I've a fine pair o' lugs, tae. This is Kinloch, mind!'

'About what time did your son go missing?'

'He never appeared for his supper.'

'Is that unusual? I mean, he is an adult. Might he have had something else to do?'

'I telt you this before, but you clearly didna listen. My boys – all my boys – are simple. They've lived wae me and my husband since they was born. They couldna survive alone. Thorbin's never missed his supper in his life.'

'Did you no' try ringing the bell for him?' said Scott acerbically.

'Aye, I did. I've been ringing it half the night – and this morning.'

'So, your sons answer to a bell?' said Daley.

'How many times? They're simple, no' quite right in the heids. They go oot tae dae their chores and when their meals are ready or it's time tae call it a day, I ring the bell tae get them back. You saw me dae it yesterday.'

'I need a description of your son, please, Mrs Doig.'

'You only jeest clocked him. Can you no' remember?'

'I need to know what he was wearing last night. His age, eye colour, height, build; just get on with it, please.'

Ginny Doig looked from one detective to the other then folded her arms. 'He's fifty-six years old. Aboot six feet tall, baldie, wae a wee coo's lick o' hair stickin' up at the top o' his heid. He was wearing a black cape o'er a blue sweater and a pair o' black dungarees – aye, and black boots. Is that enough for yous?'

'A cape? I thought they went oot wae Sherlock Holmes.' A look from Daley silenced Scott.

'It'll be enough to be going on with.' Daley put down his pen. 'Your son lost his father yesterday. Does it not occur to you that he might be distressed . . . grieving?'

'Where there's nae sense, there's nae feeling. Is that no' whoot they say?' She looked purposefully at Scott. 'Anyhow, you know fine how tae find him. Get to my daughter and ask her whoot she's done wae her brother, and why she killed her faither.'

'Can I ask your date of birth, please, Mrs Doig?'

'For whoot reason?'

'For the inquiry, please.'

'Eighteenth September, 1941. I was born in the local hospital – well, the old yin.'

'And your full name, including your maiden name, please?'

'Jennifer Elizabeth Doig. My ain name was McMaster, my maiden name, that is.' She shuffled in her seat. 'Noo can you get off your arses and away and arrest that daughter o' mine?'

Ignoring her, Daley carried on. 'Have you worked anywhere – apart from on the croft, I mean?'

'We're intae ancient history, noo? I worked as a domestic at the Royal Infirmary in Glasgow. That's where I met Nathaniel. When he came back hame, so did I.'

'And that was?'

'In the early sixties. I cannae remember the date.'

'Does your son have a favourite place to go? Near your house, or a friend's, maybe?'

'Are you deaf? My boys have nae friends. They're too stupid. Who would want tae befriend them, eh?'

Daley just nodded his head. 'So there's nowhere you can think of where he might have sought refuge from the death of his father?'

'He had me tae come tae!' She shoved her chair back and stood. 'I tell you right noo. If yous don't go and get justice for my husband and find my son, I'll go and dae it mysel'.'

'What do you mean by that?'

'You know fine whoot I mean.'

'Mrs Doig, I warn you not to approach Alice Wenger. We'll deal with this now. I'm sure your son can't have strayed far, though I'm worried he's been out all night in this cold weather.'

'See that you do. But you'll find a body, I'm sure o' it.' She turned on her heel, knocking over the chair on which she'd been sitting, and stormed out of Daley's glass box.

'She's an evil woman,' said Scott. 'If Wenger wisnae a witness to what happened tae Mr Doig yesterday, I'd swear she killed him.'

'Whatever, Brian. But it's our duty to try and find Thorbin Doig. Let's get going.'

'I'll go see if we can get the chopper fae Glasgow.'

'Right, Brian, go for it.'

Daley called Shaw and got him to round up a provisional search party. He flicked on the computer to send an email to HQ informing them of a missing person and the details to be circulated around the force. But his mouth dropped when the screen flickered into life.

The heading was simple: *Report on DCI J F Daley. DI B Scott. FAO Chief Superintendent C Symington*. Daley read the first few lines and his heart sank.

23

Mike Strong didn't like Glasgow; in fact he actively disliked it. He was even unhappier at the prospect of the task ahead. But this was the chance to make money – lots of money, and for very little effort. If he insulated himself properly, well, the risks were minimal. In his experience, the real things worth anything in life could only be attained if one was prepared to take a risk or two. He'd done since ever he could remember, never regretting a moment.

When he'd parked his dark blue Bentley on the second floor as arranged, he wound down the window. The multistorey car park was dank, dark and stank of piss, being used as an impromptu toilet by revellers who spilled from the nearby pubs and clubs most nights. He curled his nose in disgust, quickly wound the window back up, and switched on the car radio.

He never ceased to be amazed by the endless hours or print inches journalists could fill by revealing the latest scientific results of the impacts on health of drinking coffee or eating eggs. In reality, he was sure that longevity was more to do with a genetic lottery than it was a product of lifestyle, though there were extremes at both ends.

The man he was about to meet was at one of those extremes,

and not the healthy end, though Strong suspected that having reached his fifties Declan O'Neil must have come from a reasonably robust gene pool, given the way he'd abused his body with drugs, drink and depravity since he was little more than a child.

Strong drummed his fingers impatiently on the steering wheel until O'Neil appeared at the passenger window and started to open the car door.

'Wait!' shouted Strong. He produced a plastic sheet from the glovebox of the Bentley and spread it over the cream leather of the passenger seat. 'Right, you can sit down now.'

The man who entered the car had sparse fair hair, sunken eyes, and hollowed-out cheeks lined with creases and wrinkles. In his fifties he may be, but he could easily have passed for someone twenty years older.

'Mr Strong. How goes it, man?' he asked, displaying a mouth of brown, discoloured teeth, with the odd gap here and there.

'I thought this place stank, but you smell worse,' said Strong, holding a silk handkerchief to his nose. 'Are the CCTV cameras out on this floor, as you promised?

'The meter's empty, big man. I'm just away tae get a top-up. I couldnae have a bath this morning, so I couldnae. Aye, the cameras are oot. The boys dae their deals up here. They've got a thing going wae the security guys. You're like a ghost, so you are.'

'Good. When did you say you'd had a bath? Last month, judging by the smell. You can still wash in cold water, you know.'

'Fuck that! In this weather? You must be joking. It's snowing oot there, big man.'

'I know. I've just driven through it from Edinburgh.'

O'Neil sniffed back some mucus and rubbed his nose on

the back of his hand. 'See me, I love Edinburgh. Different class fae roon here. That castle an' that, pure dead beautiful, so it is.'

'Trust me, it isn't all like that.' Strong took the hanky from his nose. 'Have you done what I asked?'

'Aye. Your man will get the goods when he arrives at the place you telt me aboot.'

'And you made sure not to mention me, or anything else?'

'What dae you take me for, Mr Strong? Sure I was the best man you ever had tae defend? I might look like a heap o' shit, but I've still got it up here.' He tapped the side of his head with one gnarled, nicotine-stained finger. 'The guy that's got the guy tae get the stuff doesnae know me, never mind you. See, just like you wanted, boss.'

'Good.' Strong reached into his pocket. 'Half now, half when the job's done.'

'Hauld the bus, big man. I've done my bit o' the bargain. That's me finished – I need the dough, as you can see. I've no' had bugger all tae eat for three days. Well, apart fae they shite sandwiches and soup the Sally Army hand oot fae the van up in the Toonheid.'

Strong looked at O'Neil blankly. 'You'll do as I say, or you won't get anything. Let's not forget our little *arrangement*, Declan.'

'You're still holding that o'er my heid, eh?'

'One word from me, and you're in a nice cell for a few years. You won't have to worry about electricity bills, or food. Shit, I might be doing you a favour.' Strong grimaced.

'Right, we'll dae it your way, big man. You know me, easy-going an' that.'

Strong reached into the inside pocket of his jacket and produced a bundle of notes held together by a thick elastic band. 'You don't have to count it. As soon as the thing is done, you'll get the rest. You have my word. A small bonus, if you keep your head down and don't get into any trouble in the meantime.'

'You're a gentleman, so you are,' said O'Neil, just before he was taken by a paroxysm of coughing, his throat rattling like a machine gun.

'Right. For the time being, that concludes our business, Mr O'Neil. I have to get back to Edinburgh. Good day to you.' Strong nodded to the passenger door.

'Aye, and tae you, big man. Just give me a bell when – well, you know.' O'Neil smiled broadly and began to cough again.

Strong waited until the wreck of a human being had left the car. Between thumb and forefinger he removed the plastic sheet from the passenger seat, wound down his window and dropped it into the space between his car and the next. In a few seconds he was reversing out of the parking space, glad his latest dealing with Declan O'Neil was at an end. Though the man stank to high heaven and looked like a benighted skeleton swaddled in rags, he was one of the best fixers that Strong knew. Had he not fallen victim to drug addiction, he would now likely be worth a small fortune. But such was life.

O'Neil looked on as the Bentley swished off, passing him without so much as a nod of the driver's head. 'Aye, fuck you too, you arsehole,' he muttered under his breath as he watched the vehicle disappear down the ramp. However, he had money in his pocket now. He pulled an old mobile phone from his pocket. He pressed a button and waited for a few seconds. 'Hey, big Donnie, man, how's it hanging? I need some shit. Where are you, big fella?' He listened for the reply, muttered a few words and shuffled off in search of the next chemical release from his miserable existence.

A line of police officers and some hastily gathered volunteers were making their way up the hill behind Rowan Tree Cottage. Likewise, a string of others walked along the beach and searched the machair banks for any sign of the missing Thorbin Doig. The fields were still stiff with ice, and the boulders on the beach were frosted like cakes. In the cold clear air, the Ayrshire coast looked almost close enough to touch, making a backdrop for the dark shadow of Ailsa Craig, silhouetted by the bright sun. All of the searchers were wrapped up warmly against the elements in gloves, hats and thick coats. If Doig was to be found, he must be found soon or risk freezing to death when night fell and temperatures dropped even further. It would seem he'd already had to suffer one night out in the open.

Scott and DS Potts had been assigned to search the cottage itself. Knowing this would be an unwelcome intrusion, Daley had made sure they were equipped with a warrant from the local JP before they broached the subject of entering the domicile with Ginny Doig.

Scott stubbed out a cigarette in the ashtray and turned to his younger colleague. 'Right, son, no time like the present. Let's go and see the wicked witch o' the west in there and get this o'er with as quickly as possible.'

They stepped out of the car and made their way to the by now familiar rickety front door. Scott knocked hard with his gloved fist and the pair waited for a reply.

Sure enough, Ginny Doig appeared, staring up at them with her piercing green gaze. 'Have yous found him?'

'No, no' yet, Mrs Doig. As you can see we've an extensive search on the go. The police helicopter will soon be here tae help, so we're pulling out all the stops,' said Scott, his frozen breath billowing before his face.

'Aye, well I'll leave you to it, then.'

'As part of procedure we need tae search your home.'

'O'er my dead body. Dae you no' think if he was in here I wouldna have noticed him?'

'That's no' the point, Mrs Doig. You might have missed something; a note, some clue or other.'

'A note? You surely don't think my boys can read or write?'

'Well, that's as maybe. We need to come in and have a look, just the same.'

Ginny Doig stood stubbornly in her doorway, arms folded across her tatty apron. 'You can bugger off. You're no' wasting your time in my hoose when you should be away searching for my son and bringing that cow o' a daughter o' mine tae book for killing my husband.'

Scott sighed and produced a document from his overcoat. 'Mrs Doig, this is a warrant to enter and search your domicile. Noo, I'd much rather you cooperated, but if you don't we're coming in anyway, and if you try to hinder us you'll be detained under the terms listed here.' Scott handed the warrant to her.

'This is a travesty o' justice! There's my daughter sitting in the lap o' luxury oot at Machrie while instead of you arresting her you're persecuting me.'

'Can we come in, then, or do we go the other route?'

'You can wait until I'm good and ready!' Without warning she tried to slam the door shut.

Scott was too quick for her and stuck his foot in the crack,

174

stopping it closing. 'Your attitude is beginning tae worry me, Mrs Doig.' He pushed past her and into the cottage, Potts following in his wake.

Standing at the table, the remaining Doig sons looked on confused as their mother tried to pull Potts back out of the door.

'Come on, you useless articles, help me!' she shouted.

As though whipped into action by her words, both men lumbered out from behind the table. They were big, tall and strong, but with empty eyes.

Scott held out his hand. 'I'm a police officer. Don't come any nearer.'

'Ignore him. Get them oot o' the hoose!' shouted Mrs Doig, as she continued to wrestle with a flummoxed-looking DS Potts.

The larger of the two men made for Scott, while the other lumbered off to help his mother.

'I'm warning you. If you lay one finger on me, you'll be arrested!' shouted Scott.

As though he hadn't heard the words, the youngest Doig son grabbed Scott's throat with a vice-like grip. The policeman made a fist and punched him hard on the arm, but to no avail. Scott felt his feet being pulled up off the floor, and soon he was being propelled the way he'd come, towards the door. As he struggled to breathe, he heard Potts yelp in pain.

In seconds, Scott felt the pressure on his throat disappear as he was thrown bodily through the air and out into the yard. Potts lay bleeding near to where he'd landed. The door to Rowan Tree Cottage was slammed shut, locked and bolted.

'Are you okay, son?' said Scott, his own head spinning as he tried to pick himself up from the filthy concrete.

'No. I think he broke my arm,' replied DS Potts, grimacing in pain as he tried to get up.

'Stay there, don't move. I'll need tae get some help here.' Scott reached into his pocket and pulled out the airwave radio. 'DI Scott tae all stations. Urgent assistance required at Rowan Tree Cottage. And get an ambulance. Over!'

In Kinloch police office, Daley heard Scott's appeal over the radio. He flung his jacket over his shoulders and hurried out to his car. He'd thought that Mrs Doig would be difficult but he'd hoped that the warrant would be enough to persuade her to let Scott search the cottage. Then he remembered her sons. They looked placid enough, but they also looked big. As he started the car, Daley cursed himself for not being more careful.

'DCI Daley to all stations involved in the search. Make your way immediately to Rowan Tree Cottage!' he yelled into his radio as his car swung out of the blue gates and down Main Street.

24

Liz was getting James junior ready for nursery. He hadn't been the day before because of the abortive visit to the dentist, so she really had to take him. Her throbbing head, parched mouth and queasy stomach, though, made the task feel almost impossible. But nonetheless she dressed her son, who because he enjoyed nursery was luckily in a cooperative mood.

'Where's your other boot, James?' she asked after an exasperating search for her child's wellingtons.

'I don't know, Mummy. Maybe Daddy put it somewhere.'

Daddy. Liz only vaguely remembered him arriving back after work the night before, but she needed no reminder of what had passed between them earlier that morning. It was clear that his return to duty had brought her burgeoning problem with alcohol into sharp focus. While he'd been convalescing at home, she'd been able to please herself. Get up when she wanted, do as she pleased, safe in the knowledge that her husband was on hand to look after their son. Now she'd have to clean up her act.

Part of her wanted to go back home, let her mother take the strain while she tried to come to terms with what had happened. But that would come at a price, and that price would be to let her mother in, to tell her what had really taken place within her relationship with 'that rich dentist', as her mother called him.

Of course, her parents had seen this man as the kind of partner for life she should have chosen from the off. To them Jim Daley was of a lower class, and no matter what he achieved as a police officer it would never be good enough. He would always be a plodding millstone round their daughter's neck, stopping the rise in social status they so craved on her behalf. They'd wanted her to leave him for years, and were delighted when she had. But then, they were blissfully unaware of her many infidelities – well, she thought they were. If they did know, they were tactful enough not to mention it. More likely too ashamed, she thought.

Liz Daley needed someone to talk to: but who? Not her husband – she couldn't be as frank as she needed to be with him, and in any case he was consumed by his health problems and the return to work. She had no real friends in Kinloch besides Annie, but didn't know her well enough to share what she needed to.

There was really only one person to whom she could turn. But Liz was aware that even though she'd known the woman for so many years, it was by no means certain what reception would greet a cry for help.

She picked up the phone, after sending her son in search of his missing welly.

'Hello, is that you?' Liz listened for the reply. 'Are you doing anything this morning? I'd like to come over for a chat, if that's okay?'

The woman was as she'd always been: kind, but with a reserve Liz knew stemmed from her intimate knowledge of the state of the Daley marriage over the years. But sometimes it was better to be told what had to be heard rather than a sugar-coated version of the truth. She was undoubtedly the right person for the job.

When she had dropped James off at nursery, Liz Daley would pay a visit to Ella Scott.

Scott sat on the edge of the hospital bed as a nurse attended to a deep graze on his arm, the result of being pitched out of the Doigs' rundown cottage.

'Oh, ya . . .' He managed to contain the oath as Staff Nurse McGeachy applied some iodine to the injury.

'Try to be a brave soldier, shall we? If I remember rightly, you don't have a high pain threshold.'

'Eh? What dae you mean? I can take pain better than maist folk. I've had plenty o' it – been shot twice, you know.'

'Yes, but you didn't do too well with a peanut in your eye the last time I saw you, Sergeant Scott.'

Scott paid no attention to the mistaken rank. 'Oh, here, that was a sore yin! You see it's no' just the dunt o' the peanut you've tae consider, but these bloody things are coated wae salt. See the stinging, it went on for aboot two days, man.'

The staff nurse raised her brows. 'Well, I'm just pleased to hear you came out with your sight intact.'

Scott thought for a moment. 'You mean it could have blinded me?'

'Very easily, I would have thought. We've had some really nasty incidents with peanuts here. People scarred for life. The damned things should be banned if you ask me – like motorbikes and heroin.' A smile played across her lips.

'Here, you're jeest taking the pish, aren't you?' Scott grimaced again as she dabbed more iodine on his wound.

'I sure am.'

'Huh, what happened tae the spirit of thon Florence Nightingale, eh? I bet she wisnae cloaking aboot making a fool o' her patients.'

'No, indeed she wasn't.'

'See.' Scott nodded with pleasure at his little victory.

'She killed more people than she saved. Well intentioned, of course, but they just didn't have the knowledge back then.'

'Just as well there wisnae any dry roasted peanuts on the go, eh? We'd never have beaten they Zulus.'

'She worked in the Crimea.'

'Aye, whatever. I'm sure Michael Caine was in both films.' Scott chuckled to himself.

'Just as well you chose the police as a profession, sergeant.'

'Why?'

'Because your patter's shite.'

Scott was about to protest when Daley appeared in the ward.

'Right, Brian, I see you've survived.'

'No thanks tae Florence here. Ouch! You did that on purpose,' he squealed as the staff nurse applied a particularly large dollop of iodine.

'We have to make sure that infection doesn't set in.'

'Aye, right.'

'How long before DI Scott is ready to leave, staff nurse?' asked Daley.

'I'll just dress this and bandage him up, then he'll be good to go.' She looked at Scott. 'You never told me you were an inspector now. Well done you!'

'Aye well, it was touch and go. It was awarded for bravery in the face o' peanuts.'

*

Sergeant Shaw struggled with Ginny Doig as he took her from the van into Kinloch police office. She was to be charged with assaulting a police officer and obstructing the police in the course of their duty, as well as refusing to abide by the terms of the warrant to search her home. Under the circumstances, she'd probably never be brought to court, but it would give Daley enough time to search Rowan Tree Cottage unhindered. It had taken six officers to subdue her two younger sons, delaying the search for her eldest. And Mrs Doig wasn't happy about it.

'Yous think I'm jeest pure shite, don't you? I can see it plastered across your ugly coupon,' she said as Shaw and PC Janice James managed to get her into a holding cell.

'You'll have access to a lawyer soon, Mrs Doig,' said Shaw, out of breath after his exertions with the old woman.

'Yous are a' in the pocket o' that daughter o' mine!' she roared as the cell door was firmly shut. 'My husband deid, my son likely lying murdered tae, an' this is how you treat me and whoot's left o' my family. Yous are nothing but corrupt bastards!'

'Everything going okay?' asked Daley, newly returned from the hospital with Scott, as Shaw emerged from the custody cells.

'Just peachy, sir.'

'We should get an electric chair and fry that auld bitch while we've got the chance,' said Scott, nursing his bandaged forearm as the roaring protests of Ginny Doig echoed around Kinloch police office.

'Another PR success for Police Scotland!' said Daley. 'I can see the papers now: "Demented police inspector electrocutes elderly woman after she beat him up". Just the thing.'

'She never beat me up. That was her boy.'

'Come on, get a cup of sweet tea down you and we'll go and give this cottage a thorough search.'

'Are you sure I should be going there?' Scott was holding up his arm. 'I mean, the chances of infection, an' that. I could end up wae thon bucolic plague.'

'Bubonic, Brian.'

'Aye, that tae!'

'Have you charged them, Sergeant Shaw?'

'I have, sir.'

'Right, hold them until I give you a shout, then we'll let them off with a caution.'

'You are kidding, big man,' said Scott, looking exasperated. 'They broke Potts's arm!'

'Think about it, Brian: recently widowed elderly wife, mother of a missing son. Get into the new century. It's all about optics these days.'

'Huh, the only optics I've ever been bothered aboot had whisky in them.'

'Well, times have changed.'

'Says you!'

'If you have any problems with my decisions, I'm sure you can write them in your report, DI Scott.' Daley smiled mirthlessly.

'Noo, just you wait, Jimmy. You don't know the circumstances . . .'

Daley didn't let him finish his sentence. 'Don't worry, Brian. I get it. Just get some tea and we'll head back down.'

Daley strode off to his glass box, leaving a sheepish-looking Brian Scott in his wake.

*

The pair travelled in near silence the few miles to the Doigs' cottage. As they laboured up the last hill on their journey, Scott spoke. 'Listen, Jimmy, I had no choice but tae open that report on you. Trust me, I wouldnae have written anything detrimental. You must know me well enough by now, surely?'

Daley was focusing on the road. It was getting dark now; the bright blue of day was giving way to a dark velvet, star-twinkling sky. It would be as cold as it had been the previous night, and single-track roads like this were not a council priority when it came to gritting.

'Come on, Jimmy. Gie us a break, eh?'

'Forget about it, Brian. I have.'

'You still don't get it. If I hadnae agreed tae write this damned report they wouldn't have let you back tae work. That was the ultimatum.'

Daley thought for a few moments. 'Nothing to do with keeping your pips, then?'

It was Scott's turn to think. 'I'll no' lie tae you. Yes, that was mentioned. But I don't gie a damn aboot rank. I know I'm lucky I'm still in the job, never mind an inspector. If you think that's how I'm rolling wae this then you and me aren't as close as I thought we were, Jimmy.'

'I'm sorry, Brian. I knew they'd have eyes on me. I was just surprised that it was you who was looking. I suppose you are the obvious choice, though.'

'And just as well, don't you think? You know fine I'll no' write anything that will take you doon. Fuck, I'll let you see the bloody reports before I send them. Better still, you can write the bloody things yourself!'

'Ha! I don't think I'd manage to replicate your prose style, Bri.'

'That's a dig at me, isn't it?'

'Yes.'

Scott chuckled to himself.

When they reached the bay where Rowan Tree Cottage was situated they could see the flicker of torches on the hillside. It was obvious that Thorbin Doig hadn't been found.

'Another night out in temperatures like this, well . . .' Daley left the rest unsaid.

Constable Murray met them at the cottage, where he stood guard at the front door. Whether it was the night air, or just the low temperature, the stench of rotting seaweed wasn't so pronounced.

'Anything to report, Murray?' said Daley.

'No sir, nothing at all. Not even a trace of the missing man. Aye, and it's a cold one.' Murray looked up into the growing darkness.

'You get yourself into the support van and get warmed up. DI Scott and I are going to search the premises while the rest of the family are kicking their heels back at the office.'

'Yes, sir, thank you,' replied Murray, stomping off into the darkness, his breath rising like smoke from a campfire in the cold air.

'Here.' Scott handed Daley a pair of rubber gloves. 'Just in case, like.'

'Wow! Being a DI has certainly improved your adherence to protocols, Brian.'

'No' really. Sergeant Shaw gave them to me before we left the ranch.'

Daley pushed open the door to the cottage, and was immediately hit by the musty smell inside. A shaft of moonlight shone through a gap in the filthy net curtains, sending a stripe of white light across the room, the only illumination on offer. Daley thought fleetingly of his wife flickering through a similar one during his recent panic attack. He was still angry with her, but couldn't, he knew, take the moral high ground. His own affection for whisky had been a problem.

Scott delved into his pockets and lit one of the big storm lanterns that hung above the mantelpiece. 'There, we've got some light on the subject,' he said.

'There's a few things I'm interested in, Brian,' said Daley. 'Obviously any pointers to where our missing man might be, but also papers belonging to Mr Doig. Remember Alice Wenger told us that he spent most of his days typing? Well, it stands to reason he must have been writing something. I'd be interested to find out what that is. It might cast some light on what this place is all about.'

'No' fit for human habitation, if you ask me.' Scott curled his nose up at the smell and the general air of decay that enveloped the dwelling.

'Well, we'd better get on with it, then' said Daley.

25

Liz Daley was in her kitchen making Ella Scott a cup of tea. She'd decided to have one herself, though the temptation to have a glass of wine or something stronger was compelling. She'd been surprised how supportive Ella had been, so much so that she refused to let Liz go home by herself. With James junior in bed, the pair could have another chat.

Liz brought the tea through on a tray, along with biscuits and some chocolates she'd found in the cupboard.

'I'd offer you something stronger, Ella, but it wouldn't really be appropriate under the circumstances, I think.'

'Listen tae me. You've no' got a drink problem, Lizzie. It's what happened to you that's causing all this. Bugger me, who wouldnae hit the bottle if they'd been through what you have?'

'Jim doesn't seem to think so.'

'Does Jim know what it's like tae be raped? No, he doesnae. I'll no' condemn him, mind you, for he's had mair than his own share o' troubles.' Ella eyed Liz carefully for a response.

'I know. His health, worrying about his job – other things that you know all about.'

'Your affairs, you mean?'

Liz hung her head. 'Yes. Though it's hard for me to hear, you're right.'

'I'm no' here tae rip you tae bits. But I'll be honest, I never liked the way you treated him. I'll no' lie. Jimmy doted on you, so he did.'

'*Did* being the operative word.'

'I don't know how he feels now; oor Brian never says a word. Well, anything sensible, anyway. But you're here, aren't you? And look what he did to that – that bastard!'

'I'm here because I came here. I'm the mother of his son. I left him with no choice. He's not been in love with me for a long time. Not since . . . not since Mary Dunn.'

Ella sighed and took a drink of tea. 'Well, you can hardly gie him a hard time o'er that, eh?'

'No, I realise that, Ella.' Liz's eyes flashed.

'See, that's mair like the spirit! You cannae lie doon tae this. I know it must eat away at you every day. But feeling sorry for yourself isn't the answer. Aye, and the drink never helped anyone. I know all aboot that wae oor Brian.'

'I know. It was just a crutch to get over the hard times. To be able to forget it all for a while was bliss. Just to get some sleep.'

'As I said earlier, Lizzie, you need help – professional help. Nobody can be expected to deal with what you've had to. These days there are loads of organisations that can help. And when it comes down tae anxiety, well, the doctor can prescribe some pills in the short term – there's no shame in that.' Ella reached out and held Liz's hand. 'Remember, none o' this is your fault. And getting help is the sensible thing. I've done it myself.'

Liz looked confused for a moment. 'You have?'

Ella sat back in her chair. 'Nothing like what happened to you, though it was bad enough.'

'You mean you were attacked?'

'As I say, nothing as bad as you experienced. But it stayed wae me for years – I still think about it fae time to time. Mind, Lizzie, I've never mentioned it tae a soul.'

'Not even Brian?'

Ella grimaced. 'Especially no' Brian! I know everyone thinks he's just a loveable rogue. But see if anything happens tae his loved ones – well, I dread tae think what he would dae.'

'Will you tell me?'

'Och, it was years ago. We still stayed in the East End of Glasgow then. You'll remember the flat.'

'Yes, I do.'

'Brian was on night shift. I'd run oot o' fags. I didnae think twice aboot it. Even though the weans was just wee, they were both in their beds. The corner shop was open tae ten, so I'd nearly an hour, and it was only a few hundred yards away.' Ella smiled ruefully. 'You know me an' the fags. Anyway, tae cut a long story short, on the way tae the shop there was this wee bit o' waste ground, you know, where a tenement got blown up in the war; it's a fancy restaurant now. But at this time it was full o' bushes, auld bricks and the like. It happened in seconds. I felt someone grab the back o' my coat.'

Liz was wide-eyed. The thought of anyone attacking the formidable Ella Scott seemed almost unimaginable. 'What did you do?'

He pulled me ontae this piece o' waste ground and punched me in the face. But something in me snapped. I remembered my faither saying tae me, "Just you kick the bastard in the balls, darling." He was full o' useful information like that – especially when he'd had a drink. So as you can imagine we got plenty advice, for he was never a day sober.' She nodded her head, remembering everything. 'Mind you, I thanked the old bugger that night, so I did.'

'You managed to fight him off?'

'Aye. Just as he was hauling at my jeans, I booted him right in the haw maws wae everything I had. Went doon like a ton o' bricks, the shite.'

'Well done you!'

'I ran like I never ran before, Lizzie. I forgot all aboot the smokes and just fair pelted hame.'

'And you've never told Brian this?'

'No. But I should have done. I should have telt the polis. No man has the right, Lizzie, no man!'

As tears started to flow down Liz's cheeks, Ella Scott crossed the floor and held her tight.

While Daley was carrying out a search of the living room, Scott was making his way through the rest of the cottage. The first door he opened was the bathroom. It was surprisingly clean, not what he'd expected at all. An old iron bath sat against one wall, with a cracked sink between it and a WC. One bar of carbolic soap was perched on the sink in a soggy pool; there were no fancy toiletries, deodorants, talcum powder, aftershave or perfumes. The Doigs clearly believed in the doctrine of soap and water alone.

He opened an old tin bathroom cabinet above the sink. Five wooden toothbrushes of various colours sat in an old mug alongside a round tin of toothpowder. He remembered his old aunt using such a product, but hadn't seen anything like it for years. The antiquated dental paraphernalia aside, some disposable razors and a silver cutthroat were arranged in a pocket on the door alongside a shaving brush, its bristles worn to a stub.

All in all, the bathroom added to his feeling of stepping back in time. He checked under a bundle of towels sitting on a low white table, but it was clear there was nothing of interest to be found in the smallest room in the house.

Across the hallway was another door. Scott crossed it and entered the room, his torch flashing around in order to make sense of the place as quickly as he could. An iron double bed backed solidly on to a wall of peeling, faded wallpaper. Across from it sat a small chest of drawers and a large built-in cupboard. Scott searched amongst the few coats and jackets, checking every pocket. All he found was a couple of coins and what looked like an old shopping list.

Moving to the chest, Scott made his way through the top drawer of three. It was deep and contained four pairs of faded underpants, two tatty shirts, a couple of pairs of moleskin trousers, a thick blue jumper and some socks, three pairs all rolled up into balls. This was clearly the domain of the late Mr Doig. His wardrobe could hardy be described as extensive. But then, everything in this house seemed pared back to the essentials.

In the next drawer were the meagre belongings of Mrs Doig. A similar collection of worn underwear, three neatly folded dresses of a design that had long since become unfashionable, stockings, a couple of headscarves and a knitted shawl. Scott felt as though he was searching through the nineteenth century. These feelings aside, there was nothing of interest to be found.

The bottom drawer was different. It was a depository of odd bits and pieces: an old tobacco tin, a rusted spanner, a pack of playing cards, a rusting tube of glue, some pens, and a cardboard box half the size of a shoebox. Scott prised off the lid and delved inside, holding his torch under his chin to give him two free hands as he lifted out some old photos. One was of the Doigs taken many years ago, he reckoned. Though his only sight of Mr Doig had been when he was lying dead at the bottom of a cliff, he could still just about picture him in the younger man. Beside him, with a full head of long hair, a pretty frock but the habitual scowl, the figure of Ginny Doig, looking younger but as formidable as she had when she'd ejected him from this very cottage a few hours earlier, was unmistakable. 'Smile a while, eh?' muttered Scott to himself.

The next photograph was of four children: three boys and a girl. Scott stared at the thin little figure standing beside one of her larger brothers. Unlike her mother, Scott could see only a fleeting resemblance to Alice Wenger in the face of the child that must be Alison Doig. Her hair was lank and her dress was too big, hanging off her spare frame like the cast-off of an older child.

The three boys looked bright-eyed as they smiled into the camera. They were clearly of descending age, and Scott reckoned the largest of the three was definitely Thorbin Doig, now missing. As he stared at the photograph in the torchlight, he was struck by how alive, how vibrant they seemed compared with the bloated, blank-faced men he'd met at Rowan Tree Cottage. If anything, Alison looked the most downtrodden, with a sullen, almost vacant expression. How things had changed.

He looked through some other faded colour images of the children, all in much the same style, on the beach, in a small boat, or sitting round the table that still dominated the room

Daley was searching. In each one, it was clear that Alison Doig was not a happy child, while her brothers appeared carefree, animated and content.

The last photograph was older – much older. It was set in a small silver frame. A rough-looking man, possibly in his late thirties, stood beside two small boys, one perhaps early to mid teens, the other younger. They were standing on a hillside beside a pile of driftwood, set together like the makings of a camp fire. Scott reckoned that judging by the style of their clothes the picture must have been taken some time before the Second World War, but it was hard to tell. In the man's face he could see an echo of the Doig son who'd unceremoniously pitched him out of the front door and on to the filthy yard earlier. Grandfather, great-grandfather? He wasn't sure. But he was certain that these were relatives of the present-day Doig family.

There were only two more items in the cardboard box: a business card and what looked like the broken hilt of a knife. Scott donned his reading glasses and peered at the card in the torchlight. *Williams, Strong & Hardacre*, it read, *Solicitors and Notaries*. Though the card was old, he vaguely recognised the name of the firm, which was located in Edinburgh, and was sure that they were still in business. As a police officer, he had found that the names of legal firms tended to become fixed in the mind – even of the Edinburgh variety. He took out his notebook, and leaning on the top of the chest of drawers made a note of the firm's name and address. He then placed the business card back in the box and pulled out the knife hilt. He jumped in surprise when he pressed a small metal button near a silver band on the wooden handle and a vicious-looking blade shot from within. It gleamed in the light of the torch and had evidently been well looked after; the stiletto knife's operation was slick and well oiled.

'You could take someone's eye oot wae that,' said Scott to nobody. This place was beginning to give him the creeps. Knowing Daley wanted to leave the house looking as undisturbed as possible, he took pictures of the knife and the photographs on his phone, retracted the blade, and made sure the contents of the box were placed back in much the same order as they'd been in when he'd found them.

He checked under the base of a candleholder on the chest of drawers, then another on a nightstand, without finding anything. He was about to leave when he realised that he'd not checked under the bed. Warily, wincing at the pain in his arm from the graze inflicted when he'd landed in the yard, he knelt down and directed the beam of the torch into the dark recess.

'Fuck!' he roared as the light flickered over the shape of a body.

Having heard the oath from the next room, Daley rushed in. 'What's wrong, Brian?'

'Take a look,' he said, looking ashen-faced in the light of Daley's torch.

The big detective sat on his haunches and looked under the bed. Sure enough, he could make out a head and a rough torso. 'Here, give me a hand to get this out, will you?'

'You're keen, big man. If it's a body, should we no' just leave it where it is for SOCO?'

'Have a feel, Bri.' Daley tugged at the object under the bed, revealing the featureless head of a dressmaker's dummy. When they managed to haul it out fully, it was clear that the dummy had a metal stand in place of legs and a rough imitation of the human form made from stuffed cloth, designed to be used as a template for making or altering clothes.

'That's a relief,' said Scott. 'I thought that was your man lying deid under there, Jimmy.'

'Mrs Doig's clearly as good with her hands as she is with her fists, eh?'

'Aye, sure enough.'

'Wait!' said Daley, this time in a loud whisper.

'Eh?'

'Can't you hear that?' Daley's voice was even lower now. Above their heads, floorboards were creaking.

26

Vito Chiase was as stiff as a board as he walked down along the concourse of Glasgow Airport. He'd been through security, a process he always hated. Having no respect for authority, he found the blank-faced staff at airports particularly annoying. He wondered if it was the same in Scotland as it was back in New Jersey. For sure, there were plenty airport officials on the take at Newark. In days gone by he'd had half of them in his pocket.

Having only on-board luggage he was spared the wait at the carousel, so hobbled straight out into the growing dusk of a Scottish evening for the first time in his life. His flight had been delayed for two hours due to 'technical issues', and when he'd eventually changed planes at London Heathrow, the stopover had also been longer than he'd expected.

But, as he'd been instructed, he managed to text his difficulties to the number he'd been given to inform those awaiting his arrival of the delay. Sure enough, within seconds, he'd received the reassuring if brief reply, *No problem. Chill.* Why did people talk that way now?

He shaded his eyes from the flickering sodium lights and looked around. A thin man in a shell suit was standing with the name *Mr Chasey* written on an old piece of white card. Shrugging his shoulders, he made for the man.

'Hey, are you the guy?'

'Are you Mr Chasey?'

'Chiase, Ch-ee-ay-sie, got it?'

The young man with the pock-marked face looked him up and down. 'Aye, I've got it, man.' He smiled, displaying a set of uneven, discoloured teeth. 'This'll be a nice wee break fae the old folks' home, eh?' He chuckled to himself.

His amusement was cut short when Chiase caught him by the arm, squeezing tightly. 'Listen, kid, any more of that shit and your balls will be where your lungs are, got it?'

'Easy on! I'm only taking the piss.'

'Taking what?'

'Having a laugh, making fun of you – och, never mind. Come on, I've been here for hours waiting on you.'

'I don't give a fuck if you've been waiting half your miserable life, you cocksucker.' It was Chiase's turn to examine the man sent to meet him. 'Anyhow, where you gotta be? A date with a needle?'

'Right, o'er here!' The man walked away, Vito Chiase cursing the pain in his hip as he tried to keep up.

They walked into a car park, to an SUV parked in a bay some distance away from any other vehicles.

'Right, there's the keys, man.'

Chiase took them from the young man and pressed the button on the fob. The car bleeped and the sidelights flashed in response. He opened the passenger door.

'Hey, you'll need tae get in the other side, auld fella. You're no' in New York noo.'

This time Chiase grabbed him by the throat. 'First off, I'm not from New York, I'm from North Jersey. Second, this is a fucking stick shift. I haven't rode in one of these since the sixties.' He loosened his grip on the man's throat.

'Aye well, that's no' my problem, so it's no'. I was telt tae find you, take you to the car and gie you this message.'

'Which is?' Chiase let go of his throat.

'The goods are in the boot an' the satnav is set for where you've tae go. You sleep in the motor when you get there until the job's done. When it is, text the number you've got and the arrangements tae get you back hame will be made.' He looked around. 'Aye, an' I've tae gie you this.' He handed the old gangster a thick wad of notes – dollars, plus cash Chiase assumed was from the UK. 'Half noo, half when the job's done, as agreed, plus some dosh for expenses – nae credit cards, right? Hope I don't see you later, Don Corleone, man.' He turned on his heel and ran off across the car park, leaving Vito Chiase cursing in his wake.

'Driving on the wrong side of the road and a fucking stick shift. Shit!' Chiase was beginning to wish he'd never taken his first trip to Scotland.

Mike Strong was at home, reflecting on his day.

He'd swaggered into the plush offices of Williams, Strong and Hardacre. Karen Milne was sitting behind a large reception desk, and the sight of her made Strong feel envious and old at the same time. He knew that she and Blair Williams were having an affair. The old cashier, Phyllis Beggie, whom he'd had a fling with in the seventies, still worked two days a week. She kept her ear to the ground and her ex-lover informed.

'Mr Strong, how are you?' said Karen Milne with a bright smile.

'I'm very well, my dear. Not pretty as a picture like you, but well nonetheless.'

'Ha! You can get arrested for that now,' she replied teasingly.

'Oh, no doubt. The boys in blue make it a priority these days, I believe. You wouldn't mind making me a quick coffee, please? I'm damned parched.'

'We've got a machine now. It'll only take a couple of minutes.'

'Machine, eh?' He watched her stride off in search of the coffee machine, then looked down at the floor. Sure enough, her handbag was beside the swivel chair. He knelt down, having made sure she wasn't returning for anything.

After a few seconds: 'Ah, the very thing.' He'd found two mobile phones: one slick and expensive, the other a cheaper, much less high-end model. He slipped the cheaper device into his jacket.

She was back a few moments later, a takeaway cup of coffee in her hand.

'Ah, thank you.' He took the coffee from her. 'Mind you, I've seen the days when partners took their tea in china cups.'

Milne shrugged. 'It's coffee.'

'But the absence of crockery is always made up for by being able to cast one's eye over you, dear. I'm looking for Blair; is he in?'

'Yes, Mr Strong. He's alone. His last client left half an hour ago, but he has a meeting out of the office in about twenty minutes.'

'Well, he'll just have to be late, though I don't think our business will take too long.'

'I'll show you through.'

'Oh, I think I'll manage. After all, I have been working in this building for the last forty years.'

'Of course. Silly me.'

As Karen Milne watched him head down the corridor to the lawyers' offices, coffee in hand, she curled her lip. 'Dirty old bastard,' she muttered under her breath.

Not bothering to knock, Strong breezed into his junior partner's office. 'Glad to see you're busy, Blair.'

'Mike! I was just – just getting ready for a meeting.'

Strong smiled as the younger man hurriedly put down his mobile phone. 'Very loyal, isn't she?'

'Who?'

'Young Ms Milne; I assume she just texted you to tell you I was coming.'

'Well, it is her job.'

'I'm sure she bends over backwards to carry out your instructions to the letter.' Strong sat on the chair across the desk from Williams. 'Have you any booze? I could do with a snifter to stick in this coffee.'

Williams opened a drawer in his desk and produced a bottle of Highland Park and one small crystal glass. He poured a measure into Strong's coffee and a straight one for himself. 'Don't often drink during the day, but since you're here I'll make an exception.' He smiled nervously.

'Life is so dull now, isn't it? When I was your age we'd all go out for a decent lunch – if court wasn't dragging on, or the like. Your father was never much of a boozer, mind you.'

'My mother makes up for that.'

'She was always the life and soul.'

'Yes, I dare say.'

'About this Jeremiah business, Blair.'

'Please, don't mention it. I'm so glad you took it off my hands.' He looked relieved.

'Keeps the old brain working, you know. In any case, it's from my time, so I thought it only fair.'

'Very kind. I was dreading it.'

'I've incurred some expenses processing it all. I want you to transfer some funds from the company account.'

'Certainly, I'll have it done right away. You could just have phoned this in, no need to come in person.' Williams opened a leather-bound desk diary. 'What's the damage, Mike?'

'A hundred thousand should cover it.'

'What?' Williams's mouth was gaping.

'Don't worry; the estate is worth much more than that. We can deduct that money once everything is sorted out. Now, I take it I'll have to countersign something, yes?'

'Yes, just to keep the accountants happy, you know.' Again Williams laughed nervously.

'Old Jamieson; how is the miserable bugger?'

'Dead.'

'Really? When?'

'About a year ago.'

'Damn. I should have gone to the funeral, I suppose. Still, can't be helped.'

'He left huge gambling debts, apparently.'

'I'm not surprised. He loved the racetrack. The reason we kept the firm on. He was always so desperate for cash we could always negotiate his fees down. 'Who's in charge now?'

'Brannon.'

'At least he doesn't look as though he's catching flies. I hated that gaping mouth of Jamieson's. He was an ugly bastard. Thought he was smart, too. I'm constantly amazed by the terminally stupid – they always think they've got the better of you. And then the tables turn.'

'It's all going well, then?'

'What?'

'This . . . Jeremiah thing.'

'Absolutely fine and dandy, Blair. In fact, things should start moving quite quickly from now on.' Strong smiled beatifically. 'One last thing: I need access to the safe – the reason I came in, really.'

'What for?'

'Mind your own damn business! Now, what's the combination these days?'

In a few minutes, Mike Strong had found what he needed in the company safe and was making his way out of the office.

'Have a lovely day, Mr Strong,' said Karen Milne as he passed by the reception desk.

He stopped. 'The next time I come to visit my partner, don't dare send a message to tell him I'm on my way. Take that as a verbal warning, Ms Milne.'

'It's *Mrs* Milne, actually,' she said defiantly.

'Really? Now there's a thing.' He grinned. 'Good day to you, *Mrs* Milne.' Strong smiled to himself as he left the office. Always good to keep the youngsters in their place, he thought.

27

'Right, that's us, Brian. Better get going; nothing to be found in here,' said Daley loudly. He had taken one of the chairs from beside the table, and with a steadying hand from Scott clambered on to it just under the hatch that afforded access to the loft above.

'Aye, hang on. I forgot my gloves, Jimmy,' said Scott with a wink

The ceilings of Rowan Tree Cottage were mercifully low, so much so that Daley was now crouching as he stood on the chair, hands flat on the hatch. He gave the thumbs up to Scott and pushed hard.

The hatch wasn't hinged and just fell away to the side, allowing Daley to pull himself up into the loft space.

Scott watched his friend's feet disappear into the darkness then got on to the chair, one of his knees protesting painfully.

'Quick, Brian, get up here!' Daley shouted.

A few inches shorter than his superior, Scott struggled to pull himself into the loft, but managed it soon enough. 'I'm never oot o' bloody lofts,' he recalled.

The space looked as though it ran across the full length of the cottage. It was even mustier than the living quarters below, and also reeked of sweat and shit. The beam of Daley's torch cast light upon what looked at first glance to be a large bundle of rags. But as the policemen crouched their way forward, the rags began to move, and the flash of skin was plain in the darkness.

A muffled yelp came from the bundle as Daley grabbed a bulging arm, and for the first time the full face of a cowering man was revealed amidst a tumble of old hessian sacks. He was crouching next to a wooden support. As Scott pulled away the bags, they saw he was in fact chained to it. Nearby sat a bucket, a jug of water and a half-spent toilet roll.

'Thorbin Doig, what on earth is this all about?'

The man looked terrified, shrinking away from the light like a frightened animal.

'Don't worry, Mr Doig, we're not here to harm you.'

The man forced his back against the post to which he was chained, and promptly burst into tears.

'Wait a minute,' said Scott. 'There's no need for that. Come on, man, you're older than me!'

Daley frowned at his friend, then took the airwave radio from his pocket. 'DCI Daley to search party: send an ambulance to Rowan Tree Cottage, Thorbin Doig has been located, over.' He paused for a moment. 'And bring some bolt cutters, over.'

'Who would dae a thing like this, Jimmy?' said Scott, unable to take his eyes from the cowering man chained up in the loft of his own home.

'Two guesses, Brian.'

'Listen, you're okay, buddy,' said Scott, reaching out to Thorbin Doig in an attempt to reassure him.

Doig shrank away with a grunt, staring at the police officers, his right eye hooded by its lid.

'What happened to your eye, Mr Doig?' asked Daley.

The response was unexpected. Doig wailed at the top of his voice, a wail that turned into a piercing, blood-curdling scream.

Vito Chiase grimaced as, yet again, he crunched the gears of the SUV. He was crossing a bridge, the bright lights of the city of Glasgow to his right, the silver ribbon of the River Clyde spilling out towards its estuary to his left.

He'd examined the contents of the trunk: detailed instructions including a map and photographs, a small selection of sandwiches in plastic wrapping, a bottle of Coke, and a slim case containing a pistol, a silencer and ammunition. He hadn't taken the gun from the case for fear of security cameras, but from what he could see it looked well maintained and new.

As he pulled off the bridge following the advice of the satnav, he winced as yet again he crunched the gears. 'Fuck this!' he shouted at the top of his voice. He pictured his comfortable home in Caldwell, dearly wishing he hadn't chosen to boost his flagging finances by taking on this job. But, he reasoned, what other opportunities did he have? He'd been frozen out by his own family, the sons and grandsons of men he'd known and loved. He'd have taken a bullet for them – well, most of them.

Times had been tough for the Mafia in America. Whole crews had been taken down by new technology, forensics and the RICO Act. The FBI had been riding high until they became overstretched in the hunt for international terrorists. It had been a window of opportunity he'd hoped to be able to exploit. But after his eleven years in the can nobody cared. It wasn't as though his son had stepped into his shoes, but that pleased him. Who wants life in this thing of ours, he thought. It was done, finished. All that was left was the dregs of drugs, prostitution and intimidation that had once made him rich. Most of the young guys on the streets couldn't shake down themselves.

Having memorised some names from his instructions, he punched the wheel in frustration as he passed a large green signpost, illuminated by his headlights.

Kinloch 122.

It would take him hours just to get there. He was tired, stiff, and he hated stick-shift cars.

Vito Chiase turned on the car radio. Eventually he found a station playing the Frank Sinatra recording of a song from the fifties. 'I might as well be flying to the fucking moon!' he swore loudly to himself.

Thorbin Doig was being treated for hypothermia and shock when Daley and Scott arrived at Kinloch hospital. The pair sat patiently in chairs outside the side room while the doctor completed his examination of the man they'd liberated from the loft of his home.

'If I'd a penny for every time I've been in here, Jimmy, eh?'

'Yes,' sighed Daley. 'I hate hospitals.'

'But if it wisnae for them me and you would be six foot under.'

'True, though it doesn't make me like them any more.'

'What kind of mother chains her ain son up in the loft?'

Daley ran his hands through his hair. 'I think my question is more why?'

'That tae, big man. I mean, what had she got tae gain by it?'

'I don't know. The only thing I can think of at the moment is some kind of diversion.'

'Diversion fae what?'

The door beside them opened and a man Daley recognised appeared followed by a staff nurse. 'Dr Spence, how are you? I thought you'd retired.'

The man was stocky, thick-set, with short curly hair that had been dark but was now wound with grey. 'DCI Daley. Long time since we last met. The poor girl found dead in the bay at Machrie, I believe.'

'Yes, when I first arrived.'

'I remember it well. You never really retire from medicine, just pause. That's my experience, in any event. I'm doing my duty as a locum. Bloody hard to get GPs down to a place like this these days, you know.'

'I don't suppose they can be ordered down the way we are,' said Daley.

'More's the pity! I was bloody grateful to be sent down to such a beautiful place when I was a young doctor. I'd done my training in some of the worst parts of Glasgow. My goodness, we worked for our money there. I suppose I don't need to tell you that.'

'No.'

'Trouble is, it's all about money nowadays; cash, plain and simple. I brought my family up here. We've had a good life. I wouldn't think of moving away.'

'Can I ask you a bit about your patient, please, doctor?'

'Yes, fire away.' Spence turned to the nurse. 'That will be all, staff, thank you. Make sure Mr Doig gets some hot sweet tea.'

'So he's okay?' asked Scott.

'Nothing that a good bed for the night, some hot food and a light sedative won't help, I'm pleased to say. He'll be discharged in the morning. Chained up in his own home, I heard.'

'Yes, he was,' Daley replied.

'I've been here for forty-odd years, DCI Daley. And in all that time he's the first member of that family I've treated.'

'Is that strange?'

'I should say. In a place like this you get your hands on most families in that time.'

'Can I ask you a specific question – about Mr Doig, I mean?'

'I must respect patient confidentiality. However, in this case, I believe that I have some leeway.'

'How so?' asked Scott.

'Mr Doig is well below average intelligence. And considering the circumstances in which he was found, I'm willing to make some of my observations known to you.'

'I've noticed that he and his brothers have drooping right eyelids. Is this just a family trait of some kind . . . genetic?' asked Daley.

'Ah, yes. If you don't mind, I'd like to think about that – consult some notes.'

'Why so?'

'I don't want to say anything that is mere speculation, Mr Daley. Though I do have my suspicions.'

'How no' just come oot wae it, then?' Scott asked.

'I presume your organisation resembles mine in a small number of ways.'

'What ways are they?'

'Mainly that I need to build a reasonable case before I make any kind of judgement on what I've seen. When I've satisfied myself that what I suspect is, or isn't, the case, I'll be happy to speak further on the subject.'

'So there's something unusual, doctor?' said Daley.

'Yes, there's something most unusual; in fact, if I'm right something quite barbaric. I hope I'm wrong.'

'Can you no' gie us something?'

Spence looked as Scott levelly. 'You're the officer who suffered the peanut injury, aren't you?'

'Is no one ever going to let me forget that?' Scott looked exasperated.

'I doubt it. Not in this hospital, at least. Now, gentlemen, if you don't mind, I'll get back to you with my findings.'

Scott watched Spence walk away and turned to Daley. 'What was that a' aboot, Jimmy?'

'I don't know, but it might be significant, by the sound of things.'

'Mysterious bastards, these doctors.'

'Good memories, though.'

'Why do you say that, Jimmy?'

'Nobody seems to have forgotten your peanut incident.' Daley got up and walked off before Scott decided to swear. 'Come on, I'll take you to the County for a ginger beer and lime. I think we've earned it.'

'Changed days, Jimmy. You and me would have been heading doon the street for a few drams, never mind ginger beer.'

'We're getting old, Brian.'

'Tell me aboot it. Every time I see Symington I feel aboot a hundred and two.'

'Oh, I don't think it's all been plain sailing for her.'

'Why dae you say that?'

'Just a feeling, Bri.'

'Here, before I forget. You were wondering if those droopy eyes were genetic, right?'

'Yes.'

'Now, I'm nae expert in genetics, but is it no' fair tae say that their eyes would always have been the same – you know, that hooded way – if that was the case?'

'I suppose. Though some conditions may present themselves in later life. But like you, I'm no doctor. Why do you ask, Bri?'

Scott removed his mobile phone from his pocket. Not without some difficulty, he managed to find what he was looking for. 'I took these in the bedroom at Doom Cottage – photos fae years ago. I'll bet any money these are the Doig boys as kids, aye, and Alice Wenger, tae.'

Daley was handed the phone and scrolled through Scott's images slowly. 'Their eyes look perfectly normal on here.'

'Just my point.'

'Okay. We'll leave the rest of the Doigs to stew overnight. I'll give Shaw a quick bell. Ginny won't be happy, but a pound to a penny she reckoned we'd bring in her daughter in connection with Thorbin's disappearance. I must update Symington tomorrow.'

'Wicked auld bastard, if you ask me.' Scott plodded on in his wake.

28

Vito Chiase was tired, *very* tired when he reached the sign that said *Welcome to Kinloch*. He had wrestled with the stick shift for the first part of the journey, but eventually became proficient enough to be able to change gears without a sickening crunch. Why do they make cars like this still, he thought, as he drove into the town.

Though this was his first visit to Scotland, he was wise enough to realise that, having to sleep in the car and keep a low profile, he'd have to find a place to stop that was out of the way, unlikely to attract attention. Though he'd trusted the satnav to get him here, he pulled over now and consulted the map that had been left in the trunk, outlining his final destination, where his job was to be done.

He ran his finger through the streets of the town, roughly familiarising himself with the place. In his opinion, technology was okay as far as getting you from one place to another went, but it gave you no idea of your surroundings. A map, something you could hold, see and look around, gave a much fuller depiction of an area. And in his experience, the better you knew a place, the less likely you were to be trapped and caught.

He remembered being a kid on Bloomfield Avenue in

Newark. He and his buddies had formed a youthful crew, lifting valuables from open windows, cars, shops – anywhere. They'd memorised every lane, escape routes through gardens, public buildings, stores; they knew the centre of Newark like the backs of their hands. The cops were too busy taking bribes and drinking coffee to get to know the area they policed. Even as children it gave them a singular advantage.

Chiase sat back. He could see all their faces now, those boys, his friends who had, in most cases, grown up to be his crew. Lenny had been the first to go, shot by the police during a robbery. Carmine was next, whacked by a member of his own family for bedding a made guy's wife. These thoughts made him feel melancholy, so he decided not to think about the guys he'd never see again, not in this life, at least.

He remembered the first time he'd been taken home by the cops. He was only eight years old. Busted for stealing candy. He could see the anger and disappointment in his father's eyes. The rage of a man who'd disavowed his family's history of crime, working for a lifetime on the railroad.

'You wanna end up like my old man?'

He was a kid back then, what could he say? He didn't even know what had happened to his grandfather. He shrugged his shoulders for want of a reply. It had been the wrong decision. His father had slapped him on the head, catching an ear and making it ring.

'Don't you shrug at me! You talk, you say something, got it?' His father had him by the collar of his shirt. 'I wasn't much older than you when my father just disappeared. He was there one day, gone the next. One minute we was happy, well fed, good clothes, nice house. Next I knew, we had to move to a crummy apartment. I could hear my mother – your grandmother – cry herself to sleep every night. And do you know why all this happened?'

Chiase remembered the slap on the head and replied with a quiet 'No'.

'Because he was a wise guy, that's why. These men you admire so much – your uncle Tony, all those guys. They live on the edge, the high life one minute, lying dead in a gutter the next.' His father enveloped him in a huge hug. 'Do you know what that's like, never knowing when the axe is going to fall, looking over your shoulder every minute of every day?'

Chiase remembered the tears falling down his face on to his father's bare arm. As usual, when he came home at night, the man would strip down to his vest to relax. 'I'm sorry, Pop,' he managed to say. Then, 'Did my grandfather die in a gutter?'

His father ended the embrace, leaned his elbows on his knees and rubbed his face with both hands as he stared at his young son. 'Nobody ever knew. His brother – your great-uncle Johnny – told everyone that he ran off with some broad, but I never believed that. My mother and him, they was too close. All I know is I never saw him again. He walked out of the door and he never came back in. Is that the kinda life you want for yourself, kid?'

Vito Chiase remembered shaking his head tearfully. But even then he had known he was telling his father a lie.

He started the engine again, pulled away and made his way through the town under the glow of the streetlights. Already, having looked at the map, he felt he knew the area. He had found a likely place to pull over and sleep. He would eat what they'd provided, drink some coffee from the flask and make sure he was fresh for the morning.

Vito Chiase had things to do.

The County Hotel bar was warm and welcoming, despite the absence of a crowd. The fire glowed warm in the grate, and the familiar figure of Hamish sat at the table nearest the bar, with one or two other customers dotted around. Everyone seemed lost in their own thoughts; apart that was from Annie, who greeted them with a big smile.

'Hello, boys. How are you both?'

Daley looked around. 'Busier than you, by the look of things.'

'Och, it's always the same in late November – folk saving up for Christmas, an' that.'

'You're mair cheerful than the last time I was in here,' said Scott.

'We've had some good news,' replied Annie with a smile.

'I heard they were going to turn the place into flats,' said Daley.

'That was the plan, Mr Daley. But as Rabbie Burns says, "The best laid plans o' mice an' men gang aft a-gley," or something like that. Insna that right, Hamish?'

'Aye, it is indeed. You've a great memory for poetry, right enough, Annie. No' jeest as good for getting the change right, mind you,' he continued more quietly.

'Are you for a dram, Hamish?' Daley asked.

'Well, now, you see, that would be most gratefully received, Mr Daley. Yes indeed it would.'

While Scott sat down with Hamish, Daley went to the bar to place his order. 'A dram for Hamish, a ginger beer and lime, and a coffee for me, please, Annie.'

'You've no' signed the pledge as well, have you?' She looked at him warily.

'No, not quite. But I've to be more careful. I'd like to see my son grow up.'

'Ach, you're havering. My auld faither has had heart problems for fifty years, an' he's still going strong.'

'He doesn't have my genes, Annie.'

'No, but his might jeest fit you these days. Fair emaciated, so you are. Take a seat an' I'll bring your drinks o'er.'

'Thanks. But I've got a wee bit to go before I'm emaciated.'

'Here, this is interesting, big man,' said Scott as Daley took his seat. 'Carry on, Hamish.'

The old man drained what was left in his glass and licked his lips. 'I was remembering aboot the significance o' the name Jeremiah. Mr Scott was telling me that he'd come across it – in the line of duty, so tae speak.'

'And?' said Daley.

'A long whiles before my time, right enough. But I minded that my faither had telt me the story.'

'Hurry up before I have tae retire,' said Scott.

'Man, but it's mair impatient you're getting by the day, Brian. No' good for a man o' your age. Look at Mr Daley here, for example. Fair burdened wae care and ends up in the hospital. You should learn tae take life steadily – like me.'

'If you were any mair steady you wouldnae move at all, Hamish,' said Scott. Daley just raised his brows.

After narrowing his eyes at Scott, Hamish continued. 'By all accounts it was one o' the worst storms the west coast has ever seen. No' today nor yesterday, mark you. Way back in the 1920s.'

'So you'd be just leaving the school,' said Scott.

'I'll ignore that an' carry on.' Hamish closed his eyes and raised his head, giving him the appearance of an oriental deity. 'The *Jeremiah* was a steam puffer, no' the brightest star o' the coastal trade, but nae dunce, neithers. An auld boy called Donaldson was her skipper. One o' the McMichaels fae Dalintober was first mate – fine seamen that whole family, even though they was fae the wrong side o' the loch.'

Scott sighed.

Hamish opened one eye and looked at him balefully. 'Noo the *Jeremiah* should have been safe at berth in Oban that night, as far as her owner, a man fae Glasgow wae five puffers, was concerned. But it appeared, even though the storm was getting its dander up, Donaldson took the notion tae leave port regardless. He had passengers, they say, and they were fair desperate to get tae where they were going, storm or no storm. Ach, I'm sure the old boy knew the waters like the back o' his hand. For the coin, he'd likely have taken the risk – money was tight back then, nae social security, or the likes. A man had tae take a chance when he got one, an' no mistake.'

'How do you know about the passengers, Hamish?' said Daley.

'You hear all sorts. Even a place like Oban was tight-knit in they days. Damn near a metropolis noo. They tell me they've even got a cricket team. Can you imagine? In any event, such was the outcome of their mission – whootever that was – it stuck in the minds o' folk for years.'

'Why?' said Scott as Annie sat his soft drink in front of him.

'Well – as often is the case wae such a storm, it raged a' night. But then as quickly as it had arrived, it was gone. The next day the sea was like a millpond, thon freshness in the air.

215

To cut a long story short, the *Jeremiah* was reported missing. She was last spotted near the coast at Kilberry heading south, so the theory was she could only be heading tae Kinloch – there being no other place of any consequence in that direction. Well, unless they was heading for the Isle o' Man, but that's jeest fanciful.'

'I'm losing the will tae live,' said Scott.

Hamish carried on without comment. 'A search was begun. The lifeboats fae Tarbert, Blaan, Kinloch – even Ballycastle across the water – were all launched. The crews were all fishermen in they days, and their knowledge o' the tides an' foibles o' the coast surpassed any o' the doctors and lawyers that parade aboot noo in a' that fluorescent gear. Like great walking buoys they are.

'So, they found something?' said Daley.

'They did that. Just on the shore o' the island at the head o' the loch, within sight of the toon and safety, there she was, the *Jeremiah*, a great gaping hole in her side.'

'So that's it?' Scott sounded disappointed.

'No, it's not. On board they found four bodies – four, mark you. One o' them was a stranger, so we can forget aboot him.'

'You're a' heart,' said Scott.

'There was the poor ship's boy – a wean fae Glasgow they said – lashed tae his bunk, dead as dead could be. McMichael an' the stranger was lying below the bunks, och, jeest in a hellish condition. The engineer, whose name escapes me, was found at his station, deid as a dodo.'

'What aboot the skipper?' said Scott.

'That's where things get strange. He was found, washed up on Thomson's Point. The window o' the wheelhouse had been smashed in, and they reckoned, though I never quite

216

understood it, that he'd been flung oot in the tumult.' He paused dramatically. 'But he wasna alone.'

'Another stranger no' worth mentioning, nae doubt.'

'Not at all. The two other bodies just along the shore fae Donaldson were well quoted hereabouts. Fineas Doig – they all had odd names, that crowd – an' his younger son.'

'Wow!' said Daley, genuinely surprised.

'Aye, but there's mair. Both he and his son had been stabbed; old Doig in the back, his boy right through the heart. As I've telt yous, they had a name for being wreckers. The story was that they led auld Donaldson ontae the point wae a false light, then when they managed to board the wreck the next day a survivor put up a fight. Donaldson himself, they reckon, but I've never found that plausible.'

'How so?' said Scott.

'By all accounts he was a decent man, an elder in the church, no less, though he liked a dram or two. But any man can be forgiven for that wee indulgence. I'm sure the man above takes one or two himself, fae time tae time. Well deserved with whoot's going on in the world these days. Anyhow, they reckoned that Donaldson would never have taken the boy's life, even if he had been able tae get the better o' the faither, which is doubtful, for by all accounts Doig was a right hard bastard.'

'Were any of the remaining Doigs asked about it?' said Daley.

'They were. It was jeest the mother an' the elder son, Thorbin Doig. The father of the man that took a dive off the cliff at Thomson's Hill, as you well know. I mind o' him in his auld age. A mair hateful man never walked. Cruel – wicked, many said.'

217

'But nothing was ever solved?' asked Daley.

'No, never. Though when I thought aboot it a' – remembering, like – after you seeing the bell, Brian, well, I must admit, my mind tumbled away . . .'

Scott looked at Daley. 'Curiouser and curiouser, Jimmy.'

'Never took you for a fan of *Alice in Wonderland*, Brian.'

Scott looked puzzled for a moment. 'If I knew how you came tae that conclusion I'd be able tae reply. But then we've got oor own Alice tae think aboot, eh?'

29

Blair Williams was uneasy, very uneasy. He'd been unsettled by Mike Strong's visit; he remembered how his father had warned him about his old partner. There was no doubting his legal skills; Strong was well noted for his many successes in court. He had, though, had a darker side: malevolent and grasping, as Blair's father had described it. The words had stuck in his head, and he'd wrestled with them all night.

Just as he resolved to call his retired father for advice, the phone on his desk rang.

'It's the police in . . .' Karen Milne paused to check the name. 'In *Kinloch*. A DCI Daley.' It was clear that she had never heard of the place.

'Give me a few moments,' said Williams. He could feel his heart rate rise, and a cold sweat form on his brow. He'd only just found out about Kinloch, which hadn't filled him with joy, and now this. 'Okay, put them through.' This was not how Blair Williams had planned to spend his morning.

'You're Mr Williams?' said Daley, his voice loud over the phone.

'Yes, that's right.'

'I wonder if you can help me? An old business card issued by your firm was discovered in connection with a case I'm investigating. I'm hoping you can throw some light on it.'

Williams gulped. 'Oh yes? Where did you say you were from?' He was playing for time.

'Kinloch, in Argyll.'

'Not exactly our part of the world, DCI Daley.'

'No, but the business card was found among the possessions of a man who died the other day, Mr Williams. You'll understand that I have to follow that up.'

'Of – of course.'

'Do you know if your firm has had any dealings with a Mr Nathaniel Doig?'

Williams hesitated, letting the conversation hang in the air. 'Now, let me think, DCI Daley. I've been here for just about five years, and I can't recall anyone by that name.'

'Oh, I see. By the looks of it, this card isn't new by any means. Maybe if I take a photo of it and send it to you, someone will know roughly when it was issued?'

'Yes, good idea. One of the original partners is still working for us, albeit on more of a consultancy basis these days. I'll let him have a look when you've sent it.'

'Is it possible to have a word with him now?'

'No, I'm afraid not. As I mentioned, he only comes in when necessary. But I'll certainly try and get hold of him as quickly as possible.'

'Can I have his name, please?'

Despite himself, a smile broke out on Williams's face. 'His name is Michael – Mike Strong. One of our founding partners.'

'Yes, I see his name on the card. I'd like a contact number for him, please.'

'Oh yes, of course. I'll put you back through to our secretary and get her to pass you his contact details.' He thought for a moment. 'I hope everything is okay?'

'Not really sure,' replied Daley. 'Our investigation is ongoing, put it like that, Mr Williams.'

'I see, yes, absolutely. Well, nice talking to you, DCI Daley. Give me a few moments and I'll get you back to reception. Have a good day now.' Williams winced at his own insincerity as he pressed a button on his phone. 'Karen, give DCI Daley Mike Strong's email address and phone number, please. Mobile too.'

'Will I give him a call to let him know the police might call, Blair?'

Williams's face lost all expression. 'No, I don't think that will be necessary. Just a routine matter,' he said, knowing that it was anything but.

Suddenly Blair Williams was very happy that Mike Strong had taken charge of this particular client.

Daley placed the phone back on its cradle. As a detective, he'd spent years learning how to judge a person by tone of voice, inflection, hesitation, enforced cheerfulness. He'd heard all of that during his call with Blair Williams.

He rubbed his chin thoughtfully and stared at the numbers and email address he'd just been given for Mike Strong. He considered calling right away, but decided to leave it a while. There was every chance that Williams would tip his semi-retired partner off. But something in the young man's voice had indicted that might not be the case. Daley was sure that Blair Williams knew who Nathaniel Doig was, at the very least. The question was why hadn't he admitted it? Now the detective was even more certain that the Doig family had some secret, and to keep it they'd hired an expensive firm of Edinburgh lawyers. The question was, what could it possibly be?

He thought back to the words of his old mentor Ian Burns. *It usually comes down to love or money.* Daley could see little love in the Doig household, but even less money. Something didn't make sense. He resolved to give Williams time to call Strong, if indeed that's what he was intending to do. Meanwhile, he wanted to speak to Ginny Doig and ask her just why she'd chained her son in the loft of their home.

Liz Daley felt renewed. Ella Scott had gone just before Jim returned. The talk with the woman she'd known for so many years had helped a lot. She'd felt so alone, as though there was no one left in the world to whom she could turn – nobody likely to understand what she'd been through. But now Liz realised that had been stupid. The awful truth was that women were assaulted, maimed, raped and killed every day. Though the pain she felt, the anger, the fear, still plagued her, she now believed for the first time that it hadn't been her fault.

How many times in her head had she heard the words *you're smart, you should have known better.* Now she saw that thought for what it was: an impostor. No, she hadn't led a blameless life, but neither did she deserve to be beaten and raped for sins past. Hating her attacker was one thing; hating herself was another.

Liz had always considered Ella Scott to be indestructible, a force of nature. That she could be attacked, brought so low by an event that she wasn't prepared to tell her husband about even after all these years, perversely gave Liz strength. She wasn't weak: she could survive, and she would. She would fight to regain her dignity, her confidence. She would fight to save her marriage.

'Okay, James, time to get ready. You've had your bath, now Mummy will find some clothes.'

The little boy looked up at her, brushing his dark fringe away from his eyes. 'Where are we going, Mummy?'

'To the dentist, James.'

Elderly as she was, Ginny Doig had fought every step of the way from the cells to Daley's glass box. A prominent scratch across the face of one of the two female officers she now sat between bore witness.

'I want to question you as to the false imprisonment of your son, Thorbin Doig,' said Daley. 'You have the right to have a solicitor present during this questioning, and I strongly advise that you do so.'

She faced him, arms crossed, expressionless, but her eyes seemed to blaze with a green fire of hatred.

'Why would I need a solicitor? I've done nothing wrong.'

'I still think you should have a lawyer present when I question you formally, Mrs Doig.'

'I don't care what you think. My boys are simple but they're boisterous. One of his brothers must have chained Thorbin up in the loft for a laugh. I assure you, I had no idea.'

Daley looked at the frail woman in front of him. Not only was she stubborn, determined – violent, even – she was also clever. That was something he hadn't realised at first. It was very clear that her sons were below average intelligence, and as such an offence committed by them would be unlikely to end in prosecution. Though he was certain that Ginny Doig herself had been responsible for chaining her eldest son in the loft, it was unlikely he'd ever be able to prove it.

He smiled. 'Okay, we'll have it your way, Mrs Doig. You're smart. I know that now. But I will get to the bottom of what's been going on here, I promise you.' He addressed the officers. 'Make arrangements for Mrs Doig's release, please. I'll inform Sergeant Shaw.'

'And you'll be releasing my sons, tae.'

Daley shook his head. 'Sorry, but no I won't. You've clearly indicated to me that one of them imprisoned Thorbin. They stay here while I carry on my investigation. A great deal of time, effort and manpower was expended on the search for your son yesterday, Mrs Doig. All the time he was chained in your loft. At the very least, someone is guilty of wasting police time – perhaps more. It depends what I can glean from his brothers.'

It was Ginny Doig's turn to smile. Her teeth were brown and uneven. 'You can only hold them for so long. Dae you think I'm stupid? Anyway, the way they are, nae court in the land would convict them.'

'We'll see. In fact, because of the special circumstances, we may well be afforded more time to speak to them.'

'You dae your worst, Mr Daley.'

'No, I'll do my best, Mrs Doig.' He watched her being led away, then called her back. 'I forgot, just a couple of quick questions.'

'Whoot?'

'Have you heard of an Edinburgh law firm called Williams, Strong and Hardacre?'

'No. Why should I have done?' Her answer was casual, no signs of obfuscation.

'Okay, thank you.'

'Whoot's the other thing?'

'What's wrong with your sons' eyes, Mrs Doig?'

'Nane o' your business!' she shouted. All of a sudden she had to be restrained again by the constables. 'It's between us an' oor doctors.'

'And just who is your family GP?'

'You said I was tae be released, so jeest get on wae it. I'm no' saying any mair!'

As she was led from his office Daley smiled. Clever, but not as clever as you think, Mrs Doig, he thought.

30

Vito Chiase eyed the day with one blurry eye. Though he'd been dog-tired, he'd woken up every hour, freezing cold. He had to turn the engine of the car each time, heater on full blast, just to get warm. He swore to himself as the seat slowly regained its upright position. Yawning, he opened the door and stepped out into the cold morning light.

He'd chosen well, a little forestry car park marked on the map as being suitable for picnics. There wouldn't be many picnickers about in late November, he reckoned. With great relief, he unzipped his fly and pissed in the long grass at the side of the car before reaching back to pour the last few drops of coffee he had left in the flask specifically for his morning pick-me-up. He'd have to find some more; he couldn't function without the stuff.

As he sipped from the plastic mug Chiase stared out across the sea. He loved being down at the shore back home in New Jersey, or the many times he'd visited Atlantic City or Florida. The familiar tang of the sea was there, the shrill calls of the birds waking up to a new day – but this was different. There was a silence he'd never experienced in his life, a peacefulness that was soothing and somehow threatening at the same time. He'd spent most of his days on the Jersey turnpike between

Newark and New York. The sense of being alone here made him shiver. But perhaps that was just the chill of the morning.

He had another need. He opened the trunk of the car and located the thick roll of toilet paper his employers had so kindly provided, then stared into the trees across the car park. 'Whaddya going to do?' he asked himself as he trudged across to the trees to allow nature to take its course.

As he squatted against a sturdy stump he thought about his plans. What he had to do held no particular fear for him. He had killed dozens of times. And for this kind of money, what did one more body matter?

He finished his business in the bushes, cleaned his hands with the wipes and spray they'd provided, and took a deep breath. Then he slapped himself in the face, a way of self-motivation he'd been practising for years. He'd done it before his daughter's wedding, the day he was sent down, every time he met the boss. Every time he killed.

Alice Wenger was in her hotel room. She didn't know whether to stick or twist. But one thing was for sure: she had to get out, get away from this place for a while before she lost her mind. She decided to take a trip into Kinloch and have a meal, a drink – get smashed, if that would help. That's the way she felt. It was becoming more and more obvious that her journey back home had been a mistake. But it had been necessary. She'd watched her father die, and despite the ambivalence she felt for the man the incident would play in her mind for ever. Of that she was sure.

She was so dispirited that she rang for room service, the very thought of sitting among other people for breakfast seeming too much to bear. So she wasn't surprised when she heard the tapping at the door of her room. 'Hold on!' she shouted, pulling the cord of the dressing gown tightly around her slim waist, looking forward to coffee and croissants.

But it wasn't room service. Alice Wenger opened the door and stood still for a moment, realising she'd been half expecting the person who'd come to call. 'You better come in—'

Before she could finish, the breath was knocked from her by a sharp blow to the stomach. She staggered backwards, clutching her midriff, almost bent double. She fell back against the bed, sprawling across it just as she felt another agonising blow, this time to the head.

She was struggling for consciousness, but she felt herself drifting away, the pain, her world, disappearing into darkness. Nevertheless, she was able to grab the implement thrust into her face.

She was being pinned down. The feeling above her eye was more like pressure. Next, the pain she felt was enough to mask her throbbing head. It was as though a red-hot needle was being thrust into her eye socket.

Alice Wenger screamed in agony, then everything stopped.

Chiase had switched the satnav back on. He'd managed to change the voice imparting the instructions to that of an American woman, and the alteration had made him feel more at home. He felt more comfortable in his own skin now. The end of his job was in sight, and he was ready to do what had to be done to complete his task.

The big engine of the SUV took the gradients easily as the narrow road wound its way along the coast then disappeared into the hills, one minute a straight climb, the next a corkscrew of descending spirals. He passed by fields of sheep and cattle, stark briar, bare hedges shorn of their summer greenery and leafless trees, knotted branches reaching out like a grasping withered hand into the clear air. 'Hoboken already!' he said to himself with a chuckle.

The road rose steeply again and dropped sharply back down, the sea again visible. The day had darkened, a grey sky now lowering over the horizon.

Turn right in three hundred metres then drive for two hundred metres and you will have reached your destination.

As he followed this direction, still winding down the steep hill, Chiase could see a run-down cottage near a shingle beach. A black finger of rocks thrust out into the ocean beyond.

He recognised the place from the description in the written notes he'd been given. It was time.

Daley and Scott sat opposite the two imprisoned Doig brothers. They were handcuffed following their attack on Scott and Potts at Rowan Tree Cottage, but without the malign influence of their mother the pair appeared cowed, looking at the police officers under their brows, right eyelids both drooping in an almost identical manner. Two tall uniformed constables stood at the back of the room, just in case, and even the duty solicitor Ellis Hamilton sat further away from his clients than was his habit.

'So you don't know your names?' said Daley, already becoming exasperated by their mute silence. This was greeted by grunts from the two men.

They were remarkably similar in looks. Besides the hooded right eyes, both had tousled dark hair receding from low foreheads. The elder of the pair, Thomas apparently, had darker hair than his younger brother Inness. Inness was by a small margin the taller of the two. Both had vacant, empty expressions. They reacted with grunts, or a lowering of the head, to everything that was asked of them.

'Can yous speak at all?' asked Scott, showing more than a hint of frustration. He turned to Daley. 'For the tape, I think these are a pair of dummies.'

'I must object,' said Ellis Hamilton. 'My clients have the right to remain silent if they so wish. That doesn't make them "dummies", DI Scott.'

'What's your definition o' a dummy, then?'

'This is pointless,' said Daley. 'For the tape, this interview is at an end. I'm going to seek medical examinations of the suspects.' He clicked off the machine.

'There's no way that will be permitted, DCI Daley,' said Hamilton. 'You have no substantive evidence against these men. It's all circumstantial.'

'Aye, they just circumstantially chained their brother intae the loft,' said Scott.

'I'll ignore that.' Hamilton began to pack away his papers. 'I'm going to demand that my clients are released forthwith. And any attempt to enforce a medical examination upon them will be resisted with the utmost legal vigour. Now, gentlemen, if you will excuse me, I have things to do.' He swept out of the room without a word to his clients, who sat staring blankly at the floor.

No sooner had Hamilton left than Sergeant Shaw rushed in. 'Sir, there's been an incident at the Machrie House Hotel. It's Alice Wenger.'

'What kind of incident?' asked Daley.

'She's in an ambulance at the moment, sir. It looks as though someone tried to force themself into her room and assaulted her. Tried to remove her eye, by the looks of things.'

'Eh?' said Scott.

'The attack was disturbed by a member of staff delivering Ms Wenger's breakfast. The assailant escaped, but I believe there's hotel CCTV footage.'

'Tried tae take her eye oot! What next?' said Scott.

As Daley was about to speak Inness Doig stood and banged his cuffed hands on the table, then roared at the top of his voice. As he was being restrained by the uniformed officers, his brother joined in with a high-pitched wail.

It took Daley, Scott, Shaw and the two uniformed men to restore order, and soon the Doigs were back in their cells, though they continued to scream and shout, sounds more akin to animals than humans.

'Shaw, get two bodies up to the hospital. I want to make sure Alice Wenger comes to no more harm. Brian, we'll go to Machrie. We'll not be able to interview Wenger until she's been treated. We'll have to move fast on this, come on!'

Scott followed Daley as they rushed from the room. In minutes they were in Daley's car heading at speed for the Machrie House Hotel.

31

Chiase parked his car in a layby about a hundred yards from the lane that led to Rowan Tree Cottage. He could see the roof of the building across fields and over a small rise.

His knees aching, he managed to scale a barbed wire fence, cursing when his ring finger caught on one of the barbs and started to bleed. 'Shit!' he swore to himself as he sucked on the digit to stop the flow. 'I hate the fucking countryside. Shitting in the woods, and now this!'

He managed to focus his mind on the task in hand and moved slowly across the field, looking about to make sure nobody was watching. So intent was he on this task that he failed to notice the large cowpat before he'd stepped in it. His shoe was covered in rancid green cow shit, and, cursing as he did so, he did his best to wipe it off on the grass. His finger wouldn't stop bleeding, and now he had the contents of a cow's stomach spread across one of his expensive Italian loafers.

Much daunted, but thinking only of the hard cash, he strode on, the stench from his shoe making him want to throw up. As he edged towards the rise he lost sight of the cottage roof. He leaned into the tiny hill, and before he reached the top crouched down and craned over the rise. He could see

Rowan Tree Cottage now. The place looked deserted; no sign of life. He scanned the shingle beach, partly obscured by a large mound of rotting seaweed. A little boat was hauled up above the tideline, but that apart there was nothing – and nobody.

Chiase thought for a moment. His plan had been to grab someone, attract attention, then do what he was being paid to do, but it didn't look that easy. 'Is anything ever fucking easy?' he said to himself. Despite the chill, no smoke billowed from the cottage's single chimney, and no shadows passed behind the small, dark windows.

Slowly, Chiase crept over the rise, crouching as he went, making for the back of the dwelling, trying to stay out of the line of sight of the windows. He needed the rest of that money, and anyway, in his experience, if you walked away from a job that job would likely come back to haunt you. The people who hired men like him didn't mess about. If he didn't do what was required, he'd likely become the hunted.

As stealthily as his aching knees and hip would allow, he crouched forward. In a few more steps he removed the pistol from the back of his trouser band and held it out in front of him with both hands.

Vito Chiase might be old, but he was a stand-up guy. He could do this.

'I'm Diane Burton, the manager,' said the smartly dressed woman behind the large desk in her big office in the Machrie House Hotel. 'Please take a seat, gentlemen,' she added without getting up. The office was plush, with a picture window framing the bay and paintings of local scenes around the walls. As in most hotels, everything was underpinned by the faint smell of disinfectant that battled for dominance with Diane Burton's expensive perfume.

'I'd like to speak to the person who disturbed the attack on Ms Wenger,' said Daley once the introductions were over and he and Scott were seated.

'Donnie – Donnie O'Hara – he's only been with us for a week. He's rather shaken, as I'm sure you understand.'

'Of course, but still we need to get moving on this quickly.'

'You've got CCTV, I hear,' said Scott.

'Yes, I'll show you what we have while we wait for Donnie. He's in the kitchen with a cup of hot sweet tea.' Burton lifted the phone and spoke quietly to someone on the other end, arranging for O'Hara to attend her office. Ending the call, she typed on the keyboard in front of her, then angled a large screen towards the police officers so that both she and they could see it.

'Mr O'Hara was delivering breakfast, I believe?' said Daley.

'Yes, he was. But first I'll show you this.'

The hotel corridor looked empty, the image taken from the ceiling distorted, making everything look too close, or far away. They watched as numbers on the screen scrolled forward.

'Now, there!' said Burton, pointing excitedly at the screen.

A tiny hunched figure wearing dark trousers and a hooded top made its way towards the camera, face obscured.

'Can you pause?' said Daley.

Burton did as she was asked and the figure was frozen in mid-step.

'Whoever it is they're no' very tall,' said Scott. 'That wooden panelling comes up to my waist. I noticed it on the way in. I'm right, aye?'

'Yes, that is right,' said Burton.

'Look, their heid's just above it. This looks like a wean, Jimmy.'

'And this is the first image you have, Miss Burton?' said Daley.

'Yes, I've checked everything. There's no sign of – whoever this is – apart from this of them heading to Ms Wenger's room, then running back. Wait, I'll show you.' She let the tape run on. The small figure disappeared, there was a pause for just over a minute, and then a man in a white waiter's jacket and dark trousers pushing a trolley appeared in the corridor, passing under the camera, as had done the hooded figure. After another pause, the same hooded figure passed under the CCTV camera, this time in the opposite direction, running.

'So Ms Wenger's room was at the end, just out of sight?' asked Daley.

'Yes, that's right. As a group we feel it only right to balance the privacy of our customers against the requirements of security. I'm sure you understand, gentlemen.'

'No' quite got the right balance here,' observed Scott. 'How come this – person – could get as far as the room and only appear on one camera?'

'We'll have to establish that, DI Scott. I can assure you, the exterior of the premises is well covered by our cameras. I can't imagine why we don't have anything else.'

'And everything is working?' said Daley.

'The first thing I had checked. Every camera was in perfect working order and has been for weeks.'

'We'll need to see the recordings, nonetheless.'

'Sure. I'll give you the footage from this morning.'

'And last night,' said Scott. 'Nothing tae stop this person

fae entering the hotel some time during the night then lying low until this morning.'

'Ah, I hadn't thought of that. Consider it done.'

There was a knock on the door. It opened slowly to reveal a thin man of average height. He had sparse red hair and a pockmarked complexion. His nose was long and bulbous, a shade of purple displaying a likely fondness for alcohol – lots of it.

'Take a seat, Donnie,' said Burton, pointing to a chair at one end of her desk. The man, still dressed in his waiter's uniform, sat down. He eyed the detectives warily.

'Mr O'Hara, it would appear you did Ms Wenger a great service this morning,' said Daley.

O'Hara mashed his mouth before he spoke. 'Aye, I suppose I did.' He was wringing his hands, as though washing them in soap and water.

'Can you tell us exactly what happened? From the moment you knocked on the door of Ms Wenger's room, please.'

'I didna; knock, that is. I jeest heard screams, so I opened the door tae find oot what was wrong.' He glanced worriedly at Burton. 'I hope that was the right thing tae dae?'

'Of course!' she replied. 'I dread to think what might have happened if you hadn't come along.'

'I didna dae anything special, just walked in the room.'

'What did you see?' asked Daley.

'This wee lad on top o' Ms Wenger.'

'A lad, as in boy?'

'Aye, I think so.'

'But you're no' sure,' said Scott.

'No, I didnae see a face, or that. I suppose I just thought it

236

was a boy. He – it – had a hood up, but looked just like a young fella. You know, shape an' that.'

'So you never saw any features at all?'

'No. The hood was up all the time. Ms Wenger was jeest lying there – like, oot o' it. The boy – or whatever – jeest took off, pushed past me. I was going tae try and catch – it – but I thought I'd better look after Ms Wenger. I got on the phone as quick as I could. I'm sorry if I didna dae the right thing.' He looked from the police officers to his boss.

'You did exactly the right thing, Mr O'Hara. Your duty was to ensure the well-being of your guest. It's our job to catch whoever did this,' said Daley.

'Is she going tae be okay?'

'I hope so. We'll be off to the hospital as soon as we finish here.'

'Her face was bleeding – it looked nasty.'

'Apart from Ms Wenger – helping her, I mean – did you touch anything?' asked Daley.

'The phone – the one on the bedside.'

'We don't permit our staff to carry their mobiles when they're on duty, DCI Daley,' said Burton.

'Did the assailant leave anything behind, Mr O'Hara?'

'Aye, something fell on the bed.'

'You didnae touch it?' said Scott.

'No, I'm no' that stupid.'

'What was it?' asked Daley.

'Like a wee hammer – something you'd use for model-making, or that kind o' thing.'

'A wee hammer?' Scott looked bemused.

'Aye, jeest that.'

'We sealed off the room as your desk sergeant advised. I think your team are up there now, Mr Daley.'

'Yes; we'll join them shortly. Thank you, Mr O'Hara. If you remember anything else, you know where to find us.'

'At the station in Kinloch, aye, I do. I hope the lady recovers okay.' He stood and walked to the door. He turned to face them. 'Aye, an' I hope you catch her that did it, tae.'

'Her? You said you thought it was a boy,' said Scott.

O'Hara shuffled from foot to foot. 'Boy, lassie – you know whoot I mean.'

'Thank you, Mr O'Hara. Please go home, take the rest of the day off. I'll pass your address on to the detectives here, just in case they need it.'

'Aye, thank you.' He nodded and left the room, closing the door behind him.

'Right, gentlemen, if you give me a moment I'll take you to Ms Wenger's room.' Burton picked up the phone from her desk and spoke quietly to whoever was on the other end.

'What did you make o' this O'Hara, Jimmy?' said Scott, leaning into his colleague's ear.

'A small wager, Brian?'

'Nah, the odds don't look too good. He's at the madam, no mistake.'

'We'll give him some time to relax, then we'll pay him a visit.'

'Right, that's me ready. I'll show you to Ms Wenger's room.' Burton stood and held her office door open for the police officers.

Chiase was within a few yards of Rowan Tree Cottage when he heard the distant rumble of an engine. He threw himself to the ground just as a taxi turned on to the rutted lane that led to the dwelling.

Chiase swore to himself. He was partially hidden by a hummock of grass, but if anyone looked in his direction they'd be able to spot him. He considered trying to slither back the way he'd come, but reckoned that movement was more likely to catch the attention of those arriving at Rowan Tree Cottage. Things were most certainly not going the way he'd envisaged.

He squinted as one tall and one small figure emerged from the taxi. The shorter of the two looked like an old woman, the other a middle-aged man, though with his eyesight it was hard to be absolutely sure. He looked on as the woman handed money to the driver before both she and the other passenger made for the cottage. Neither of them looked in his direction. He lowered his head and sighed with relief. The taxi was reversing quickly back up the lane and on to the main road. Chiase remained still, observing Rowan Tree Cottage. The taxi disappeared back up the hill towards Kinloch.

He approached the corner of the house, hopefully out of sight of the windows. He held his pistol firmly now, and could feel his legs tremble. This was a sensation he'd become used to over the years. Whether it was down to fear or anticipation, he'd never been sure. The feeling had unnerved him at first, but now he realised that having a hit of adrenalin was essential if he was going to get the job done.

He was at the rear of the cottage, sliding his back along the rough wall. He had to think what to do for the best – how he was going to gain access to the place.

The waves hissed off the pebbles in the small bay and a gull cried mournfully overhead while Chiase worked things out in his head. He had been assured that the family barely left their home, yet he'd just seen two of them arrive in a cab. Just as he made up his mind, a noise from behind made him turn quickly.

Two shots rang around the hillside, sending a flurry of birds squawking into the sky.

32

Liz had left her son at nursery and she and Ella Scott were heading for lunch in the County Hotel. As she drove across the head of the loch she felt much better than at almost any point since returning to Kinloch. Though their relationship had often been a strained one, it appeared as though they had bonded over their mutual experience of being attacked by men. Ella chatted away cheerily as they drove up Main Street.

Liz parked in the patrons' car park behind the hotel, and they made their way into the County by way of the back door, around which lay cigarette butts stubbed out carelessly by those addicted to nicotine and now banished to pursue their habit out of doors.

'Would you look at that,' said Ella Scott. 'Dirty buggers. They could at least put them in that big ashtray.'

They carried on up a flight of stone steps and into a corridor. When they entered the bar there was a buzz that neither woman had expected. In fact, the place was busy, certainly for lunchtime.

'What's the occasion?' said Liz, forcing her way through the bar to where Annie held court.

'Lovely tae see you, Liz. You've not been in much – you know, since you came back,' replied Annie, being as diplomatic as she could. Everyone in Kinloch knew what had happened to Liz, it seemed.

'I'm feeling much better, Annie, thank you. Ella and I thought we'd have a bite to eat, but you seem rushed off your feet.'

'It's a big day. We're jeest waiting for Charlie Murray tae come back fae the council meeting in Lochgilphead.'

'Oh? I know he's a pillar of the community and all that, but I'd no idea how important he was.'

'This is a special meeting, Liz. No doubt Mr Daley will have telt you that the owners are wanting tae turn this place intae flats.'

'Yes, he did as a matter of fact. I was so sorry to hear it. Here was – well, it was like a second home to us when I first arrived. In fact, Jim was living upstairs.'

'Aye, that he was.' Annie smiled.

'You're looking quite chipper on it, despite everything,' observed Ella.

'That's why everyone's here. Charlie Murray has raised an official objection. You know, for planning permission. This hotel's been here for well o'er a hundred years. And being right in the centre of the toon, well, he thinks they'll knock it back.'

'That would be great,' said Liz.

'It would be bloody fantastic! Noo, whoot can I get you ladies?'

As the pair ordered drinks and perused the menus they were greeted by another familiar face.

'Hamish, how are you?' said Liz.

'Mair tae the point, how are you?'

'I'm fine. This is all very exciting.'

'Aye, well I pray they get what they're hoping for. I had a bad dream aboot a' this last night. Just me sitting wae a dram amongst a pile o' rubble.'

'That must have been upsetting for you, Hamish.'

The old man nodded his head sagely. 'It wisnae all bad. I'd a fair bumper o' a dram, and every time I took a sip at it, damn me if it didna jeest fill itself right back up again. Canna say much for the surroundings, right enough.'

'Oor Brian used tae have a glass like that,' said Ella with a sniff.

'There's plenty o' room at my table if you ladies would like a seat.' Hamish pushed his way through the throng. 'Jeest you move aside, Johnny Rocks; can you no' see there's ladies present?'

The younger man moved hurriedly. 'I'm jeest making a wee post for Facebook, Hamish. So folk that's no' here can see the place getting its reprieve.' Johnny grinned.

'Well you're in the way, Cecil B. DeMille. And I hope your phrasebook mates don't get a fair gunker.'

'No way, Hamish. You know oor Charlie, everyone on the council hangs on his every word. They'll no' stand up tae him, that's for sure.'

As Liz, Ella and Hamish sat at the table, Ella leaned in so the old man could hear her. 'Is that his real name, Johnny Rocks?'

'No, no' a bit o' it. He's been the skipper o' two fine boats, and damn me, he's sunk them both. Hence "Rocks".'

'You can find a name for everything in Kinloch.'

'So we can, Ella. And this gathering, tae me, should be called counting your chickens before they're hatched.' He sipped on a dram that didn't replenish itself.

'This is what you're looking for, sir,' said the officer in the white suit, one of those examining the room where Alice Wenger had been attacked. He handed Daley a plastic evidence bag holding, as described by O'Hara, a small red hammer. 'It was found on the bed, sir. Just here.' He pointed towards the end of the bed. The duvet had been messed up, and the light carpet stained with drops of Alice Wenger's blood.

Daley held the hammer up to the light of the window. 'No prints?'

'No, sir. The assailant must have been wearing gloves.'

'So you've nothing significant?'

'We're looking for fibres now, but it's a long shot. You know hotel rooms, no matter how clean they look there's bound to be contamination from previous guests.'

'I used tae have a hammer like that,' said Scott when Daley handed him the bag.

'When you were studying gnome carpentry?' said Daley.

'Naw. It was part of my Meccano set. You must have had one. I made a lorry.'

'Impressive, Brian.'

'No' really. The wheels fell off on the day I made it. I started tae build the Eiffel Tower, but my father had tae pawn the kit before I'd finished the base. The drunken auld bastard.'

Daley turned to his forensics man. 'No sign of the blade, or whatever it was that caused the injury to Ms Wenger's eye?'

'Nothing, sir. Though we're pretty sure that was caused by something other than the hammer, as you say.'

Daley examined the bag again and stroked his chin, deep in thought.

'What's on your mind, big man?'

'Just something the doctor said, Brian. We can't do much here. We'll get back to the office and start someone off getting this CCTV footage analysed. You never know. Then it's off to the hospital again.'

'We're never oot o' there, Jimmy.'

'I know. I've read books like that – cops never out of hospitals. Think how poor Alice Wenger feels.'

'The hotel should gie her a discount. She's spent mair time in there than she has here.'

'Let me know if you turn anything up,' said Daley as the forensics officer went back about his business.

33

The old woman ran as fast as she could along the slick pebbles of the beach. As she panted with the effort the wheeze in her throat became more pronounced. She was fit for her age but too old for this, she had no doubt of that. As she ran, tears were stinging her eyes, her throat aching with the pain of shock and loss.

She stumbled towards a large rock, and slipped behind it, trying desperately to catch her breath, back pressed against the cold stone as her spare chest heaved. She tried to gather her thoughts. She was in no doubt as to what she'd seen as she looked round the back of the cottage. A man she did not recognise had appeared from nowhere and killed her son. Two sharp shots, one to the heart, the other to the head, had felled her boy like a great tree being hacked at by a saw. He had entered her home; she had no choice but to seek sanctuary along the beach.

She felt desperation, something that had become a stranger during the course of her mundane life over the last few decades. Now that life could be nearing its end.

She peered around the rock with one eye, looking down the beach the way she had come. Distantly she could see the man standing sniffing the air, looking around, searching – searching for her!

She held her breath now, feeling almost as though she would black out. If he came nearer she faced the almost impossible task of scaling the cliff in order to escape. The only other option was the sea, and she was no swimmer. Taking a deep, rasping breath, she leaned round the rock again. To her great relief the man was walking away from her, back towards the cottage.

Ginny Doig said a silent prayer and slid down to her knees. What was she to do now?

Alice Wenger was in the same room she'd occupied following the death of her father. This time, though, one eye was covered by a large white patch, through which a speck of blood had leaked and dried brown. Her face was pale – grey, almost. When Daley and Scott came through the door she barely acknowledged them, staring blankly into space with her one good eye.

'Ms Wenger, I'm so sorry this has happened to you,' said Daley, standing at the end of her bed.

'I'm sorry I ever came back,' Wenger replied flatly. 'It's been the biggest mistake of my life; that and being born.'

'I've spoken to the doctor. It would appear that there is no permanent damage to your eye.'

'No. That's twice I've been lucky.'

'What do you mean?'

'Ask the doc. I've been attacked that way before, Detective Daley.'

'By whom?'

'You must be pretty dumb if you can't work that out.' She sniggered mirthlessly.

247

'Please indulge me, Ms Wenger.'

'Why do you think I ran away in the first place? When I was a kid, I mean.'

'I don't know. You've not exactly been forthcoming on that subject, Alice.'

'Take my brothers, for example; you've seen them. Tell me what you think.'

'I don't know them well enough to form any opinion.'

'They're morons, detective. All three of them are like . . .' She didn't finish the sentence.

'Were they always like that?' asked Scott, remembering the photographs of three bright young lads he'd seen at Rowan Tree Cottage.

'Hell no, they were just normal kids – like me. Hey, they picked on me, teased me a little. I was a girl, you can imagine what it's like growing up with three brothers, right?'

Daley and Scott nodded.

'But there was no harm in them. It was just being kids, like I say.'

'So what happened?' asked Daley.

Wenger ripped the patch away, making Scott wince at the sound of the tape being prised from her forehead. Already her eye was swollen and discoloured as a result of the attack. 'You see this?'

'Yes.'

'She failed the first time with me, so she thought she'd come back and finish the job.'

'Who? What job?' asked Daley.

'I don't know – something she learned when she worked in the hospital. She and my father learned.'

'Eh?' said Scott.

248

'Hell, I don't know the name for it, I just know what it does.' Alice Wenger looked suddenly scared. Gone the down-to-earth Southern manner. The years appeared to drop away, revealing the frightened girl she had once been, the teenager who thought she had escaped her tormentors. 'It takes away your mind, Mr Daley. It destroys you.'

Daley decided to leave Alice Wenger to rest. Instead he and Scott made for Dr Spence's office. The elderly clinician was staring at his computer through a pair of half-moon glasses.

'Well timed, gentlemen,' he said as the detectives entered his office.

'How so?' asked Daley.

Spence beckoned them to join him behind his desk. On the large computer screen an image was frozen, clearly a paused frame of a video he'd been watching. 'I hope you have strong stomachs,' he said. 'I found this on YouTube, of all places.'

'My stomach isn't particularly strong,' said Daley.

'Nevertheless, I'm sure what you're about to see will be of great interest to you as far as your investigations are concerned, I'd say. Are you ready?'

Daley took a deep breath and nodded, but just as Dr Spence was about to press play Scott held up his hand.

'Hang on – I need my specs. I cannae see bugger all withoot them these days.' He fished in his pocket, found his spectacles and placed them on the end of his nose, in a manner not unlike Spence's own.

'Ready now?' asked Daley.

'Aye, batter on, doc.'

Daley narrowed his eyes as the footage sprang into motion. The film was in black and white, poor resolution, perhaps from the fifties or sixties judging by its venerability. Daley reckoned that monochrome was no bad thing as he took in what was happening. A man, drugged in some way but still conscious, was strapped to a gurney by thick leather bonds. He was naked to the waist and his shaven head lolled about as though he was blind drunk. Two nurses sporting the headwear of the time secured it with a belt across his forehead, pulled tight like a massive watchstrap. The semiconscious man protested feebly, but to no avail.

From behind the nurses appeared a taller figure, a man with short, slicked-back hair, most of his face obscured by a surgical mask. He was wearing a white coat and held two medical instruments, one in each hand.

Though the sound quality on the video was poor, Daley could make out his words as he asked the nurses to stand back, while the camera zoomed in closer on the head of the man strapped to the table.

'This is the interesting bit,' said Spence, engrossed by the on-screen proceedings.

'Oh, great,' said Daley, feeling his stomach churn.

The man in the mask and the white coat leaned over the subdued patient. In his left hand he wielded something long, probably metallic, which he placed on the eye socket of the man on the gurney. In his other hand he held something Daley couldn't quite make out for a while, until a movement of the hand revealed a small hammer.

'That's just like what we found in the room at Machrie, Jim,' said Scott.

Daley was about to reply when a wail emanated from the computer. Despite his obvious sedation, the patient strapped to the operating table screamed as with a few taps of the hammer the instrument held against his eye socket was visibly inserted into his head, hammered there like a nail. The patient's wail turned into an agonised scream as the instrument was pivoted swiftly from side to side before being removed as quickly as it had been inserted. At this point the film stuttered and the screen went blank.

Daley felt sick, really sick, his knuckles white as he gripped the back of Spence's chair. He tried to speak, but words wouldn't come.

'What the fuck was that?' said Scott, doing Daley's job for him.

'That, gentlemen, was a trans-orbital lobotomy. Barbaric, of course, but at one time considered to be cutting edge, if you pardon the pun.'

'You mean the people doing that were proper doctors?' asked Daley, still looking shaken.

'Very much so! The old way of doing this operation was to trepan the skull, then remove the frontal lobe of the brain – a messy, costly, dangerous business. Then it was discovered that the skull was at its thinnest at the top of the eye socket. A quick tap, and in you went. A few well-directed slashes, and job done. Of course, the procedure more often than not ended in complete disaster, as did much of the so-called "psycho-surgery" of the time. The patient was usually left with the mind of a child – or dead.'

'What kind of doctor would countenance that?' asked Daley.

'Curious ones, Mr Daley. In those days almost anything went in the name of science and development. No matter what the cost.' Spence removed his glasses. 'In the end the operation was being performed by nurses, or even orderlies.

Usually took place in those awful institutions in which they incarcerated the mentally ill. We've come a long way in a relatively short time, you know.'

'Yous have? They took my auntie Jenny's leg off no' that long ago and she died on the spot. You've maybe no' come as far as yous think.' Scott pursed his lips.

'It's monstrous,' said Daley, still staring at the empty screen.

'You're telling me, Jimmy. She was a lovely auld dear. Ninety-six, tae.' Scott shook his head while Daley looked at him with an expression that could best be described as *please shut up, Brian.*

'Indeed. Hard to believe that it was still being used when I started my training. Mind you, that's not yesterday.' Spence polished his glasses with the end of his tie. 'They had a nickname for it – used most of the time in fact, even by professionals.'

'What was that?' asked Daley.

Spence placed his glasses back on the end of his nose and looked at Daley over the rim. 'An ice pick lobotomy, DCI Daley.'

'So wait,' said Scott. 'Dae you think that's what this – person – was trying to do tae Alice Wenger, doc?'

'More than that, Inspector Scott. I think it was done to her brothers – the one I examined, at any rate. I had hoped it wasn't the case, but now I'm almost certain. It will require brain scans to confirm this, but in the light of what has just happened to Ms Wenger – well, a sound bet, I'd say.'

'I believe Mr Doig trained as a doctor,' said Daley.

'Yes, and specialised in mental illness, by all accounts. Never qualified, though.'

Scott made a face. 'Bloody Frankenstein stuff this, Jimmy.'

Daley nodded. 'If you could keep a close eye on Ms Wenger for us please, Dr Spence, I'd be much obliged. I'm so glad whoever tried to do this to her didn't succeed.'

'Yes. Very mysterious – the whole thing is bizarre.'

Leaving Spence to his work, Daley and Scott walked into the corridor at Kinloch police office.

'That's a shocker, big man. What now?'

'Get Shaw to round up Ginny Doig. She's got a lot of questions to answer. And our waiter from Machrie House Hotel, get him brought in too. But just for "further enquiries", if you know what I mean.'

'Nae bother.'

'Meanwhile – and please don't lecture me – I need a quick drink.'

'After that, so do I, Jimmy.'

Daley smiled. 'Just a swift one for me and a ginger beer and lime for you, Brian, eh? Alice Wenger has a cop at her door, and as for her brothers . . .'

'No wonder auld Doig took a heider off that cliff, eh?'

'You would think. But let's go through the process, Brian.'

As Scott called Sergeant Shaw, Daley went to the toilet where he was copiously sick. For the first time since his rehabilitation, he felt seriously ill. He'd always had a weak stomach, but seeing that operation performed with such ruthless, uncaring efficiency had made it literally churn. He hoped the sensation would pass, though the images of what had been done would stay with him for ever. Like so much else he'd seen, he reckoned.

34

Vito Chiase cursed his luck. If the man he'd killed hadn't surprised him he'd have been able to get into the house and do the job he'd come to do. But why were there only two people there? That wasn't what he'd been led to expect.

The old woman had disappeared and he had neither the will nor the knees to pursue her. This was a shit job in the arse end of the world. He hated himself for being so stupid, loathed himself for his greed. He'd have got by – he had enough. But he dreaded ending up in some shitty retirement home. One thing was for sure: his kids wouldn't come to the rescue. The more he reasoned, the more he came to terms with what had just happened – what he'd done. But it was time to go, time to leave this place. It wasn't his fault that the job wasn't finished. Whoever had planned this was a useless cocksucker.

Chiase ducked across the fields to his SUV, just in time to hear the phone he'd been given ring. He opened the door and answered the call.

'No, I only got one of them. The old woman fucked off down the shore.'

'This isn't the kind of professionalism we're paying for, Mr Chiase.' The voice on the other end was calm. He recognised the Scottish accent, though in this case it was much weaker than in the guy he'd met at the airport: cultured, almost.

'You pay me, or I come and find you. You think I'm some punk? There was nobody here when I arrived. These people – only two of them – arrived in a cab. Whaddya want me to do, conjure the rest of them up outta thin air, asshole?'

'What I want you to do is lie low. You finish this job, or we finish you. I hope I'm clear.'

'You threatening me, you prick?'

'Hide somewhere and wait for my call.' The line went dead.

'You—' Chiase was about to throw the phone to the ground, but thought better of it. Instead he got back into the car and drove off.

There were plenty of people in the County Hotel when Daley and Scott arrived, but nobody was speaking. The patrons were all staring into space, or swirling the remainder of their drinks in glasses. Daley waved to his wife and Ella Scott, who were sitting beside Hamish at the back of the bar. The old man at their side looked like a sail bereft of wind. He was sitting forward, staring into an empty glass that had no doubt once contained whisky, no smile crossing his face, no tall tale on his lips.

Annie greeted them mirthlessly, her eyes red-rimmed.

'Yes, gentlemen, what can I get you?'

'I'm sorry,' said Daley. 'Have we walked in on a funeral reception?'

'Aye, yous have in a way.'

'Who's deid?' asked Scott.

'This place.' Annie gestured airily around the room with

one hand. 'This'll likely be someone's lounge, or shower room. The planning permission has been granted. Charlie Murray's jeest off the phone from the council meeting in Lochgilphead. The County Hotel will soon be extinct, so enjoy it while yous can.'

'That's shit,' said Scott. 'What will you dae?'

'Och, I'll be okay. There's a job going at the petrol station. Better hours, but less money, mind you.'

Scott looked around. 'But the craic's bound tae be better than this. Even o'er a gallon o' unleaded.'

'Can I have a large malt please, Annie?' said Daley. 'And whatever my wife's table are drinking.'

'You're fine, Mr Daley!' shouted Hamish. 'I'm jeest going tae take a walk back hame. I've nae heart for drinking this day.'

'What about you two?' Daley didn't need to shout to his wife and Ella, such was the prevailing silence in the bar.

'I think we'll be off shortly, tae,' said Ella. 'It's no' exactly a' the fun o' the fair in here.' She rolled her eyes.

'Ginger beer an' lime for me, Annie,' said Scott. 'I just hope they dae that as well at the Douglas Arms as you dae it in here.'

Daley looked at Liz, who was staring at the floor. She'd seemed happier that morning, more like her old self. Now she bore the haunted, troubled look he'd become so used to since her attack. 'Darling, anything?'

'No, I'll take Ella and Hamish back home. Young James will soon be out of nursery anyway, so it's time to get moving.'

Annie handed Scott his drink and the large dram in a small glass for Daley. 'On the hoose,' she said.

'Are you sure?' Daley asked.

'Aye, I am. I've never taken as much as one penny fae that

till in a' these years, but noo – well, if oor good customers can't get a thank you for all their business, who can, eh?'

Daley looked round as he put the glass to his mouth. This was undoubtedly the quietest he'd ever seen anywhere in Kinloch, never mind a public bar – the library was louder than this.

He tilted back his head and drank the whisky in one. The spirit warmed his throat as it went down; he hoped it would also banish the pictures that were playing across his mind of the unfortunate man tied to the gurney. He thought about the Doig family: a dead father, three sons who'd possibly suffered terribly, a distraught, estranged sister and Ginny Doig.

Daley remembered Dr Spence's words. *In the end the operation was carried out by orderlies.* He shuddered at the thought of the tiny woman with the piercing eyes going about the business of removing her children's minds. It all fitted: her husband had worked as a trainee doctor in a hospital for the mentally ill, where she had worked as a domestic assistant. There could be no other explanation. Systematically, the Doigs had destroyed the lives of their own. But why? It was as wicked as almost anything he'd encountered in his career. 'Come on, Brian. This isn't quite the light relief I had in mind. We better get back up the road and see what Mrs Doig has to say for herself.'

'Aye, I'd rather stick my heid in a buckct o' pish than stay in this morgue any longer,' replied Scott under his breath, making sure Annie wouldn't hear.

The pair said goodbye to their wives and the rest of the down-in-the-mouth patrons of the County Hotel bar and made their way back to Kinloch police office.

*

Alice Wenger was dozing when she was roused by the knock on the door of her side room at Kinloch hospital. She had to squint with her uncovered eye to identify the person now entering the room with a large bunch of flowers.

'I hope this is okay, Ms Wenger?' said the tall policeman at her side.

'Sure, she's one of my oldest friends – the oldest, in fact.'

'Alison – Alice. How are you?' said Sheena McKay. 'I came as soon as I heard.'

'That's kind of you. The flowers are lovely. Take a seat, Sheena.'

As her old friend brought a chair to the side of her hospital bed, Alice did her very best to smile, anything not to show her true feelings. This became harder when Sheena started to sob.

'I'm sorry. It's just – what with you losing your father, and now this – well, it's brought back memories.'

'You know me, Sheena. I ain't no shrinking violet. Never have been, never will be.'

'I know you're strong – goodness knows, you've had to be. But all this; you must wish you'd never come back.'

'The thought had crossed my mind.'

'I remember when you used to come to my house – you know, when you were so upset about what they were doing to you.'

'Sorry?'

Sheena McKay cleared her throat and lowered her voice. 'Don't you remember? You told me about what they used to do to you.'

For a moment, Alice's mind was blank. Then, slowly she recalled conversations she'd had with her friend, the woman who was now sitting in front of her. It all seemed so, so long ago. She had forgotten she'd confided in anyone.

'You've got some memory, girl,' she said. 'Imagine you remembering all that shit.'

'I suppose you've blocked it out of your mind.'

'I guess.'

Without warning, Sheena rushed from her chair and enveloped her old friend in a hug. 'I don't care – whatever you need, just ask. It's been so good to see you after all this time – to know you're alive. Whatever we have is yours, Alice.'

'That's so kind of you, Sheena. But as soon as I get the all-clear from here I'm going back to California.'

'Won't the police want you to stay until they find who did this to you? What if they try again?'

'I'm safe now – there's a cop at my door. And when I get out I'll be much better off away from – well, away from here. Anyway, I have a good lawyer, so they can't keep me by force; he'll see to that. I'll come back for the trial. Once that witch who calls herself my mother gets her dues.'

'I'm sure you're right.' Sheena hesitated. 'Can I ask you a question?'

'Sure, go ahead. If it's about my eye, don't worry. It's going to be just fine.'

'No, I mean . . . what happened? When you went away?'

'I told you.'

'No, about – well, you know.'

'I don't know, Sheena.'

Sheena McKay paused for a moment. 'You were pregnant. What happened to the baby – your baby?'

The colour drained from Alice Wenger's face, leaving it almost as pale as the patch that covered her eye.

'I'm sorry. I shouldn't have said anything. That was thoughtless of me.'

'No, no, it's okay. I suppose, like you say, I've kinda blocked things out – bottled them up.'

Sheena looked at her sadly. 'What did happen to the child you were carrying?'

'I was a kid, right? I was in a strange country with nobody to help me. I met these nuns. They took me in. When I had the baby, well . . .'

'They gave it up for adoption?'

'Yeah, that's what they did.' Tears began to fall down Alice's face.

'I'm so sorry. I should learn to keep my mouth shut.'

'No, it's not your fault, Sheena. You just forget these things on purpose. It does no harm to be reminded of reality now and again.'

As her old friend hugged her tight, Alice Wenger's face was expressionless. She was remembering the past.

35

Daley and Scott arrived back at Kinloch police office, a short walk up the road from the misery that was the County Hotel. Sergeant Shaw was busy at the front desk filling in custody forms.

'How are our guests?'

'The Doig boys? Fine, sir. I'm just waiting for word from the officers I sent out to pick up Ginny Doig. O'Hara is on his way, but I think he's suspicious.'

'How so?'

'Keeps saying he told you everything in Machrie, apparently.'

'He should have said less, then we might no' have smelled a rat. Coffee before we start, Jimmy?'

'Tea, please, Brian. It looks like we're in for a busy time. I'll have to let Symington know what's happening.'

Leaving Scott to the beverages, Daley made his way to his glass box. He sat back heavily, and leaned his face towards the ceiling. He was happy to be back at work, but, as had always been the case, he knew that certain aspects of the job would never cease to horrify him.

He worried about Liz. He had hoped she was on the mend, but in the solemn surroundings of the hotel she had looked as miserable as ever. Perhaps she was just falling in line with the rest of the gloomy clientele. He supposed he'd find out for sure when he went home.

He puzzled over Ginny Doig. The family had endured a terrible reputation for ruthlessness for generations, but if Dr Spence was right, what they had done was beyond ruthless. To destroy the lives of others was bad enough, but to mutilate one's own children was of another order altogether.

He could see the malevolent face of Ginny Doig staring at him in his mind's eye. How could any mother do that to her children? He wondered again. He supposed he was dealing with just another evil individual. Man's inhumanity to man never ceased to appal him.

The phone on his desk rang.

'Sir, we have a situation at Rowan Tree Cottage.' Shaw's voice was tight with concern.

'Another one?'

'It's Thorbin Doig, sir. He's dead.'

Mike Strong ended the call. He was now deep in thought. The situation he was facing was more complicated than he'd envisaged.

He looked at the cheap mobile in his hand. He almost keyed in a number, but clicked the device off in the nick of time, remembering he must never make this particular call from anywhere near home. If things were beginning to run off course, it was time to build some precautions into the plan. Old age and experience had taught him that, at least.

He walked across to the table where sat two bottles of malt whisky and some crystal glasses. He poured a large measure and thought about the future. All his life he'd been careful, staying just on the right side of the law, observing the accepted protocols his position demanded. Now he was straying into unknown waters.

He thought of his partners: one dead, the other fading away like a dying grape on the vine. He sipped at the expensive malt thoughtfully. That he wasn't in control of events was true, but he could still influence them. He pondered briefly on the end of his life, and the fact he had no child to pass on his genes. Was that the ultimate demise, nothing left of you in the universe? This was an old ache, but like chronic pain it was one Strong had learned to ignore.

He sat back behind his desk and mulled things over. Desperate problems required desperate measures. He pocketed the cheap mobile, drained his glass and left the study. In Mike Strong's experience, it was always possible to turn things in his favour.

Scott's suit was covered by a white paper overall as he knelt over the body. Dressed likewise Daley stared at the corpse of Thorbin Doig from a standing position under the bright arc lights set up by the SOCO team. A police photographer was taking shots, the flash from his camera bright in the fading light of the cold evening.

'One tae the heid, one tae the heart. This is a pro, Jimmy,' said Scott, his voice muffled behind his mask.

'You would think so, Brian. But who – Ginny Doig? She might be wicked, but this . . .'

'Well, there's nae sign o' her, that's for sure.'

'So, we think that she cuts up the brains of her kids and treats them like slaves for years, before she chains one of them in the loft then shoots him like a professional assassin. Really?'

'Folk dae strange things. Me and you know better than maist aboot that.'

'True.'

Daley stared at the body of the overweight, middle-aged man. If Ginny Doig was responsible he'd got it wrong, very wrong. He had never suspected she would do this. He wondered if he was just no longer up to the job. Then again, Scott had been thinking along the same lines: realising that Ginny Doig may be a monster, but not tagging her as an imminent danger. In retrospect, he supposed they had both been naive. But still he felt guilty that he'd let Ginny Doig go free, though it was hard to think how he could have held her in custody at the time.

'We're ready to move the body, sir,' said a white-suited SOCO officer.

'Right. Time we all got out of this cold. Good work, Sergeant Jackson.' Daley stared down at the face of Thorbin Doig. He'd only ever seen him wearing a vacant expression, apparently devoid of any sense or feeling. But the eyes of the dead man that now stared blankly into the inky black sky seemed – even in death – to be filled with terror.

'We'll have tae call off the search for that auld harridan, Jimmy. It's getting too dark.'

'Yes, Brian. But the pickup is still here, and that wreck on the bricks hasn't moved for twenty years by the look of things.'

'You're right. There's grass growing up through the front seats.'

'Has anyone been in there?'

'In the van? No, sir, not to my knowledge; the boys shone a torch inside when our dead man here was missing. But that's it,' said Jackson, getting ready to remove the remains of Thorbin Doig.

Scott rolled his eyes. 'How dae you know Mrs Doig's no' hiding in there?'

'Not my responsibility, DI Scott. I'm just dealing with the forensic evidence.'

'It's like the auld Rootes Group o'er at Linwood. Dae you mind, Jimmy?'

'Chrysler, you mean?'

'Aye, that was after. One guy put on the wheels, and another blew up the tyres. If you did anything but that, oot they'd all go on strike. I had a friend that worked there – made Hillman Imps.'

'Really?' said Daley, feigning interest.

'Aye. At the madam, so he was. The security had their eye on him for years – checked him and the wheelbarrow every time he went off-site.'

'Did they find anything?'

'Nothing. Twenty-two years and they never caught him. Made a packet on the side, mind you.'

'How?' asked Daley suddenly puzzled.

'Stealing. How do you think?'

'If they were checking him every night how did he manage that?'

'He was stealing wheelbarrows. Every bugger in Renfrewshire had a wheelbarrow they bought fae Davie. He was a clever bugger, right enough.' A look verging on admiration crossed Scott's face.

'Don't you think you should have investigated that,

Brian? I mean, after all, you are a police officer.'

'I only heard the story at his funeral. Poor bastard was killed in a car accident.'

'What happened?'

'He got knocked doon by this bloke driving a Hillman Imp.'

'Oh,' said Daley. 'Poetic justice, then.'

'Eh?'

'Never mind, Brian. Come on, we've got more than wheelbarrows to worry about. We'll have a look in this van. Should have been done long ago.'

Scott pulled his torch from his pocket, and the pair headed to the wreck of the old Transit. The vehicle was propped up on bricks, a long crack across the windscreen. It was missing one passenger window, while the other had been taped up.

Daley pulled open the driver's door. It creaked and cracked so much that he began to wonder if it might come off in his hand, but with a bit of force he managed to prise it open. 'Here, give me your torch, please, Brian.'

Scott handed his friend the torch and Daley looked round the cab. The seats were perished, and looked as though some creature might well have been gnawing at them. There was some detritus on the floor; mostly ancient drinks cans, almost as rusted as the vehicle itself. A faded newspaper sat next to a shrivelled plastic carrier bag, the name it once bore bordering on invisibility. Daley pulled the bag from under the passenger seat and shook it, but it proved to be empty.

Leaning on the steering wheel, he realised how over-sized it felt. He'd driven vans exactly like this when he was first in the police and this was the first time such a thought had struck him. Fashions changed in everything – even steering wheels, it seemed. He supposed that with power-assisted steering much smaller ones were all that were necessary. It was also strange to see it devoid of the buttons and gadgets to be found in contemporary vans and cars. Daley couldn't help wondering if people were the same; does everyone get to the point where they are no longer fit for purpose, left behind by a younger, fitter, more tech-savvy generation who marvel at the antiquated nature of those who went before?

Scott had managed to crack open the passenger door and was examining the contents of the glove compartment. 'Not a thing in here apart fae a spanner and an' auld Green Shield stamps book. I'd forgotten they things existed.'

'Huh, me too,' said Daley with a shrug. 'Come on, we'll have a look at the back.'

As Daley pulled at one of the back doors, instead of producing the sound of rusted metal and cracking, it opened with nothing more than a squeak.

'That's strange. Been used recently – and often, eh?' said Scott. 'Here, I'll get in the back – just in case you take a heider off something.'

'Thanks for the vote of confidence, Brian.'

'I know you've lost weight, but you're still as tall. I'm a better fit. Try and be so sensitive in your auld age, Jimmy.'

Daley made a face as he handed Scott the torch and watched his DI climb into the back of the van, flashing the beam about as he went.

'Empty, apart fae this.' Scott directed the torch down upon an old metal box secured by a stout padlock. It was waist height, but reasonably long. It didn't look as decrepit as the vehicle in which it sat, but something about it made Daley think it might be older.

'Can you move it, Brian?'

'Aye, but it's heavy.' Scott strained as he tried to move the box along the back of the van.

'I'll get some bodies and get it back to Kinloch. We'll have tae get the padlock off with a pair of bolt cutters, anyway.' Daley marched off to find some help, as the stars of a late November evening began to twinkle over the black croft.

36

Mike Strong parked his car in the leafy Edinburgh street. The call he made was from the cheap mobile. The response of the person he called irritated him, and he had to threaten more than cajole to make sure that he was making his point. That done, Strong left the car and headed for the three-storey town house that was home to his young colleague Blair Williams.

'Mike, how are you?' said Amy Williams as she opened the front door, letting a warm glow from the hall illuminate her caller on the doorstep. She made a great play of kissing him, smacking her lips and making the 'mwah' sound that so irritated him these days; not that Amy wasn't attractive. She was slim and tall, with flaxen hair tumbling over her shoulders. Her blue eyes were piercing – not unlike those of her husband, he thought, although the theory that people with similar features were attracted to one another was a hoary old one. Even so, Strong couldn't work out why his junior partner was bedding the secretary when he had Amy to come home to.

Then he remembered his own life.

She led him through the wide hall, down two steps and into a cosy lounge where classical music was playing – well,

Stockhausen, which was certainly not to his taste. If Strong ever fancied being highbrow he preferred the Baroque period, the atonal meanderings of this twentieth-century composer leaving him cold. He'd always thought that cultivating a taste for such music was akin to admiring the emperor's new clothes, or enjoying Shakespeare. And anyway, he was a child of his generation, and much preferred the Rolling Stones and Jimi Hendrix to just about anything.

Following the usual pleasantries she got up from the leather couch. 'I'll get Blair. He's just putting the children to bed, but I can take over with storytelling, though they always prefer Daddy for some reason.'

Because he's better at telling stories than you are, thought Strong as he watched her leave the room. He took the cheap phone from his pocket, turned it on to silent, got up from his chair and slid it under the couch on which she'd been sitting. He pushed it as far back as he could, feeling his age as he struggled to his feet and sat back down where Amy had left him.

'Mike, this is a surprise. I was just getting the sprogs down.' Blair Williams entered the room in sweat pants and a T-shirt. Noticing the older man's appraisal of his clothing, he smiled. 'I'll be going for a quick session in our little basement gym before I have a glass of wine or three. Can I get you something?'

'I'd like to say a large malt, but the way things are now it had better be coffee. I had a couple earlier. At least it'll keep me awake on the way to Dudingston village. The peelers are bloody dedicated to stopping everyone having a good time nowadays. Back in the sixties I used to wake up and wonder how the hell I got the damned motor back home.'

'Well, changed days and all that, Mike. I'll go and get you a coffee – espresso do?'

'Yes, with a touch of sugar – brown, if you have it, none of that white garbage.'

'Of course. I'll just be a tick. We've got a bloody ace coffee maker. I don't know what we did without it.'

Mike Strong was pleased to have the chance to sit back and rehearse what he'd come to say – not that he was going to say much. He'd done what he'd come to do; the rest was just window dressing.

Eventually Williams came back bearing a small espresso mug on an equally delicate saucer. 'Enjoy, Mike,' he said, handing the cup to Strong. 'Now, how can I help? Nothing wrong, I hope?'

Strong enjoyed worrying Blair Williams, though he was aware that his colleague would be a damned sight more worried if he had any idea what was really going on. However, he adopted a serious expression and took a sip of the coffee. It was good, he had to admit. He wondered what beans Williams used, then realised how boring his life was becoming in old age. 'Things aren't going just as we expected with our deceased friend on the west coast, if you get my drift.' He hid a smile as he watched the expression change on Williams's face.

'Fuck! I mean, in what way?'

'Tricky to explain, and I'm sure you'll agree that the less you actually know the better.'

'Oh, yes – of course.' Williams paused, clearly thinking. 'I hope this won't impact on the partnership. Is it something I should tell Daddy about?'

'No, I wouldn't worry too much about it. It's tricky, but

it means I'll have to take off down there for a while. Make sure that everything is properly in place, that sort of thing.' Strong leaned forward, espresso mug in one hand, saucer in the other. 'Not the kind of thing your father would condone, but we can still make good money, as you are aware. That's why I popped over – you know, rather than discuss this on the phone.'

'I understand.' Concern was now etched across Williams's face. 'Is it worth it, Mike? I mean, it's not as though we're all poverty-stricken.'

'This is the difference between you being stuck here or being able to have that place on Lake Como you've always wanted; the chance to send your children to a good school.'

'We have them on the list at Fettes.'

'Bugger Fettes! Eton, Harrow – proper schools. Trust me, by the time they're ready to take that step you'll want as much distance between you and them as possible. Teenagers are bloody irritating bastards. Let the school take the strain and knock them into shape. Give you more time with the good lady, or . . .'

'Or what?' Williams looked suddenly alarmed.

'Anything else you want to get up to, young man.' Strong smiled in an avuncular way, leaving Williams unsure as to the meaning of his last statement. The older man was enjoying every moment of this and it made him happy.

'How long will you be away for?' Williams asked. 'We need to keep in touch; I'll worry myself sick if I don't know what's happening.'

'Oh, don't fret about that. I'll give you regular updates,' said Strong, knowing he would do nothing of the kind.

'That's a relief, at least.'

'I'm glad. And don't worry. If I need you, I'll be on the phone straight away. But it won't come to that. Just needs a gentle nudge in the right direction – and us to keep our nerves.'

Blair Williams got up and walked to a cabinet from which he produced a bottle of wine and a glass.

'Giving up the idea of the gym tonight?'

'Yes. I've lost the enthusiasm, rather.'

'Quite right. A friend of mine fell off an exercise bike recently. Damn near killed himself. I'm sure you get enough exercise elsewhere, eh?'

'Sorry – what?' Williams looked flustered as he struggled with the wine cork.

'Better get going. At my age, sleep is a must, especially if there's a journey on the cards. Don't worry, I know the way out. Please give Karen my best.'

'Amy, you mean.'

'Yes, Amy, of course. Sorry. I'm getting old, Blair, damnable bloody stuff. We'll speak soon.'

As Strong walked up the two narrow steps and out of the room, Williams managed to open the wine. He poured himself a large glass and drained it in one go.

'Darling, you didn't let it breathe,' said Amy Williams, returning from her storytelling duties.

'Bugger that. I need a drink.'

'Has Mike gone?'

'Yes, he's gone. I swear I wish he'd die off or something. The man's a bloody menace.'

'Oh? In what way?'

'In every bloody way.' Blair Williams poured himself another large glass of expensive Shiraz.

*

O'Hara faced Daley and Scott in the interview room at Kinloch police office. It was well into the evening, and the hotel employee was noticeably jumpy, irritated at the wait and clearly concerned by what more the police wanted from him.

'Now, Mr O'Hara,' said Daley. 'Sorry to have kept you; we've been out of the office.'

'Could you no' have jeest asked me to come down when yous were here? I've been waiting for hours.' It was clear that O'Hara's meek manner had changed since his interview at Machrie House Hotel.

'Sorry, couldn't be helped,' said Daley. 'I just want you to go over what you told us earlier, please.'

O'Hara rolled his eyes. 'Jeest like I says. I was about tae deliver Ms Wenger's breakfast when I heard noises from her room.'

'Screams, and the like?'

'Aye, that's it. Shouting and screaming.'

'And you heard this plainly from the corridor?'

'Aye, that's why I rushed in.'

'Some of our colleagues have taken statements from the other guests on that floor. Nobody heard a commotion at all, and three of the other rooms were occupied at the time.'

O'Hara shrugged his shoulders. 'Whoot dae you want me tae say?'

'Well, it's rather strange that if someone was screaming they weren't heard by anyone else, don't you think?'

O'Hara opened his mouth to say something, but Scott spoke before he had the chance.

'How do you get to work, Mr O'Hara?'

'On the bus fae Kinloch. Why dae you ask?'

'And you got the bus the day Ms Wenger was attacked?'

'Aye, at six. Gets me there just in time for breakfast service.'

'Did you come to work alone? I mean not wae any o' your colleagues, or that?'

'No, jeest me. Hold on. I don't know whoot yous are trying tae get at, but I don't like it. It was me who helped the woman!'

'Yes, and she's very grateful for your intervention,' said Daley. 'But you'll understand that we have to examine everything very closely. This was a serious attack on Ms Wenger, and it's still unclear just how the attacker entered the premises.'

'Aye, I suppose.' O'Hara appeared to see the logic in this.

'It's a matter of routine, but we'll have tae have a look at your bank account, Mr O'Hara,' said Scott.

'Whoot? So, I save someone and noo I'm the one under suspicion? This isna right!'

'Just procedure,' said Daley. 'It's the kind of thing we do after a serious attack. We're just looking for answers. And there have been developments elsewhere that mean this case has taken on another, much more serious aspect.'

'Like whoot?'

'I'm afraid I can't tell you that at the moment, Mr O'Hara.'

'And what if I say no to yous looking at my bank account?'

'Under those circumstances, and because of the nature of the assault on Ms Wenger, we would seek a warrant.'

O'Hara stood up, scraping the chair he'd been sitting on along the hard floor. 'If I'm under arrest I want a lawyer.

Your cops jeest told me they wanted mair information. This is starting tae sound serious tae me.'

'You're free to go, sir,' said Daley. 'Do we have your permission to have a look at your bank account?'

'Aye, if yous must. But I tell you this. The next time I hear someone screaming fae anywhere, I'm jeest ignoring it!'

'We can have a car drop you back home,' said Daley.

'Naw, you're fine. I need a walk tae help me calm doon after this shite.'

Scott showed him to the door and closed it. 'What do you think, Jimmy?'

'He's been up to something. We'll get in touch with the bus company in the morning. I want to know who was on that six o'clock bus to Machrie.'

Mike Strong was packing a bag when his wife arrived back from her reading group. She looked at the scatter of clothes and toiletries and regarded her husband with a puzzled expression.

'A holiday I don't know about, Mike?'

'No, wish it was. Bloody business.'

Samantha Strong sat heavily on the sofa and watched her husband with great interest. She'd flourished on joining the readers' group. They had guest authors from time to time and their message was the same: 'Observe everything around you. You have five senses, so use them, describe what you see, how you feel, et cetera.' The last author had also been a hypnotist, and had promised to come the next day to regress her. Secretly she was pleased that her sceptical husband would be elsewhere. And, after all this time, she didn't really care what he got up to.

She'd been married to her lawyer husband for almost forty years, and reckoned he'd probably clocked up a similar number of conquests in that time. Though she'd known about his affairs almost from the beginning of their marriage, she had decided not to make an issue of it as long as it wasn't flaunted in her face. He'd been careful enough not to do that; she refused to think of it as being considerate.

This time, though, she sensed something different. There was a determined urgency to the way he was packing, a job she normally did for him. 'Going somewhere nice?'

'Bloody Argyll.'

'Oh, it's lovely there. What part?'

'Is this twenty questions?'

'So it's a secret, then.'

'Sam, do me a favour, will you? I'm in a hurry. I just want to get this done, catch a couple of hours' sleep and head off.'

'You're leaving tonight?'

'Early morning, more likely – very early.'

She smiled. 'I'll leave you to it. Remember to take your pills, won't you, Mike.'

As she left the room he shook his head. He could – should – have left her a hundred times. But she had money, and Mike Strong had always coveted money.

As Sam closed the bedroom door behind her, she leaned against it and smiled. Getting rid of her husband for a while was just what she needed.

Daley and Scott stared into the low metal box they'd brought back from the old Transit at Rowan Tree Cottage. The padlock had been a stout one, but an equally robust constable equipped with a pair of bolt cutters had managed to dislodge it, though not without some effort.

On top of the open box sat an antiquated manual typewriter in a neat black leather box. It looked to be from the sixties or seventies, a Remington, the type journalists would take with them to write up a story; from a bygone age, Daley considered.

Under the typewriter were reams of paper, all neatly typed, but of varying ages, judging by the colour of the A4 sheets. Some were yellowed with age, others bright and fresh-looking. The papers seemed to be in no particular order, old and new mixed together. Scott picked up a sheet and began to read.

'Gobbledygook tae me, Jimmy. Here – have a look yourself.'

Daley took the sheet from Scott and cast an eye over it. Though the grammar and spelling were sound, the subject matter appeared rather impenetrable, with lots of long Latin words and complex descriptions. 'It's like some massive medical dissertation. But I want every page studied. This must be the work of the late Mr Doig. We wondered where the typewriter Alice talked about had gone. Now we know.'

'I hope you don't expect me tae dae it. I've got needles tae stick in my eyes by way of relaxation instead.'

'We'll get some of the DCs on it in the morning. Looks like we'll need some expert guidance in any event.'

'It's been a long day, Jimmy. Fancy a wee snifter – Douglas Arms, maybe? We're no' going tae find Ginny Doig tonight.'

'No thanks. But you're right. She'll know this area better than any of us. We'll start asking about tomorrow. Leave that box for the early shift with some instructions, please, Brian. I'm off home. Bloody knackered.'

'But you're feeling okay, aye?'

'Yeah, fine, just tired. Don't worry, I'm not about to expire, Brian.'

'You're coping well, big man. This isn't exactly the quiet easing back intae work you were expecting.'

'Nothing's ever as we expect, is it?'

'Aye, true. I'll away hame tae. No point sitting in Hotel Misery either – it's bad enough drinking ginger beer as it is without all that gloom. See you in the morning, Jimmy.' Scott left to compose instructions for the early shift regarding the box and its contents.

Daley drove home under a carpet of stars. The roads were already slippery; another frost was about to set in. The loch glistened, bright with the lights of the town and the twinkling heavens above, church spires like looming monoliths in the moonlight. Daley had always liked this time of year: cold, crisp weather, cosy nights by the fire and the build-up to Christmas. He'd impressed himself by the way he'd managed to slot back into the routine of being a police officer again. But the Doig case was becoming more and more complex, and he felt his stomach churn again when he thought of the footage of the 'ice pick lobotomy', and the body of Thorbin Doig he'd seen earlier. How could anyone do that to another human being, never mind their own children?

As he bumped up the lane to his house on the hill he noted the place was in darkness and reasoned that Liz must be in bed. When he parked the car and made his way into the house he was startled by the lone figure sitting motionless on the couch in the moonlight, staring blankly into space.

'You okay, Liz?'

'I don't know,' she replied wistfully. 'And don't worry, I haven't been drinking.'

'I never said you had.' Daley sat beside her and slipped his arm round her shoulder.

She leaned into him. 'Do you know, that's the most affectionate you've been since – well, since I've been back.'

'I'm sorry. I know how hard things have been for you.'

'I had a meltdown at the dentist the other day – or at least outside, in the car.'

'Shit! I was supposed to take James. Sorry, it slipped my mind. What was wrong?'

'Dentists.'

Daley sighed in realisation. 'I'm so sorry. I should have remembered. That was really insensitive.'

'Don't worry – I was just being stupid. I took him this morning and we were both fine. I've been having great chats with Ella.'

'I was surprised to see you two in the County earlier.'

'Why?'

'You've not exactly been bosom buddies over the years.'

'No, but with age comes wisdom. I felt fine until I sat in the hotel. It was so depressing.'

'Tell me about it!'

'But I'm going to be okay, promise.'

'I'm glad to hear it, Liz. For your sake, I mean.' He pulled her close and the pair of them sat in an embrace in the moonlight, feeling a quiet companionship hitherto alien in their marriage.

37

Ginny Doig was glad to see the dawn as it broke across the North Channel. It had been bitterly cold in the tiny shepherd's hut, and the little store of firewood the family left there had been exhausted well before the sun appeared over the horizon.

She felt safe here, though. When the man who had killed her eldest son had walked down the beach away from her hiding place she'd held her breath, back pressed firmly against the rock until she could stand it no more. Then she sneaked along the sand, staying as low as she could, and made her way up the hill through the low gorse bushes and clumps of heather to where she knew she'd find sanctuary. Her sons left basic food and some water and a kettle in the little hut they used when the sheep were on the hill. She had drunk tea to warm her during the night, boiling the kettle over the small fire, her mind in turmoil, hatred in her heart.

There must be no mistake now. The woman – her daughter – who had made such an unwelcome return had made her life a hell on earth. First her husband; now she'd lost a son. As the morning broke bright over the frost-fringed heather, Ginny Doig made her plans. She couldn't rely on the police – her daughter had them in her pocket, she was sure. An end must come to every life, and she cared little now for her own. She'd lived a life that had suited her, isolated with her family by the restless sea and the hissing pebbles.

But Ginny Doig wasn't quite ready to give up yet.

Annie counted the small bottles of tonic water, bitter lemon and fresh orange juice as she'd been doing for as long as she could remember. But her heart wasn't in her work today. If it hadn't been for the loyalty she felt to her customers – her friends – she would have walked away and left the owners of the County Hotel to wind down their own business. She would have to look out Christmas decorations soon, and dreaded the thought.

Everything comes tae its natural end. Has its time and place, Anne. She could see her grandfather in her mind's eye, smell rolling tobacco and his musty cardigan. The old man had managed to get her a job as a waitress in this very hotel when she was still a schoolgirl. She remembered smiling at him as she waited for an order to appear through the hatch of the bar that was now her domain. He sat in the same seat every day and had three drams and a half pint of beer. After he died, she couldn't face looking into the bar. She always felt that she'd see him sitting there, alive and well. But when she gathered her courage and walked through the door, his seat was as empty as her heart. That was how she felt today.

The ringing of the bell at reception made her lose count of the mixer bottles, and she cursed to herself as she walked from the bar to the little reception desk. A tall man in his mid-forties was standing there. He smiled at her.

'I'm sorry to bother you. I wondered if I could have a room for a couple of nights? I know it's too early to take up residence, but if you have a vacancy, I'd be grateful if you would hold on to my bags until I can check in properly.' His accent was a soft American one – or Canadian; Annie could never tell the difference.

'You're in luck, sir. We're damn near empty as far as guests are concerned. I can gie you the keys tae a room right noo. I'll need a credit or debit card number, or cash up front if you're so minded.'

He handed her a credit card and smiled again. 'Thank you. I hope this will do?'

She studied the card, didn't recognise the bank, but saw the Visa logo. 'Aye, that's just fine, Mr . . . ?'

'Macmillan – Tom Macmillan. I've wanted to visit this town for years, and now here I am.'

'You've picked a quiet time of year. We get a wee turn jeest before Christmas, but up until then it's like a ghost town.'

'Suits me.'

'Are you here on business?' Annie regarded him suspiciously, thinking of the surveyors and how she'd welcomed them with open arms, only for them to pull the rug from under her feet.

'Yes and no. To be honest, I'm not sure. I have some thinking to do.'

'Aye, well, you'll have plenty time tae think here.'

'This place has been around for a long time.'

'Aye, but not for much longer.'

'How so?' His expression changed, smile suddenly gone.

'In their wisdom, the owners intend tae turn the hotel intae flats. We'll close after the New Year.'

'Wow! I'm so sad to hear that, I really am.'

'We all are. It's been a shock, I'll no' lie.' Annie handed

her new guest the key to his room on its large wooden fob. 'There you are, room fourteen. You get a good view o'er the Main Street. Jeest up the stairs and turn right. Any problems just gie me a shout.'

'Much obliged to you, ma'am,' he said in the American fashion.

As Annie watched him heft his holdall on to a broad shoulder she reckoned there was something familiar about Tom Macmillan, but she couldn't quite put her finger on it.

Bin day. Sheena McKay hated it, mainly because she could never remember which bin was to go out on a particular week. Peering from the kitchen window of their modest home on one of Kinloch's private estates, she saw that her neighbours' blue bins were missing from their respective back gardens. So it was recycling bin day. She congratulated herself on this small triumph as she slipped on a pair of crocs and her jacket in order to take the bin to the collection point at the end of the road.

The cold hit her like a slap in the face, but it was refreshing, too. Everything seemed new and clean under the blanket of white frost. Its pattern glinted in the morning sunlight, and looked quite beautiful, Sheena thought. She dragged the bin wearily along the back path, remembering the times when the bin men came and did that themselves, in the days when everyone only had one bin to worry about. Now, she had to send her husband to local recycling points with their empty wine bottles. This was Kinloch, and she knew that the contents of their bottle bin would be noted and discussed if they looked to be in excess of what was considered normal consumption. What hypocrites, she thought. Her husband had told her of the long line of cars in the local supermarket car park on the day before the bottle bins were collected. Shifty-looking people doing their best to disguise the fact that they were doing just what he was. But, she supposed, it was nice to be part of a tradition, no matter how contrived and bizarre.

She left her blue bin neatly beside the rest and, watching her step as the paths were treacherously slippery, began to make her way towards her own back garden again. She was thinking about Alison – Alice Wenger, remembering how her friend had suffered in her early life: penniless, abused, unloved, the product of a family who didn't care. Her own life had been privileged in comparison, up in the old mansion overlooking the loch. As she regarded her present home, she reflected upon the dispiriting nature of a life that had moved backwards instead of forwards. There was Alice, glamorous, attractive, rich, while she was a dowdy housewife in a home that more nearly resembled a box than a mansion. But then she thought of her family – husband, children, dog – and instantly felt better.

If Sheena McKay heard the thud of the muffled shot that hit her in the back of the head, nobody would ever know. Had any of her neighbours been peeking through their net curtains they would have seen her pitch forward in a spray of crimson blood, ending up face down on the frosty path, all thoughts of houses, bins, bottles, old friends, husbands, children and dogs gone in an instant.

38

Brian Scott eyed his toast with displeasure. It was 'over-brown' as his mother would have said, when she really meant burnt. He looked across at his wife as she downed a glass of orange juice in one. He shook his head and sighed.

'What's up wae you?' said Ella.

'Just remembering how great it is no' tae wake up wae a drooth or a thumping heid every morning, dear.'

'Oh, aye. Well, you've got plenty o' experience tae draw on, since you were battered oot o' your napper for the best part o' thirty years.'

'That's a bit o' an exaggeration, Ella.'

'No' from where I'm standing it isn't.'

'It was part o' the job back in those days. You had tae take a drink or no bugger would trust you. Everybody was the same.'

'I cannae mind Jim Daley commandeering an ice cream van tae take him hame, drunk as a lord.'

'That was a friend o' mine!'

'He wisnae very friendly when you got him oot o' his bed tae drive you all the way across Glasgow at three in the morning.'

'I paid him.'

'How much?'

'I bought a double cone wae a flake.'

'And he near lost his trading licence.'

'That was his own fault.'

'In what way?'

'He should have telt me no' tae press that button.'

'You fell on the button, Brian.'

'Pressed, fell – what's the difference?'

'Five pints o' heavy and half a bottle o' whisky, that's the difference. They chimes o' his were always deafening enough during the day, never mind at that time o' night. Yous woke everybody up fae the Broomielaw tae Shettleston.'

'I cannae mind much aboot it.'

'No, but I mind me and him trying tae get you up the close stairs while "Greensleeves" was banging away oot in the street.'

'How did he no' turn the chimes off?'

'Because you'd broken the switch. The poor man was beside himself. Half o' the neighbours didnae speak tae me for weeks.'

'You just remember all the bad stuff, never anything good.'

'Aye, like the time you asked my big cousin Jane when her wean was due?'

'That was me being nice.'

'She was fifty-nine! Poor woman had been battling wae her weight for years. That took a lot o' putting right, I'll tell you.'

'Ach, don't take your bad temper oot on me, just because you've got a hangover. It isnae my fault.'

'Huh!'

'How's Lizzie, anyway?'

'A poor bugger, like me.'

It was Brian Scott's turn to roll his eyes and look at his

wife askance. He was about to think up a suitable retort when his phone rang. It was DC Fleming who had taken the place of the unfortunate DS Potts while he was recuperating from his broken arm, inflicted by one of the Doigs. 'Aye, what is it, son?' said Scott through a mouthful of toast.

'Sir, we have a dead body in Dalryan Terrace.'

'There's a lot o' aulder folk stay up there. It's this cold, they drop like flies, the poor buggers.'

'Not this one, sir. Someone shot her in the head. DCI Daley is attending from home. He asked me to inform you, too.'

Scott put the phone down, looking pale.

'What's up, Mr Whippy?'

'Some poor woman's just been shot deid o'er the other side o' the toon.'

'Bugger me. We'd be safer staying in the Bronx.'

Scott took a gulp of tea, stuck a piece of toast in his mouth, shrugged on his jacket, and hurried out of the kitchen.

Mike Strong was tired. The drive to Kinloch was longer than he'd remembered, and he hadn't managed to get much sleep. The forestry car park was in the middle of nowhere. He needed some breakfast and especially a large shot of coffee. Strong was more irritated when he looked at his watch and realised the person he'd come here to meet was nearly half an hour late.

He was listening to the Rolling Stones track 'Thru and Thru' when an SUV appeared from the main road.

'Where have you been?' said Strong, winding down his window to talk to the man advancing towards him from the other vehicle.

'You asshole,' said Vito Chiase. 'You get me over here to do one job, and I end up having to clip half the population. You better have my money.' He wagged his finger angrily in Strong's face.

Mike Strong reached behind into the back seat of his Jaguar and produced a bulging A4 envelope. 'You take this and pay it into the account in the bank on the note enclosed. When you get home, it'll be wired to the business you told us about, no questions asked, just as we agreed.'

Chiase fingered the envelope. 'It seems okay,' he said with a shrug.

'I have another proposal to make.'

'You crazy? I'm outta here. Even in this shithole place the cops won't be long in figuring out who did it.'

'I have a boat ready to pick you up and take you to Glasgow as soon as it's done. I can offer you the same again.'

Chiase looked at the heavy envelope. 'As this, you mean?' He looked about, taking in his surroundings, thinking. 'I dunno.'

'Strictly speaking, you didn't fulfil your contract.'

'Strictly speaking, I'll blow a hole in that smug face of yours, cocksucker.' Chiase made for the waistband of his trousers, revealing a pistol.

'No need for that. It's your choice, take it or leave it.'

'So a hundred grand, just for one more job?'

'Yes. You have my word.'

'And how do I know you won't just disappear?'

'You don't. But I'm here now, am I not?'

Chiase thought for a few moments. 'Same deal – with the notes and the bank transfer, yeah?'

'Yes. Just go in the bank, ask for Vicky and hand her

the bag. Wait until she gives you the receipt of transfer. That's all there is to it.'

'As long as the bank's not in the middle of that shithole town, I'll do it.'

'Good man.'

'Until then, what am I gonna do, just sit here?'

'I'm going into Kinloch. I'll bring back some food and coffee, then we can talk.'

'You got it, old man.'

Mike Strong eyed Vito Chiase up and down. 'What age are you?'

'Never mind. Just go get the fucking coffee.'

Again Daley and Scott were wearing white paper suits, their shoes covered, masks over their mouths. The local personnel were doing their best to secure the scene while they waited for SOCO to arrive from Glasgow. But as the morning began to warm and the frost melted, time was of the essence. Daley looked on as a young DC took pictures of frosty footprints on the path. She looked pale. Daley knew this was her first murder scene and made a mental note to have a word with her when there was time. He remembered well his revulsion as he stared into the blank eyes of the first person he'd seen murdered. It wasn't pleasant.

Sheena McKay's body was spread-eagled on the path, a dark red pool of blood stark against the white frost like the frame of a picture. Her arms were outstretched, the back of her head missing, the jagged edge of her skull a darker shade than the brain tissue that lay at the heart of the wound.

'I hate tae say,' said Scott, 'but this looks like the work o' a pro as well.'

'But she's just an ordinary housewife. We're trying to get hold of her husband, but he's away with his work and isn't answering his phone.'

Daley remembered the mixture of horror and sheer anger he'd felt when Liz had told him about the attack she'd suffered. He found himself sending a silent prayer of thanks for the fact that she'd made it and wasn't lying here in a pool of her own blood and gore.

'Close range, tae. Must have only been a few feet away,' said Scott.

'Judging by the footprints he was about three metres away from her when she was shot.'

'Metres? I hate that bollocks. Aboot three yards, you mean?'

'Have you not been touched by any part of the modern world, Brian?'

'As little o' it as possible, Jimmy. I cannae see how things have improved in any way. Folk are all o'er the place now. The youngsters don't even go oot for a pint. The experts might think it's progress, but I'm no' so sure.'

'Maybe we spent too much time going out for pints, Brian.'

'Maybe we had a life – met folk, had friends, shared a laugh. No' just staring at a screen all day. Kids are like zombies these days.'

'And so endeth the lesson from the Reverend Brian.'

'Look at this, for instance. Poor woman oot at her back door, then – well, then this.'

'Looks like she'd been putting out her bin.'

'Bins! There's another bloody thing. Soon you'll need a garden three times the size o' the one you've got just tae fit a' these bins intae it.'

Daley ignored the rant. 'We can't forget that Sheena McKay is one of Alice Wenger's best friends. Someone tries to kill her – or scramble her brains, at least – then her brother is killed, and now this. I want her out of that hospital and placed somewhere safe – if she's fit enough to be discharged, that is.'

'Where? The hotel?'

'Nah. The hotel's not safe, as we've found out.'

'Three choices then: the office, a safe hoose, or tell her tae bugger off back tae California.'

'No, I want her here. All this is going on and she's at the centre of it. I want to clear it up once and for all.'

'You don't think it was that torn-faced auld bitch, do you?'

'You have a real way with words, Brian. If you think this is the work of Ginny Doig . . .' He shrugged.

'She's the common parameter, Jimmy.'

'Denominator, Bri.'

'Shit. I just learned that word, tae.'

'But you're right, she is – but this, and murdering her son? I can't see it. She's no professional killer.'

'How dae you know? I wouldnae put anything past her. If you came up an' telt me she was Auld Horny himself I widnae be surprised.'

'No, there's a third party, and he or she knows exactly what they're doing.'

'But who, and why are they doing it, Jimmy?'

'There are two people at the centre of all this, and they're mother and daughter.'

Scott pulled the mask off his face as they walked away from Sheena McKay's body. 'I was thinking last night.

Whoever it was that had a go at Alice Wenger – you know, tae scrub her brains, an' that?'

'Yes.'

'She was small, right?'

'She?'

'I think it was Ginny Doig.'

'She was in custody, remember. We let her go that morning.'

'Aye, but at what time, eh?'

'I can't remember, Brian, but before the attack on Alice. But she wouldn't have the time – would she?'

'And if it was her, surely the victim would recognise her ain mother right enough.'

Daley nodded slowly, taking on board what Scott had said. It would have been tight, but he supposed that Ginny Doig could have made it to Machrie in time to attack her daughter. But how did she get into the hotel?

The young DC Eva Welsh approached them. She was as white as the frost, but wore a determined look.

'Sir, we've taken images, as you'll have seen.'

'Yes,' said Daley.

'We have isolated two clear sets of prints. Mrs McKay was wearing quite distinctively soled shoes – crocs.'

'She likely kept them at the back door for going in an' oot. That's what Ella docs – easy tae slip on,' Scott suggested.

'And the other set?' said Daley.

'Mrs McKay is about a size four, as far as we can judge, sir. The other set of prints are larger, size nine, ten, something like that. But they have no tread, so not trainers or anything.'

'Dress shoes – like wae a leather sole?' asked Scott.

'Yes, sir. That's what I thought.'

'Thank you,' said Daley. 'How are you holding up? This is your first murder, yes?'

'I'm okay, thank you, sir. We all have to go through it.'

'We do, but it's never pleasant.'

'I've only ever worked in rural areas. So not many murders.'

'Aye, until you came here,' said Scott.

Two things happened simultaneously. The distinctive buzz of a helicopter sounded in the clear cold air overhead, and Daley's mobile rang.

'Here's the cavalry,' said Scott, recognising the aircraft carrying the SOCO team as it came into view over the loch.

'Yes, John?' Daley's call was from an old friend at the forensic department. He listened intently, putting one finger in his ear to block out the sound of the helicopter. 'Okay, much obliged, mate. Ping me over the report and I'll have a look.'

'Who was that?' said Scott.

'John Hartley at ballistics. They have a match for the bullets that killed Thorbin Doig. The same gun's been used in two shootings in the last year.'

'Where?' said Scott.

'Glasgow. Used by the Trimble family – we think.'

'Eh? Why would they be involved down here?'

'Now that's a good question, Brian.'

As the helicopter passed noisily overhead they looked on, collective breath rising like steam in the frosty air. Meanwhile, the body of Sheena McKay lay stiff in the pool of dark congealed blood.

39

Ginny Doig stumbled across the frozen ground. She knew these hills like the back of her hand, but knowing the terrain and getting from one place to another were very different prospects. Her knees ached, she couldn't feel her hands and she was beginning to feel tired. Even with her limited medical knowledge she discerned the first signs of hypothermia.

She knew that she had to get to the smallholding just over the hill as quickly as she could, but her legs refused to work, to obey her commands. She was staggering now, the world becoming a confusion of bright sky, cold air and frozen heather that tore at her ankles.

She stopped, hands on her knees, gasping for breath.

'Mother?' The little boy looked at her intently. He was dressed in the moleskin trousers and jumper she'd made for him.

'Thorbin, you away and get a coat on. You'll catch your death of cold.'

'I'm dead already.'

Ginny stared into the child's face. His thick dark hair was roughly cut, sticking up in untidy clumps; she'd done it herself with her dressmaking scissors. She hobbled towards him, hand held out.

'You can't touch me now.'

'Why not?' Her voice was stern. Ginny Doig hated her children disobeying her.

'You can't touch dead people.'

Just as her trembling hand reached out to his face, a trickle of blood like a small tear began to meander down his face from one eye. The trickle became a torrent, and soon his whole face was covered, a bloody mask. Only his eyes stared out, bright blue and alive.

'Thorbin, stop that!' she shouted. The image began to shimmer. The boy smiled at her through the gore of his own face and disappeared.

Ginny turned round. She couldn't see her oldest son anywhere. Nothing made sense; she just wanted to sleep. As the sky began to spin she sank to her knees, barely feeling the fast-frozen heather and the hard ground beneath. Her eyelids flickered, heavy, impossible to keep open.

'Ginny.' The voice was her husband's.

'What?' she asked weakly, her head buried in the heather now.

'This isn't how it ends; this isn't what we do. We fight!'

'I've fought my fight, husband. So have you.' Ginny Doig felt warm now, cosy, as though she was lying in her bed under a pile of thick blankets on a cold winter's night. She knew it was freezing outside, but she was comfortable, ready to sleep. With her bony hand she reached through the heather to nip out the candle that wasn't there. The effort was enough to see her eyes close tight shut. She was breathing slowly now, her brain curating her end like the gentlest nurse.

Everything was warm, everything felt safe; everything was slipping away.

She could feel herself being taken up, strong hands pulling her body free of this earth, as though she was being taken from this life to another realm.

'Mrs Doig!' the man shouted as he lifted her frail body from the ground. 'Quick, Gordon, get her in the tractor. Help me!'

Ginny Doig's head lolled as two pairs of brawny hands gripped her by the shoulders and feet and placed her in the cabin.

The man in the dark suit could have been of any age between thirty and fifty. He was well dressed: an expensive suit, pristine white shirt, silk tie and Savile Row tan shoes. His naturally light hair was flecked with subtle blond highlights, gelled back from his head. He was around six feet tall, slim and wiry. He made sure the Range Rover was locked before he walked the few yards up to Kinloch police office.

Despite the cold day, he felt refreshed, quite comfortable in just a suit and tie, though a less robust individual would doubtless have preferred a thick overcoat or jacket on such a chill November morning.

He bounded up the few steps and into the police office. Behind the front desk, the desk sergeant stood up, his mousy hair showing grey at the temples, not looking entirely comfortable in the black T-shirt that now formed part of his uniform.

'Yes, sir, how can I help you?'

'I'm Grant Dunwoody. Here to see DCI Daley – my card.' He tossed the business card across the desk, where Sergeant Shaw managed to catch it just before it fell to the floor.

'I'm afraid DCI Daley is busy working on a serious

incident. I don't know when he'll be available, sir.' Shaw's face was devoid of expression. Though he'd read the card, the man before him needed no introduction. Grant Dunwoody was one of Scotland's – the UK's – most prestigious lawyers; he was also prodigiously expensive. Either way, his notoriety stormed before him.

'I'll take a seat, will I?'

'Can I ask what your business is with DCI Daley, sir?'

'If you must.' Dunwoody sighed, as though reluctant to speak to such a lowly mortal. 'I'm here representing my client, Alice Wenger.'

'I see. Well, I suggest you take some time out to go and see her. She's still in the local hospital. And as I say, DCI Daley will be quite a while.'

'I know where she is, man. I've just come from the hospital. Please don't tell me my business. I demand to see the DCI the minute he's available. I hope that's clear?'

'I'll tell him, Mr Dunwoody. I can show you through to the family room if you'd prefer. Much more comfortable.'

'I'm fine here. But tell Daley this is a matter of the utmost importance.' Dunwoody sat on one of the four chairs facing the tall reception desk. Without further discussion he brought out a smartphone and began to flick through email messages.

'I'll let him know you're here.' Shaw walked to the rear of the office to call his boss.

Donnie O'Hara hadn't enjoyed the best of luck during the course of his forty-eight years. He'd married one woman who told him on their honeymoon that she'd made a mistake. The marriage ended a few weeks later.

His second marriage had started off much better, but his drinking and inability to hold down a job began to irk his hard-working new wife. So, with two years of less than blissful wedded life behind them, that relationship too came to an unceremonious end.

He'd met Tracy in a pub. With a reputation in Kinloch for drunkenness, idleness and being a less than caring partner, his chances of finding love locally were limited. So, during periods of intermittent employment, but still on a limited budget, he made the occasional trip to Glasgow in an attempt to find someone willing to take him on. Mostly, though, he lengthened the odds by staying in cheap hotels and seeking comfort amongst the city's prostitutes until either his holidays or his money ran out, usually the latter. However, on one particular evening, he hit lucky.

Sitting on his own counting out enough change to buy a last couple of drinks in a rundown pub in the city centre, he'd been joined by a woman who sat at his table and asked him for a cigarette. At first O'Hara thought she was another prostitute – they used the bar frequently – but it soon became clear that she, like him, was a lonely soul seeking the company of a member of the opposite sex.

They met again on his next trip to the city, by which time he'd managed to lose his latest job. When he told Tracey that he wouldn't be able to see her again until he could find more work, she offered to come down and stay with him in Kinloch.

Donnie O'Hara thought long and hard about this. His last two relationships had caused him so much grief that he had been happy on his own, able to take 'comfort' where he found it on his trips to the bright lights. He even considered making the move to Glasgow himself. But such was his perpetual impoverishment that he relied on his family to prop him up at regular intervals, and no such support network existed in the city.

After much thought, he decided to take Tracey up on her offer, and soon they were sharing a turbulent, threadbare existence in one of the proliferating one-bedroom flats in Kinloch's town centre. Tracey seemed able to find jobs more readily than he, but was equally adept at losing them. In the main, they spent their days arguing, drinking cheap wine or strong cider and watching the best Netflix had to offer.

When the man had contacted them and asked them to perform the strange task, Donnie had worried. He'd only just started work at the hotel, after all. But when he heard it was only a prank – a practical joke – well, for the money, it seemed as easy as falling off a log.

Now he was regretting every minute of the whole thing as he sat chewing his nails in the room that overlooked Kinloch's Main Street. He wasn't sure whether it was the noise of the cars, or the bell ringing on the shop door downstairs, but he'd managed to attain a state of watchful calm, though he dreaded a phone call, or a knock at the door. He'd always been wary of the police; now he had reason to be, despite being unable to work out what had happened at the Machrie House Hotel.

Tracey was still in bed, sleeping off a bottle of vodka. They had a little cash now, but Donnie O'Hara wasn't sure if it had all been worth it.

When the knock sounded on the door it seemed almost inevitable. He knew the gimlet-eyed police inspector with the Glasgow accent could see right through him, so instead of fear he felt a certain relief as he went to answer it, as though surrendering to the inevitable.

The man in the close didn't look much like a police officer, though. He was certainly in his sixties, at least, and his sallow lined face and clothes looked out of place in Kinloch.

'Can I come in?'

'What for?' said O'Hara, slightly taken aback.

'I have something for you. You know, something more – for your trouble the other day.'

O'Hara pinpointed the New Jersey accent. He watched loads of films featuring men who talked like this. He was about to slam the door in the man's face when, from somewhere, he found the courage to say, 'I want mair money. The police are on my back, and if you want me to keep my mouth shut – well, you'd better pay up!'

The man at the door held his hands out in surrender. 'I hear ya, buddy – that's why I'm here. We know you need a little extra. Things haven't gone just like we planned. Some people . . . let's just say, they don't have any sense of humour.'

O'Hara thought for a moment. 'How much mair money?'

'C'mon, you wanna discuss this with me on the doorstep like some salesman? Hey, I ain't no Willy Loman, my friend.'

'Who?'

'Never mind. Let me in and we can do a deal, kid.'

O'Hara reluctantly nodded and walked away from the door.

Vito Chiase followed him inside, making sure he closed the front door quietly behind him. He passed the kitchen, where piles of unwashed dishes sat in a sink above a floor of cracked, stained linoleum.

'Can I get you a cup of tea or something?' O'Hara had his back to the American, picking up some empty cans of cider from the table in an effort to make the flat look semi-presentable.

'No, I'm good, thanks.' Chiase reached into his pocket and produced a ring of cheese wire. In an instant he had looped it over O'Hara's head and down on to his throat. He was about to pull it tight when a shrill scream rent the air. Momentarily distracted, Chiase looked behind him. At first he thought a child was standing in the shabby room, but on closer inspection it was clear that this was a small woman.

'I'm calling the polis!' she shouted at the top of her voice, darting to a mobile that lay on a nearby chair.

As he took this in, Chiase felt a blow to the side of his face as O'Hara's elbow connected with his cheek. The American staggered back, but managed not to fall, though his head was spinning.

With one hand over his face he made for the door. He could hear the woman shouting down the phone to the operator to put her on to the police. Half blind, head throbbing, he made it out of the flat and stumbled down the stairs. Not sure if he was being pursued, he dashed down Main Street, knocking over Mrs McKechnie as she pulled her shopping trolley towards the newsagents.

Chiase, working on instinct now, turned the corner into the side street where his SUV was parked outside a barber's shop. He jumped in and pressed the button that engaged the engine. As the car sputtered into life, with one eye shut he struggled to find the right gear. Again, he cursed stick-shift automobiles before eventually he made it into first and with screeching tyres sped away, but not without attracting the attention of a few curious locals in the process.

As he turned left and headed for the seafront, he cursed and banged the steering wheel with his hand. 'You fucking asshole! You never did know when to quit while you were ahead!'

Chiase sped along the esplanade gathering speed, anxious to leave this small town far in his wake.

40

Dunwoody observed a number of things all at once. A middle-aged man he vaguely recognised rushed past his seat near the front door of Kinloch police office. Though the man was clearly in a hurry, he stopped, turned round and faced the lawyer.

'I hope they're keeping you waiting.' He shook his head, then dashed out of the door.

'Who's that?' Dunwoody enquired of the desk sergeant.

'DI Scott, sir.'

Scott. He thought for a moment. 'You mean Brian Scott?'

'Yes, sir.'

'A bloody DI! No wonder things are bad in policing these days.'

'Brave man. He's been shot twice in the line of duty.'

'Third time lucky, eh? We can always hope.'

Shaw just had time to glare at Dunwoody before the phone rang. Though the policeman mumbled, the lawyer could still hear the urgency in his voice.

Distantly, a police radio was spouting forth. He couldn't pick up all that was said, but, remembering his basic knowledge of police incident codes, Dunwoody quickly realised that there had been a shooting locally, though the where, when and whom remained unclear.

The door was thrust open again, this time revealing a chief superintendent. Though he felt he should, Dunwoody didn't recognise her. She went straight to the main desk, where Shaw had just ended his call.

'What on earth is going on? The back gates are locked. My driver can't park the bloody car.' Her accent was of the refined Yorkshire variety, Dunwoody realised. He'd had a great-aunt who had lived near Scarborough and spoke in much the same way.

He looked on, increasingly intrigued, as the desk sergeant whispered to her conspiratorially. The lawyer had been trained over a number of years in the observance of people, whether police officers, judges, sheriffs, members of the jury, witnesses or clients. The fact that he had a top-of-the-range Range Rover sitting down the road, a large house in the leafy suburbs of Glasgow, a plush London apartment and a villa in Tuscany spoke to the proficiency he had acquired. In short, he knew an incident of note when he saw one.

He watched the superintendent's complexion change as she hurried off into the bowels of the police station.

'Trouble, sergeant?' he said to the harassed man behind the desk.

'Nothing we can't handle, sir.' It was clear that Sergeant Shaw was of the old school: steady and dependable, especially in a crisis.

'I'll just step out, if you don't mind. I have a couple of calls to make.'

As Dunwoody took the few steps down to the pavement, two police cars rushed down the hill, sirens sounding, lights flashing. He was here to make sure Alice Wenger was free to leave Kinloch and return to the USA, and goodness knows she'd paid him handsomely enough for the privilege, but something about all this activity made him uneasy. He knew he'd get nowhere with the local police, but there was always a way. Members of the press – depleted as they may be – were still the best people to shine light into dark corners and expose the truth.

He dialled a number and put the phone to his ear. 'There's something big on the go at Kinloch, Douglas. If you need a few anonymous observations, I'm happy to oblige. If I were you I'd get down here pronto.'

'I'm sorry, Jim. This isn't the kind of return to work we'd planned for you, is it?' Symington chewed her lip as she sat across from Daley in his glass box.

'No, not exactly, but that's the job, isn't it? Brian and I were just saying the same thing. If we knew what was before us every day it would be a piece of cake.'

'So, to recap: you have a dead woman in her back garden, now a man almost garrotted in his own flat. To add to that, one of the Doig sons has been murdered, the father killed himself, and Alice Wenger has been assaulted. Does that sum it up?'

'We also have a frantic woman who was present when the man in the flat, her partner, was assaulted – probably saved his life, in fact. Plus an elderly woman with cuts and bruises who was knocked over in what we presume was the assailant's bid to escape. Brian is off to bring them all in now. Oh, and we can't find Ginny Doig, Alice Wenger's mother.'

'Shit!'

'My thoughts exactly.'

'Who is the guy sitting in reception? I managed not to catch his eye, but I recognised his face from somewhere.'

'Grant Dunwoody; he's here to represent Alice Wenger.'

'Shit!'

'That's a lot of shit, if you don't mind my saying, ma'am.'

'I'm sorry, Jim. I've heard of him: quite the reputation. What is he here to achieve?'

'He wants us to allow Alice to go back home. I've managed to avoid him so far.'

'And why can't we do that, Jim?'

'Well, she's been a witness not only to the attack on herself, but also to the death of her father. The fact that her brother has been killed and her mother is now missing also comes into play. Her best friend is the woman lying dead in the backyard, and the man who's just been half strangled in his flat is the person who rescued her from her attacker at the hotel. Are you still with me?'

Symington opened her mouth to speak then closed it quickly.

'It's okay, I know what you were going to say.'

'How are you holding up, Jim?'

He shrugged his shoulders. 'Fine – this is what I've been doing for most of my adult life. Though I must admit, this case is a challenge.'

'So, tell me what you think?'

'I honestly don't know. At first we thought Ginny Doig was at the centre of everything. But the hits on Sheena McKay and Thorbin Doig were both the work of a pro.'

'Alice Wenger worries me.'

'She comes on holiday only to be assaulted, and for her

father, brother and best friend to be killed, you mean?'

'Yes. But she has money – big money.'

'And with money comes influence.'

'It sure does. But where does she fit in?'

'That I don't know.'

Symington thought for a moment. 'Right, I'll take care of Dunwoody. There's no way Alice Wenger can go home at the moment.'

'It'll be hard to stop her.'

'I'll think of something.'

'She's been a victim in all this.' Daley shrugged.

'We'll just have to hope we can break through what's happening.'

'You said it.'

Ginny Doig was sitting in an armchair beside a roaring fire, covered in a blanket. When she opened her eyes she was momentarily disoriented, but soon recognised the front room of her nearest neighbour's home. The big farmer held out a cup of tea to her in his paw of a hand.

'Here, this will help you warm up, Mrs Doig.'

'Thank you, Malcolm,' she said weakly.

'Whoot on earth were you doing out in this weather on the hill? You were blue with cold.'

Ginny Doig pretended she was too weak to reply. She'd watched her son die at the hands of a gunman, and she didn't know whom she could trust. However, her options were limited. She had to find somewhere relatively safe so she had time to think. 'Would you mind if I stayed here for a while, Malcolm?'

'Don't you think you should go tae hospital?'

'No!' Suddenly her eyes flashed. She spoke more quietly. 'I'll be fine wae a bit o' rest.

They both started at the loud knock on the door.

'Are you expecting visitors, Malcolm?'

'No, I rarely get any. Since Minnie died, me an' Gordon have lived here right quiet, like. Never see a soul.'

Again, there was a loud knock at the door.

'Don't let on I'm here, Malcolm. I canna tell you why, but I'm in bother. Don't tell anyone – especially the polis.'

When Malcolm Pirie opened the door to his small farmhouse two constables stood at the door, one woman, one man.

'Sorry to bother you, sir,' the woman said. 'We're looking for one of your neighbours.' She produced a photograph from her pocket. 'Mrs Ginny Doig – I take it you know her, yeah?'

'Aye, I know her fine,' replied Malcolm, uneasy in the presence of the police as he wasn't averse to poaching from the nearby estate. 'Canna tell you the last time I set eyes on her, mind you.' He lowered his voice. 'They're an odd lot, the Doigs – ask anyone.'

'Do any of them ever visit, you know, or drop in now and again? Maybe at New Year?'

'Ha! No, no' had a glimpse o' them for long and weary. I used to meet Mr Doig on the road in that auld pickup o' his. But other than that – nothing.'

'Well, if you do see her we'd be very grateful if you contacted us immediately.'

The tone of her voice gave Malcolm Pirie pause for thought. 'Has she committed a crime, or that?'

The police officer smiled. 'We just want to speak to her at this time. Sorry to bother you; we'll leave you to your day. If you do see or hear from her, please give us a call on this number.' She handed Pirie a card with a prominent police logo imprinted on it.

He closed the door and walked back into the lounge. 'What have you been at, Ginny?'

'Me? It's that daughter of mine. She killed Nathaniel, you know.'

'I'd heard he'd gone, and that she reappeared – after a' these years too, eh?'

'I need tae trust you, Malcolm. She's got a pile o' money noo – has the polis in her pocket. You know fine whoot it's like wae these bastards up at the estate. If you've got money you can dae anything you bloody want.'

Malcolm Pirie nodded in agreement. 'Aye. They stole those fields off me – gave me a fraction o' the price I should have got.'

Ginny Doig nodded in satisfaction. She knew she'd found an ally in Malcolm Pirie.

41

Symington at his side, Scott looked at Donnie O'Hara. The erstwhile hotel porter looked sullen and miserable, his dark hair standing up in untidy clumps, eyes bloodshot, unshaven. The strong smell of stale alcohol soured the small interview room. The duty solicitor grimaced when O'Hara leaned in to him for some private advice.

'You were on the six o'clock bus fae Kinloch tae Machrie on the day Alice Wenger was attacked.'

'I telt you that already.' O'Hara looked back defiantly. 'I take the bus tae my work.'

'Do you always take your partner, Miss Ferguson, tae your work wae you?'

'She was just wanting a wee look at the sea.'

'At six in the morning?'

'The sea's there a' the time.'

'It's in the loch, tae. Why go all the way tae Machrie first thing in the morning tae look at the sea when you can just walk doon the street?'

'Change o' scene.'

'What height is your partner, would you say, Mr O'Hara?'

'What's that got tae dae with anything?' He looked at the solicitor, who looked back apologetically.

'Just answer the question, eh?'

'She's wee. I dunno, maybe five foot one, or something. I don't know.'

'I've got a statement here from a Mr Ron Hamilton. He's the chef at Machrie House Hotel.'

'I know.'

'He tells us that you was right keen tae know aboot a' the security cameras in the hotel. In fact, he nearly reported you tae the manager.'

'Aye, but he didna.' O'Hara shook his head. 'I'm sick o' this. It was me that got attacked in my ain flat! Whoot are yous doing aboot that?'

'We're investigating that, you can rest assured, Mr O'Hara,' said Symington.

'I've got an idea,' said Scott. 'I think you were interested in they cameras for a reason. I think the small person who went intae Alice Wenger's room and attacked her was Tracey Ferguson. How much money did you get?'

O'Hara hung his head. 'I know my rights. I'm no' sayin' nothing.'

'That's okay. Tracey's telt us the whole thing, so you're just getting yourself deeper in mair trouble by lying. But go ahead; I like a good story just as much as the next man, son.'

'That stupid cow! I should never have brought her doon here. She's a bloody alkie!'

'So, how much did you get?'

O'Hara had a resigned look on his face. 'This guy phones me up. Tells me he wants tae play a joke on a friend o' his.'

'What did he sound like, this guy?'

'Posh, like. I don't know.'

'Did he give you his name, his number?'

'Nah. He jeest telt me there would be some money coming through the post the next day if I promised tae dae as he asked.'

'How much?'

'Three hundred quid!' said O'Hara as though he was describing a fortune.

'So for this three ton, you were just supposed tae give Ms Wenger a fright.'

'Aye. We had it a' planned. I smuggled Tracey intae the hotel – away fae they cameras, an' that. I was due tae take Ms Wenger's breakfast up, so that was the perfect opportunity.'

'Then Tracey knocked the door and attacked Alice Wenger. Doesnae sound much like a joke tae me.'

'She was just tae kind o' jump on her, you know? Then I was tae come straight in an' save the day. Jeest like I did.'

'So how do you explain the injury to Ms Wenger's eye?'

'I dunno – must jeest have taken a knock in the carry-on. Tracey never meant tae harm her.'

'What aboot the wee hammer?'

'That was part o' the joke. She was tae take that in and leave it on the bed.'

'What on earth made you think anything about this would be funny, Mr O'Hara?' said Symington.

'He was just thinking how much booze he could buy wae that money,' said Scott.

'I'm sorry. I jeest didna think. I never meant tae hurt the woman.' O'Hara looked at his lawyer.

'As you can see, my client is quite distressed. He's just been attacked in his own home. I think this interview should end now.'

'Aye, don't worry. We've got what we need.' Scott ended the interview formally and he and Symington left the room.

'I didn't know Tracey had confessed,' said Symington.

'Has she? Good stuff,' replied Scott.

'But in there you said—' She stopped in mid-sentence and shook her head. 'Brian, what on earth am I to do with you?'

'A fully paid holiday in the Bahamas?' Scott winked at the chief superintendent.

Mike Strong had been sitting in his car across the road from O'Hara's flat when he saw Chiase hurry from the close and knock down the old woman with the shopping trolley and run round the corner. He sighed and sat back to watch events unfold.

In a few minutes the police arrived. Shortly afterwards he watched with great disappointment as O'Hara and his partner were taken into an ambulance and rushed away back up the hill.

Things go wrong – that's why you insulate yourself, he thought by way of reassurance. He'd taken steps. He knew what he was doing. It would be fine. He kept saying this to himself as he drove into the remote forestry car park, where the New Jersey gangster was waiting.

Strong got out of his car. 'That was a disaster! What went wrong?'

'I got blindsided, and she was on the phone to the cops. Whaddya going to do?' Chiase shrugged his shoulders, a large lump already appearing under one eye. 'You never told me I was dealing with a pair of fucking junkies.'

'Harmless drunks – she's tiny! I have to say, I'm disappointed by all of this, Mr Chiase.'

The American grabbed the lawyer by the collar and forced

him against the side of his Bentley. 'I don't give a fuck how disappointed you are. I want my money and I want out of this shithole, the way we discussed.'

'I'll give you half,' said Strong, his face reddening as Chiase squeezed his throat.

'Half?'

'You didn't do the job!'

'I should just clip you now, you piece of shit.'

'Then how will you get home?'

Chiase let go of Strong's collar and shook his head while the lawyer caught his breath, scarlet-faced. 'You and me, we're too old for this shit. I told you that before. We should be sitting by a fire some place with a big drink, or on a beach. I've been doing this since I was a tyke.'

Strong was still breathing heavily. 'Maybe you're right.'

'But you're just like me, ain't you? Enough is never enough, right?'

Strong nodded. He supposed that though they'd had very different lives, the Edinburgh criminal lawyer and the New Jersey gangster, there was a similarity in nature. 'But what do you do – just lie in your bed and die?'

Chiase smiled. 'No, you go on as long as you can until you drop off the fuckin' end. That's how it works. It's the same for every poor bastard, paupers and kings. We all gotta fade away one way or the other.' He looked round, feeling the lump on his face with one hand. 'Okay, half – just get me the fuck outta here.'

Strong thought for a moment. 'Family's important to you Italian Americans, isn't it?'

'Yeah, of course – it's all there is. When we first came to America – my great-grandfather – we all had to stick together.

We was treated like shit. We laboured, we made money where we could.'

'And then?'

'And then some of us got pissed off with the situation. We brought over lots of traditions from the old country, my friend.'

'The Mafia.'

'I dunno what you're talkin' about.' Chiase smiled.

'I think it's only right you know this, Mr Chiase.' Strong fished a small card from the inside pocket of his overcoat. 'Here, take this.'

'What the fuck?' Chiase looked at the faded, stained business card. 'Where did you get this?' His eyes were wide.

'From the family that killed your grandfather.'

Chiase gulped, looking at the card in disbelief. *Chiase Olive Oil – Frank Chiase.* 'This was my grandfather's company. He disappeared when my father was just a kid. They was left with nothing.'

'He was branching out from olive oil.'

'How do you know this? It was years ago, back in the Prohibition days.'

'Yup. Your grandfather was here – well, near here. He was buying whisky. Not only that, he was buying distilleries.'

'He was?'

'Yes, he was. In fact, the man you shot was the great-grandson of the man who killed him.'

'I can't fucking believe this.'

'The family – Doig is their name – they took the mob's money. Lots of it, too.'

'The fucking assholes! By all accounts he was a sweet man. My grandmother never looked at another guy when he went.

What happened to the money? These assholes obviously spent it on shit, judging by where they live now, in that cottage.'

'No, in fact they were very careful with it. It was all in gold bullion.'

'You're breaking my balls. Whaddya mean, gold bullion – like gold bars, right?'

'Yes, exactly. Notes weren't so easy back then. Cash, especially foreign cash, attracted attention. There was a real little smuggling racket going on between here and the likes of Atlantic City and New York. The US government was breaking up stills and breweries. Your grandfather and his cronies needed booze for their speakeasies, and it was from places like this they got it.'

'All this time my family thought he ended up in a concrete block under some bridge, but he died here.' Chiase looked around, shaking his head sadly at the thought. 'So they still have this gold, these cocksuckers – my inheritance!'

'No, I do – well, at least I know where it is.'

'How much we talking?'

'These days – millions.'

Chiase smiled. 'So, we cut a deal – me and you.'

'I can do that. But first we have things to do.'

'Like what?'

'Like wipe out the last of the Doigs. I can't have any of this come back on me, and I don't know who knows what.'

'You're their attorney, aren't you? You chose me for this shit on purpose. The link with my grandfather, and all.'

'Yes.' The reply was flat.

Chiase flung his head back and laughed heartily. 'I've never trusted attorneys my whole life.'

'But you can trust this one.'

'What do we do, Mr Attorney?'

'We have to be careful. The police will have you on CCTV from earlier.'

'But we can get round that, right?'

'Yes, with some careful planning – and time.'

Chiase wagged a finger in Strong's face. 'As from now, I got all the time in the world, my friend.'

42

Daley left Dunwoody to Symington. She was much better at the art of dealing with such people than he was. And anyway, he had to think.

Scott was busy checking through O'Hara's phone records, while other officers checked out the town's CCTV cameras. Whoever had attacked the waiter was pivotal to what was going on, but how did this man fit into the bigger picture?

Daley thought about Ginny Doig, Alice Wenger, the Doig sons with their blank stares and ruined minds. Then there was the apparent suicide of Nathaniel Doig. He was staring at two photographs. One of Ginny Doig taken on her recent arrest, the other her daughter, a screen grab from her company website. 'What do you both know that I don't?' said Daley to himself.

He picked up the phone on his desk and dialled the number for the ACC's office. He was surprised to be transferred so quickly to the senior officer who handled Police Scotland's dealings with law enforcement agencies around the world.

'DCI Daley, how can I be of assistance?' said Franklin. He was a Londoner, well respected, and his current position in Scotland was seen by most as a stepping-stone to the top job at the Met.

'I would like to speak to the FBI. It's about a case we're involved with down here.' Daley went on to explain what he required.

'Leave it with me, Daley. I know things are difficult with you. I'll try to pinpoint the right person to speak to about this.'

'Thank you, sir.' Daley ended the call just as Scott arrived in his glass box.

'You're no' going tae believe this, Jimmy.'

'Me? I'm prepared to believe anything right now, Brian.'

'We got a decent image o' O'Hara's attacker fae CCTV.'

'Yes, and?'

'Ran it through the UK database – nothing.'

'Disappointing.'

'Then I took a shot at the international database. Here, take a look for yourself.' Scott handed a piece of paper across the desk to Daley, who peered at it for a few moments.

'Vitorio Chiase, a capo in the New Jersey mob.' Daley looked at Scott.

'Been inside for a decade. Got out a couple o' years ago. Looks like he's fallen on hard times.'

'And that's why he's here?'

Scott shrugged. 'He's working for somebody, that's for sure.'

Daley thought for a moment. 'Alice Wenger? She lives in the States, but surely that's all that connects them?'

'Worth asking the question, big man, eh?'

'It is.'

'And another thing. The boys up the road have traced the phone used tae call O'Hara tae arrange oor wee "joke" at the Machrie. It's an address in Edinburgh – posh, too. Owned by a Blair Williams; ring any bells?'

'Oh, yes, Brian. Oh yes.'

Blair Williams hated being hauled out of work. But his wife sounded very nearly hysterical, and when the police were mentioned he flung on his jacket and in moments was behind the wheel of his Maserati, weaving through the Edinburgh traffic. Silently he cursed Mike Strong. This had to be something to do with his machinations; there could be little doubt about that.

After a fraught drive blighted by road works, suicidal pedestrians and arrogant cyclists, he pulled up outside his state-of-the-art home, sweat forming on his brow despite the chill of the day. He was dismayed to note two strange vehicles in his drive. One was a nondescript saloon, the other a small van bearing Police Scotland markings.

'Shit!' He swore loudly to himself, banging the wheel with frustration.

Inside he found his wife with three police officers. One was a middle-aged man in an ill-fitting cheap suit; the archetypal detective. The other two were in police boiler suits. One of them was holding a device in his hand akin to a remote control for a toy plane – his son had one.

'Mr Williams, I'm DS Boyle.' The detective held out his hand, which Williams shook limply. 'These officers are from our technical forensic department.' Boyle's accent was heavily Edinburgh, making Williams's lip curl in distaste. Still, he was shocked.

'What?' His face was now deathly pale. He couldn't work out what on earth these forensic officers were looking for.

'An attack was perpetrated in Kinloch. The instruction to the attackers was made via a call from a mobile phone.

We have reason to believe that phone is here in your domicile, Mr Williams.'

'That's rubbish! How on earth did you come to that conclusion? I'm afraid you have me mixed up with my colleague, Mike Strong. He is currently on business in Kinloch.'

'Really?' Boyle nodded his head with interest. 'Well, we have a choice to make here, Mr Williams. I don't need to tell you that if you refuse to cooperate we shall have to raise a warrant to search your home. On the other hand, if we have your permission we can get on with it now. Sooner the better, eh?'

'Why my house?'

'The signal from the phone was traced to this address, sir.'

Williams thought frantically for a moment. 'He was here the night before last – Mike Strong, I mean. He must have had the phone in his possession.'

Boyle looked thoughtful. 'What makes you think your colleague – partner, I believe – would be involved in arranging an assault in Kinloch?'

'He's handling a case down there – a will, of sorts. He's acting on the instruction of a client of ours – a deceased client.'

Boyle looked confused. 'Okay, we can talk about that later. In the meantime, do we have your permission to search your house?'

Blair Williams felt slightly relieved. It was just the kind of mistake Strong would make. He wasn't tech-savvy, of that his young partner was sure. 'Go ahead; don't let me impede your investigation. If Mike Strong has been up to something, clearly it's in my interest to know as much as possible – as far as the firm is concerned, I mean.'

'Thank you, sir.' Boyle nodded to one of his colleagues. 'Go ahead, Brendan.'

At this, the officer with the hand-held device pressed a button, and almost instantly a bleeping noise emitted from it. As he moved round the room, the bleeps became either more or less frequent. The technician was meticulous, following the sounds, his face etched with concentration. Eventually he arrived at the large sofa. Suddenly the rapid bleeps turned into one long tone. He looked at Boyle. 'Here, gaffer.'

'You don't mind if we have a look at this, sir?' said Boyle.

'Yes, of course. I mean, I don't know what you think you'll find . . .'

The third officer, wearing thin rubber gloves, went about his work. He removed the sofa cushions and slid his hand into every nook and cranny of the piece of furniture. His task over, he looked at Boyle and shrugged.

Blair Williams's face took on a haughty expression. 'You see, I told you there was nothing to be found.'

'I'd like to move the sofa, please, sir,' said Boyle.

'To where?'

'Just to have a look underneath. I hope you don't mind. We have to be meticulous.'

'If you must. But I think it's pretty clear your gadgets aren't as clever as you think.'

'Well, we'll give this a go, eh?'

The two officers lifted the sofa to one side. Williams's wife gasped at the sight of a small cheap-looking red mobile phone lying on the carpet directly below where the sofa had sat.

Blair Williams had to take a seat. Not only was he shocked at the sight of the phone; he recognised it.

Boyle produced his own mobile from the inside pocket of his jacket and pressed the screen a couple of times. Sure enough, the phone on the carpet burst into life, vibrating on the carpet.

Ending the call, and pulling a rubber glove on one hand, Boyle bent down and lifted the red mobile from the carpet. 'So, any idea how this got here, Mr Williams?'

'No – none at all.' Beads of sweat were now plain on his brow. 'I can only think that Mike put it there.' The reply sounded less than convincing.

'Still some battery – let me see.' Boyle pressed some buttons on the red mobile. He read something from the screen as everybody in the room fell silent, Williams's wife looking at him with a mixture of panic and incredulity.

'Do you know someone called Karen, sir?'

'Yes, Karen is our secretary.' Williams gulped.

Boyle showed him the phone screen. Williams read the words *I'll be round in half an hour. Been thinking of fucking you all day. B.*

'You recognise this message, sir?'

Williams nodded his head, then stared at the floor.

As DS Boyle cautioned him, Amy Williams stared at her husband in disbelief. 'What have you done?'

As handcuffs were placed on his wrists, Blair Williams shot his wife a sad glance, but said nothing. He was led away by the police officers.

'I'm going to phone your father!' she shouted after them as her husband was taken from the house.

43

Daley gazed at the whiteboard. On it were pinned photographs of the Doig family, both living and dead; the estranged daughter, Alice Wenger; Sheena McKay, lying dead on the back path of her own home; and a single image of Blair Williams standing companionably at some function or other, sporting a glass of wine. The dead-eyed stare of Vitorio Chiase looked out from a monochrome prison mugshot, a number displayed underneath.

'That's aboot the oddest collection o' folk I've ever seen, Jimmy,' said Scott.

'What do you mean? We have a reclusive local family, two of whom are dead; an upmarket Edinburgh lawyer; a dead housewife from Kinloch; and a notorious member of the Mafia from New Jersey. What's unusual about that, Brian?' Daley smiled.

Symington appeared through the door of the glass box. She looked weary, her face pale and dark shadows under her eyes. 'He's a tough bastard,' she exclaimed, sitting down beside Scott opposite Daley.

'Grant Dunwoody? He's well known for it. That's why I afforded you the pleasure, ma'am.'

'Gee, thanks, Jim.' She ran her hand through her dark hair. 'Well, the upshot is, we have a problem.'

'We've always got a problem, me and him. Have you no' noticed that yet?' Scott took a slurp of tea.

'I have, come to think of it.' Symington smiled wanly. 'We can't keep Alice Wenger in the country. I've tried everything. She's a victim, not a suspect. Dunwoody has undertaken to give us full access to her – even said that she'll come back if reason dictates. But as for compelling her to stay here in Scotland, that's out of the question. And the bosses have given that the nod, too.'

'There's a whole lot of things that still aren't clear, ma'am,' said Daley.

'I know, Jim. I pointed that out to HQ, but they're not having it – plain and simple.

'What aboot Spence? He's old-school: could we no' ask him tae find a reason tae keep her in the hospital for a whiles? Just to gie us some breathing space, an' that.'

Symington looked at Scott askance. 'I'll pretend I didn't hear that, Brian.'

'Sometimes you have tae piss . . . use what you have, ma'am. And who knows, the lassie might no' be well enough tae travel. She'd a right dunt tae the heid.'

Daley nodded. 'I know you don't like the idea, Carrie, but it might be worth a try.'

'Do we suspect her of anything?'

'To be honest, I don't have a clue what's going on. Do you?'

Symington bit her lip. 'You buggers are going to get me in right trouble one of these days.'

'John Donald used tae say something similar, ma'am,' said Scott.

'And look how things panned out for him!'

'Aye, but they was extentional circumstances.'

'Exceptional,' said Daley.

'Aye, that tae, big man.' Scott nodded sagely.

Symington stood up. 'Do what you must, while I go and work out what other job I could do.'

'My advice, for what it's worth, ma'am?' said Scott.

'Go on.'

'Best no' tae worry aboot things until they happen. That's my . . . what do you call it, Jimmy?'

'Burying your head in the sand.'

'Naw. Thon other word. That Beatle was never done using it.'

'Mantra, do you mean?'

'Aye, that's it. Get some o' that mantra aboot you, ma'am.'

Symington raised her eyes, a resigned look on her face. 'I'm off before I tacitly sanction anything else that could lose us all our jobs.'

As she was leaving, Scott turned round in his chair. 'So you don't want me tae put this in the report I'm writing aboot the big man?'

Symington looked from one to the other. 'I don't know what to say.'

'That can be your mantra,' said Daley with a smile.

Scott looked at his old friend when she left. 'I'll get up the hospital, see what I can dae.'

'Best of luck, Brian.' Daley looked back at the whiteboard. He knew he was missing something, but for the life of him he didn't know what it was.

*

Ginny Doig felt much better now. She'd been fed and watered by her neighbours, and the feeling of relentless exhaustion had been all but banished. She sat and thought about her family. Her dead son, the other two, still in custody for all she knew, and finally her daughter. Her eyes narrowed and a flinty expression crossed her face.

'Malcolm, I know I owe you a great debt of gratitude.'

'Don't be stupid. I couldna leave you oot on the hill tae freeze tae death.'

'Aye, but the polis as well. You lied tae them. I know you're an honest man. It must have been hard.'

'Think nothing mair aboot it. Have you decided whoot you want tae do?'

'In a way. I wonder, could you dae me another wee favour?'

'Aye.'

'Could you take a look doon at the cottage for me – see if there's any sign o' life?'

'That's nae bother. Dae you think the boys might be hame?'

'I don't know. I just want tae know if the polis is still poking aboot, or the like.'

'As you know, I'm no friend tae the polis. I'll be happy to take a look.' He got up stiffly from his chair. 'But this weather fair stiffens me up these days, Ginny.'

'Same here. It's oor age. Folk is no' meant tae live long lives like we've done, Malcolm.'

'I'm seventy-eight in February.'

'Just a wean, then.' She smiled.

'I'll off an' take a look. I'll take the Land Rover. They say it's going tae snow. I wouldna be surprised. My boy won't be back until later; he's got a young farmers' meeting in the toon.

You know where stuff is. Feel free tae get yersel' tea, or anything else.'

'You're a good man. I thank you for it.'

She watched him drive down the farm lane under the heavy skies. There was always something about the clouds when snow was on the way, a kind of luminous quality, as though what sun there was was shining through the heavy burden about to fall in flakes. She waited until the old Land Rover was out of sight and then made her way into the lobby. A stout metal cabinet stood there, a small padlock holding it firmly closed.

Beside the cabinet was a scallop table on which sat a china figurine, a Jersey cow on a heavy base. Ginny lifted the ornament up. Sure enough there was a small key. She'd observed Malcolm quietly as she'd recovered. She'd seen him remove a gun from the cabinet and place the key back under the Jersey cow.

Ginny Doig unlocked the padlock. Inside the cabinet were a double-barrelled shotgun and a hunting rifle. She removed the rifle and the box of ammunition that sat beneath it.

Outside, a Subaru pickup was parked by a byre, the keys in the ignition; normal practice for farmers who couldn't keep track of the mountain of keys needed for their various farm vehicles.

She placed the rifle on the back seat, started the pickup and drove off down the lane as the first flakes of snow began to fall from the heavy sky.

Dr Spence looked at Scott over his half-moon spectacles. 'That would be most irregular, inspector. You know that, don't you?'

'Aye, but you wouldnae want yon lassie jumping on a jumbo jet unless you were sure she was a hundred per cent. I mean, heid injuries can be nasty.'

'Nearly as bad as peanuts, I dare say.'

Scott shook his head, a flat-lipped expression on his face. 'Enough wae the peanuts already!'

'I dine out on that story.' Spence laughed.

'Well, what aboot it then?'

'Okay. In fact, I'm genuinely not happy that Ms Wenger should endure a long-haul flight in her condition. But I can't justify keeping her in hospital. Beds are precious, and she's well enough to go back to the hotel. I'll have a district nurse check on her every day for a week or so, then we can think about letting her travel, all being well.'

'You're a star, doc.'

'No, I'm a professional. Don't confuse the two. And don't forget, she's not a prisoner. She's free to do as she pleases, regardless of what I say.'

'Understood. Right, well, I'll off and see how the patient is.'

'She's very upset, as it happens. Just found out about her old friend being killed, I understand.'

Scott thanked Spence again and made his way down the corridor. He nodded hello to the police constable guarding Alice Wenger's room and knocked gently at the door. Hearing a quiet 'Come in', he entered the small room.

Alice was lying in bed. Her face was pale, and a large bruise ringed one eye. She turned her head to look at Scott, and then wearily stared back at the wall. 'Oh, it's you, inspector.'

'Yes, nobody o' any importance,' he replied.

She sat up in bed, the expression on her face changing. 'Where were you when Sheena was killed?'

'It was a terrible thing. We couldn't possibly predict that she was in any danger.'

'Huh! Same as my big brother, then.'

'You have oor sincere condolences. Honestly, this isnae what we expected at all.'

'I told you what my mother was like! You chose not to listen.'

'So you think everything is doon tae her? I mean, this has all happened since you appeared . . .' Scott's voice tailed off.

'You're trying to blame me? Mr Dunwoody will love that.'

'I cannae go into details, but we think your brother and your best friend were victims of a professional killer.'

'Shit! I've lived in some of the worst places in America. You're telling me they have professional killers in Kinloch? Please.'

Scott ignored the barb and carried on. 'Dr Spence is coming to see you in a while.'

'Gee, my day just got so much better.'

'He doesnae think you're fit tae fly – what wae the head injury an' that.'

'I don't care what he thinks. I'm outta here, honey – first available to LA. My people are on it right now.'

'You're a rich woman, right?'

'You're smart. How much detection did it take to work that out?'

'Am I no' right in thinking that with someone like yourself they airlines wouldnae be very happy if anything happened tae you on the flight? You being ill, an' all that. I mean, it would cost them a fortune – if there was a claim, or the like.'

'And you'll make sure they know. You and your doctor friend down the corridor, right?'

'It's our duty tae look after your wellbeing.'

'Tell that to Sheena.'

'Anyway, I just thought I'd pop my heid in.'

'Oh, you're so kind. Now do me a favour and pop your "heid" back out again.'

Scott left Alice Wenger and the hospital behind. Outside it had begun to snow heavily. The roads and pavements were already slathered with a veneer of white flakes. He pulled up the collar of his overcoat and plodded off to Kinloch police office.

44

Mike Strong was sitting in the front seat of his car, seat reclined, the music of Jimi Hendrix washing over him, bringing back fond memories of his youth and those long summer days that never seemed to end.

Butterflies and zebras and moonbeams and fairy tales.

Was it really so long ago? It seemed like only a couple of years. But he knew he was about to get old – very old – and the thought saddened him.

Strong wasn't surprised when his mobile phone rang. He'd been expecting it after a distraught call from the secretary back in the office in Edinburgh to tell him that Blair Williams had been arrested. He'd enjoyed Karen's discomfort, knowing full well it would multiply when she found out that her 'other' phone had been the cause of his incarceration, never mind what else that device contained. People were so careless with their property these days.

'Mike Strong, how can I help you?' He turned on the wipers to remove the film of snow covering the car's windscreen.

'It's DCI Daley at Kinloch police office. I understand that you're in the area on business, Mr Strong. I'd like to have a word with you at the office, if you'd be so kind.'

'Yes, I am in Kintyre. But can I ask what business you have with me?' Why make it easy for the police, he thought.

'You may not be aware, but one of your partners was arrested a short time ago.'

'Yes, I have been informed of that. While it shocks me in one way, in another I'm not surprised.'

'Oh? Why not?'

'He's young and very careless. I'm only here trying to clear up the mess he caused in dealings with a client. But I can tell you more about that when I come to see you, DCI Daley – within the parameters of client confidentiality, of course.'

'I'm investigating two murders, Mr Strong. I'll decide about the nature of confidentiality. Will an hour or so be okay?'

'Perfect. I'm looking forward to meeting you.' Strong ended the call, a smirk on his face at the thought of Williams's plight.

He watched as Vito Chiase padded across the car park, huddled into his jacket, his grey hair already crowned with snow.

'What the fuck? I'm dying of cold over here.' He waved airily with his hand in a typical Italian American gesture.

Strong wound down the window and handed him a piece of paper. 'Put this address into your satnav. Make sure not to take the route through the town. It's a cottage, booked and paid for. The keys are under the mat. Nobody will bother you. Keep your phone on. I have to go and see the police in Kinloch.

'The cops are on to you? Oh, Marone!'

'It's nothing. I have everything under control. Think of the money, Vito.'

'This joint better have some food and a fire. I'm freezing my nuts off.'

'It has everything you need. Better get going; this snow is getting worse.'

'Huh! This ain't snow. Go to South Jersey – it's like winter fuckin' wonderland down there. I know all about snow, my friend.'

Strong watched as Chiase hurried back to the car. In a few moments he was gone, as was the lawyer. Though he was heading to Kinloch police office.

Daley picked up the call. 'DCI Daley. Thanks for getting back to me so soon.'

'Sure thing, sir. I'm Special Agent Jackowsky. I'm at Langley, FBI HQ. We've been having a look at Alice Wenger, as you asked.'

Daley was pleased that this man sounded all business. He didn't have time for small talk. Something told him that every moment counted; he had to get to the bottom of things, and quickly. 'Have you turned anything up?'

'Wenger herself, from what I have now, is clean as a whistle. She's had a green card for thirty years. One thing: she'd been beaten up quite badly by an ex-boyfriend when she first arrived in our country, according to our records.'

'Yes, she mentioned that,' said Daley, disappointed that there wasn't something more tangible on Alice Wenger.

'I've got our field officers in Louisiana making enquiries. You never know what they'll turn up.' It was clear that Jackowsky had picked up on the deflation in Daley's voice. 'I do have some news for you about her business, though. Wenger Leisure, right?'

'Right. What about it?'

'They aren't doing as well financially as it would appear. They've been filling losses – big losses too – with the IRS in the last couple or three years.'

'And before then?'

'They were flying high.'

'Some kind of recession?'

'We're past all that over here. I don't know about you guys in England.'

Daley ignored the mistaken geographical reference and carried on. 'So why the downturn?'

'That's what I personally am looking into for you. Give me twenty-four hours, I'll have an answer.'

'Thank you. This is much appreciated, I assure you.'

'Don't worry; it's my job. Who knows, we might find something of interest to us. We'll speak soon. Pleasure doing business with you, detective.'

The call over, Daley looked again at Alice Wenger's image on the whiteboard. He stroked his chin. 'What do you know that I don't know?' he said aloud.

The snow was still heavy as Strong parked his car by a lawyer's premises and walked the few yards up the hill to Kinloch police office. He remembered dealing with that lawyer about twenty years ago. A pleasant man, he recalled.

Having spent a lot of his career in police stations, the prospect of being in another didn't bother him. Preliminary research on the DCI he was about to meet indicated that he was a meticulous, tenacious individual, but he'd come across lots of policemen like that. Though they worked hard, he usually found himself in a superior intellectual position.

He'd made a career of it.

The desk sergeant was courteous and efficient, commenting on the weather as he showed Strong through to a familiar scene: a CID office with detectives busy at their desks. The buzz in the place made it obvious that they were dealing with urgent business. He recognised the ebb and flow of police procedure.

Strong was shown to a partitioned-off glass box sitting in the centre of the room, blinds down so that no one could see inside. The desk sergeant knocked quietly, opened the door and introduced the lawyer to a tall, rather grey-faced and gaunt-looking man behind a large desk. His clothes hung off him as if he had been ill or on a crash diet. Ill, thought Strong, as he was invited to take a seat; the lines and hollow eyes were good enough indications of that. He noted that two whiteboards had been turned round so that he couldn't see what they displayed. So this detective was at least smart enough to do that – he'd known many who weren't.

'Mr Strong, thank you for coming in.' Daley shook his hand with a tight grip.

'It's my pleasure. Personally, I'm mortified that Blair Williams has been arrested. I don't know any details, so I'd be grateful if you could fill me in.'

Rather than answer directly, Daley asked a question in return. 'I spoke to Mr Williams a while ago. He was very keen to implicate you in any investigation into his actions. Why would that be?'

Strong ran his hand through his silver hair. 'He's been out of his depth for a while with the affairs of a client of ours. I'd rather not go into details, but it's fair to say he should have informed me of what was going on long before he did.'

'That client being the late Nathaniel Doig?'

'Yes. I'm prepared to confirm that, though the exact nature of the wishes of our deceased client must remain confidential.'

'As you know, Mr Strong, if I deem it necessary I'll seek a warrant compelling you to reveal the details of those "wishes".'

'That's up to you, DCI Daley. However, in the meantime we are where we are.'

Daley nodded and consulted his notes. 'Are you aware that your partner Blair Williams has dealings in Glasgow?'

'No, I was not. We have our hands full with our part of the world without branching out into Glasgow.'

'But you took on a client from Kintyre?'

'That is a long-standing arrangement made by our client with a late colleague of mine, a lawyer named Hardacre. For whatever reason, he saw fit to inform young Williams of the case before he died. He should have come to me, the senior partner.'

'Why do you think he didn't?'

'I don't know. Hardacre was very ill – cancer. He had a brain tumour; I can only imagine this malady affected his judgement.'

'We believe that Blair Williams arranged for an assault on a visitor to this area. Does that surprise you?'

Strong raised his brows. 'In recent weeks, much of what Blair Williams gets up to has surprised me. But I must confess, this revelation is a bit of a shock.'

'So you know that he's been having an affair with your secretary.' Daley looked down at his notes. 'One Karen Milne, I believe.'

Strong sighed. 'Yes, I was aware of this . . . relationship, DCI Daley. Rather tawdry for a married man with children and a lovely wife. But he's a grown man. I might be senior partner, but I'm not the keeper of his morals.'

'So you didn't see this affair as a source of potential problems for your firm?'

'I did, as a matter of fact. A marriage break-up – well, it can make the best of us unstable. I'm sure you agree. Especially a junior member of staff.' He smiled at Daley, letting him know that he'd done his homework. 'I had intended to have a word with him, but events rather got in the way.'

'We are in possession of a mobile phone that we believe was used to arrange this assault. It was found at his home. I believe you visited there recently.'

'Indeed I did. I had to find out how much he knew about our client before making the trip to Kinloch.' Strong rubbed his chin as though thinking what to say next.

'What?'

'I did think he seemed rather jumpy – not himself, if you know what I mean. I put it down to the fact that he'd made such an arse of the things I'm now forced to deal with. But in the light of what you tell me, well, it's obvious why he looked rather stressed.'

'I see.' Daley consulted his notes again. 'Mr Williams has been interviewed by our colleagues in Edinburgh. He is of the opinion that you planted the phone in his lounge on the night of his visit.'

Strong laughed. 'How ridiculous! From what you tell me, I imagine this device is the source of your information pointing to his affair with Ms Milne. I assume that it contains intimate conversations of one kind or another. How on earth would I come into possession of such an item?'

'Yes, we did wonder about that, too. Mr Williams also

told us that you withdrew a considerable sum of money from the company coffers recently. Would you care to elaborate?'

'I have a company credit card. Why on earth would I want to withdraw funds in cash?'

'Mr Williams tells us that you told him it was in connection with your visit here.'

'Sounds to me as though young Blair has lost the plot, or is involved in some nefarious project to which I am certainly not privy. I would have thought what was contained on his phone, not to mention his handling of our late client's affairs, would be enough to confirm that he's hardly to be trusted.'

Daley paused, looking Williams straight in the face in silence for a few moments. The lawyer met his gaze unflinchingly. 'Are you aware of a gentleman named Vitorio Chiase?'

'Doesn't sound like a chap from Morningside, does he? No, I have no knowledge of such a person. What has he got to do with this – with Blair Williams, I mean?'

'Like you, there are certain things I'm not at liberty to discuss, Mr Strong. I take it that you are still unwilling to divulge the nature of your business with Nathaniel Doig?'

'I think the reputation of my firm is in enough jeopardy without my making known to all and sundry the private affairs of our clients, don't you?'

'In that case I do intend to pursue a warrant.'

'I wish you good fortune, DCI Daley. The correct procedure, I agree.'

'Indeed. Can I ask you how long you intend to spend in the area, Mr Strong?'

He shrugged. 'I don't quite know – as long as it takes. I believe that there are complexities within the Doig family of which I was hitherto unaware. I'm sure you know more than I do. In fact, I need to book an hotel. Do you have any recommendations, DCI Daley?'

'The County just down the Main Street is as good as any.'

'Yes, I passed it on the way here. I'll take your advice.'

'Good. Please stay in touch, Mr Strong. We may have to speak to you again, as I'm sure you realise. So let me know when you intend to leave.'

'You have my word, DCI Daley. I'd better get booked into this hotel before the snow gets worse, eh?'

Daley stood and shook the lawyer's hand. He watched him leave, all expensive overcoat and well-cut suit. From what he knew of Blair Williams, the younger man sounded young and foolish. His senior partner most certainly did not come into either category.

Daley got up and turned the whiteboards back round. Again he stared at the faces, but they still weren't talking.

45

Grant Dunwoody looked exasperated as he sat on the chair beside Alice Wenger in Kinloch hospital. She was sitting with her arms folded, a determined look on her face.

'To offer to do this, well – it's madness!' he said.

'I pay you to do what I want, not to tell me what to do. Take my proposal to DCI Daley. I know he'll want to take the option.'

Dunwoody shrugged. 'If you say so, but I must register my concern regarding this course of action.'

'You be as concerned as you want. Just do as I ask. And while you're at it, tell the doctors that if they won't discharge me I'll do it myself.'

'Your choice!' Dunwoody walked out of the room.

Alice Wenger bit her lip. Everything seemed to be collapsing around her. Now was the time to be proactive. Now was the time to do what she always did in these situations – find a way to make a difference.

Scott shook his head when Daley told him about the meeting with Strong. 'Aye, I've heard o' that mob. Supposed tae be shit-hot criminal lawyers in their day, but mainly dae corporate stuff noo, yes?'

'So it appears.'

'News from the hospital, Jimmy: the results of the scans on the two Doig ... boys.' Scott shrugged as though he didn't know the best way to describe the unfortunate men with the minds of children.

'As we thought?'

'Yep. Well, getting by all the medical jargon, both have scar tissue tae their frontal lobes, and signs that the skull above their eyes has been broken at some point. That's how they're no' playing wae the full deck. Old Spence was right!'

'It's truly disgusting.' Daley's face had blanched.

'So, your man knows that the daughter has come tae expose his brutality and takes a heider off the cliff. Simples!'

'Ginny Doig must have known. Are we any further with the box full of his papers?'

'Hard going, big man. From what the guys are telling me, there's everything there from wild theories aboot the world to observations on the weather and the like. No mention o' any ice pick lobotomy, or that. But we're only just a third o' the way through it.'

Daley pondered on this. Surely the reason Alice Wenger ran away was to avoid the same fate as her brothers. It made sense. As children they must have gone to school, and any medical intervention such as Scott had described would have been picked up instantly. So, for whatever reason, Nathaniel Doig waited until his children had left school and then took their minds. He still couldn't come to terms with the monstrosity of it, but he'd come across so much inexplicable horror in his long career that this was just one more gruesome movie to play in his head.

He looked at his watch. 'Shit! It's time for my meds and

343

I left them at home. Hold the fort, Bri, and I'll pop up and get them.'

'I'll go, Jimmy. Just you sit tight and work this little lot out.' Scott nodded to the whiteboards.

'It's all right. I could do with some fresh air and time to think.'

'You're okay though, aye? I've got tae say, you're a bit pale aboot the chops, like.'

'I'm fine, Brian. You know, that's the strange thing. I dreaded coming back – to work, I mean – but I've not had a twinge, nothing, since you picked me up and we went to Rowan Tree Cottage.'

'The black croft, you mean.'

'Don't spoil the moment, Bri.' He smiled. 'Nothing on the searches for Ginny Doig or Chiase?'

'Gone tae ground, buddy. But they can't get far, surely. There's been a roadblock at Tarbert ever since this all kicked off. I cannae see thon auld hag piloting a boat, can you?'

'But Chiase?' Daley left the question open.

'I'm mair intae a straightforward crook, me. All this stuff is bursting my heid!'

'Mine too, Brian, mine too.'

The handsome guest Tom Macmillan had just arrived for lunch in the County Hotel. As Annie fussed over him, asking how he'd slept and taking his food order, Hamish eyed his tall figure from his seat near the bar, sucking thoughtfully on his unlit pipe.

'You'll be Canadian, I reckon,' he stated sagely.

'You're very observant, sir. I know in this country most folks find it hard to tell us from our neighbours to the south.'

'Not at all; I've always noted a wee hint o' good old Scots in the Canadian tongue. I heard it in your voice when you were busy ordering the fish there. The Americans don't have that – well, maist of them, at least.'

'You'll be telling me you know my name next.' The man smiled at the elderly fisherman, whose face crinkled into a smile.

'I wouldna presume tae tell you your ain name. But if I was tae take a guess, I'd say you were a Macmillan.'

Momentarily there was a silent competition between Annie and the new guest to see whose jaw could drop the furthest.

'How dae you know that, Hamish? I hope you've no' been looking at the guest book.'

'No, no guest book. You're the spitting image of your faither when he left here. I would have spotted you anywhere.'

'Amazing!' Tom Macmillan was clearly impressed. He leaned over and held his hand out to Hamish. The old man shook it enthusiastically. 'People do say that, mind you. But to spot it out of context like this, that's an impressive feat, sir.'

'Hamish. Just call me Hamish. Och, I knew your faither passably well, even though his time was spent driving lorries and mine aboard a boat. He married auld Willie's daughter – your mother.'

'He did. They emigrated to Canada before I was born.'

'I dare say there was plenty mair room on they Canadian roads for lorry drivers.'

'Yeah, there sure was. He set up his own company in Toronto. I'm very proud to say that I run it now, since – well, since he passed away.'

'I'm fair sad tae hear that. You have my condolences, son. He was a fine man.'

'Which "auld Willie" are you on aboot, Hamish?'

'You knew this man's grandfaither as well as yoursel'. He was your boss for a wee while, sure.'

'My grandfather owned this place. When he left it to my uncle, my mom and dad decided to take their share of what he'd given them and start a new life. Now I come here and discover that the place is to be turned into flats. It makes me very sad.'

Annie sighed. 'I remember noo. I was just a lassie then. It's by pure chance that you caught us in time. In a few months this place will be nothing mair than a building site.'

Tom Macmillan looked from the old man to the woman behind the bar. 'This makes you guys sad too, right?'

'No' jeest sad, son. Damn near a tragedy, if you want my opinion. There's been an inn on this site for a good three hundred years. No' the fine establishment you see now, but a convivial place o' welcome in one way or t'other. Noo, well, it'll just be some holidaymakers, or them wae too much money wandering aboot wae the ghosts, wae no idea o' all the tall tales an' grand deeds that took place within these walls.'

Tom Macmillan took a sip of his beer. 'I know my mother will be devastated. She bangs on about the County Hotel all the time.'

'It's a great pity it went tae her brother. I mind your mother well – a bonnie lassie, so she was. You be sure tae pass on my regards next time you're talking.'

Before Tom could say more, a stocky man with silver hair and a smart overcoat appeared in the bar. 'I've been ringing the bell. I wonder, could I have a room for a few nights?'

'I am sorry, sir,' said Annie. 'We were jeest reminiscing aboot old times.'

'Nothing wrong with that,' said Mike Strong. 'I do it all the time.'

Daley knew James junior would be at nursery. If truth be told, he was uneasy as to what scene would greet him as he opened the front door to his home on the hill and made his way down the hall and into the lounge. He prayed that Liz was managing to maintain her sobriety of recent days.

'Shit! You gave me a fright, darling,' she said, looking up from the paper on which she was writing. She was sitting at the big dining table at the far end of the long room, her reading glasses balanced on the end of her nose.

'Are you writing your memoirs?'

She removed the spectacles and shot him a sad smile. 'I'm writing to my mother.'

'Oh.'

She shrugged. 'I have to tell her what really happened. I know she's been beside herself. You know what she was like the last time she was here.'

'Worried.'

'Yes. It's only fair that I tell her. I know you've never liked her, but she's been good to me. She deserves an explanation, don't you agree?'

'It's never been a case of me not liking her. She's always hated the fact that you married beneath you. If there's been any hating done, it has come from her.'

Liz nodded sadly. 'You're right, of course. But you know why that is, don't you?'

'She's a snob.'

'She came from a scheme in Glasgow.' Liz stared at her husband levelly.

'What? I thought she went to a private school, then uni – where she met your father.'

'No, that didn't happen. She was a barmaid at the uni bar. That's when she met my father.'

'You mean, after all these years . . . I mean, you've all been lying to me. Why?'

'That would take a long time to explain. Why don't we talk about it tonight?'

Daley looked at his watch. 'Yes. I've only come back to get some tablets.' He was about to say more when his phone rang. 'Yes, Brian . . . Okay, I'll be back in a few minutes.' He ended the call and turned to Liz. 'To be continued, yes?'

She nodded and got back to her letter writing.

46

Daley entered Kinloch police office to a commotion. The urgency on everyone's face was obvious. Even Sergeant Shaw looked flustered.

'Brian's in your office, sir.'

Daley nodded and hurried into the CID suite. Two detectives were wearing bulletproof vests. Daley noticed how young they looked, their faces a mixture of fear and excitement. For a split second he was reminded of the first time he'd carried a gun, the feeling coming back unbidden, making him shiver.

Scott, himself decked out in firearms kit, was standing in his glass box looking at a map on the wall.

Daley didn't need to ask the question: Scott got straight to the point. 'A few things, Jimmy. First of all, an auld farmer up in the hills has reported both his truck and hunting rifle missing, aye, along wae the ammunition. He was questioned yesterday by two uniforms who were looking for Ginny Doig, but he lied to them. He picked her up on the hill, near dead wae the cold. It would appear she's recovered.'

'She took the vehicle and the rifle?'

'Aye, she did that. This auld fella thought better o' it and called us.'

'Is that the few things? The truck and the rifle, I mean?'

'No, there's mair.'

'Great.'

'I've had a phone call from Grant Dunwoody.'

'If Alice Wenger wants to get on the next flight to the States it would be for the best. There's only one person her mother will be looking for.'

'The opposite. She wants to stay – be a decoy to attract her mother, Jimmy.'

'That's ridiculous.' Daley looked blankly at the wall for inspiration.

'Big man, there's also the matter of her two sons; we have them here, remember? Would you put it past her tae try and break them oot?'

Daley shook his head. 'No, I wouldn't put anything past her. She has ammunition, right?'

'She has that – and plenty o' it, tae.'

'Where's Symington?'

'At a local council meeting. Mind, you were supposed tae go, but she stepped in.'

'Get her back, Brian. I need to go to the hospital to speak to Alice Wenger.'

'No need. She's in the family room with Dunwoody.'

'This is madness. Now we have two armed and dangerous individuals roaming free.'

'I've got the helicopter on its way, but they're no' happy wae the snow. It's off at the moment, but if it comes back on – well, they're grounded.'

'This truck that Ginny Doig has. Surely it won't get through a blizzard?'

'Aye, it will. It's a Subaru SUV. And he's got snow chains

on it. Put them on when the snow started. She's likely mair mobile than us.'

Daley couldn't fathom it all. One murdered man, one murdered woman, both with connections to Alice Wenger. Nathaniel Doig's suicide; his lawyer complicit in, well, something. Then there was the attack on Alice Wenger, her financial problems in America. Not to mention a New Jersey gangster on the loose.

Every time he asked himself the question, the same three names presented themselves: Alice Wenger, Ginny Doig and the USA. But what was the connection?

'Okay, Brian. I see you've got a team together. I take it you've put out an alert for this Subaru?'

'Yup. Dae you want me tae get on the road, see if we can find the woman?'

'Hang tight until the chopper arrives. We can only assume that she's after Wenger or her sons, and they're all here.'

'True.'

'Secure the office: gates, front door, the lot. Nobody in or out without authorisation from you or me.'

'Symington will love that.'

'See if you can get her on the mobile, Bri. I'll go and speak to Alice Wenger.'

'Spot on, big man, spot on.'

With no little difficulty Vito Chiase found the cottage that Strong had arranged for him. It nestled in a small valley, everything shrouded in a carpet of sparkling snow. When he walked through the door scented logs were ablaze in a large fireplace. The warmth washed over him like a hot bath.

He walked to the flames and rubbed his hands before the

fire, feeling every joint in his body loosen up, the dull ache in his knees and shoulders slowly disappear.

He pulled the cell phone from his pocket. He had a signal. He plugged the phone into a socket near the fireplace and went in search of food. Though the kitchen was small and cramped, the cupboards were full. He opened a large packet of potato chips and devoured them ravenously.

In another cupboard he found a big loaf of home-baked bread. In the fridge were some cold cuts and cheese. He placed them on a plate, together with a knife and some butter. Before going through to eat this impromptu meal by the fire, he opened the last cupboard. This contained the necessities of life, well, certainly as far as he was concerned. A large jar of coffee and two mugs stood by a bottle of Scotch and a small crystal glass.

It took him two trips to bring everything through to the lounge. He placed the food and the whisky on a small table beside a chair by the blazing fire. The coffee could wait. He wanted a drink – he needed one.

He poured three fingers into the glass, set it down on the table, ate some of the bread, cheese and cold meat and then sat back, letting the heat wash over him again. He took a large gulp of whisky and his relaxation was complete.

As the spirit warmed his body and soothed his brain, his mind began to wander. White-wall tyres, a beautiful girl with silky smooth legs in the back seat of his Lincoln; on the tables with his crew in Atlantic City; a man's head disappearing in a spray of blood; an iron bar over a security guard's knee as he yelled in agony; throwing piles of money into the air like confetti.

He took another sip of the whisky – it was good. Deep and

mellow, with a bite of spice at the back of his throat that reminded him of Christmas.

Vito Chiase was surprised to feel a fat tear meander down his cheek. In his world you didn't show any emotion. In the funeral parlour, yeah, you got a pass. But everywhere else it was all bravado: terrible jokes, breaking balls – being a stand-up guy.

The taste of the spirit mixed with the cold cuts took him back to his favourite restaurant in Caldwell. A friend of his from school had taken over a joint that had been built up by his grandfather and father before him. Originally they made the peasant food of southern Italy that the immigrants to the new world so craved, but as the years passed and palates became more sophisticated, the restaurant became one of the best places to eat in the tri-state area – certainly if you were Italian. He could see it, smell it and taste it.

All these memories brought back by a hunk of bread, some meat and a little booze. Life was strange; he couldn't remember such a mix of emotions. But here, in this strange country in the middle of nowhere, he was reliving his past. It was playing out across his mind's eye like a movie that never ended, but just went on and on and on.

He remembered the picture of his grandfather that stood on the mantel above the fire in his grandmother's house. She used to kiss it every morning, and say a prayer and a Hail Mary, working the string of beads through her fingers as tears slipped down her face. He remembered her doing this from when he was a kid until the day she could no longer stand and had to be taken to a retirement home, the best in North Jersey, the one he paid for gladly, the one where the photograph of his grandfather sat by her bedside. In her last days, when she could barely breathe, all she could do was stare at the man with the thick dark hair and the broad shoulders – like Victor Mature, he'd always thought. That he had died here, in this place – it made Vito Chiase feel nauseous.

People watched too many movies. Those in *this thing of ours* were invariably portrayed as monsters – and some were, but they were in the minority. Most of the guys he'd grown up with wanted the best for their families, wished their kids to lead any life but the one in which they found themselves. Everybody knew the risks and the rules; they were soldiers, they obeyed orders. Amongst their own, when the gloves were off, anything went. If you were a made man you had some leeway, but if a boss wanted you clipped, you might as well have been some punk on the street.

Memories: they were beautiful and haunting at the same time.

He drained the glass and felt the whisky warm his gullet.

His last thoughts were of his beautiful wife.

He didn't have time to realise that his heart had stopped.

The glass dropped from his hand and rolled across the wooden floor.

Dunwoody sat like an owl on the sofa in the Kinloch police office family room beside Alice Wenger. His gaze flitted between Daley and his client through expensive round horn-rimmed spectacles.

'It's me she wants,' said Wenger, the large bruise over her eye now yellow at the margins.

'What about your brothers?' said Daley.

Before she could reply Dunwoody held his hand in the air, ending the exchange. 'I must say at this point that my client is most certainly going against my advice. I—' He wasn't given time to finish the sentence.

'You keep it shut, honey. I'll tell you if I want an opinion,' said Wenger emphatically. 'If you put me in that house, she'll come after me. You know it's true, Mr Daley.'

'I know it's a ridiculous idea, and a dangerous one.'

'So you'd rather have my mother roaming free with a hunting rifle and enough bullets to start a war. She's going to come find me – and this is where she'll come.'

'I think we can handle your mother.'

'And what about the guy who killed Sheena, not to mention the person who arranged that little "joke" at the Machrie House Hotel?' She pointed to her injured eye. 'Some joke, yeah?'

'We have the people who did that.'

'But you don't have the person who paid them to do it.'

'I can't say anything about that at this time.'

She laughed mirthlessly. 'You might want to sit here like a turkey before Thanksgiving, but I don't. We put an end to this now. I've spent too many years with horror of what my parents did to my brothers – tried to do to me. It has to end!'

'Not that way,' replied Daley wearily.

'You tell them about your journalist friend, Grant?'

'What?' said Daley.

'Not a friend, merely an acquaintance, DCI Daley. As I'm sure you know, in my profession it sometimes pays to have a contact amongst the gentlemen of the press.'

'So?'

'He knows everything: about my client's upbringing, her brothers – the events of the last two days. More pertinently, about the utter incompetence you and your officers have displayed in dealing with this case.'

'And a little bird told them this, yes?' said Daley, feeling his heartbeat thud in his chest.

'Lots of little birds in places like Kinloch, I find. This will make headlines on both sides of the Atlantic. My client has a reasonably high profile amongst the business community in the United States of America.'

'The answer is still no,' said Daley.

'No to just what, exactly?' said Wenger. 'You have no power to hold me here. I can leave and go anywhere I damn well please.'

Daley shrugged.

'Good, that's agreed then. Grant, let's get the hell outta here, boy.'

As Daley opened his mouth to object, there was a knock at the door. Symington appeared, her face a mask of concern. 'A word, Jim.'

Daley left the room and walked a few feet down the corridor with his boss.

'First, I know what she wants to do, and second so do the bosses.'

'Meaning?'

'Meaning they think the idea will work. Dunwoody plays golf with one of the ACCs.'

'Typical.'

'We can't just sit here like fish in a barrel, Jim. Plus the helicopter is snowbound in Glasgow, and the road's closed by heavy snow on the rest. Our options are narrowing.'

'So we use Alice Wenger as a decoy to trap her own mother. Bizarre!'

'But it might work. We'll have plenty of bodies tucked away. She won't get anywhere near Wenger.'

'What about Chiase?'

'The considered opinion is that they're working in tandem, Jim.'

'What's Blair Williams saying?'

'Nothing. He claims that he left everything to Mike Strong.'

'But the phone used to contact O'Hara was in his possession.'

'He says Strong planted it.'

'How convenient.'

'But it makes sense when you think about it.'

'Okay, so there's lots of money at stake, apparently. Though where this money has come from nobody knows.'

'And Nathaniel Doig is riven by guilt when he sees his daughter for the first time in nearly four decades. He knows why she's come – to seek vengeance for the way her mother and father brutalised her brothers, and would have treated her if she hadn't run away.'

'And Ginny Doig is the brains behind all this, Carrie?'

'We know what she's like.'

'But the whole hotel thing doesn't make sense.'

'Why? It was a warning, plain and simple.'

'And the attacker just happened to be the same height and build as Ginny? Did you know Wenger's company is in trouble?'

'It is?'

'The FBI is looking into it. They're getting back to me.'

'But what would that prove? We know Alice Wenger didn't kill her brother or Sheena McKay. We also know from the Greek witness that her father simply fell backwards from the cliff, just like she said.'

Daley sighed. 'But this decoy idea – it's still madness.'

'We have enough bodies. We stick her in the cottage, let the gossips do the rest. My guess is Ginny and Chiase will turn up – and there we go.'

'He's a pro, ma'am. In the bloody Mafia.'

'He's an old man. Look at the mess he made of the O'Hara business. Frankly, if we can't round up two OAPs in these circumstances, we might as well give up.'

'What I say doesn't matter, does it?'

Chief Superintendent Carrie Symington shrugged. 'It doesn't matter what either of us think. The decision has been made. Alice goes to the cottage with a minder; we spread the word, get in position and wait for events to unfold. As soon as they show themselves we nab them.'

Daley was tired; tired and horrified. He had two men in his cells whose minds had been taken away in the most brutal fashion. He had two murder victims. Everything pointed to Ginny Doig and Chiase. 'Okay, we do it your way, ma'am. But I'm interested to know how an elderly woman who has hardly left her croft in the middle of nowhere for years gets in touch with an American gangster. They don't even have a phone at Rowan Tree Cottage.'

'I hear you. But if we catch them things will become much clearer, eh? And remember, this is not my way, Jim.'

'Whatever.' Daley rubbed his face and walked off. He wondered yet again why his organisation bothered with middle-ranking officers, when it appeared that decisions were being made behind desks nearly two hundred miles away. It wasn't the first time this thought had crossed his mind, and it wouldn't be the last, he reckoned.

47

Mike Strong sat on the edge of his hotel bed tying his tie. It was dark outside, and while the snow had stopped in Kinloch he saw on the television that the adverse conditions had brought much of the central belt of Scotland to a halt.

In any case, he was hungry and thirsty. He cursed himself for not having brought a decent malt to enjoy in the privacy of his room. But he was bored hanging about in this dingy place, and reckoned that an hour or two in the bar surely couldn't be that arduous; it would at least break the monotony, and he might pick up some information. He knew how small towns worked.

He stood and opened the old net curtains to stare down on Main Street. On the road, snow had been turned into a muddy-brown slush, but the pavements, though dotted with footprints, were still white. A movement caught his eye, and he realised an old woman was waving at him from the bus stop on the opposite side of the road. Instead of returning the gesture, he pulled the curtain to, cursing his luck at being stuck in this place. Then he thought of the reward.

Mike Strong shrugged on his blazer, checked his hair in the mirror one more time, and made for the small bar of the County Hotel.

'I cannae dae it,' said Brian Scott to his wife.

'Why not? Have you taken a vow o' silence?'

'No. I'm a policeman, remember?'

'I remember fine,' said Ella. 'Don't you dare tell me that the polis don't go intae pubs, get half cut and tell anyone who'll listen all they know. I've been about one o' them for a' these years, after all.'

'But I don't drink, dearest.' Scott was doing his best to be pleasant. He realised that any other strategy would end in disaster.

'So, I just rock up in the County, stand on a stool and tell everyone this Wenger lassie is holed up in her mother's hoose. What's it called again, Christmas Tree Cottage?'

'Rowan Tree Cottage.'

'Right. And don't raise your eyebrows, Brian Scott. You get paid tae be a polis, no' me!'

'All you need tae dae is go up tae Hamish or Annie and gie them the whisper. The whole toon's on aboot what's been happening. They'll lap it up. It'll be all over the place before you can say gie me a large gin and tonic.'

'No, it won't. That's the first thing I'm going tae say.'

'So you'll dae it!' Scott smiled widely.

'I'll need tae be rewarded in some way. I'm no charity, you know.'

He sidled up to her and kissed her neck. 'Don't you worry aboot that, my dear.'

'You can keep your hand on your ha'penny! I mean a new dress, or some nice shoes. A roll in the hay wae you has long since stopped being any kind o' reward.'

Scott looked rather crestfallen. 'Aye well, if that's what

it takes. Meantime, I'll away and swallow some bleach – just to get oot o' your way, like.'

'You'd be better wae the drain cleaner. Much mair powerful, I'd think.'

'My mother telt me you had a cruel streak.'

'Aye, she was right, then. Poor old bugger thought everyone had a cruel streak after a' they years wae your faither.'

'Always a dig at my faither.'

'He drank every penny he ever earned, just aboot. I'm sure you had tae burn the doors tae keep warm – no' tae mention eating your pets.'

'It wisnae "pets", it was just Thumper. My rabbit.'

'Just as well yous never had a dog.'

'We were poor, but we were happy. We wanted for nothing. There was folk in oor street much worse off than us!'

It was Ella Scott's turn to raise her eyebrows. 'Poor bastards.'

Mike Strong was pleasantly surprised by the conviviality of the little bar at the County Hotel. Though he'd attracted a few glances when he first walked in, the other customers soon returned to their own conversations. In fact, he detected a conspiratorial buzz about the place; little wonder, he reasoned, following recent events in the area.

The barmaid was efficient and polite, despite her strong accent. He noted that an old man in the corner near the bar, with a pipe and a thick fisherman's jumper, was following his every move through hooded eyes, but that was a minor irritant.

He chose a table at the back of the bar and sat down with a very large malt whisky. A fire was blazing in the hearth, and an artificial Christmas tree that had seen better days stood at its side. Its branches were, in places, bare of faux greenery, and the wire from which they were constructed could be seen drooping under the weight of gaudy, unfashionable baubles. However, what with the snow, the whisky and the leaping flames, Mike Strong couldn't help but feel an encroaching festive spirit.

He thought about what to do next. Chiase was safely tucked away. He was the weapon of war that Strong needed. A shield between himself and what was happening. He felt a fleeting sadness that the old mobster had spent his last Christmas in New Jersey. Then he reasoned that Vito Chiase had removed Christmas from many people during his life of crime.

A couple entering the bar caught his eye. The man was of average height, and had short dark hair peppered with grey. His wife was slim, but not in a healthy way. She looked like many of his less affluent clients of the past, thin through necessity rather than choice: a lifetime of cigarette smoking and pecking at poor food, no doubt. He decided that, despite her neatly dyed hair and well-cut coat, this woman had seen hard times.

He supposed this was a product of his years as a lawyer; it was impossible for him not to notice people, to weigh them up. He'd done it in the courtroom, and more recently across the corporate boardroom. Everybody had a weak point. If you observed them for long enough, you could detect a raised eyebrow here, a change of pallor there; dry lips, a tight throat, trembling hands. It was all part of his art.

Suddenly the man caught his eye and stared at him. Though Strong couldn't be sure, he thought he saw the same process going on behind that gaze, as though he was the one now being evaluated.

He put the glass to his mouth and ignored the notion. He had enough on his plate without perceiving problems that didn't exist.

'Hello, you two,' said Annie, with a smile that was perhaps too broad to be absolutely sincere. She liked Ella, but had to work hard at hiding her latent feelings for her husband. 'Are you in for a meal?'

'No such luck,' replied Ella Scott. 'There was nothing on the telly, and I didn't want tae spend another night staring at this yin's coupon.'

Annie laughed, but anyone who knew her would have detected a mirthless quality in the sound. In fact, the old fisherman sitting at the table nearest the bar reckoned that the chatelaine of the County Hotel would be quite happy to stare at Brian Scott all night, TV or no TV.

'It's yourselves,' he said, his face creased in a grin. 'My, but it's chilly oot there tonight, ch? But we've had it easy – the rest o' the country's in blizzard conditions.'

'Snow. You can keep it, as far as I'm concerned,' said Brian Scott.

'We went skiing once. I'll no' even go intae it,' said Ella with a grimace.

'Oh, come on, you canna leave us hanging, Ella,' said Annie.

'Tae cut a long story short, yer man here was on the nursery slopes.'

'Did you hurt yourself, Brian?' said Annie, staring at the detective.

'Och no, he was fine. The poor wean he ran over wisnae so jolly, right enough. The job I had calming the mother doon.' Ella glared at her husband.

'Let's get things straight here. First off, I didnae want tae go skiing in the first place. One o' oor weans bought Ella some o' they dry slope lessons in Glasgow, and after that there was no stopping her. We had tae go tae Austria.'

'Where you near beheaded a wean.'

'The wee bugger slid oot in front o' me.'

'He was skiing. You were sliding, Brian.'

'Ach, whatever.' Scott gestured dismissively with his hand. 'I wanted tae go tae Torremolinos, but no; come February, there we was freezing oor bollocks off trying no' tae break anything.'

'I gied the wee boy money. That sorted him oot,' said Ella.

'He was at it! I've nae doot he was running intae novice skiers a' the time just so as he could make a bob or two.'

'His folks were loaded!'

'You know how fly weans are these days. Likely picked it up on thon YouTube.'

'Aye, that View Tube is tae blame for the end o' society, as far as I'm concerned,' said Hamish. 'That an' a' this Place Book and Twatter. Folks canna have a decent conversation in the street; they're a' looking doon at they damned phones. Malky Maloney near knocked me in front o' the Blaan bus the other day. Too busy talking tae his brother in Toronto, apparently. It's a' very well being sorry, but what good would that dae if I was flattened by the bus, eh? Aye, an' the folk heading for Blaan widna have been too happy neithers wae the bus being late. And let me tell you, they're a glum lot at the best o' times.'

'He didnae offer you fifty quid, though, I bet,' said Scott.

'Here we go wae the money again,' said Ella under her breath.

'No, but he offered tae hypnotise me.'

'What?' said Scott, bemused.

'He lost his job a whiles back. They put him on this course tae learn thon hypnotism. Though dear knows whoot he'll make o' that.'

'What did he dae before?'

'He was a plumber. Ach, no' a very good one. It took him three goes tae unblock my toilet a couple o' years ago.'

'What an image,' said Annie.

'It was no laughing matter, I'll tell you. I was just standing – doing my business, as you'll be aware, Brian. I had this fit o' coughing, and damn me but my bottom set shot right doon intae the lavvy.'

'Oh, for Christ's sake, Hamish' said Annie, wincing.

'Did they no' jeest get stuck at thon U-bend. I tried tae get my hand doon, but I'm no' as supple as I once was. Had tae get Malky in – what a performance.'

As Annie continued to recoil, Ella looked more sympathetic. 'Did you get another pair free? I know fine what dentists are like these days.'

'Thankfully, there was no need. At the third go Malky Maloney managed tae get them oot. I soaked them in some Sterident o'er night and they were as good as new – see.' He parted his lips in a rictus grin and pointed to his bottom teeth.

Annie retched as Ella looked on in disgust.

'In fact, they fitted better after the event, so I did myself a favour.'

'Here was me wondering if you was talking pish all this time, when in actual fact you have been.' Scott laughed.

'At least I never brutalised a poor wee boy on the ski slopes, Brian Scott.'

'I ran intae him an' knocked him doon. Don't get so dramatic.'

'Huh! So you admit it. You've been blaming that wee soul for the last ten years.' Ella looked triumphant. 'Can I have a large gin and tonic please, Annie? My husband is paying.'

'I need to go to a place,' said Scott, nudging his wife out of sight of the others.

'Aye, okay, steady on, Rambo.' Ella waited until Brian Scott had left for the Gents before she leaned across the bar. 'Here, Annie, have you heard aboot a' this carry on?'

'Aye, jeest terrible. Sheena McKay was a lovely lassie. As far as them fae the black croft – well, I'm saying nothing.'

'It gets worse,' said Ella, lowering her voice.

'How can it get worse, at all?' said Hamish, now standing at the bar, ear cocked.

'The bold yin – her fae the States. She's only moving intae the cottage.'

'Alison? You are kidding?' said Annie.

'No' a bit o' it, Annie. Bold as brass.'

'I mind o' her, right enough,' said Annie. 'She was a bit older than me, but when she ran off, well, the whole toon was on aboot it, weren't they, Hamish?'

The old fisherman sucked at his unlit pipe. 'Aye, it was a terrible thing. I think maist of us thought she was deid – well, until she turned up the other day, that was.'

'Don't tell Brian I said anything. I'll have my heid in my hands, I'm sure yous understand.'

'My lips are sealed,' said Hamish.

'Aye, an' your teeth are pish,' remarked Annie. It was only then that she noticed the man with the grey hair and the expensive overcoat standing behind Ella. 'Mr Strong, I'm sorry tae keep you waiting. Whoot can I get you?'

48

Daley trudged up the steps to his house on the hill. Before entering he turned round and looked at the twinkling lights of Kinloch reflected in the still loch, shimmering fires in the cold darkness of the water. The covering of snow added a luminous glow from the hills looming ghostly now over the town. The air was sweet and clear, the tang of the sea ever-present, and the smell of smoke from coal fires took Daley back to his youth. Chilly nights at play with his friends, almost magical under the blanket of stars not obscured by the orange glow of Glasgow's sodium lights.

But that was a long time ago – a different life. In short, he loved this place. Kinloch was his home now both in fact and in his heart.

Wearily, reflecting on the events of the day, and the plans to lure Ginny Doig to Rowan Tree Cottage, he walked down the hall. All was in darkness. Peeping into the room he again shared with his wife, he saw her and his son snuggled together, heads just above the duvet. While Liz looked serene in repose, the little boy's eyelids fluttered and he murmured in his sleep. No doubt the sparkling lights of Christmas, Santa and presents were occupying his childish dreams – or so Daley hoped.

Again he remembered being a child: the warmth of the big fire in the grate of their council house; Christmas stockings bulging with gifts arranged around it for him and his siblings. Though they weren't as poor as some – Daley's father eschewed drink in the main, and his mother still earned money by taking in typing and the like – they were by no means rich. But there was always a goose on the table, with all the trimmings – his father hated turkey. The smell of Christmas with its spices, cooked fowl, stuffing and burning logs had stayed with him from that day to this, though it was with no little melancholy that he reflected on the faces from his childhood he would never see again.

But life was a bittersweet business.

He decided not to disturb his wife and son and headed for the spare room. Soon in bed, he caught the midnight news on Radio 4, listened to the Book of the Week, then was soothed by the almost poetic mantra that was the shipping forecast. *Tyne, Dogger, Fisher, German Bight*. It was a cerebral tour the British Isles, a lullaby that had – for as long as he could remember – calmed him before sleep; a constant in his life that cosseted him through the very worst of times.

As was his habit now, he took his pulse; reasonably steady, if rather faster than he would have liked. That, too, preyed on his mind. His own mortality was the last thing he thought about before he slipped into the arms of Morpheus, and – after a blissful split-second of sleep-befuddled wakefulness – the first thing to cross his mind in the morning. He'd often wondered how those suffering from terminal illness managed not to scream; to cry out every minute of what was left of their lives at the injustice of it all, the thought of everything being taken away; the prospect of eternal darkness.

Jim Daley now had a notion of how that felt, and it stalked him.

He switched off the radio and settled his head on the pillow. Sleep soon followed.

One minute he was answering the phone, the next he was standing in Main Street. The harsh glow of streetlights illuminated the scene. He was holding a gun, conscious of someone standing behind him. He could almost feel the breath on his collar.

As Daley looked up the street, he saw a pallid-faced woman being held round the neck by a man, whose face was in the shadows. At their side lay a body, large, misshapen, grotesque. Man or woman, he couldn't be sure – he didn't care – but he saw a crimson stain of blood in the dirty snow billowing out around a head that lay face down on the cold ground.

He knew he should recognise the captive woman, but he couldn't place her. Like someone he hadn't seen for a long time, her name wouldn't come to his lips. All the same, he felt a desperate need to save her. Not just from the man who held the gun to her head, but something else – a forgotten tragedy that wouldn't form in his mind.

'What are you going to dae now, arsehole?' The man's face was still in shadow, but Daley knew the voice.

'Leave her alone!' It was feeble, but all he could find to say.

'Oh, aye, just you gie it your best shot, Jimmy boy. You always were a useless prick. Lucky, that's all you've ever been, eh? But everyone else has had tae pay the price. Well, no' this time, wanker!'

The young woman struggled in his grasp, her blue eyes wide, pleading.

'You can't save her, Daley. Like he said, you've been lucky until now, but your luck has just run out. I always knew it would.'

Still holding the gun out straight ahead, Daley turned to face the figure behind him. John Donald sneered, a malicious, venal expression. He was enjoying this, Daley could tell. 'I know I'm dreaming, John,' said Daley, his voice wavering.

'You think you know everything – you always did. How can you be so sure? Life isn't the same for you these days – not for any of us. Can't you see? You're hovering, Jimmy, hovering between two worlds. You know that, I know that.' He paused. 'And they know that.' John Donald nodded to the menacing figure and his struggling prisoner. As he did so, the man with the gun held to the blood-red hair of the woman stepped into the light. It was James Machie.

The woman let out a whimper. 'Please help me, Jim.' She looked at him, all the sadness in the world reflected in her wide blue eyes.

'Come on, what are you worried about? Take the shot, arsehole! You've done this before, you piece of shit. Try it again!' Machie held out one arm, as though beckoning Daley to fire. 'You might hit me, then again, you might kill her. You've killed us all already, so what does it matter?'

'He's right, do it!' said John Donald in Daley's ear. His breath reeked of death and decay, the smell that had stalked the detective since his first visit to the mortuary as a young cop.

'I'm going tae make your mind up for you. One, two . . .' Machie forced the pistol against the woman's skull, making her scream. Distantly a bell rang, echoing around the buildings of Main Street.

Daley closed his eyes and pulled the trigger.

He felt something fall at his feet. He looked down. The girl was lying on the road beneath him as the pistol smoked in his hand, blood flooding down her face like an enveloping mask. She mouthed some words. Daley knelt by her side to hear what she said with her last breaths.

'You killed me,' she sobbed. Then the light left her eyes.

The two men stood in front of him, Machie beside Donald now, both clapping slowly, the crack of their applause syncopated with the distant toll of the bell.

'It's time to pay your dues, Jimmy boy,' said Machie. The pair howled with laughter.

'Jim!'

He was sitting up in bed drenched in cold perspiration, his wife holding him to her chest. In the doorway, his son stood in the shadows, a teddy bear hanging loose in one hand.

'I'm okay,' said Daley. 'It was just a dream.' But he could feel his heart throbbing in his chest, see the pulse in his eyes as it raced, making him feel light-headed.

'You're sweating,' said Liz. 'I'm going to get the doctor.'

'No doctors!'

'Who is Mary, Daddy?' asked his son.

'Nobody. Go back to bed!' replied Daley sharply.

In the doorway, James Daley junior began to howl.

Back in his dingy room in the County Hotel, Mike Strong dialled the number once more – still no reply. He knew he shouldn't have arranged to have whisky left in the cottage for Chiase. Strong resolved to rise early and call again. If the worst came to the worst, he would have to go and get the man personally. Who knew how well mobile phones worked in this bloody place.

But despite his irritation at the lack of contact with the American, he felt as though, at last, he was about to achieve what he'd come here to do. There were still obstacles to be overcome, but at least he now knew the road ahead.

He lay in bed, revelling in the thought of his cocky young partner Blair Williams spending the night behind bars. He wouldn't be there for ever, but by the time all was revealed Mike Strong would be far away. Far away from his irritating wife, far away from the rain and biting cold of Edinburgh, far away from a slow decline into old age and back to – as close as he could reconstruct it – his youth. After all, you could do anything with money, just about. He knew he had some years left, and he intended to ensure that those years were going to be the best of his life.

He switched off the bedside light and turned on to his side. Outside, even at this late hour, cars swished through the wet slush. He could hear laughter and singing coming from late night revellers in the street.

Mike Strong closed his eyes. These were mere distractions. As always, he had the big picture in mind.

Though the Subaru was cold, Ginny Doig was able to switch the engine on from time to time, turn the heater to maximum. She'd found a rug tucked behind her seat, and was now wrapped in it. The hunting rifle was cradled to her breast like an infant. But her thoughts were far from maternal; rather those of hatred and revenge.

The vehicle was on a narrow forestry track amidst the trees that faced on to Thomson's Hill. As she stared into the shadows, the bright moon illuminated the snow-covered cliff from which her husband had plunged to his death. It loomed like a ghost in the pale moonlight. Beyond, the sea shimmered, cold and black on this winter night.

Ginny Doig had seen many winters, maybe too many. She wasn't particularly bothered if she saw any more. All that mattered was to rid herself for good of the daughter she so despised. She'd always known Alison was alive. Parents could tell instinctively, she was sure. So Ginny was also unsurprised when her runaway child returned. To her, it had always been inevitable.

She could see Nathaniel in her mind's eye, standing with his arms outstretched, toppling slowly backwards to his death as the police had described in their written report.

He wouldn't be the last person to meet their end before this business was over – not if she had anything to do with it.

She pictured her home, out of sight far below the cliff of Thomson's Point. No smoke from the chimney this night. Her eldest son and her husband dead, her other sons in custody, there was nobody left to light the fire. As she drifted off, flames at the edge of the cliff spat and swirled in her dreams, while out at sea an unfortunate mariner saw the light and rejoiced, not knowing his end was nigh.

Alice Wenger was back at the Machrie House Hotel. A chink of light escaped the heavy curtains, shining directly on the corner where she had tried to save the fly from the spider's web. She lay staring at the spot, draining the last drops of a glass of whisky. She didn't often need something to help her sleep. But tonight – well, tonight things were different.

She'd packed up her belongings ready to head for the first home she'd known in the morning. She recalled its drab, damp misery; the ridiculous rules that her parents had made for her and her brothers. She could smell the rotting seaweed; hear the rats as they scratched in the walls at night; feel the cold damp sheets against her thin, frozen body, which could never find warmth. She could hear the summoning toll of Jeremiah's bell.

The whisky soon did its job and sleep came. Alice tossed and turned as in her nightmare three pairs of arms held her down. But this was no surprise; she'd gone to sleep to that same horror every night for more than thirty years. It had long since lost its power over her.

Ella Scott was applying cold cream to her face as her husband struggled to untie his shoes. 'You're like an old man, all that puffing and blowing, Brian.'

'I am an old man.'

'You're in your fifties, man. Your uncle lived until he was eighty-five.'

'Billy?'

'Aye, Billy.'

'The rest didnae dae very well – look at my faither!'

'He'd a liver the size o' a medicine ball! He drank the East End dry – aye, maist nights, tae.'

'He liked you.'

'He used tae call me Helen.'

'He was getting on.'

'He was forty-seven when I met him! He was puggled. His brain was like a sponge wae all the booze.'

'You're getting more hard-hearted the aulder you get, dae you know that?'

'No' hard-hearted enough no' tae worry aboot what you'll be doing tomorrow.'

'I'll be taking a back seat, Ella.'

'You will? It'll be the first time.'

'They'll have somebody fae the Tactical Firearms Unit babysit thon Wenger lassie.'

'I'll believe it when I see it.'

'I dae what I have tae.'

'Is it no' time Jimmy put himsel' in harm's way?'

'He just managed off that pontoon and nae mair. I think he's had enough excitement for a while.'

'What is it John Donald used tae call you?'

'What did he no' call me?'

'Jimmy's loyal wee dog – that was it.'

'That was one o' the nicer things he had tae say, aye.'

'Brian, you'll never learn.'

'Och, I'm off tae sleep. I cannae be listening tae this pish.'

'Sleep well.'

'You too.' There was silence for a few moments. 'And I didnae run o'er that wee boy at the skiing. Just a bump, that was all. I was trying tae stop.'

'You ran right intae him and the two o' yous went hurtling doon the slope. You're supposed tae have your skis in a V shape tae stop. Yours were like a pair o' tram tracks.'

'I couldnae control my legs!'

'No' for the first time, neithers.'

'Right. Goodnight, Ella.'

'You promise me you'll stay oot o' danger tomorrow.'

'I'll be sitting wae a cup o' tae watching it all on some video feed. Mind I'm an inspector these days. Inspectors don't get their hands dirty.'

'No' the ones called Brian Scott.' She sighed, switched off the light and snuggled into her husband's back. Though their bickering made it sound otherwise, she loved him to the ends of the earth. Then he began to snore, so she poked him just hard enough to rouse him sufficiently to stop the racket.

49

A grey dawn greeted the new Kinloch morning. The skies had cleared overnight making the lying snow and slush freeze into a treacherous surface for those earliest on the go.

Jay Blue the bakery driver was the first victim as he slid his length outside Black's toy shop. He cursed as he got to his feet, damning the weather, as once more snow clouds gathered over the town.

Felicity Watson, who regarded herself as indestructible, left for her early morning run, only to find herself in Kinloch hospital with a fractured ankle, sustained when she slid on a patch of black ice and toppled over a bench on the seafront, much to the amusement of Charlie McLean the milk boy as he made his deliveries.

Jim Daley too was awake. He'd spent half the night sitting up in bed staring into the darkness. Not only did the nightmare haunt him; worries about his health and what was to happen later that day fought for prominence at the front of his mind. The nearer the clock ticked to seven, the more thoughts of Alice Wenger and Ginny Doig kept him awake.

Sick of trying to find sleep, he padded on bare feet across to the window. Throwing the curtains open wide, he was greeted by a scene from winter wonderland. What wasn't still covered by yesterday's snow was now coated in a blanket of hoar frost. The sky was filling in again, and already tiny flakes were beginning to fall.

He donned his dressing gown and headed for the shower, the reassuring low hum of the central heating easing his shivers. Nonetheless, as he towelled himself down, he could feel a knot in the pit of his stomach, and he noticed that his hand trembled as he tried to shave.

He opened the bathroom cabinet and sorted through various packets and small bottles until he had a collection of pills of varying shapes, sizes and colours in his large hand. A red and white capsule for his blood pressure and to help keep his heart pumping, a tiny pill to hold his pulse steady, a white one to counter the side-effects of the first two, tablets to make him pee. The list went on. But for Jim Daley, this was now his life.

He could picture Rowan Tree Cottage – or, as he preferred to think of it, Hamish's black croft. He resolved to ensure that the papers contained within Nathaniel Doig's metal box were all read and noted before the attempt to lure Ginny Doig and Vito Chiase to the remote dwelling began.

He hated the thought of this operation, and willed the skies to open and send a blizzard over south Kintyre. At least that would give him time to think, plot and perhaps persuade his superiors to dump their ridiculous plan. But back in the bedroom, as he dressed in a shirt, suit and tie, he saw only a flutter of snowflakes. The weather was bad enough to be a nuisance, but not bad enough to stop everything in its tracks. The worst of both worlds, he reckoned.

'Coffee, Jim?'

Daley was startled by the question as he walked into the

lounge. Liz was sitting at the dining table, nursing a steaming mug. 'So you couldn't sleep either?'

'No, I couldn't.' Her voice was short and sharp.

'I can't help what I dream, Liz.'

'Took me ages to get our son to sleep. Do you ever wonder what he thinks?'

'I can barely remember anything from when I was that age, can you?'

She shrugged. 'Well, that's okay, then.'

'I'm not doing this today. You know how I feel – you must know what I'm going to say.'

'About me being a hypocrite, you mean?'

It was Daley's turn to shrug, though he chose not to reply.

'The difference is that those men – whatever – they didn't mean anything to me.'

'Oh, nice.' The reply oozed sarcasm.

Liz persisted. 'You loved her; you can't deny it. You still do!'

He held his hands in the air in a gesture of surrender. 'I have a lot on my plate today. I'm buggered if I'm doing this shit before I even get to work.' He left the room in search of his overcoat. Now he'd lost so much weight he felt the cold as never before – or maybe it was just another symptom of his heart problems.

'That's it, run away, as always. Let's pretend there's nothing wrong.' Liz followed him into the hall.

He turned to face her. 'Yes, I learned to be very good at pretending there was nothing wrong, remember? If you don't recall, that happened every time I found out who you were sleeping with, every time I heard my colleagues sniggering as they passed me in a corridor, every night I waited up for you

379

to come home with some lame excuse about where you'd been. I could smell the sex on you, Liz. Do not dare try to bring me to your level.'

'This isn't going to work. I've known it all along.'

'What you really mean is *you've done your bit, Jimmy. I can go back home and carry on where I left off.* That's it, isn't it?'

'I don't want to leave you!'

'Well, what the fuck is wrong with you then?'

'Apart from you pining for that dead girl, you mean?'

'Yes, apart from that.'

'Think about it for a minute, Jim. Do you really want our son to be brought up here – educated in the schools in this backwater?'

'What's wrong with them?'

'Huh! Do I have to spell it out?'

Daley walked towards her, staring sadly into her eyes. 'That's your problem, Liz.'

'What?'

'You just can't help yourself. You're a snob, plain and simple. You want our son to be a clone of you, or people like your brother-in-law. Pains in the arse; shallow bastards with letters after their name, but no soul.'

'So it's better to have letters before your name, *DCI* Daley?'

'I'd rather that than be a rapist or a philanderer. My son stays with me.'

She shook her head and turned on her heel.

Daley opened the front door and headed into the frozen morning.

*

Symington was busy in her office when Daley knocked on the door. She looked grave when the DCI entered.

'Problems, ma'am?'

'The road is blocked at the Rest, and there's no chopper because of the weather. It's still much worse up there.'

'Good. So we can put an end to this little charade.'

'No, we go ahead, Jim. That comes from above. We have some extra manpower – enough, they reckon. We proceed with care, but the operation still has the green light.'

'Ridiculous! It was bad enough before, but this is just madness.'

'They want an end to this before anyone else gets killed.'

'What about our officers? Let's not forget we have a ruthless professional killer out there, not to mention a deranged woman who saw fit to stick knitting needles into her children's eyes to make them pliant.'

'My hands are tied, Jim. So are yours.'

He pulled up a seat at the desk that used to belong to John Donald, the man who had been so vivid in his dream the night before. 'Okay, you tell me, then. Who, how and when?'

Brian Scott was tucking into a bacon roll and a large mug of coffee in Daley's glass box when his friend pushed the door open, walked in, and slammed it shut behind him.

'Trouble at mill, big man?'

'Yup.'

'When is there no'?'

'Brian, I have to ask you something.'

'I never touched they biscuits you've got in that drawer.'

'Never mind the biscuits. Everybody is snowbound up the road – there's no chopper – you know the score.'

'And?' Scott had placed what was left of the roll on a paper towel on Daley's desk.

'Symington wants you to accompany Alice Wenger to Rowan Tree Cottage.'

'No chance! I'm an inspector, Jimmy. I shouldnae be up tae these capers.'

'I volunteered, but she wouldn't have it. You're experienced, she trusts you – what can I say?'

'*I'm going tae shoot you tae put you oot o' your misery* would sound quite good right noo.'

'Okay, it's not the TFU, but we've got plenty of good bodies about. The place will be under scrutiny. As soon as Ginny Doig and Chiase appear, we'll have them. You're safe as houses in the cottage.'

'I'm no' so sure, Jimmy. We're assuming a lot here.'

'Like what?'

'Like how do we really know the two o' them are in cahoots? I mean, he killed her son, or so we think.'

'She took her son's mind away, Brian.'

'And you trust this Wenger lassie. I'm here tae tell you, me an' her didnae exactly hit it off.'

'I don't have a choice, Brian. All I can suggest is that you go in and tell Symington you're not up for it. Nobody could blame you. You've been shot before in the line of duty. Use that.'

Scott sat for a few moments with his elbows on his knees. He shook his head. 'We both know I won't dae that, big man.'

'I thought you'd say that.'

'You thought right.'

'You'll go in dressed as a cop. Once you get the big jacket on with the collar up, and a cap, Ginny Doig will think you're just some woodentop.'

'How dae we no' just find her and take her oot?'

'Because, if she and Chiase are acting together as we suspect, in the event of us finding one of them the other will open fire. You know the landscape round there, Brian. The only chance we've got is luring them both to the cottage at the same time. Then we have them both.'

Scott rubbed his chin thoughtfully. 'Just don't tell Ella, that's all I ask.'

50

Mike Strong threw the mobile phone on the hard mattress of his bed in the County Hotel. He still couldn't raise Chiase and it infuriated him. This man was still pivotal to his plans, even though he would be jettisoned as soon as he'd outlived his usefulness.

He showered, shaved and changed into the warmest clothes he had: a V-neck cashmere sweater under his suit jacket, his heavy overcoat and a woollen scarf. His room was cold enough; he dreaded to think what the temperature would be out in the wilds of Kintyre. Judging by what he could see through the faded net curtains, today was worse than yesterday. He was glad he'd found Chiase a cottage on a road that was gritted by the council. He'd asked the owner when he'd rented it, which he'd done using an assumed name and the credit card he kept for emergencies. It was a legacy of his philandering days. He was glad nostalgia had encouraged him to keep it.

He sat alone at breakfast in the big dining room, save for a tall dark man – American, he reckoned, hearing snatches of his accent as he ordered his meal. The man nodded hello across the room, which Strong returned with a smile. He wasn't in the mood for conversation or pleasantries. As he waited for his full Scottish fat-fest, he buried his head in the largest newspaper available at reception.

He tried Chiase once more, but again there was no reply. Sleeping it off, he thought as he chewed on a lukewarm sausage from a plate that could have melted gold. He'd often wondered how hotels managed to serve up tepid food on such molten platters – another mystery that would doubtless remain unsolved.

He drained the last of his coffee and headed out into the cold Kinloch morning. Chiase was only five miles or so away. In the end, he supposed, this was only a minor irritation. In any case, it gave him more time to plan what he was going to have the gangster do. He'd already decided how to despatch him when he'd completed the tasks in hand.

Soon, his car was purring from Kinloch. He turned right on to a side road, as the Kinks' 'I'm Not Like Everybody Else' pounded from the sound system.

Scott was in uniform again, and he didn't like it. He'd found an unexpected pleasure in donning the braided cap and pips of an inspector's uniform, and being in the garb of a constable brought back memories of cold nights in search of cups of tea at friendly dosses and much else besides.

'You'll wear this,' said Symington, holding up a bullet-proof vest.

'I thought I was as safe as hooses oot there.'

'It's a precaution. You know that, Brian.'

Daley looked on as his friend yet again prepared to be in the line of fire. This plan still nagged at him. He had five officers reading the rest of the documents from the metal box left by Nathaniel Doig. He was determined to find out as many of its secrets as he could before sending his best friend to the black croft.

'Don't even think o' laughing, Jimmy,' said Scott as he pulled on a thick police anorak over the rest of his uniform. 'By the way, this is luxury. Remember they wafer-thin raincoats we got issued wae back in the day? It might as well have been taps aff in the winter when I was a sprog.'

'They gave me a greatcoat,' said Daley.

'Aye, me tae. But mair often than not it got wet. Not only did you smell like a dog, but it was like walking aboot wae a duvet on. Nah, I just got cold.'

'Thankfully, times have changed,' said Symington.

'Have they, though?' Scott looked at her levelly. 'I'm still heading off intae the unknown here wae the southern belle. That wee poison dwarf on the loose wae a hunting rifle.' He placed a pistol in the shoulder holster under his jacket.

'There's half an army between you and her.'

Scott looked at some of the fresh-faced detectives who would be his first line of defence against Ginny Doig and Vito Chiase. 'Mair like the Boys' Brigade. I reckon no' one o' these weans will remember who John Noakes was, even.'

'Who?' said Symington.

'See!' Scott looked balefully at Daley.

'Is this a required operational qualification, Bri? I can't see how knowing who John Noakes was will help with the matters in hand.'

'It just proves how young a' these kids are.'

'They're all highly trained, responsible officers, Brian,' said Symington.

Scott looked round the room again, just as one detective

picked his nose and examined the bogey with great interest. 'Huh! What aboot *pick it lick it roll it flick it* o'er there?'

Symington shook her head. 'I'm off to give the ACC a quick Skype briefing – tell him we're just about ready for the off. I'll also give Alice Wenger a call. We'll have the cops at Machrie House bring her in shortly.'

'We?' said Scott, as she disappeared.

'Don't worry, Brian, I'll be there. Surely you trust me by this time?'

'You've been a bit shaky lately, Jimmy. What if you come o'er all Emergency Ward Ten when I'm in my hour o' need, eh?'

'Thanks, Brian,' said Daley, flat-lipped.

Strong had to admit that the scene before him would have graced the most expensive Christmas card. The little glen in which the log cabin sat was shrouded in snow that glittered in the cold morning air. There was a glimpse of the sun, though luminous white clouds filled most of the sky, creating a strange, yet not unattractive, light. Branches of pine trees were ghosted in white. All they lacked was a few fairy lights and baubles to turn them into magnificent Christmas trees.

In a nearby field, the coats of a small herd of sheep looked shabby, a dirty shade against the pristine white snow. High above, a bird of prey soared, ensuring the sky was empty of any other creature. As the raptor circled on the thermals, the rest of the local bird population sought sanctuary amongst the heavily laden branches of the trees, sending the odd flurry of displaced snow silently on to the white ground like sugar into a cup of milky tea.

Strong was dismayed to note the absence of smoke issuing from the cottage's chimney. It was clear that Chiase was not up and about, more likely in bed sleeping off a whisky hangover. He cursed under his breath as he pulled up beside the gangster's SUV and made his way out of the warm car. Instantly his breath billowed out in front of him like a cloud in the cold air. Strong pulled up his collar and made his way along a small path, following only one set of footsteps, now shallow and almost invisible, nearly obscured by the earlier flurries of snow. No doubt they were made by Chiase on the previous evening as he headed into the small dwelling.

Though he had a key – one of two sent him by the owner – he tried the door. Clearly the New Jersey man had reckoned there was little danger to be found in this remote place, as it had been left unlocked and opened readily on to a tiny hallway.

Strong shivered. The cottage was as cold inside as it was out. Having studied the layout of the place from the online brochure, he knew the lounge was straight ahead. Indeed, the door was slightly ajar, and he could just see a dark fireplace. He knew the only bedroom was to his right, so he looked in, expecting to see the sleeping figure of the gangster, tucked up against the cold. But the bed was empty.

Frowning, he made his way to the lounge. To his left, the narrow kitchen was devoid of life, though various cupboard doors had been left open. He pushed at the lounge door. The slumped figure was still in the big chair by the long-dead fire, a surprisingly full bottle of whisky on a small table beside the chair, an upturned whisky glass lying a few feet away on the wooden floor.

'Chiase, wake up, man!' called Strong as he walked towards the motionless figure. He was about to shake him awake when he noticed the blue lips and the blackness under the fingernails – and recognised the stench of death already tainting the air.

Strong pushed Chiase's head back, revealing cold, lifeless eyes in a blackening face.

It took the lawyer a few moments to come to terms with the scene, but when he did he swore loudly, steadying himself with a hand on the arm of the chair occupied by the corpse of Vito Chiase, a sudden flush of dizziness making him feel wobbly on his feet.

He walked across the room to where a leather sofa covered by knitted blankets was set against a wooden wall. He sat down heavily and studied the lifeless man with burgeoning despair.

'You had to die now, you worthless piece of shit!'

Then something dawned on him. Though there were no obvious signs of foul play, how could he be sure Chiase's death was a natural one? Suddenly the breath caught in his throat.

Quietly, Mike Strong got to his feet and walked once more across to the body of the hitman he'd hired. This time he did so on tiptoes. With no little distaste, he pulled aside the dead man's jacket. As expected, a pistol lay tucked in a holster under his arm. Barely breathing, Strong removed it and placed it in his pocket.

He stood still for a few moments, listening for any sound. Then satisfied that he was alone with a dead man, he left Vito Chiase for someone else to find. He hadn't removed his leather gloves, so he was confident that he'd left no trace of his presence in the house save for footprints, which could have belonged to anyone. Anyway, by the time Chiase was found he planned to be far away.

The only problem now was that he was going to have to pull the trigger himself to get what he wanted.

When he walked out of the front door, the flapping wings of a bird set his heart thumping.

As he pulled away from the cottage Cream's 'I Feel Free' blasted from the speakers. Chiase was, and soon he would be, too. But it was in sheer frustration that he banged the leather steering wheel of the Bentley again and again.

51

Dressed in the expensive bad weather gear she'd bought in Kinloch and walking between two tall police officers, Alice Wenger made for the police car parked at the rear of the Machrie House Hotel. A third officer stayed back, automatic weapon in his arms, surveying the scene. They travelled the five miles from Machrie in a van and a car, Wenger crouched in the back seat of the latter.

She'd slept fitfully the night before, watching the dawn as it broke over the dark, cold sea that frothed on to the beach, where snow still lay. The coast across the sea was a thin grey line under the heavy sky today, the flashing of the Antrim light punctuating her thoughts. They had drifted to the times she'd spent at that very beach, years ago, with her friends. They'd travelled to Machrie by bus. She didn't possess a bathing suit, but Sheena had found one that fitted her.

As they neared the town, thoughts of her dead friend played across her mind, and her gaze shifted to the footwell of the car.

Soon they were in Kinloch. Wenger heard the big blue gates swing shut as her small motorcade swept into the station's car park. Still watchful, she was hurried through a security door and into the warmth of the office. She was observed closely by men in dark clothing, armed officers, as she was led into a partitioned-off glass box in the middle of a larger room. Behind a desk she recognised the tall policeman. Wenger respected Daley; he was clearly nobody's fool. The expression on his face today was one of resignation, a reluctant acceptance of the facts. She knew she'd been the one to push for this, and he knew the risks involved. Every line of his face and the look in his eyes told her that.

Beside him, standing in an adorned uniform, was Chief Superintendent Carrie Symington. She held her chin high, staring straight into Wenger's eyes.

'Well, Ms Wenger, you have what you wanted. Though I must inform you that we don't have the team we'd hoped for. The snow is much worse in Glasgow, so they couldn't get here.'

'You don't appear short-handed, honey,' said Wenger, and was pleased to see the irritation on Symington's face.

'With respect, how would you know if we were "short-handed" or not?'

Wenger answered the comment with a smile. 'Then you'd rather wait for my mother and her friend to kill more innocent people like Sheena?'

'We have no evidence to prove that your mother had anything to do with the death of Mrs McKay.'

'But you sure as hell know that she is out there somewhere, armed and evil. Who else would hire a man to kill for them? You got a town full of psychos here?'

'Be in no doubt,' interjected Daley from his seat behind the large desk, 'this is not how I wanted to resolve this situation. Though I too am concerned about further incidents.'

Wenger laughed. 'I love cops. *Incidents*. That's how you

describe the death of my friend and my brother – their murders? Let me tell you, all that was keeping my mother in her place was my father. And he was as mad as a hickory stick on fire, too.'

'But not as mad as your mother?' said Symington.

Before Alice Wenger could reply, the door swung open. Brian Scott, dressed in the ordinary uniform of a police constable, entered the small space. She turned round and looked him up and down.

'This is the officer who will accompany you into the cottage,' said Symington.

'You're kidding me, right?'

'No, I'm deadly serious.'

'Hey, don't think I was a volunteer,' said Scott. 'Between you and your auld dear, you gie me the shudders.'

'DI Scott!' Symington snapped.

The phone on Daley's desk burst into life. He put the handset to his ear. 'Yes, Sergeant Shaw.' He listened for a few moments, then ended the conversation and looked at the chief superintendent. 'You'll have to excuse me. I've things to attend to.'

As he got up to leave, Symington gave him a questioning look. Daley shook his head almost imperceptibly and left his glass box.

'So when we gonna get this show on the road, boys and girls?' Wenger asked.

'We leave for Rowan Tree Cottage in ten minutes. Does that suit you?' Symington's tone was sarcastic.

'It would suit me better if you could rustle up a cup of coffee, honey.'

'I'll see what I can do.' Symington too left Daley's office, leaving Wenger and Scott alone.

Wenger stared at the policeman. 'I thought you had some fancy rank?'

'Don't you worry aboot me, darlin'. Just do your bit and stay put in that hellhole when I tell you. I don't care how much money you've got, I'm in charge, right?'

'Okay, officer, sir. You're *da man*.' She laughed.

'Aye, you'll no' be feeling so merry when that mother o' yours is at your heid wae a knife trying to cut your brains oot.'

'She's tried that before.'

The door opened again, this time to admit a constable bearing a steaming cup of coffee.

'At least somebody can do their job in this place. Thank you, boy.' She took the coffee and sipped it.

'Where's mine?' said Scott.

'I didn't think, gaffer.'

'Well start thinking. I might be dressed as though I'm fresh oot the wrapper, but I'm no', remember?' Scott watched the young man leave, then sat heavily on Daley's chair, looking miserable in his constable's uniform.

'What is it, Jim?' asked Symington. Daley was standing in the corridor examining two sheets of A4 paper: one yellowed with age, curled at the edges, the other white, almost pristine.

'Here, read for yourself, ma'am.' He handed them to Symington.

She began to read. The typeface was that of an old-fashioned manual typewriter, mistakes crossed out, corrections handwritten above. It was dated 4 March 1973.

It's hard to come terms with some things. I faced it when I was in medical training. In fact, it was during my education at university that I realised there was something far wrong with my family.

My father was a cold and brutal man. He confided to me on his deathbed that he'd killed his own father and younger brother. Whilst I was surprised by this confession, perhaps I shouldn't have been. My family have been in the trade of death for profit for a very long time, though I feel none of this evil in my own soul.

I look at my own sons, and I see cruelty; the taint of the genes stretching back who knows how far. It makes me sad – sick to the heart. But I know these boys will turn out to be as hateful and wicked as my father. The way they bully in school – behave at home. It's in their every fibre, the youngest learning from the eldest.

I learned much in my time at university. I left because my father thought it a waste of time. I'm sure he would have hunted me down had I continued on the road to a career in medicine. But still, I learned a lot.

You may think this wicked in itself, but here is a solution to my problems, though I fear I'll never be able to put it into practice and rid my family of the cancer at its core . . .

As Symington read on, her face became more pallid. 'This is monstrous, Jim! I know you explained the theory of it to me, but to read it here in black and white is . . . it's inhuman. He obviously found the wherewithal to carry out this procedure on his own sons, despite his reservations here.'

'Ice pick lobotomy. Yes, it's horrendous, ma'am. But read this.' Daley handed her the much newer sheet of paper. It had clearly been written on the same machine, but the letters were less bold, as though the ribbon was old and running low on ink, or perhaps the strength in Nathaniel Doig's fingers was ebbing away with old age.

I fear that I've been wrong about many things. I'm a rich man, you see. I've never wanted this wealth – it's blood money. But blood money, or no, it can still work for good. I have a number of ideas that will help put right the damage done by the Doigs over centuries.

But at the heart of this family there still lurks horror. I must think. I need more time.

The writing stopped abruptly. Symington looked at Daley. 'This is dated the day before he died, Jim.'

'It is, Carrie.'

She looked at the two missives written so far apart. 'I get the first one, but what does he mean by the second?'

'We must presume it's his wife. We don't even know if he knew Alice was back home when he wrote this.'

Symington thought for a while. 'This doesn't really change anything.'

'It doesn't?'

'What else have we turned up so far?'

'A real mix: cod psychology; observation of the seasons; thoughts on politics, that sort of thing. To me, this guy is seriously troubled. So far, though, this is the most personal material.'

'Okay, tell them to keep digging.'

'And?'

'We go ahead as planned. This doesn't change anything.'

'There's motive now. He writes about his wealth for the first time, as far as we can make out, and he dies the next day.'

'He took his own life, Jim.'

Daley nodded, but his face spoke of other emotions.

'We go ahead as planned. We have plenty of protection in place for everyone concerned.'

'And Brian?'

She hesitated. 'We don't tell him about this.' Noting the irritation on Daley's face, she placed her hand on his arm. 'It'll just make him jumpy, and this rambling doesn't prove a thing.'

'If you say so, ma'am.'

'I do, DCI Daley, I do.'

They made their way to Rowan Tree Cottage in an unmarked car, Scott driving. Anyone looking on would have thought them to be quite alone, but as they progressed along the gritted roads, past white fields on one side and a grey sea on the other, police officers were quietly taking up position out of sight, but within range of the low dwelling.

They parked in the yard beside the cottage. Scott grimaced at the stench of seaweed as they made their way to the front door.

'Welcome to my childhood, detective,' said Alice Wenger.

'Don't worry, mine wisnae milk and honey either. No' the same stink, though.'

Once inside, Scott surveyed the scene with the same distaste he'd felt on the last occasion he'd been in this place. 'Did yous no' even have a telly?'

'We had nothing. The Bible, some other religious stuff.' She stared at him. 'You have no idea.'

'Well, make yourself comfortable. I'll light the fire.' He spotted the brimming coal scuttle to one side of the cracked hearth.

'No, I'll do it. It'll be like old times. That was one of my chores every morning before we picked up the bus to school. Since I was – well, since I was old enough to remember.'

Scott watched her as she piled coals into the fireplace. She did so expertly, leaving enough room between the black lumps to allow air to circulate. He remembered his mother doing the same thing, though she'd used the wound-up pages of old newspapers in between as an accelerant. 'How are you going tae get it going wae nae firelighters, or that.' He tossed her a box of matches from his pocket.

'You can't teach this family much about lighting fires, trust me. Is it okay for me to go to the kitchen, or do you have to come with me?'

'I'm here tae keep you safe, no' as your gaoler. If you want tae go ootside and let that auld dear of yours take pot-shots at you – well, that's your lookout.'

'My knight in shining armour.'

She returned from the rudimentary kitchen with a small bowl and showered sugar on to the coals, lending them the temporary look of mountains in the snow. She struck a match, which lit at the first attempt, and in a cupped hand held it against the fuel in the fireplace, blowing gently as the flame caught the sugar and grew.

'You've got that down tae a fine art. No' forgotten after a' these years, eh?'

'Some things you just don't forget.' She sat on an old chair backed with an off-white antimacassar. 'So, what do we do now?'

'We wait, that's what we dae,' said Scott, unfurling himself in front of the fire in the hope of at least some warmth.

Outside, light snow fell from a low sky on to the roof of Rowan Tree Cottage.

52

Ginny Doig had left the relative comfort of the Subaru and headed out into the elements, all the time making sure she was obscured by the treeline of dense firs. She knew that the police would be searching for her, but there were lots of places to hide on the Kintyre peninsula. They'd have to flush her out; she wasn't stupid. It came as no surprise at all when she watched the car pull up in the yard of her home, and shortly after saw a small white thread of smoke issue from the chimney. She'd concealed herself in a tiny cave, a place probably forgotten by most of the local population, apart from the Doigs, that was. This small, dank space had come in handy for many years; had hidden contraband, weapons, plunder. Her husband had told her the stories, and she'd paid attention. Though he was dead, she could still hear his voice in her head, as he guided his widow to the places she'd need to find if she were to succeed.

Down the glen – you're out of sight all the way because of the bushes on either side. Be careful, though: the stones at the bottom of the burn are slippery, but you can steady yourself by holding on to sturdy overhanging branches. I hid from my father for near a week there one summer.

As she trudged through the small freezing stream she did

as he'd told her. With the hunting rifle cradled in one arm, she only had the other to grab hold of branches with which to steady herself. The stones were even slicker than she remembered, whether the product of frost or melting snow it was hard to tell, as the dry coiled branches of wintering bushes writhing above her almost blocked out the light. In summer, when everything was in flower and leaf, this place was almost a tunnel, the natural canopy closing it off from the rest of the world.

Before you come out on to the shore, you'll see the wee path. Take it. It's steep, but generations of our family dug our feet in hard to chisel out footholds, almost like a small set of stairs.

She was on that steep path now. The old footholds were still there and helped, but her old knees ached, and only the hatred in her heart drove her on, her wrinkled face now numb with cold as she wound her way down to the sea.

Turn right when you reach the bottom. You can be seen there, but only from the sea, and who will pay any attention to you from out in the North Channel? There are some big boulders to get over, but the largest of them you can skirt round.

She remembered the first time he'd taken her there. It had been a balmy summer's day, not long after they'd wed. They were young, and the world smelled sweet, the sun bathing them in heat and light. Today, though, its cold light was only visible as a pale disc, like a hole to a brighter world almost hidden behind the snow clouds.

Ginny Doig reached one of the big boulders, a rock almost twice her height. She approached the tight space between it and the cliff with a lump in her throat. As she remembered, it had been a tight squeeze all those years ago, her husband almost having to force his thin frame between the rock and an equally hard place. There was no choice, though; the ground in front of the boulder fell away about twenty feet on to the shore. To her surprise, though, it seemed the years had taken flesh from her bones and she was able to slip though easily.

Carry on until you come to the gate at the end of the machair. It's almost obscured by trees, but if you look, you'll find it.

She was old, but her eyes were still keen. The ruined gate was lying on the rough ground, almost covered with snow, but the gap it left afforded her access to the sheltering safety of old oak trees. She heard an animal scurry away as she made her way between the trunks, their branches reaching out like fleshless fingers into the lowering sky.

The stone looks ancient, but it's not – maybe a couple of hundred years, or so. Planted there by my family as a mute signpost. It served its purpose well, for it saved the necks of many of them – without it, what lies below would be almost impossible to find in the undergrowth, especially when the chase is on and fear blinds the bravest soul.

Look below, and you'll have what you need.

She was breathless now, weary after her exertions, but she had no intention of stopping. With her free hand she groped for the small torch she'd taken from the boot of the car she'd stolen. It was there. She turned it on, but in the gloom of the woods it helped only a little. Nonetheless, when she pulled away some loose branches and turf, there it was, a metal cover complete with a stout handle. She silently thanked her husband, who she knew had maintained the family's old escape routes from the excise men of long ago. It was one of the reasons he walked every day. She knew he had never been proud of the Doigs' ignoble tradition of wrecking and smuggling, but something drove him to keep everything in working order.

'You never know,' he would say mysteriously, almost as though he knew this day might come.

She pulled at the steel handle. Though it took effort, the cover opened with relative ease. Ginny froze for a few seconds. She could have taken this escape route in reverse when the man with the gun had killed her eldest son, but to do so would have placed her within a few feet of the killer as he moved to the front door of the house. She supposed she could have played a game of cat and mouse, waited for him to look round the other side of the building, but her nerve had failed her. All she'd wanted to do was run.

Now it was time for others to taste that fear.

Ginny Doig disappeared into the darkness.

The cottage had warmed up considerably, the fire's soporific effect making Scott feel tired. He yawned widely and stretched out his arms.

'You take a nap, honey,' said Alice Wenger. 'Ain't nothing happening here.' She looked at him intently as his eyes almost closed, but then he shot up in the old chair.

'Near nodded off there.'

'No wonder. This is like two nights in Kentucky.'

'I've never been.'

'Don't, would be my advice.'

'I could fair go for a cup o' tea – coffee – anything hot.'

'Now that's something that will certainly be here.'

'What?'

'Tea. Both my parents drank gallons of the stuff. Doubt there will be any milk, though. Well, not that you could drink.'

'You set the fire, I'll away and get some tea. Even black. It's better than nothing.'

'Oh yeah? And just how do you mean to boil a kettle?'

'Oh, right enough. Nae electricity.'

'See that hook above the fire?'

'Aye.'

'Let me show you.'

Again Alice Wenger headed for the kitchen. She arrived back with a blackened kettle that wouldn't have looked out of place in a Dickensian tableau.

'At least they have a cold tap now. When I was young the only water we had was from the little burn that came down from Thomson's Hill.'

Scott screwed up his face. 'Wae a' thon sheep shit and that floating in it? No thanks.'

'Everything was boiled. We survived.'

'Aye, yous did well,' said Scott sarcastically, looking around.

Wenger hung the heavy kettle on an equally blackened hook. 'Now all we do is wait.'

'We've got one o' they new fancy kettles. You just fling the water in oot the tap and before you can say c'mon the Rangers, the water's boiled. It's a great thing.'

'Wow, you sure know how to live it up in bonnie Scotland.'

'The fridge defrosts itself, tae.'

Alice Wenger rolled her eyes. 'I'm sure the long winter nights just fly by in your house, DI Scott.'

'It's no' bad, what wae Netflix an' a' that.'

'I see.'

As they sat with nothing else to say, the hiss of water boiling in the old kettle was all that broke the silence.

53

Daley was on his stomach in some bushes about five hundred yards from Rowan Tree Cottage, beside him Constable Fearns with a sighted rifle. Though he was wrapped up in two jumpers, a thermal fleece and a heavy jacket, he was still frozen. As he watched the cottage through a small pair of binoculars, his gloved hands trembled with cold.

He was listening to radio traffic coming from various officers around the scene and at both turns to the Doigs' home from the Main Road. But all the observations were the same – nothing to report.

'You okay?' he said to Fearns.

'Yes, sir. Though I think my chances of having more children are diminishing by the second. This cold is penetrating the parts nothing else can reach.'

'Huh. You sound like Inspector Scott, son.'

'Nobody sounds like Inspector Scott, sir.'

'This is true. Well spotted, constable.'

Daley turned his ear to the airwave radio once more, again to no avail. I knew this was a stupid idea, he thought, calculating how long this little charade could continue. Especially given the weather.

In the meantime, shivering and miserable, he stayed put.

Ginny Doig knew she was close. She'd been at this end of the tunnel much more recently. She'd known of its existence for most of her married life, and always feared that something unpleasant might be lurking not far from where she slept. That being the case, she regularly descended a few feet with a lantern in search of signs of mice or, worse still, rats.

So when she reached the short flight of steps hollowed out of the rock she knew she was nearly there. Leaving the rifle at the bottom, she ascended the steps with the torch. Carefully, she pushed open the hatch. It was hard work, as both she and her husband had checked regularly to ensure that it was as well disguised as the hatch at the beginning of her journey. But with a little effort she managed to push it open a crack, making only a tiny creak.

The day had seemed dull before she entered the tunnel, but she was about to emerge into absolute darkness. Though it was hard to tell from this snail's eye view of a world of black, Ginny knew exactly where she was. The smell of damp and camphor was familiar: comforting almost.

Anyone watching would expect her to come from the road or over the fields to the front of the house. As she knew, the shoreline was effectively closed off at either end of the cottage: on one side by the boulder that had hidden her from the gunman who had killed her son, on the other by the sheer cliff over which her husband had tumbled to his death. The only other approach from that direction would have been via the sea, and even the policemen she had met recently would have been able to spot that.

She cursed her husband for being so weak. They should have presented a united front when their daughter had reappeared after such a long absence. Instead he'd taken the coward's way out. But she'd seen the light disappearing from his eyes over a number of years, and knew that the many secrets he carried in his head weighed him down. Alison's return had been the last straw. That's why he spent his days wandering the hidden paths and tapping out his feelings on that damnable old typewriter.

Closing the hatch carefully, she crouched down to retrieve the rifle. With the small torch held between her teeth, Ginny Doig ascended the steps again. She knew she had to be brave now, even reckless. She pushed firmly at the hatch, letting it fall open quietly against the wall, displacing some of the old rags they had used to hide it.

With her heart in her mouth she took the last two steps, rifle in hand, and emerged into darkness in the cupboard of the bedroom she'd shared for so many years with her husband.

Ginny Doig was home.

Daley felt the mobile phone vibrate in his pocket. He struggled to remain hidden in the undergrowth as he tried to wrestle it from his pocket. 'Hello,' he said quietly.

'Sir,' said Shaw from the office. 'I've had the FBI on the phone from Langley. The Special Agent would like to speak to you urgently. I wasn't sure how you were placed to take the call.'

Daley thought for a moment. 'Text me the number; I'll call him. Are you sure it's that urgent?'

'He sounded pretty keen, sir.'

'Okay, send it over. If I get a chance, I'll ring him back.' He ended the call just as the radio burst into life.

'Hotel Three to all stations. A vehicle, looks like a Bentley, has pulled up on the verge about half a mile from subject cottage. No movement yet, over.'

'Daley to Hotel Three, keep a watching brief. Let me know the minute you see anything.' He thought instantly of Chiase.

'Roger, will do, sir.'

Daley pondered for a few moments. There were few explanations. Unless Ginny Doig had managed to steal another car, which he thought unlikely, this could just be a member of the public taking in the scenery, or it could be the American gangster. They couldn't close the road to the public or the matriarch of the Doig family would have known she was entering a trap. In any event, he was still fervently hoping that nothing would happen and the whole operation would be called off. It would mean a hunt for Doig and Chiase, but that was by far the better option. This was just too risky.

His radio crackled into life again.

'Hotel Three, male IC1 leaving the vehicle, just climbed the fence, over.'

'Intercept, Hotel Three! To all stations, assist Hotel Three immediately! We'll maintain our position observing Rowan Tree Cottage.' Daley heard his order being confirmed by the various officers nearby. If this was Chiase, he couldn't take risks.

Scott and Alice Wenger sipped at black tea from two cracked old mugs. It was without sugar or milk, but at least it was warming and might just keep him awake, he thought. They'd both heard the radio traffic, and the atmosphere in the room had changed.

Wenger was staring into the fire, its flames reflecting in her blue eyes.

'Penny for them,' said Scott.

'It'd cost more than a penny for these memories, detective.' She took another sip of tea, still not taking her eyes from the fire. 'That isn't her.'

'How dae you know?'

'My mother isn't stupid. She knows this place like the back of her hand. She knows you guys will be searching for her.'

Scott thought about relating this to Daley, but reasoned that he would have his hands full with whatever was happening. He looked again at Wenger. 'Best no' tae dwell on memories, that's my motto. Nothing but baggage we all carry aboot.'

'I could be like my brothers. I'm sure they remember nothing.'

All Scott could do was nod in silence. Remembering the blank faces of the Doig sons, he did not doubt she had a point.

'Hotel Three to all stations, we've lost visuals on subject. Repeat, we've lost visuals.'

'Shit!' said Daley. This was what he had feared. All the officers he had available were firearms trained, but not part of the tactical unit snowbound in Glasgow. 'Update, Hotel Three!'

'Sir, we saw him cross the field, but by the time we caught up he was out of sight.'

'There's snow on the ground. Can't you follow his footsteps?'

'Hotel Three to DCI Daley. Mainly boulders, sir. The sea has washed the snow away in most places.'

Daley cursed himself for the stupid comment. Of course the snow on the beach would now have been melted by the incoming tide; that was obvious. He was about to contact Scott when the radio burst into life again.

'Hotel Four to all stations. We have eyes on subject. Heading north on the beach, over.'

'Daley to all stations, apprehend, I repeat, apprehend!'

In Rowan Tree Cottage, Scott listened intently. It was a bit like following football on the radio, he thought. He was busy picturing the scene and those involved. He removed the pistol from the holster under his arm. 'You cannae be too careful,' he said to Wenger, who was now looking more than a little alarmed.

'Are you sure your guys are up to this?'

'Oh aye, nae bother. But belts an' braces, me.'

'This is a guy, right? On the beach, I mean.'

'Appears tae be, aye.'

'So what about my mother?'

'Good question,' said Scott, feeling the heft of the firearm in his left hand.

Daley was holding his breath, waiting for more from his teams on the beach. In police work, the old maxim that no news was good news just didn't apply.

'What do you reckon, sir?' asked the constable beside him.

'Not sure, son . . .' The crack of a shot carried on the cold air stopped him in mid-sentence. 'Hotel Three, Four, report, over!'

The silence was agonising. Daley could feel his heart thump rapidly in his chest; for him, not a welcome sound.

Then, 'Hotel Four to all stations, subject apprehended. I repeat, subject apprehended.'

'Hotel Four, arrest subject and remove him from the locus, over.'

'Yes, sir, over.'

'Is it Chiase?'

'Negative, sir. The subject doesn't match the image we have of Chiase. Armed with a semi-automatic pistol, which he has been relieved of, sir.'

'Is everyone okay?'

'That's affirmative, sir. Including the suspect, out.'

'There you are, eh? I wonder who the hell that was? How many enemies have you got?' Scott placed his weapon back in the holster.

'Plenty,' replied Alice Wenger.

Behind them, the old door creaked open.

'Jeest stay where yous are, right!' In the doorway stood the tiny figure of Ginny Doig, a large hunting rifle held out before her.

54

'So, Mom, you made it. Where have you been, hiding in the walls?'

'You shut up, Alison. You should have stayed in America.'

'Right, Mrs Doig,' said Scott. 'Just put the weapon down. We can sort this withoot the gun.'

'Huh, you! Could they no' find anyone of any use tae guard my daughter? My boys made short work o' you and the skinny laddie you were wae the last time. I see I'll have tae dae the business myself noo.'

Scott made to stand.

'Sit back doon or I swear I'll shoot you. I'm an auld woman. I've lost my husband and my eldest son. Come tae that, I lost all my boys a long time ago.' She glanced at Alice Wenger. 'And here's the very one I was quite happy never tae see again, bold as brass.'

'You sure ain't changed, Ma.' Wenger sat back in the chair. She looked calm, almost untroubled by her rifle-toting mother.

'No, you can rely upon that. And I still have the same regrets I've had all these years.'

'Oh yeah? Are you gonna keep us in suspense?'

Looking on, Scott admired Wenger's sangfroid. She spoke

in even, moderated tones, a hint of a smile playing across her lips. 'Right, that's enough of this!' he said.

'No' until you hear the truth, officer.'

'We can dae that back in the office in Kinloch. You're only making things hard for yourself, Mrs Doig. It's just going tae get you the jail.'

'As I said, I've nothing tae lose. But my daughter has. She's many a tale tae tell.'

'You mean how you treated me in this – hovel?'

'You were a little whore, nothing mair!'

Scott noted that Alice Wenger's expression had changed. Her calm, almost serene expression was now one of growing fury.

'Tell the detective what you let them do to me, Mother!'

'They never touched you! You tell him what you did to them, Alison.'

'Don't call me that. How many times?'

'I'll tell him what really happened,' said Ginny Doig.

'See if I care, you mad old bitch,' retorted her daughter.

'Tell me without the rifle, Mrs Doig.'

'No, nor will I. But you'll sit down – the both of yous – and you'll listen.'

'Let her ramble on, detective,' said Alice Wenger. 'She and my father are born liars.'

'She couldna keep her nose oot o' anything. She knew her faither was writing stuff, so she had tae read it.'

'Crime of the century, Ma.'

'One night, she got a hold o' sleeping tablets fae that posh Cunningham lassie. Her mother was troubled wae her nerves, as I recall. She crushed them up and put them in oor last cup o' tea before bedtime.'

'This is priceless,' said Wenger.

'Shut up!' Ginny Doig pushed the rifle in her direction.

'Was this how you managed tae run away?' said Scott.

'No, she did that later. She had tae punish us all first.'

'How?'

'She took her brothers' minds away, that's how!' Tears were now streaming down Ginny's face, the rifle shaking in her hands. 'She took a knife tae their brains, that's whoot she did. They've been like the walking deid ever since.'

Alice Wenger stood, facing her mother, towering over the tiny woman with the hunting rifle. 'But you let them do what they wanted to me. I was only a kid, but you didn't care. My father knew the truth, but he wouldn't stand up to you.'

'Ach, it was a bit o' rough an' tumble – a carry-on. You were always a sleekit wee lassie, telling tales, making up stuff.'

'Oh yeah? Sure, I had every right to tell tales. This wasn't just "rough and tumble", as you put it. You know what they did, Mother, and they did it again and again!'

'Shite, you're a liar.'

'You wondered why I ran off, didn't you?'

'I was glad you went.'

'I ran away because I was pregnant, Mother, pregnant by one of your precious sons. And don't ask me which one, because I've no idea. Oh yeah, I took their minds. I wish I'd killed them. All you could do was pin me down and try to do the same thing.' Wenger touched the lump over her eye. 'But like everything else, you were too stupid to know what to do.'

Scott looked from one to the other. Ginny Doig had advanced into the centre of the room, the rifle to her eye, equidistant between Scott and her daughter, who was now standing in front of a grubby window.

414

'You're lying, Alison.'

Wenger began to cry. She looked at her mother in desperation. Her voice was weak now, almost a pleading whisper. 'Why, after all these years, won't you believe me? You're my mother. And you're also the grandmother of my son.'

Slowly, Ginny Doig looked defeated. She appeared to fold in on herself, letting out the agonised sigh, the silent scream of a tortured soul, someone for whom life had been a struggle between truth and denial.

As Scott looked on, he saw her lower the rifle, her chest heaving for breath. But before he could move, Alice Wenger reached behind her back and advanced on her stricken mother. As he went for his shoulder holster, he saw Wenger swing her left arm through the air. With a loud clang, the object clutched in her hand connected with the old woman's head in a splatter of blood. Ginny Doig dropped the rifle and sank to her knees, then fell prostrate on the cracked wooden boards, her body twitching silently.

Her face impassive, Alice Wenger let Jeremiah's bell fall to the floor with a clang.

Scott rushed to Ginny Doig's side. He could feel a faint pulse. 'Quick, hand me my radio. I'll need tae get help or your mother will die. You gave her a hell o' a dunt there.' Scott looked up, only to see Alice Wenger standing over him, the hunting rifle held to her right eye.

'Sit down, detective. You and me have business.'

Daley's face had turned the shade of snow when he finished the call.

'Anything wrong, sir?' said Fearns.

Daley lifted the airwave radio to his mouth. 'DCI Daley to DI Scott, come in, over.' The silence was deafening, only a crackle of static to be heard from the device. 'Brian, come in, over!' There was desperation in Daley's voice. Then, 'To all stations, attend Rowan Tree Cottage, now!'

He didn't issue any orders to the constable beside him. He burst from behind the rocks and bushes that had been their hiding place and ran across the snowy field towards the road, slipping and sliding on the slick ground. He could see stars in front of his eyes and felt dizzy, but carried on until he reached the fence, gasping for breath.

His young colleague soon caught up with him. 'Quick, get to the cottage,' said Daley through gulps of air. He watched the youthful policeman vault the fence, and with as much speed as he could muster did the same.

His nagging doubts had been justified; they rarely let him down. He'd been wrong – they'd all been wrong. Why had he ignored his own instincts?

The rifle still close to his head, Scott made for the chair, hands held high.

'Listen, Alice, whatever you did was a long time ago. You were a kid – you were abused. We can sort this all oot.'

'I know how cops "sort things oot", detective. You have no idea what I know, how I've had to fight to survive. I've always hated my family, but I needed the Doig genes. They've made me who I am.'

As Scott turned to sit, she caught him a vicious blow to the side of his face, so that he fell on the old chair with a thud, groaning in pain. Wenger put the rifle on the floor and from her handbag pulled out a smaller bag.

Scott was drifting in and out of consciousness. The room seemed to revolve around his head and he felt sick. Desperately, he tried to stand, but he simply slumped further back in the chair.

Alice Wenger loomed over him now, two small metallic objects in her hand. 'This is the best thing my daddy ever taught me. Leastwise, he wrote it down. I'll make sure my mother won't survive, and by the time I'm finished with you you won't remember jack shit. I'll blame everything on her, just like she deserves.' She knelt on the knee of the squirming policeman, pinning him to the chair.

Desperately, Scott tried to push her away, but he could see the darkness of unconsciousness pooling in his eyes.

Wenger appraised him with a smile on her face, her head canted to one side, the way a mother would look at a child. 'By the time your buddies arrive I'll have hit my head on the wall a couple of times, and you'll be a zombie. The brave cop who gave his mind to save the poor woman he was guarding.'

As Scott struggled underneath her weight she thrust something sharp into the gap between his left eye and his eyebrow. 'Time to say goodbye, detective.'

55

As Daley neared the end of the long lane to Rowan Tree Cottage he could see his colleague turning the corner into the yard. When he arrived there himself there was no sign of the young constable.

Looking around desperately, he stumbled to the front door, still gasping for breath. It was half open, so he pushed his way inside, hearing the wail of police sirens in the distance. He had to focus to remember the layout of the cottage as he gulped air. He heard a noise coming from behind one door. When he opened it he saw the still body of Ginny Doig on the floor, while Constable Fearns was struggling with Alice Wenger, who was brandishing a small knife. But it was the sight of the slumped figure in the chair that almost made him cry out. Brian Scott looked lifeless, a stream of blood pouring from one eye.

He caught Wenger by the scruff of the neck and pulled her backwards, making her yell furiously while Fearns wrenched the knife out of her hand and applied the cuffs. As soon as that was done, Daley ran to his stricken colleague.

'Brian, can you hear me? Brian!' He knelt over Scott and pulled back his head. One side of his face was now covered in blood, and his eyes were rolling in their sockets.

As more officers piled into the room, Daley shouted orders. 'Check Mrs Doig and get an ambulance here now! Brian, help's coming, I promise.' He looked into Scott's face once more. He thought he caught a spark of recognition in the uninjured eye, though his friend's mouth was gaping open like a dead fish. 'Brian!' Daley tapped him gently on the cheek with his paw of a hand.

Without warning Scott focused on his face, but Daley could see no recognition in that stare as he tried to examine the damaged eye. It was impossible to see how badly injured he was, so all Daley could do was fish a hanky from his pocket and hold it against the wound to try to stem the bleeding. Scott's mouth moved as though he was trying to speak, but only an unintelligible garble of words could be heard.

His face pale and hatred in his eyes, Daley looked round at Wenger, now prostrate on the floor, screaming her hate and fury. 'I swear to you,' he roared, 'if you've harmed this man . . .' He looked at the rifle on the floor nearby. He felt a weak tap on his arm and turned round to face Scott.

'Steady on wae a' the shouting, big man. I've got one hell o' a headache here.'

Carrie Symington sat in front of Mike Strong, Daley at her side. 'For the record, can you confirm you do not want the services of a solicitor, Mr Strong?'

'I am a bloody solicitor. Who on earth could you conjure up in this damnable place fit to represent me?'

'Good, then we can proceed. How did you get in touch with Vito Chiase?'

Strong sighed. 'Listen, I know I'm up the creek without

a paddle. I'll tell you everything you need to know. In return for a plea bargain.'

'You know I can't give you any guarantees on that,' said Symington.

'Maybe you can tell us how you first came into contact with Alice Wenger?' Daley said.

'She contacted me about some financial problems. She knew about the money her father had stashed away. She'd read about it in some of his writings, or something. The man was a bloody oddball.'

'But he trusted your firm with the money,' said Symington.

'The rest of them – my firm – have nothing to do with this. I was acting entirely on my own initiative.' He paused. 'Can I have a drink or something? I'm parched.'

Symington nodded to the constable at the door of the interview room, who went off in search of a beverage for Strong.

'She's clever, you know. But as ruthless as they come.'

'I think we've realised that, Mr Strong,' said Daley.

'Had problems with extortion, plus the financial crash – money in the wrong places, that kind of thing.'

'The FBI tell us her son was blackmailing her. She killed her first husband in America and the boy was taken into care. It was put down to self-defence, but he was old enough to remember what really happened, and she abandoned him shortly afterwards. Not the story she used for public consumption. I take it you knew that?' said Symington.

'No, as a matter of fact I didn't. But if the boy waited all those years to get his revenge by blackmailing her, he sounds as bad as she is. It's clear the Doig genes are strong.'

'Which is why Nathaniel Doig wanted to make sure that the bloodline stopped,' said Daley.

'Ah, but he didn't reckon on his daughter. And she had good cause to be the way she was. Abused, beaten, raped by her brothers. No wonder she did what she did, DCI Daley.'

'That's true. She had an awful background, and for that I blame not just her parents but also some of my colleagues from that time. Her life was barbaric, as were the consequences. A tragedy that only ends now, after all these years.' He paused. 'But how did *you* end up the way you are, Mr Strong?'

The disgraced lawyer looked up, his craggy face breaking into a smile. 'You wait until the day you realise there's not much time left. You'll look back on your life and wonder what the hell you did with it. I just wanted to spend my last years living the high life. Selfish, but there you are. I told you I'd be frank.'

Daley squirmed in his chair at the thought of the end of life, but kept his focus. 'And Alice Wenger, how well did you know her?'

'She was smart – very smart. She took notes of addresses, of people's names, when she was still a kid. One of them was our law firm. She knew we were dealing with her father's affairs, and about Chiase and his family history. She'd researched the lot, worked things out. You know these Italians: they'll avenge family even if it takes generations. And he needed the money. But the man didn't live to see it.'

'They reckon he had a heart attack – initial findings, but probably reliable,' said Symington, making a sweat break out on Daley's brow at the thought. 'And he was your muscle?'

'Yes, though it was Ms Wenger who told him what to do.'

'You weren't involved?' said Daley.

'I was a mere facilitator.' Strong thought for a moment.

'Like the attack she arranged on herself at the Machrie House Hotel.'

'Done to attract attention to her mother,' said Symington.

'Exactly. Small figure, the famous ice pick lobotomy – or attempted, at least. I'm afraid she didn't chose her associates very wisely.'

'And Sheena McKay?' said Daley.

'She knew too much. Alice had forgotten she'd told her friend that she was pregnant all those years ago. It would have been easy for anyone to trace her son, then boom!' Strong made a gesture with his hand to imitate an explosion.

'So the plan was to wipe out the family and profit from the money that would then belong to the sole survivor, Alice Wenger.'

'Her plan, not mine.' Strong smiled.

'But a considerable sum,' said Symington.

'Yes. Millions in gold bullion today.'

The constable arrived back and laid a cup of steaming coffee in front of Strong.

'And Vito Chiase would be a handy scapegoat. His grandfather was killed by the Doigs, which gave him motive. You split the cash with Alice Wenger and live your life of luxury, yes?'

'That sort of thing, though my part in it all was a very junior one.'

'But Chiase wasn't ever going to survive, was he?' said Daley.

Strong shrugged. 'I have no idea. I found him, paid him, the rest was up to Ms Wenger.'

Daley sat back in his chair. 'That's where things kind of unravel for me, I'm afraid.'

'How so?'

'If you were "a mere facilitator", then why were you running down the beach towards Rowan Tree Cottage?'

'I'd come to my senses, DCI Daley, simple as that. My conscience got the better of me. I just wanted to put a stop to the whole damned thing. I overheard a conversation in the County Hotel. How Alice was going to the cottage. Must say, too many loose lips in your operation, eh?'

'Why not just tell us when you had this change of heart?'

'And implicate myself? Not likely. Though I dare say I could have batted off any accusations from Wenger – clearly a madwoman. That would have been easy.'

Daley smiled. 'I have a theory, Mr Strong.'

'You do?' Strong returned the smile.

'I think that Chiase dying suddenly put paid to all your carefully laid plans. You wanted to be the last man standing and pocket the lot. After all, apart from Wenger, you were the only person who really knew how much money there was to be had once the Doigs had been wiped out.'

'Mere supposition.'

'We spoke to Blair Williams. He had no clue how much the Doig estate was worth, nor did his retired father. No documentation at your law firm, or your home. That's why, in desperation, you thought you'd go to the cottage and do what Chiase was supposed to do. You had no notion we were setting a trap for Ginny Doig and your friend from New Jersey.'

'I have no further comment to make other than that if you think that will hold up in court, you're more stupid than you look.'

'Oh, I think we have sufficient evidence against you to put you away for a long time, regardless of whether we can prove my theory or not. More time than you have left, I'd say. So much for living it up in your golden years, Mr Strong.' Daley smiled.

'Interview ends at three fifteen p.m.,' said Symington.

'I wish you good luck with your theory, Mr Daley,' said Strong as Daley shrugged on his jacket.

'Oh, there was another thing I was going to tell you. It slipped my mind,' said Daley.

Symington frowned at her DCI.

'We had to collect DNA – normal in these cases, as you know.'

Strong shrugged, draining the last of his coffee.

'Blair Williams is your biological son. You do know that, don't you?'

Strong dropped the plastic cup and stared up at Daley, opening his mouth to say something, but words wouldn't come.

Epilogue

Three weeks later

The party in the bar at the County Hotel was in full swing. A large Christmas tree replete with baubles old and new sat beside a roaring fire. New decorations festooned the place, making up for the lick of paint so badly needed. Customers clustered at the bar and tables, the Christmas spirit in full flow.

Alistair the butcher and his wife were singing an old Scottish song, with many joining in. Elspeth McCall from the post office looked rather worse for wear; she wasn't a habitual drinker and two rum and Cokes saw her squinting at the assembled throng through one eye. Charlie Murray was singing heartily if somewhat tunelessly, while Jessie Duncan was tapping out the beat on the spoons.

Hamish was wearing a moth-eaten Santa hat that drooped over one half of his face. He was smiling benignly, looking at his fellow revellers with what could best be described as an expression of sublime contentment. Three large drams were lined up on the table in front of him beside his unlit pipe.

'There you are, Mr and Mrs Daley. I didna think you'd make oor wee celebration the night,' he said.

'How could we miss it?' said Daley. 'Where did all the new decorations come from?'

'That'll be the new owner, Mr Macmillan. That's him o'er there at the bar speaking tae Annie. Does she no' jeest look like the cat that's got the cream?'

Daley had to admit that before the change in ownership he'd thought his visits to the County Hotel were numbered.

Her conversation with her new boss over, Annie made her way to their table, a broad grin spread across her face. 'Liz, Mr Daley, it's a pleasure to see you both. What can I get you? Aye, an' he's no' needin' any mair.' She raised a brow at the large measures in small glasses lined up in front of Hamish.

'You could put a frown on the face o' the happiest man in the world, Annie, and that's a fact,' retorted the old man.

They ordered their drinks and Annie threaded expertly back through the crowded bar to get the drinks.

'They tell me Ginny Doig is making a good recovery, Mr Daley,' said Hamish.

'So it would appear.'

'As you know, I've never cared for the woman, though someone has tae keep tabs on those poor sons o' hers. Dear knows whoot will happen tae them when she's gone.'

'Nothing's ever easy,' said Liz, glancing at her husband.

'No, but you have the right o' it there, Lizzie. You're looking right bonnie, tae. If an auld man is permitted to compliment a woman these days.'

'Thank you, Hamish.'

There was a flurry of activity at the door and Ella Scott appeared wearing a red dress and huge Christmas bauble earrings. Behind her, in a dark suit and wearing a pair of sunglasses, came her husband.

'Bugger me,' said Hamish. 'Roy Orbison is alive and well, right enough.'

'I'll have you know I've tae wear these on doctor's orders. You don't know how close I came tae walking aboot like the living deid,' said Scott.

'Here's me thinking you've been at that for the last thirty years, tae,' said his wife, with a wink in Hamish's direction.

'I'm just pleased you're okay,' said Daley, patting his best friend on the shoulder.

'Aye, things could have been much worse, right enough. But, yet again, here I am. Me and you are survivors, Jimmy.'

Daley nodded in agreement, though in his mind, despite the occasion, he felt every beat of his heart.

Annie arrived just as Alistair and Agnes stopped for a break, and music from the bar began to play in order to keep the festivities going.

'Here. I saw yous coming in an' took a guess,' she said, handing Ella a large gin and tonic and Scott a ginger beer and lime.

'Aye. Happy Christmas,' said Scott, eyeing his drink through his dark glasses with a distinct lack of enthusiasm. He saw Liz Daley smiling broadly and followed her line of sight. It was directed at the handsome Canadian who'd just bought the County Hotel. Then Scott's gaze attracted her attention, and she smiled weakly back at him.

Knowing she couldn't see his eyes through the dark glasses, he just shook his head. It was a moment only noticed by the two of them.

Liz grabbed her husband's hand under the table and whispered in his ear. 'Are we okay, Jim? You know I love you.'

Daley smiled back and kissed her on the forehead. 'Yes, we're fine, Liz.'

Just as he said the words, a Blue Nile classic drifted out from the hotel's sound system and over the chatter, laughter and merriment. Jim Daley's heart sank.

Annie tried to ring the bell behind the bar. New owner Tom Macmillan wanted to make a speech. But her attempt to bring the room to order failed when the rope attached to the bell came away in her hand.

'It's broken, after all these years!' she lamented.

'A bad sign, if you ask me,' opined Hamish.

'Here, I know where you can get another bell,' said Scott.

A Note from the Author

Campbeltown and Prohibition

As a result of pressure from temperance societies to prohibit the manufacture, sale and transportation of intoxicating beverages, the Volstead Act came into effect in 1919; despite a rocky road through the House of Representatives, the amendment to the Constitution was in full force by one second past midnight, 17 January 1920. The United States of America became alcohol-free – dry. Or so the legislators hoped. The initial signs were positive: consumption dropped by around a third, arrests for drunkenness fell and the price for illegal alcohol rose dramatically. However, the rigorous enforcement of Prohibition was matched by the ingenuity of the bootleggers who knew that not every border or illegal drinking venue could be controlled. Criminals (not yet particularly organised but getting there) became increasingly inventive.

Speakeasies rapidly sprang up across the country. Gangsters like Johnny Torrio, his protégé Al Capone, Nucky Johnson, Charles 'Lucky' Luciano, Albert Rothstein and Meyer Lansky became synonymous with the provision of illegal alcohol. This activity made them rich, and entrenched organised crime in the USA for decades. Luciano was pivotal in establishing the so-called National Crime Syndicate (a loose confederacy of the Italian-American mafia and the Jewish mob), and later founding The Commission, the Mafia's governing body which was run by five powerful New York families.

In short, the Volstead Act proved to be disastrous for the country and established the tentacles of organised crime that exist to this day.

The east coast of the USA was perfect for smuggling. As depicted in HBO's *Boardwalk Empire*, the real Nucky Johnson made sure that Atlantic City, of which he was the de facto boss, was at the epicentre of 'rum running' or 'bootlegging'. As briefly mentioned in this book, Captain William McCoy, a former fisherman who knew the coast like the back of his hand, became one of the most effective mariners on 'Rum Row'. He was able to evade US Coastguard patrols and smuggle whisky, rum, wine and other forms of booze onto the Eastern Seaboard with relative impunity. He is remembered in the saying, 'the real McCoy'.

Alcohol from across the Atlantic was also smuggled into the USA via its northern border with Canada. Much of this ended up in Chicago, from where it filtered out to the rest of the country. Johnny Walker and Canadian Club are still two of the bestselling whiskies in America today – surely no coincidence.

Illicit booze came in two distinct forms: that produced in opportunistic distilleries and breweries run by criminals in the USA, and the real thing smuggled in from either Europe or Canada. The latter became much sought after, and the name Campbeltown was synonymous with high-quality and luxury whisky. The town's location made for convenient transatlantic deliveries, and its thirty-four distilleries were a great resource. Al Capone famously stencilled 'Campbeltown Whisky' on casks and printed it on labels of homemade gut rot in order to persuade his customers of its quality. Stories persist in local folklore that Capone, a keen golfer, visited Campbeltown on more than one occasion, and even played at Machrihanish. Likely apocryphal, but by no means beyond the realms of possibility.

Of course, the clandestine nature of this trade has ensured that very little written evidence remains of Campbeltown's role in thwarting Prohibition. But perhaps it is no coincidence that the fortunes of the town's many distilleries went into rapid decline after the Prohibition laws were relaxed and the Volstead Act was repealed in 1933. Though it has to be said, the three distilleries that remain are of *the* highest quality, still more than justifying Campbeltown's place as one of Scotland's whisky regions.

Transorbital Lobotomy

After a chance meeting with Portuguese neurologist António Egas Moniz (who had first attempted this procedure in 1935 in Lisbon), at a conference in London the same year, neurologist Walter Jackson Freeman II, along with neurosurgeon James W. Watts, became responsible for the introduction of frontal lobe psychosurgery to the American health system. The basic concept was that disrupting the prefrontal lobe of the brain by surgical intervention would cure mental health conditions such as schizophrenia, mania, insomnia and depression.

Initially the procedure was carried out by drilling holes in the skull in order to access the frontal lobe. But that required an operating room, anaesthesia and trained neurosurgeons. Freeman soon realised that using an ice pick to break through the thinnest part of the skull, just above the eye, was far quicker and easier, and could be done without anaesthesia or trained staff. The lobe would be 'scrambled', rendering it ineffective as far as its function in the brain was concerned. Vigorously promoted by Freeman and Watts, the idea quickly took off, and between 1940 and 1944, almost 700 lobotomies were performed in the US. In total, around 40,000 people were lobotomised in the US, many of whom were women.

The efficacy of the surgery was doubtful from the beginning, considered crude and hazardous by many scientists, and although some patients appeared much improved following the operation, little or no attempts were made to follow up on their welfare. The procedure spread to the UK, where Sir Wylie McKissock was its greatest advocate. In the beginning, operations took place in hospitals around the country but they were soon performed in mental hospitals and institutions, often by nurses and staff with no medical qualifications. (McKissock stated that it was 'not a time-consuming operation. A competent team in a well-organised mental hospital can do four such operations in 2–2½ hours.')

By the late 1950s and 1960s, however, many were expressing serious concerns, and the practice fell out of favour. Henry Marsh, one of the UK's most eminent neurosurgeons, recalled the many patients he encountered who had been lobotomised thirty or forty years before. He commented in 2011 that it was 'very bad medicine, bad science, because it was clear the patients who were subjected to this procedure were never followed up properly'. Their cognitive abilities were seriously impaired and, consequently, their lives as social human beings were ruined; they became listless, disinterested and detached from life.

This barbaric treatment has thankfully been consigned to the past. But the struggle to help those with mental illness continues to this day.

Acknowledgements

As I've said many times before, writing is not the solo occupation many imagine it to be. The rise of social media means that writers are in daily contact with their readers. I would like to thank the army of bloggers and those who run and participate in book groups around the world on the likes of Facebook and other platforms.

As I write, we are in the midst of one of the most virulent pandemics ever encountered by humanity. It would be remiss of me not to mention the many, many health professionals across the world who bravely risk their lives in order to save others. I hope, as a species, we will learn something from this.

Huge thanks to all at Polygon who continue to bring Daley et al out into the world. I'm indebted to my copy-editor, Nancy Webber, and editor-in-chief, Alison Rae. I also owe a great debt of gratitude to outgoing agent Anne Williams of Kate Hordern Literary Agency. Her advice over the years has been invaluable. And a big hello to my new agent, the ebullient Jo Bell of Bell Lomax Moreton. We've already achieved such a lot in a short space of time. You're a star!

Thank you to the many writers who provide a grand resource of help and advice – notably Douglas Skelton, with whom I now present the podcast SBooks. It's always a blast.

Last but never least, gratitude to my wife Fiona and the community of neighbours and friends in our lovely village, all of whom make the place special. And, as always, to the people of Kintyre – always home – who continue to inspire. Without them Daley would not exist.

D.A.M.
Gartocharn
April 2020

The DCI Daley thriller series

Book 1: *Whisky from Small Glasses*
DCI Jim Daley is sent from the city to investigate a murder after
the body of a woman is washed up on an idyllic beach on the west
coast of Scotland. Far away from urban resources, he finds himself
a stranger in a close-knit community.

Betrayal, fear and death stalk the small town of Kinloch, as
Daley investigates a case that becomes more deadly than he could
possibly imagine.

Book 2: *The Last Witness*
James Machie was a man with a genius for violence, his criminal
empire spreading beyond Glasgow into the UK and mainland
Europe. Fortunately, Machie is dead, assassinated in the back of a
prison ambulance following his trial and conviction. But now, five
years later, he is apparently back from the grave, set on avenging
himself on those who brought him down.

Book 3: *Dark Suits and Sad Songs*
When a senior Edinburgh civil servant spectacularly takes his own
life in Kinloch harbour, DCI Jim Daley comes face to face with the
murky world of politics. To add to his woes, two local drug dealers
lie dead, ritually assassinated. It's clear that dark forces are at work
in the town. With his boss under investigation, his marriage hanging
by a thread, and his side-kick DS Scott wrestling with his own
demons, Daley's world is in meltdown.

Book 4: *The Rat Stone Serenade*

It's December, and the Shannon family are heading to their clifftop mansion near Kinloch for their AGM. Shannon International, one of the world's biggest private companies, has brought untold wealth and privilege to the family. However, a century ago, Archibald Shannon stole the land upon which he built their home – and his descendants have been cursed ever since.

When heavy snow cuts off Kintyre, DCI Jim Daley and DS Brian Scott are assigned to protect their illustrious visitors. But ghosts of the past are coming to haunt the Shannons.

Book 5: *The Well of the Winds*

As World War Two nears its end, a man is stabbed to death on the Kinloch shoreline, in the shadow of the great warships in the harbour.

Many years later, the postman on Gairsay, a tiny island off the coast of Kintyre, discovers that the Bremner family are missing from their farm.

When DCI Daley comes into possession of a journal written by his wartime predecessor in Kinloch, he soon realises that he must solve a murder from the past to uncover the shocking events of the present.

Book 6: *The Relentless Tide*

When Professor Francombe and her team of archaeologists find the remains of three women on a remote Kintyre hillside – a site rumoured to have been the base of Viking warlord Somerled – their delight soon turns to horror when they realise the women tragically met their end only two decades ago.

It soon becomes clear that these are the three missing victims of the 'Midweek Murderer', a serial killer who was at work in Glasgow in the early 1990s. DCI Jim Daley now has the chance to put things right – to confront a nightmare from his past and solve a crime he failed to as a young detective. However, when Police Scotland's Cold Case Unit arrive, they bring yet more ghosts to Kinloch. *The Relentless Tide* is a tale of death, betrayal, Viking treasure and revenge set in the thin places where past, present and future collide.

Can Daley avenge the murder of his colleague and friend?

Book 7: *A Breath on Dying Embers*
When the luxury cruiser *Great Britain* berths in Kinloch harbour, the pressure mounts on DCI Jim Daley. The high-powered international delegates on board are touring the country, golfing and sightseeing, as part of a UK government trade mission. But within hours, one of the crew members vanishes and a local birdwatcher goes missing.

The lives of the ship's passengers and the residents of Kinloch, as well as the country's economic future, are soon in jeopardy. And as Daley faces a life-and-death struggle of his own, DS Brian Scott – reluctantly back at sea – comes to the fore.

Could this be Daley's last throw of the dice?

One Last Dram Before Midnight: The Complete Collected D.C.I. Daley Short Stories
Published together for the first time in one not-to-be-missed volume are all Denzil Meyrick's short stories and novellas.

Discover how DCI Daley and DS Scott first met on the mean streets of Glasgow in two prequels that shed light on their earlier lives. Join Hamish and his old mentor, skipper Sandy Hoynes, as they become embroiled with some Russian fishermen and an illicit whisky plot. And in present-day Kinloch Daley and Scott investigate ghosts from the past, search for a silent missing man, and follow the trail of an elusive historical necklace that still has power over the people of Kinloch.

All of the DCI Daley thrillers are available as eBook editions, along with an eBook-only novella and the short stories below.

Dalintober Moon: A DCI Daley Story
When a body is found in a whisky barrel buried on Dalintober beach, it appears that a notorious local crime, committed over a century ago, has finally been solved. However, the legacy of murder still resonates within the community, and the tortured screams of a man who died long ago still echo across Kinloch.

Two One Three: A Constable Jim Daley Short Story (Prequel)
Glasgow, 1986. Only a few months into his new job, Constable Jim Daley is pounding the beat. When he is seconded to the CID to help catch a possible serial killer, he makes a new friend, DC Brian Scott. Jim Daley tackles his first serious crime in an investigation that will change his life for ever.

Empty Nets and Promises: A Kinloch Novella
It's July 1968, and fishing-boat skipper Sandy Hoynes has his daughter's wedding to pay for – but where are all the fish? He and the crew of the *Girl Maggie* come to the ~~conclusions over Kinloch~~ fangled ~~superne~~ herring.

First mate Hamish comes up with a cunning plan to bring the laws of nature back into balance. But little do they know that they face the forces of law and order in the shape of a vindictive fishery officer, an exciseman who suspects Hoynes of smuggling illicit whisky, and the local police sergeant who is about to become Hoynes' son-in-law – not to mention a ghostly piper and some Russians.

Single End: A DC Daley Short Story
It's 1989, and Jim Daley is now a fully fledged detective constable. When ruthless gangster James Machie's accountant is found stabbed

to death in a multi-storey car park, it's clear all is not well within Machie's organisation.

Meanwhile Daley's friend and colleague DC Brian Scott has been having some problems of his own. To save his job, he must revisit his past in an attempt to uncover the identity of a corrupt police officer.